FIRST
DATE

BOOKS BY SUE WATSON

Love, Lies and Lemon Cake
Snow Angels, Secrets and Christmas Cake
Summer Flings and Dancing Dreams
Fat Girls and Fairy Cakes
Younger Thinner Blonder
Bella's Christmas Bake Off
We'll Always have Paris
The Christmas Cake Café
Ella's Ice Cream Summer
Curves, Kisses and Chocolate Ice Cream
Snowflakes, Iced Cakes and Second Chances
Love, Lies and Wedding Cake

Our Little Lies
The Woman Next Door
The Empty Nest
The Sister-in-Law

FIRST DATE

SUE WATSON

bookouture

Published by Bookouture in 2020

An imprint of Storyfire Ltd.
Carmelite House
50 Victoria Embankment
London EC4Y 0DZ

www.bookouture.com

ISBN: 978-1-83888-512-0
eBook ISBN: 978-1-83888-511-3

For Nick Watson, my best first date.

CHAPTER ONE

'I've always wanted a yellow Labrador,' I say, trying to bite into a piece of garlic bread without butter running down my chin.

'No?' He smiles. 'That's crazy!'

'Why?' I'm struggling with the pasta and splashing arrabbiata sauce everywhere. Not a good look.

'You know how people talk about white picket fences, and 2.4 kids?' he says.

My heart sinks, this was going so well, but here it comes, the usual commitment-phobe comment. 'Mmm…?'

'Well, I don't care about the white picket fence. I just want the Labrador and three kids.'

'Three? No way. Me too!' Warmth floods my veins. I've had a good feeling about this guy ever since we started talking, and did he just mention kids? On a first date? I'm blown away.

I'm trying to eat with dignity and not sound over keen, I don't want to mess this up. It isn't every day you meet someone who wants everything you do, whose hopes and dreams match yours – even down to the breed of dog you want. But I mustn't get carried away. Not yet.

'So… music. Who do you like?'

'Mmm I love the nineties, reminds me of being young. I'm a big fan of Oasis.'

'No? I LOVE Oasis,' I say.

'Favourite album?' he asks.

'*What's the Story, Morning Glory?*' we both say in unison, and laugh.

'Has to be – "Wonderwall" is on it,' he says.

'Yeah, I love that too,' I say, amazed. 'So – let's test this further – where's your favourite place to go on holiday?' I ask eagerly.

He thinks for a moment. 'I guess the guys you usually go out with go to cool places like Hawaii, or, I don't know, Iceland?'

I shake my head.

'I'm going to be very boring, I'm afraid.' He sighs. 'But my favourite holiday destination is probably Devon…' He considers this for a moment. 'Yes, Devon, we had some great holidays there when I was a kid. I keep thinking I'd love to go back.'

'Really? Me too.'

'This is getting weird now.'

'Yeah! I *love* Devon. Haven't been for ages, but only recently I was saying to my friend Jasmine that I'd love to go back for the weekend, rent a little fisherman's cottage by the sea, then eat Devon cream teas until I'm so full I can't move.' We both giggle at the prospect. What I don't mention is the fact that I'd told Jasmine I wanted it to be a *romantic* weekend, and I'd wished I had a gorgeous man to go with. And now, as we gaze across candlelight, I'm marvelling at how life sometimes gives you exactly what you wish for.

'Okay, so we both want dogs, three kids and Devon?' He smiles. 'What's your favourite kind of food? I love French food.'

'Ahh that's a shame, my favourite is Italian, perhaps we're not soulmates after all,' I tease.

'Well, there's still a chance. I love Italian too.' He finishes the pasta primavera on his plate as if to prove this, and takes a sip of Merlot.

'Yeah, I love pasta,' I say, pointlessly, my voice fading and insides melting as he directs his gaze into my eyes.

'Okay, perhaps we *could* still be soulmates then.' His eyes smile independently of his mouth, as if he has this amusing secret he wants to share but daren't. I want to know *all* his secrets.

I imagine us walking along a beach together next summer, we're holding hands, walking into an orange sunset, later returning to that romantic little cottage with roses around the door. I feel a shimmer of excitement at the thought.

He's sitting back now, observing me, that secret still laughing in his eyes. 'So, Hannah Weston, are we meant for each other?' He leans forward, and his hand brushes mine on the table, causing electricity to shoot up my arm.

'Do we really want the same things in life, or have you been lurking on my Facebook page and that's how you know my favourite breed of dog, and my passion for the south-west coast of England?' He screws up his eyes in mock suspicion, and resting his chin on his hands, makes like he's scrutinising me.

He smiles and takes another sip of wine, he'd ordered the bottle before we arrived – apparently his favourite, and it happens to be mine too. How many signs do we need to tell us this is fate? Why doesn't he just ask me to marry him now and be done with the small talk? I want to laugh at my madness. I'll admit I did look him up on social media, but there was nothing about Labradors or Devon on his Instagram, just anonymous, moody landscapes and the odd selfie. Alex pours more wine for both of us while telling me about his work as a solicitor at Boyd and Walker, a big legal firm here in the Midlands.

'It must be very interesting,' I say, rather lamely. I'm not good under pressure. I have this tendency to make meaningless small talk. I don't want to say something stupid and send the evening on a downward spiral after such a brilliant start – I need to stay calm and get to the end without knocking over a wine glass or oversharing my life story. I need to keep a little back and not throw myself at him until I know exactly who he is. Given some of the awful men I've met, I'm looking for the flaws, but so far, so good.

It's well documented that the online dating world is fraught with danger, from dinner with potential serial killers to outings with bad boys and mummy's boys. I'd been put off this kind of matchmaking, having spent my twenties going on dates with strangers off the internet. The first date often started well – let's face it, no one is going to reveal their weird habit, real age or secret wife on a first date. But things would soon start to slide, like the gorgeous guy who on our first and only date seemed funny, intelligent and charming and, after a wonderful dinner, invited me back to his for coffee. I jumped at the chance, but arriving at his mausoleum-like home, he took me upstairs and asked if he could brush my hair with his mother's hairbrush. She'd been dead ten years. I shudder now at the potential psychodrama I may have opened up, or if I'd even be here today, if I hadn't made my excuses and left.

So far, Alex is intelligent, good-looking, and hasn't mentioned his mother once. Nor has he referred to his 'beautiful' ex or introduced me to his 'love truncheon' under the table, as a previous potential mate did on a first date. It seems that Meet your Match, an app that states reassuringly that 'your soulmate is only ten minutes away', might just have the magic formula I've been seeking all these years. Hard to believe this Adonis before me was almost binned for an Indian takeaway and a night with Jasmine in our pjs watching Netflix. And it's Jas I have to thank for this, really. I wouldn't have even started online dating again without her encouragement. At thirty-six, I felt it was too late. But the way Alex is looking at me over his glass of wine, I'm beginning to think there might be someone for me after all.

'Have you been on many online dates?' he asks now.

'I was in a relationship for a while, so I'm new to Meet Your Match, but I went on quite a few dates in the past.' I roll my eyes. 'And, trust me, they weren't my soulmates. I haven't done this for years,' I add, gesturing from him to me. 'The last guy – who shall remain nameless – seemed nice enough. On our first date he told me he shaved his legs every day because he was a keen cyclist. Turned out the real reason he liked his legs smooth was because he liked wearing women's clothes. Now I have no problem with—'

'Men in tight dresses?'

'Honestly, I have no problem with that, you do you. But if something's such a big part of your life it is worth a mention before you invite anyone back for coffee.'

Alex laughs, so I plough on with the story, hoping it will amuse him and he won't think I'm mean.

'He took a particular liking to a leopard-print top I was wearing – he even asked if he could try it on!'

He stops drinking and looks horrified. 'While you were on the date? In public?'

'No, when he invited me back—' I stop, realising that this might give him the wrong impression, and that an invitation for coffee leads to my immediate abandonment of clothes. 'It was just coffee. That's all,' I add.

He smiles, and goes on to ask about my job, and I fill him in on the life and times of a social worker, how rewarding – and frustrating – it can be.

'Some of our clients need so much support, but we can't give it to them because of the slashed budget. I work with teenagers, and some of the shit that they've had in their lives is horrifying, and they're kids… still just kids.'

He shakes his head slowly, gazing at me, fascinated. I like the way he makes me feel.

'I was twenty-two when I got my first job and thought I could change the world.' I sigh. God, I sound like such a bloody cliché. I think it has more to do with erasing my past than making a difference, but I don't want to hand him my baggage at this early stage in proceedings. 'After fourteen years of battling, I've had to manage my expectations.' I take a sip of wine. To my surprise, he hasn't nipped into the silence with a story of his own like people often do. He's waiting to hear what I say next. 'Anyway, I now know I was deluded to think I could change *anything*,' I say, putting down my glass. 'There's not enough money or time to take every kid from every potentially abusive situation. And once we've pushed through all the red tape, sometimes it's too late.'

He's still listening intently. *I think I'm in love.*

'And... the kids are still being abused and neglected,' I continue, as he nods sympathetically. I feel indulged. After being ignored for such a long time in my previous relationship, I'm beginning to realise how it *could* be – how it *should* be. 'Sometimes I go home to my flat after a day of fire-fighting, and I feel so – pointless.' I probably should stop slurping the wine because I'm talking too much and I mustn't mess this up. 'Sorry,' I say, touching the stem of my glass and moving it away slightly.

'Don't apologise, you're driven – and that's a *good* thing. But I'm sad that it makes you feel that way.' He says this with such sincerity, that I know he means it. He isn't bored by my rant, he's *moved* by it.

'Jasmine, or Jas, as we call her, is my boss – and my friend – and she's always telling me I shouldn't get so involved. She says it can affect decision-making. And that I'd find the work easier if I was more detached...'

'Detached?' He laughs. 'Life would be so much easier if we were *all* more detached – but we're human, it's what we do. I take it your boss is a robot?' His eyes are laughing again.

'No.' I smile. 'She's one of the good ones.'

'But saying you need to be more detached seems a little harsh. I mean, it's your kindness, your caring that shines. If you stepped away, cared less – well, it wouldn't be Hannah – it wouldn't be who you *are*,' he says, as if he's known me forever. I feel like he has.

'I just need to be more professional. I react to situations with my heart, not my head,' I admit.

'I can relate to that.' He sighs. 'As a lawyer it's the same in my work, when I lose a case it really slays me, especially if I know someone's innocent. I feel I've let them down. I'm afraid I don't understand people who say "think with your head". That's for bankers and city types... and your boss.' He sighs again. 'Not me.'

I agree – it seems there's nothing we don't agree on. It's a strange but not unpleasant experience to finally meet someone who seems so in tune with me. I don't want this date to end and I'm more than happy to order dessert and make the evening last longer. He asks if I'd like to share one and I say no, because I love dessert and I want it all to myself, which makes him laugh.

When our desserts arrive, I give Alex strict instructions not to come anywhere near. He eats his portion of sticky toffee pudding, giving me a running commentary. 'It's sticky and sweet and warm... Oh the depth of that toffee, the reverberant echoes of earthy chocolate,' he gushes, closing his eyes in mock ecstasy.

I laugh, not only is he gorgeous, he's funny.

'What a shame you decided not to share your chocolate mousse with me. I might have shared this with you,' he teases.

I play along. 'Can I just try a teeny-tiny bit?' I say, making out that I want some, which actually I don't because my heart is sitting somewhere between my chest and stomach.

He shakes his head. 'Nuh-uh.'

'I don't want your pudding, anyway, I'm loving my mousse,' I tease, pretending to sulk.

'What's your very favourite dessert,' he asks, 'if you could have anything at all?'

'Mmm, probably pistachio ice cream.'

'Oh, nice,' he says, 'but this is better.' He tenderly lifts his spoon towards me.

Our eyes meet, and I take the sickly sweet treacly sponge from his spoon into my mouth. It feels intimate, sensual, and I welcome in the lush sweetness as it melts on my tongue. It's delicious, but I don't want any more, yet Alex is insisting and gently pushes another loaded spoonful of stickiness into my closed mouth. I have no choice, I either take it or end up with toffee goo all over my lips, so I open up and in it goes.

We both linger over coffee, and I get the feeling he wants to make things last longer too. But when we finally look around, we're suddenly aware there's only us left in the restaurant and the staff look like they want to go home. We get up to leave. I go on ahead, and turn to see him discreetly pick up my used coffee spoon and napkin, and push them into his trouser pocket.

I look at him, smiling quizzically as a bored waiter stands holding the door open for us. 'Did I just see you steal cutlery?' I murmur, under my breath.

For the first time all evening he loses his composure slightly and seems a little flustered. For a moment I wonder if I've spoiled everything by even mentioning it, he obviously hadn't realised I'd seen him, but as we step out into the cold night air, he seems to find his smile again.

'I'm short of teaspoons,' he says.

'Isn't everyone?' I giggle and don't mention my used napkin. I don't want to embarrass him, nor do I want this perfect evening to be tainted by anything weird. So I leave it. For now.

An hour later, as we stand in the inner doorway of my block of flats, Alex says I still have some toffee on my cheek. He touches my face, and with his other hand pulls me towards him gently, but firmly. I melt into him, he smells of pine forests and leather – and a subtle undercurrent of something else, smoky, and dark. I breathe him in as he kisses me deeply, taking me somewhere else, filling my head with wonderful nonsense, and I close my eyes, drifting off into the night. And then, to my absolute surprise, in the middle of all this, he pulls away. I open my eyes, and he's just looking down at me. It's dark, and as hard as I try I can't see his face properly to work out what's happening. I feel confused, abandoned, he's now holding me away, his hands on my shoulders.

Then he suddenly kisses me on the top of my head and says, 'Goodnight, Hannah, it's been lovely.'

I long for him to say more, to pull me in again, to tease me with more kisses, to take things further, but he doesn't, he just turns and walks away.

I think I might cry with disappointment and confusion as I watch him go, the street lamps providing a grainy light over the road and houses and a dark figure walking away. It reminds me of his photos on Instagram, bleak, unreadable, rain reflected in pavements. I stand in the cold for a long time after he's gone. Tonight, I've been adored and rejected within a matter of hours, and now my chest is wide open, and my heart exposed – visible for anyone who might be passing to see.

CHAPTER TWO

When I woke this morning, the first thing I thought about was last night. I made a pot of tea, and thought about his eyes; microwaved some porridge and analysed everything he'd said, every facial expression, every nuance. I've pushed away the kiss that ended so abruptly, and tried not to dwell on the spoon and napkin he slipped into his pocket. Instead, I'm reliving the best parts of the evening. Driving to work, I almost ran a red light remembering how his hand brushed mine, the way he looked at me, and listened. Really listened.

'How was last night?' Sameera calls when I arrive at work, popping her head out from the office kitchen expectantly.

'Good, good,' I answer, grateful for the camaraderie and support from my colleagues, but wishing at the same time they didn't have to know everything. My fault, I overshare – but what I don't tell them, Jas does, so Sameera and Harry, my other colleague, pretty much get filled in one way or another.

'Did you get laid?' Harry asks.

'Like I'd tell you if I did!' I laugh.

'Oh no, were you catfished?' He laughs. 'Was he really a seventy-six-year-old with a heart problem and a harem of young brides?'

'He was lovely actually.' I smile.

'Any gaffer tape and scissors in his car?'

I smile, and stick my tongue out at him.

In this profession, you get close to your co-workers quickly. When you're dealing with the mess of life, you need support, and you give it too. There are just four of us in the office, we go through a lot together on a daily basis, and our bond is deep.

'So, how did it go?' Jas mouths through the glass pane of her office. I'm now checking my phone to see if he's called, or texted. He hasn't. 'Come on, spill the beans, I want to know everything,' she calls, beckoning me in with her finger.

Jas has taken it upon herself to be my 'dating coach'. After my horrible break-up with Tom last year she's encouraged me to meet new men. Jas lost her husband, Tony, in a car accident more than ten years ago, and I can only imagine how devastated she must have been to suddenly become a widow in her thirties. I think Jas is almost scared of finding love again in case she loses it, which explains why she only seeks casual relationships, and wants to live vicariously through me. Now she wants a blow-by-blow account of last night. But it doesn't matter how well I think it went, the fact we haven't made arrangements for a second date makes me feel I may have got it all wrong. I so want to believe it went well, but why did he pull away from the kiss? Did I misread the signals? I'm torn between feeling elated and wondering if I'll ever see him again.

Margaret, our receptionist and admin assistant, waves at me from across the office. 'Was he as good looking as his photo?' she asks, having studied his online profile in some detail, along with the rest of the office, last time she popped up on her break.

'Better looking, if that's possible, Margaret,' I call back.

She smiles and gives me a wink. She's like the office mum, even bakes cakes for us all on our birthdays. 'I was never lucky enough to have my own children,' she once said to me, 'but the universe has a way of giving you what you need.'

Last night, the universe gave me Alex. But now it's playing twisted games and might have plans to take him away. As the minutes tick away with no word from him, my heart is beginning to feel slightly tender.

'Thing is,' I say to Jas, after I've given her the highlights of my date, 'I'm not sure he feels the same.' I told her about the kiss, but haven't mentioned the spoon and napkin 'theft'. It isn't important, and she'll only turn it into a drama. 'Why do you think he didn't invite himself to come in for coffee, Jas?' I know she'll have a theory.

'Oh girl – it *has* been a while, hasn't it?' She sits back in her chair, plonking her Converse-clad feet on the desk. Jas loves throwing her energy into my non-existent love life, it's probably a welcome break from the traumatised teens and lost adolescent souls we deal with every day.

'Men these days don't want to come over as pushy, they're scared of being accused of some heinous crime. Or perhaps he was just playing games with you by making you *want* him, then pulling away?'

'Two solid theories, but what if he just didn't fancy me?'

She laughs.

'I mean... my photos on the app make me look quite attractive, but what if he thought I was horrible in the flesh? Do I look older, fatter?'

'Hannah,' she says, 'please stop with this constant self-flagellation. It's boring. But if he didn't mention a second date, then his loss – he doesn't appreciate how amazing you are. Men never do – you're *gorgeous*, and don't you forget it.'

'And you're kind – or blind.' I roll my eyes, I'm not good at taking compliments. 'It *seemed* to go so well though. I *thought* he liked me. But I drank a lot of wine – Merlot – turns out that's *his* favourite too. Honestly, Jas, we have so much in common, it's mad.'

'Merlot, eh? I hope you're not going to start drinking Porn Star Martinis with *him*, that's *our* drink,' she jokes.

'No way. You'll always be my Porn Star Martini partner.'

'He probably wasn't that great anyway,' she says as a softener. 'You saw him through the bottom of a wine glass. It's easy for them to come over as a dream guy on a first date, but, trust me, a few dates down the line and you'd have seen a different guy to the one you saw last night.'

I know she's only trying to console me, but it isn't working. Jas was the one who suggested I go on the bloody dating app, so it's annoying that she's doing her 'no fish in the sea worth having' speech now.

'Jas, if you'd been there, if you'd met him, you'd know what I'm saying – we just *fit*.'

'I'm sure you do and, hey, there's nothing to stop you giving *him* a call,' she suggests.

'Mmm, I could,' I murmur doubtfully.

She raises her eyebrows and, lifting her long, denim-clad legs off the desk, brings the conversation to a close with her body language.

Harry's in the doorway waiting to see her, so I get up and move to the door.

'Have you two finished discussing… no, dissecting, the men you slept with last night?' Harry asks.

'Cheeky sod,' I say, laughing. 'I didn't sleep with *anyone.*'

'Probably just as well, because he *will* kill again,' he says in an American accent, while slowly putting his hands around my neck.

I waft him away, like a pesky fly. Harry's only twenty-six, and sometimes it shows. We all love him, but sometimes he's like an annoying little brother.

'Let me know if you hear anything, or if you decide to call him,' Jas says, ignoring Harry completely. 'I mean, it's not the 1940s.'

'I know, but I—'

'When you two have finished with the dating therapy, we have a nine thirty.' Harry gestures towards Jas with his head.

Jas rolls her eyes. 'Come in.' She turns back to her desk, and I have to smile as I close the door and hear her say, 'So, have you told Gemma that you love her yet?'

Jas loves getting in people's business, and when she's not being the boss, she's the office agony aunt. Last year she convinced Harry to break up with Natalie, his childhood sweetheart, said they weren't right together. Then, after going into Brown's Bakery one day, she spotted Gemma working behind the counter and decided she was 'the one' for Harry. His budding romance with Gemma has been like a daily soap ever since, with Jas tutoring him at every turn.

'I might become a matchmaker if this social work thing doesn't work out,' she jokes. But it seems Jas has good instincts for romantic couplings, because Harry's been with Gemma for almost a year now, and they're madly in love. Harry's always looking for excuses to go to the café to see her, and one of those excuses is to pick up something delicious and high-calorie, which he offloads on me on his return. I'm not complaining though, Gemma bakes a mean cake and I rarely resist.

Harry's young and makes fun of his female colleagues' romantic aspirations, but deep down I think he's as starry-eyed as the rest of us. He told me once how when they were first together, Gemma made him a batch of mini doughnuts, and before she put each one to his mouth, she kissed it. I think that's probably the most romantic thing I've ever heard. At the time, I was still with Tom, and seeing Harry with Gemma just confirmed for me how far away we were from love. I thought last night I might actually be on to something but now it looks like I'm no further on.

Later, when Harry and Jas have had their meeting, Jas wanders over to my desk. Her dark, curly hair is fizzing around her face, her lips are a questioning pout enquiring without words if Alex has called, but I shake my head before she asks.

'He just didn't feel the same, obviously,' I mumble, lifting my head up from the computer screen.

'Yeah, he obviously found you repulsive,' she says, deadpan.

I must look surprised at this, because she lets out a belly laugh, her perfect white teeth framed by red lips. I start laughing too, and now Harry and Sameera are looking up to see what all the noise is about.

'Jas says I'm boring and ugly,' I say to them.

'Tell me something I don't know.' Harry shrugs, slipping into his default mode as the teasing younger brother.

Sameera throws a ball of paper at him. 'You're gorgeous, Hannah!' she says, frowning at him.

Having ducked the paper, he's now pretending to concentrate on work, but a dimple forms on his cheek. He's trying not to laugh, and I can see by his face he's thinking up a far worse punishment for Sameera than a rolled ball of paper.

Jas and I roll our eyes at each other, at the two 'kids' in the office.

A psychologist I worked with once told me that within a group of people, a family unit always emerges. However long they've known each other, people subconsciously take on familial roles, and I see this in our small team every day. Jas is in her early forties, she's in charge and very much the alpha, the big sister of the group. I don't think anyone would argue with my theory that at thirty-six, I'm the next big sister, while Sameera and Harry, both in their twenties, are the unruly kids.

I watch Jas as she answers a query from Harry about one of his clients. She's so 'on it', knowing exactly who he's talking about and responding clearly, in bullet points. She practises 'controlled emotional involvement', something we all know is the secret of a good social worker. She cares, she understands, she empathises, but doesn't allow emotions to cloud her judgement. Unlike me.

Despite a pile of paperwork on my desk and at least five home visits to do today, all I can think about is Alex, and my emotions are clouding *everything*. I watch Jas through the glass of her office and wonder if she's right that he's like all the rest. As she said, I know it's not just up to him to get in touch – but I want him to *want* a second date enough to call and ask me, rather than have me chase him.

A couple of hours later, I look up from my computer screen and realise, with a sharp sting, that he still hasn't called. I wonder if he's like me, and doesn't want to be the one to call. How many great love affairs have been dashed on the rocks before they began because neither had the courage to make that first move?

I'd given up on men, until Jas told me about Meet your Match. She convinced me that I should 'get back on the horse after Tom'.

'Even if it's just a bloke you can go to the cinema with, sleep with, someone to put your bins out,' she'd said.

'I want more than that,' I'd replied, as we sat at the bar of The Orange Tree that night.

'There's no such thing as a man who wants commitment. They all just want a one-night stand,' she said, as we sipped on Porn Star Martinis – 'our' drink.

'But I want a home, a family, three kids and… a Labrador. I want a big garden with a trampoline and holidays in Devon, like we did when I was a kid… and…'

'Pina coladas and walks in the rain?' She'd sighed. 'That's why you can't find anyone. I mean, talk of Labradors and kids would scare any normal man off. I think you need to be a bit more like me and lower your standards. All I ask is that a man is good in bed, makes a mean cheese on toast, doesn't ask too many questions… and who needs a dog and kids anyway?'

Jas is 'seeing someone' but not in a relationship. She's recently been hooking up with a teacher she met while working on a family case. They live their own lives and just meet up now and then, which she says she's happy with, but recently he hasn't been returning her calls, and she told me she thinks he's seeing someone else. I didn't think it would bother her too much, she's always said she isn't looking for commitment, doesn't want to be married again, but I sometimes wonder if she's lying to herself. She's forty-two and she loves kids, and whatever she *says*, I worry she might regret not being a mother. Perhaps I'm just imposing my fears on her, because I very much want marriage and kids and I'm not playing games with myself pretending I don't. I know it might sound old-fashioned, but that's what I want, a family of my own, and someone who's committed enough to stay with me beyond next weekend.

Jas's weekends are spent drinking too much wine, catching up on work and cleaning her house. Her place is pristine, the surfaces shiny, with a permanent smell of bleach and every little thing in its place. She says it's because of her past.

'I was a bit of a tearaway, slept with a lot of guys,' she once told me. 'I was underage and wild. I did it to get at my dad. He was so strict, he'd try and lock me in my room, so I'd climb out the window.'

'At least he cared?' I'd offered.

'Too much,' she said, and I'll never forget the look on her face. 'That's why I don't have a door on my bedroom.'

I remember putting my arm around her, and it was then I realised that, in very different ways, we shared lost childhoods. Hers was spent escaping home, and mine was spent searching for one.

I was nine years old when I moved into my first foster home. Mum couldn't cope, but I believed it was my fault, and living with strangers was my punishment for causing her distress. I didn't understand then that her drug addiction was the reason she couldn't function as a mother, it's only now I realise how my life was blighted.

Meeting Alex last night gave me a little glimmer of hope that I could meet someone with whom I could make a life I've always dreamed of, and even a real home. I just have this feeling he wants the same things I do, and I finally have the chance of having something good in my life. If only he'd call.

'Go on the app, prove me wrong and find Mr Right.' Jas had laughed through a haze of alcohol that night weeks ago in The Orange Tree. As the evening had worn on, she'd become more tipsy, and more keen for me to try it out. I distracted her for a while by putting 'Wonderwall' on the jukebox and singing along to it with her, but she's like a dog with a bone, is Jas.

'As your boss, I'm here to tell you that you work too hard, so it's time for you to chill, have sex and have *fun*.'

'I *do* have fun,' I'd protested.

'Oh yeah, I'm sure you do, sitting at home every night writing up reports, checking up on teenagers to make sure they're in their own bed and not someone else's?'

'That's why I'm in this job, to try and keep them safe.'

'Well, I think you should get out more. Ooh, he's hot.' She pointed to a photo on the app. 'A handsome solicitor, living minutes away and gagging for a thirty-something woman to complete his life? Yes please,' she gushed. 'Hannah, he's only just gone on the app – it's like buying a house, when a great one goes on the market, you need to pounce.'

'I'm not pouncing.' I laughed. 'I've online dated before – and it's not for me.'

'Look, just click "yes" now,' she yelled impatiently (she's always loud in bars), 'and if it doesn't work out, I'll have your sloppy seconds, he's gorgeous!'

So, fuelled by her enthusiasm, and alcohol, I clicked, and about fifteen minutes later he clicked on me. I suddenly felt nervous. What was I letting myself in for? I told Jas I'd changed my mind, but – typical Jas – she wasn't having that.

'Just give it a go, Hannah. You're going on a date, not marrying him for God's sake.' She'd laughed. 'Have some fun, and then, when we both get to sixty and we're still single and childless, we'll move in together.'

I laughed, hoping against hope that wasn't all I had to look forward to. I love Jas, but she isn't everyone's cup of tea. She has so much energy but sometimes doesn't know when to stop. She can take over if you let her, which is often irritating, but sometimes in life you *need* someone to take over, to pick you up and brush you off and tell you in a loud voice to your face that it's going to be all right. And after my break-up with Tom, she did all that, and she fixed me.

I'd been so crazy about Tom at first, I asked him to move in with me after a few weeks. But I realised pretty early on that this had just been infatuation on my part, and once I'd got past the blue eyes and the killer smile, there was little else. He'd wander in from work, turn on the TV, spread himself across the sofa, open a beer and be on his phone all night. I'd hoped for more – sustained eye contact or a conversation would have been a start. But things didn't change, and after the first few months what little flame there had been just sputtered and died. It was like living with a flatmate; there was soon nothing between us.

I gave it almost a year. Thing is, he just didn't know how to be a partner. He never listened to me, and often on a Friday he'd hand me a cheap bunch of flowers and think that made it okay for him to spend the weekend at the pub. As Jas pointed out at the time, 'He's just a rubbish boyfriend, and he won't ever change.'

So one Friday night, when everyone at work had been talking about their plans for the weekend, and I'd realised I didn't want to spend mine with him, I asked him to leave. It was really difficult because, as he'd said, he hadn't actually done anything wrong. But I told him I had too much work and didn't have the time for a relationship – but in truth I just didn't love him. 'You're just tired,' he'd said, and turned the TV volume higher to drown out my words. Which said it all really. Eventually he'd agreed to pack his bags and left that weekend.

I'd felt guilty, but I was also relieved. I didn't want to spend the rest of my life with someone who didn't give me anything. I felt I deserved more.

After he'd left that Saturday, I immediately called Jas, who'd reassured me I'd done the right thing. But Tom started phoning in tears, begging me to take him back, and even turned up at work and asked if he could walk me home. By then, he was sleeping on a friend's sofa and I felt so bad about making him homeless, I began to think it might be easier to just let him move back in. But Jas gave me the strength to say no – with kindness. And later when he turned nasty, and said it was my fault he'd been suspended from his job, she was there for me every step of the way, and without her support I don't know what I'd have done.

Jas was right, of course. The relationship would never have worked and I had to end it. But I saw Tom in a bar a few months back and he looked sad and rather dishevelled, and I worry that the break-up had a more lasting impact on him than I'd realised.

But I push away troubling thoughts of Tom, when I see the phone on my desk flashing. I pick up and catch my breath. It's a voicemail message from Alex.

CHAPTER THREE

'I wondered if you'd like to meet up again? Er… if you did, please call me.'

Short, sweet and possibly life-changing? I never expected Alex to call me at work. I didn't give him the number. He must have googled it. Just hearing his voice makes me want to do a little dance in the middle of the office – but I resist.

I check the next message, it's from him again. A moment's silence, no slick, scripted lines, just lovely flawed sentences, broken words.

'I… just realised, I left you a voice message and didn't leave my number. Don't feel under pressure to call. I like you, but I understand if… look, I've read situations wrong before, so no worries… Oh I'm rambling now. Sorry. Anyway, call me back if you had a good time, we could go out again, tonight, tomorrow, next week? Call me…' Reciting his number, he was clearly about to put down the phone, and I was about to melt into a puddle on my desk, when he said, 'Oh… also, you'd told me where you worked, so I thought it better to call and leave a message rather than call your mobile.' He paused, and I realised I was smiling from ear to ear like an idiot. 'That way, you can ignore the message. If that's what you want to do. And… if we bump into each other in the street, then you can pretend you didn't see me or you didn't get the message. Bye.'

I am seduced by his honesty, the way his words just tumble out, no façade, no bravado – it's so refreshing. He seems so sincere, and how sensitive of him to do it this way, not putting me in a difficult position if I wanted to say no.

I call him straight back from the work phone. He answers immediately, and I feel all squishy inside, as if I'm thirteen again and talking to my first crush.

'Hey, Alex, it's Hannah. I'd *love* to see you again,' I say.

'Great… that's really great, Hannah. I wasn't sure you'd call.'

His vulnerability touches me. 'Of course. I had a great time.'

'Me too. So… when are you free?'

'I'm free whenever.' He's not playing games, so neither am I.

'Tonight?' he suggests.

'Yeah, why not?'

'Great, great. Shall I come to yours and pick you up?'

'Why don't I meet you outside the wine bar, like last time?'

'Perfect, see you at eight?'

'Perfect.'

I put down the phone feeling as if I've just been wrapped in pink, scented cashmere. As hard as I try to manage my expectations, to prepare myself for disappointment, I'm also willing it to work. Having told myself for a long time that I don't need anyone but me, I now realise that I'm right – I don't need *anyone*. But I would like *someone*. And Alex might just be that someone.

'Oh God, it was the sweetest message,' I tell Jas over lunch.

We're having sandwiches from Greggs at her desk. She has a fancy coffee machine in her office so the two of us usually sit in here on the rare occasions we have time to eat. Today, we have about seventeen minutes before my next home visit and her meeting with the local head of social services, so it's a little rushed.

'I'm telling you, Alex is genuine,' I say, enjoying his name on my tongue. 'He's amazing, thoughtful, sensitive, and he listens… he actually listens, Jas.' I smile, warmed by the thought of him.

Jas gives me a warning look. 'Sounds too good to be true. And when someone seems too good to be true – that's because they are.'

'You've got to stop being so cynical,' I say, disappointed that she's not joining in on my excitement. 'Why are you suddenly against this – *you're* the one who suggested I go on Meet Your Match in the first place! You said it was just what I needed.'

'Yeah, but I meant to have fun, not to take it too seriously. You've only had one date with this guy and you're all over the place, talking dogs and kids and… It was the same with Tom, within days you'd fallen hook, line and sinker and moved him in. That makes you vulnerable, which is why Tom played you, Hannah. You did everything for him, and he gave you nothing back.'

'Tom was different. Alex is—'

'Yeah, I think we know all about Alex by now.' She rolls her eyes. 'You were supposed to go on the dating app for fun, that's all – so you could do something other than watch *The Great British Bake Off* every evening.'

'It isn't on every evening,' I say, a little stung by her words.

'You know what I mean. Sorry, didn't mean to sound like a bitch, it's just – you're already talking like you're madly in love and you don't *know* the bloke. Don't get yourself into another Tom situation.'

'I just told you, Alex isn't Tom,' I say defensively.

She sighs in exasperation. 'No, but this one…' She pauses, raises her eyebrows. 'I think the fact he didn't ask for another date *on* the night, but kept you waiting, then called your work phone randomly the next day is a big red flag, babe.'

'No it isn't.'

Jas takes a big bite of her sandwich, as I argue my point.

'If you heard him, Jas, you'd know what I mean – his honesty, is… well, it's quite disarming, and I believe him when he says he didn't want to put me on the spot. Trust me, this is a considerate guy who doesn't want to pressure me, that's all.'

She shrugs, as if to say *that's what you think*.

'So you're going out with him again?' She plonks her sandwich down and gets up to make coffee.

'Yes I am going out with him again.'

'When?' she asks.

'Well, he suggested tonight.'

Her lips purse, she's not pleased.

'What?' I press.

'Nothing,' she mutters, her back to me as she makes the coffee, then she turns round. 'It's – just that we were supposed to be going to the cinema tonight, to see that new Ryan Reynolds film.'

'Oh… God! I didn't realise we'd said *tonight*?' I'm sure we didn't make any arrangements. It was a vague conversation last week about how we must see the film. But still.

'Look, it doesn't matter if you've already arranged to see *him* tonight, it's okay. We could go another night, I suppose.'

'Do you mind?'

'Would it make any difference?' She puts a just whisked frothy coffee in front of me.

'Of course it would, don't be like that, Jas.'

'It's fine, I was just messing with you,' she says, but I don't think she was. 'If he's as gorgeous as he looked on his Meet Your Match profile, I don't blame you wanting to see him rather than me.' She plonks herself back down on her chair with her coffee and takes a sip. 'I might get a job as a barista if this doesn't work out,' she says.

'I thought you were going to be a matchmaker if social work isn't for you?' I joke, trying to lighten things. I feel guilty now. She's ambushed me slightly with our supposed cinema arrangements; what I thought of as a vague idea, was clearly seen by Jas as a booking. 'Jas, I really am sorry, I wouldn't have said yes to Alex if I'd thought you and I had made a firm plan.'

'It's fine, it's fine.' She drops the remains of her sandwich onto the desk. 'But it's not about me or the cinema – I just think you *so* should have suggested meeting tomorrow. Don't be so willing. "Make them wait" is my motto.'

'Yeah, but if he's honest, and doesn't play games, then why should I wait?' She doesn't respond. I think she's more pissed off about the cinema than she's making out.

'Look, Jas, I'm sorry about the cinema.'

'I don't care about the cinema – I can go with someone else.' She clearly does care.

'You don't *have* to go with someone else. *We* can go tomorrow night,' I say firmly. 'And I take on board what you're saying. Yes, I get involved easily, I fall fast. But I'm not applying your "controlled emotional involvement" rule to my personal life.' I smile to soften the irritation in my voice.

'That's not what I'm saying. All I ask is that you don't leap into another relationship and regret it, hon. Jeez, I sometimes feel when I'm talking to you like I'm talking to one of our teenagers.'

I ignore this, sometimes she pushes it too far. Likening me to some kid who's making bad choices is hardly fair.

'You know how you're always saying to me that I shouldn't get so involved with my clients' cases?' I say, biting into my tuna baguette.

Jas looks up from her coffee. 'Yeah?'

'Well, perhaps I am too involved. But it's because I have nothing else to fill my mind. And going out with a really nice guy like Alex will give me some perspective. So instead of worrying about clients, I'll have someone else to think about, won't I?'

'I suppose,' she says, throwing her sandwich wrapper in the bin, a full stop to our conversation. 'Sorry, babe, I have to get on with work now. I'm going to have to throw you out.'

'Of course.' I stand up and move out of her office, clutching the remains of my baguette and cup of frothy coffee. I know Jas too well: she can't hide her feelings and she's angry with me for being what she would see as 'weak'. She doesn't want us to argue, though, so she's going to work through her feelings – I know this because she told me that her therapist has said she must isolate herself when people make her angry or hurt her. I haven't intentionally hurt her, but from her perspective I have, by not taking her advice. She's complicated. Childhood abuse does that to a person. And Jas's sudden anger is just one of the emotional responses in an adult who's been sexually abused as a child.

We deal with damaged children all the time in our work, and that's what we are, Jas and I – we're damaged children who've grown up. But that doesn't define us. Most of all we're friends, and we understand each other. We both want the other one to be safe and happy, and she's just looking out for me, as I do her – I just wish she'd trust me to make the right decisions sometimes. And when it comes to Alex, I really believe this is the right decision.

Waiting outside the bar for Alex is hell. I rushed home from work after a difficult day, including a call-out from Chloe Thomson, a sixteen-year-old with slight learning difficulties. Chloe also has a challenging home life: her parents split up when she was younger and her mother, a drug addict, has just moved another of her boyfriends into the tiny flat they share. When I visited them today, her mum had a black eye, apparently caused by 'walking into something', which, of course, I don't believe. I tried not to think about poor Chloe as I showered, dressed and applied lipstick. I undid my hair, letting it fall loose around my shoulders, and pulled on a black polo-neck jumper, which I thought looked good with my blonde hair. I then ran all the way from my flat to the wine bar in the rain, and when I arrived, my umbrella had turned inside out and given up the ghost, so I threw it in the bin and stood outside under an awning. And now my hair is damp, frizzy and nothing looks good with it!

I've been waiting here for Alex for twenty-three minutes. After ten minutes, I checked inside to see if he'd already arrived, but I couldn't see him. I contemplated sitting at the bar, and ordering a drink, but there was a man standing by the bar staring at me, and when he pulled out a stool and patted it, I walked out. It's so cold and rainy, I consider going back inside, but what if Mr Weirdo is still waiting with my bar stool? Oh, I wish Alex would hurry up. Now I'm wondering if he's even going to turn up, and just as I'm about to call him to check I have the right place, he appears in front of me. He's twenty-seven minutes late, but full of apologies: 'I have this really big case on at the moment, and one of the lawyers I'm working with wanted me to meet her at 6 p.m. to discuss the case. Can you imagine?'

I bristle slightly at the thought of him not wanting to let down a female colleague, but seemingly happy to leave me in the rain.

'I wanted to say, "I'm meeting this really hot woman for a second date, so do you mind if we meet another day?" But, of course, I couldn't.' He rolls his eyes.

I force a smile. Work? Is that his only excuse? 'I was just about to leave,' I say. 'It's not how I expected to spend this evening, waiting in the freezing rain!'

His face drops. 'Oh, Hannah, I'm so sorry. I didn't have your number, so I couldn't let you know, but I should have called the bar, shouldn't I? Have I screwed this up already?'

I smile, softening at him clearly realising his error. 'Not yet, you're on probation though.'

'Promise I won't break the terms of my probation. Just give me a chance?' He's half-joking, but I can see this matters to him, that he cares that he was late. He isn't playing me, but I think Jas's warning has rattled me more than I realised, and it's made me actively look for negatives where there aren't any.

We decide to go into the wine bar for a drink, and while there, we chat about our respective work days, then he suggests a pizza. I'm starving, so we drink up and head for the door, but just glancing outside tells me the rain is now pretty torrential.

'We'll get wet through,' I say as we huddle together in the doorway.

'Where's your umbrella?'

'I don't have one.'

'Yeah you do. I mean… I thought…' he stutters, 'I just… I just *know* you'd be the sort of person to have one.'

'Actually, I did have one, it's in the bin.' I nod over to the bin on the pavement, the umbrella jammed in, looking like a dead crow, the spikes sticking up like feet. 'It died.'

'Oh dear.' He laughs and, taking off his jacket, gallantly holds it over my head. 'The pizza place is only about five minutes from here, isn't it?' he says into my ear. The brush of his lips on my earlobe is electric. 'Shall we make a run for it?' he asks, with a smile.

After a mad, splashy dash to the pizza restaurant, we are taken to a table, where we order Merlot. He refers to it as 'our usual', and I like how that sounds, like the two of us already have a history, we belong. Despite a little glitch at the start, when he arrived late and I was irritated, he's allayed all my doubts and this feels right.

I don't taste the pizza, I can barely remember what I ordered, something with mushrooms? I just can't stop looking at him, and his eyes are constantly on mine. Whatever Jas might say, if she was here right now, she'd *know* this is the real deal.

'So, you do criminal work?' I ask between mouthfuls, wanting to know everything about him.

'Yeah.' He smiles. 'Not the prettiest or most glamorous of practices, and I do end up spending a lot of time at the police station out of hours, drinking nasty tea and being sworn at.'

'Ahh, sounds fun,' I say, exaggerating the look of doubt on my face and thinking how even that sounds more pleasant than dealing with Chloe Thomson's mother. This afternoon, when I apparently asked one too many questions, she told me to 'F the F off' and slammed the door in my face.

'Yeah, it's okay actually. Today in court I managed to prevent a young guy going to prison. He'd been forced by his older brothers to help them steal cars, the charge sheet was endless and I used every trick in the book to try to get him a suspended sentence. In the end, all he got was a fine and community service – and you know what he said after the case?'

I shake my head.

'"I wanted to go back inside, mate."'

'Ouch. I think I'd be tempted to say, "Fight your own case next time!"' I put down my knife and fork; I don't want any more pizza, I'm too full.

'Yeah, but these kids don't stand a chance, do they? It's like the minute they're born, their lives are mapped out: peer pressure, poverty, drugs, prison, abuse…'

'That's where I come in.'

'Yeah, I guess you do.' He's shaking his head sadly, remembering what happened. 'And then… it was raining when we walked from the court. He had on a T-shirt and no money for a bus or a train.'

'That's sad,' I say, knowing from my experience that, for some, bus fare is a luxury.

'So I ended up giving him a lift home.'

I feel my heart swell at this. 'That was kind of you.'

'Yes, I hope in some way it helped him feel like I cared beyond the court – not just as someone paid to do a job.'

'I'm sure it did, some people have never known simple kindness.'

He nods. 'And how is anyone ever expected to free themselves from a life of crime when they have nothing, and no hope of anything? He's nineteen and he already feels like he has no future.'

I nod, I know exactly what he means. 'Gosh, you sound like me. I wrote a piece for a social-work blog recently and said exactly that.'

'Did you? I'd love to read that sometime.'

I blush slightly, loving the fact he's taking such an interest.

'I dropped him off at his flat,' he continues. 'Peeling paint, the smell of urine… I gave him thirty quid, it was all I had on me, but, do you know, I swear I saw tears in his eyes. I sometimes wonder why I didn't become a wealthy, corporate lawyer – but *that's* why – for kids like him, who have no faith, and no one fighting for them.'

He looks at me, and I feel a physical tug. This guy is truly wonderful.

He shrugs, and takes a breath. 'So, are we having dessert again today?' He lifts the menu, dismissing his heroic act of kindness.

Modest too.

I can't eat any more, my stomach is in knots, my appetite always diminishes when I fall for someone. It's all or nothing with me, I'm either fat and single or skinny and in love.

'I'm too full for dessert,' I say.

He reaches his hand across the table. The tips of his fingers touch mine. It's so erotic. He looks into my eyes. 'I know it's only our second date, but it's… good – this.' He gestures to me and back to him and I nod eagerly.

'Yes, it's good,' is all I can utter. I want to say so much more, I want to tell him how I haven't felt like this for years, how my ex barely noticed me, how I didn't think I'd ever be able to love someone again, and it's all so quick but right now I think it's happening. But of course I don't say any of this, I need to take this gently and don't want to scare him off.

But when he kisses me outside my door a little later and suggests we meet again tomorrow night, I tell him breathlessly, 'I can't wait.'

I run up the steps to my flat, while he watches me go in – he's so sweet, making sure I'm safely inside before leaving. But just as I get inside and walk towards my door, I hear something outside. I turn and a sudden banging on the door scares me half to death. I know I shouldn't just open the front door, but it might be Alex back to take me in his arms, and even if it isn't Alex, the banging will wake my neighbours in the downstairs flat.

I go to the door, and open it cautiously – and, to my deep relief, it's him. I half-expect him to try and kiss me, but he doesn't.

'Sorry, Hannah, I don't have your mobile number!' He's leaning in the doorway, breathless, sheltering from the rain. I laugh, relieved it was him, and we swap numbers before he runs off into the rainy night, stopping briefly to wave at me as I stand on the doorstep watching him trip between puddles, lit momentarily by a street light or a passing car.

When he's finally out of sight, I go inside and dash up two flights of stairs without even feeling it. Falling in love even makes exercise bearable – I could run up twenty flights tonight if I had to! Once inside, I put the kettle on, make a camomile tea and relive the evening in my head. It's like watching a favourite old film again and again, remembering every nuance, every word, the way his smile gives him a twinkle in his eyes, causing his face to light up suddenly.

I shake my head. It's early days; I need to stop thinking about him all the time, Jas warned me about that. Oh crap. Crap. *Crap. Jas!* I promised to go to the cinema with her tomorrow evening, and I've just arranged to see Alex. Oh God, I would never be *that* woman who dumps her friend the minute a man comes along. But, then again, I don't want to cancel on Alex either. This is new and I don't want him to think I don't like him or I've changed my mind – or that I'm unreliable. What the hell am I going to do?

CHAPTER FOUR

It turns out there's no way Jas would have let me stand her up tonight. She's already booked two cinema seats and is even talking about what kind of popcorn we'll be eating during the film, and it's only 10 a.m.! I'm going to have to text Alex, I can't even call him because she'll hear and I don't want her to think I was even *considering* seeing him tonight because it will hurt her feelings. I'm wary of not wanting another lecture from her. Jas's heart is in the right place but she simply wouldn't understand what's already between me and Alex.

So, I text Alex, wanting to let him know as early as possible that I can't see him tonight. I explain that it's something I'd previously agreed to and suggest we do something later in the week. He doesn't get back to me straight away, he's probably busy.

Harry arrives in the office a little later, carrying a warm almond croissant in a napkin. 'For you, madame,' he says, throwing it on my desk.

'Ooh thank you, but you shouldn't,' I say.

'I *should*, it's your favourite. Gemma had some extras, so I grabbed one for you.'

'You're right,' I say, biting into the moist croissant. 'It is my favourite. When are you going to marry this girl, damnit?'

He laughs, as he saunters over to his desk. 'I'm too young for marriage. We're fine as we are.'

'Sameera's usually here first, is she not in this morning?' I ask. She's closest to Harry.

'Sameera?' he says, looking over at her desk. 'Oh yeah, she's, er…' He has to rack his brain. 'Doing something boring, like getting fitted for a wedding dress, tasting the bloody cake for the hundredth time.'

I laugh. 'You're such a lad, Harry.'

'Well, it's a load of rubbish, isn't it?'

'You might think that, but us ladies of a certain age dream of *rubbish* like that, I know I certainly do.'

He laughs and shakes his head.

'Do you ever see you and Gemma getting married?' I ask.

'Nope.' He's still young, but I'm surprised by his determined reply; he seems so happy with Gemma, so focused on her.

'Why not?'

'Dunno, I've never really thought about it. And Gemma's never asked me.' He shrugs.

'Yeah, she's just using you for your body, I reckon.'

'Let's hope so, eh?' he says absently, as he sorts through his post.

I log onto my computer. 'I was like you once, but as you get older, your perspective changes. I used to think marriage was patriarchal, archaic and all that – but now I think I really could see myself in white lace.' I don't mention that in my mind's eye I'm standing next to Alex, who I only met in the flesh a few nights ago.

Harry looks up. 'Slight flaw in your plan though – you need to find a groom to match the dress.'

'Yes, there is that minor point. But the latest contender is looking pretty promising.' I smile.

'Oh, really?' I can see he's not that interested. I wish Sameera were here, she's getting married in the New Year and loves talking weddings.

'Yeah. I like him,' I say, understating my feelings. 'It's early days – we've only had two dates – but I'm… hopeful.'

'I thought you said after whatshisname you weren't going out with anyone again,' Harry says, his eyes drifting back to his computer screen, bored of the conversation already.

'I did, but never say never.' I pick up the croissant he gave me and change the subject. 'Thank you, but you mustn't keep giving these to me, Harry, I'll get fat.' Really, it's a godsend – I never have time for breakfast before I leave, and who knows when I'll get lunch today.

He smiles and starts typing, apparently our rather one-sided wedding chat now over.

I take a bite of croissant and make a mental note to buy him something in return for all the sweet treats he keeps bringing us all. I check my phone. Alex has texted me back about tonight.

> *That's a shame ☹ but no worries, you enjoy the cinema. I had been thinking I might cook you dinner tonight. I need to make it up to you for me being late on date 2. So how about dinner at mine tomorrow night – if you'd like?*

I text him back straight away.

> *Yes. Thanks, sounds great. I'll look forward to it. X*

This time his reply is instant.

> *Me too! X*

I feel good. I've managed the situation and kept everyone happy, which, for an inherent pleaser like me, is all that's required. Alex is proving to be as perfect as I thought by taking it in his stride, and also confirmed a third date, *and* he's cooking. He's doing everything right.

Later, as Jas and I enjoy the cinema, I realise that I can juggle my slightly needy but well-meaning friend with my new boyfriend, I just have to be sensitive, and not go on about him. We both lust after Ryan Reynolds instead.

'God, what I would give for fifteen minutes with him,' Jas says as we leave the cinema and walk to the wine bar for a last drink.

'Yeah, me too,' I echo, not really feeling it. What I really think is that I'd rather spend fifteen minutes with Alex, which I know sounds crazy.

'I loved it, but I felt like the mother in that movie was totally one-dimensional,' she adds.

I agree, and we sit down with our drinks and talk about the representation of mothers in the media.

'Mothers get a bad press,' I say.

'Yeah, but they're not all Madonnas.' She sighs. 'Look at our mothers.'

'I find it hard to deal with my mother and my past.' I sigh. 'I'd rather think about the future, it helps me overcome the past.'

'Good luck trying to overcome *my* past. It's what shapes us, Hannah, and it doesn't matter how positive we all try to be – our past is who we are.'

'Yeah but our lives aren't pre-destined. Just because my mum was an addict doesn't mean I am, I've fought tooth and nail to have a different life.'

'Mmm, sadly my life's a cookie cutter of my mother's. That guy I've been seeing, Richard?'

'Yes,' I say.

'I was right. He's shagging someone else.'

'Oh, Jas, that's crap. Do you *know* that for sure?'

'Yes.' She looks down. 'I know we were casual, but I thought we were heading somewhere.'

'Yes, but either way, it was a conversation he should have had with you,' I say, feeling protective of her. On the surface she seems so strong, always looking out for everyone else, fiercely guarding her friends – yet she's so vulnerable herself.

'Exactly. Anyway, I confronted him last night, told him I'd seen some texts on his phone. Hannah, the thing that hurts most isn't the betrayal. It's the fact he'd clearly wanted me to see them. And after he'd "confessed", he said he felt so much better.'

I shake my head. 'Sorry. I didn't know you'd actually found proof – texts.'

'You've been busy,' she says pointedly.

'Not too busy for you,' I say, feeling guilty now.

She shrugs and takes a large glug of her drink.

'I didn't realise you were exclusive…' I pause.

'What do you mean?' She quickly turns to look at me. 'It wasn't that regular, but… it still bloody hurts.' The flash of anger in her eyes surprises me. It isn't like her to be snappy, she must be upset.

'I'm not saying you're not hurting,' I add quickly, putting my hand on hers. 'I just think sometimes you push people away until they go, and then you're surprised. But it doesn't sound like he was someone you'd want to stick around anyway,' I say, back-tracking slightly to spare her feelings. 'I mean, you said yourself it sometimes felt like a booty call… for both of you,' I say clumsily, and want to bite my tongue as the words tumble onto the table.

She glares at me. 'Wow.'

'I'm sorry that came out all wrong, I was trying to console you, make you feel like you hadn't actually *lost* anything but…'

'But instead you managed to trivialise my relationship *and* my feelings in one sentence. Nice one, Hannah.' She takes another large, angry glug of wine.

'I didn't mean—'

'You know what I think?' she interrupts.

I'm not sure I want to hear this.

'You've had *two* good dates and suddenly you think you're the authority on what constitutes a relationship.' She throws the rest of her wine down her throat and orders two more.

'I'm not. And I really wasn't trivialising—'

She lifts up her hand in a 'stop' gesture, and I go back to my drink, knowing when she's like this it's best to stop apologising, because I'll only dig a deeper hole. Jas's calm work persona is quite different from her personal one, where a rather fiery undercurrent sometimes flares up when she's hurt, or angry.

I realise how I must sound to Jas's cynical ears, and I don't blame her for being angry, she probably thinks I'm being a smug know-all. Which I'm not, but I change the subject anyway, and we talk again about the film.

But being Jas, she can't let it lie, and wounded by what she sees as criticism about her single status, she soon swoops back to me and Alex. 'So, how *is* everything in Camelot?' she asks.

I pretend I don't hear the sarcasm in her comment, just the humour. 'Great. He's cooking for me tomorrow,' I add, wanting to share this with my friend but at the same time feeling guilty for my happiness.

'You'll be moving in next week.'

'No, that would be too soon.'

'I was joking,' she says tartly.

'So was I.' I smile. But inside I'm disappointed in Jas's reaction. She's supposed to be my best friend and I would love her to support me on this. 'Jas, I know the timing's crap, you've just finished with Richard,' I say going along with her relationship narrative, 'but I wish you could be a tiny bit happy for me. You've always been so encouraging before, but this time you seem, I don't know, really quite negative.'

The penny seems to drop and her face changes, then she puts her arm around me. 'Babe, I'm sorry, you're right, I'm being selfish. It's just that sometimes I look around and see other people in settled relationships, and it reminds me of how I used to be before…' her voice trails off and I realise I should have known this negativity isn't about me and Alex. It's about Tony. She doesn't speak about him much because it's still so painful, probably always will be.

'I know you still miss him, even after all this time,' I say, touching her arm.

She nods. 'People expect me to be over it, but when someone you love dies, you never get over it. Hell, it's been years, I was a different person when I was married – but he'll always be here.' She touches her chest.

'I can't begin to understand the pain.' I sigh.

'Sameera getting married makes me think about my wedding day, all the hope, and the optimism. And you've met this guy who *seems* great—' She puts the emphasis on 'seems' and I wince slightly. 'And when I say things, it isn't because I'm being negative about him – I just don't want you to get hurt. So please don't take my "negativity" as anything more than just me trying to look after my friend.' She smiles and squeezes my hand. 'I am happy for you – just cautious.'

'I know. But I'm good – and what's the worst that can happen? He could turn out to be as rubbish as Tom? But I want to enjoy the fun and the butterflies bit while it lasts… And I need my bestie with me.'

'I'm there for you, girl, but you can be naïve – and, let's face it, I'll be the one picking up the pieces if this one falls apart, won't I?'

I bite my tongue. Her comment has annoyed me, but the ice-cold Pinot soothes my hot throat, taking the edge off slightly.

'I think we both need to start prioritising ourselves,' I say to Jas. 'And you, madam, need to stop worrying about everyone else's love life and concentrate on your own.'

'What love life? Everyone but me has one. Even bloody Harry's in a long-term relationship.' She laughs mirthlessly. I reckon it's a hazard of the job: she's great at other people's relationships but seems to have so much disappointment in her personal life. I'm the same when it comes to clients and friends: I care too much about everyone else and don't always consider my relationships. Perhaps that's what happened with Tom and me. If I'd been more present, and not immersed in my job, he might have become a better partner, a more caring, more engaged boyfriend. After all, it takes two.

'I might go and see that shrink again,' Jas says, playing with the stem of her glass.

'Yes, that might help.' I nod, feeling doubtful. In our line of work, we have access to therapy, but it didn't really work for me. 'My problem with therapy,' I say, 'is I feel guilty about how *my* guilt is affecting the therapist. How's that for irony?'

'Silly cow.' She laughs. 'I told you, anyway, you don't need a therapist. You can just talk to me.'

'Yeah, thanks, Jas,' I say, but it seems that my friend's support comes with conditions. I'm still smarting slightly from her earlier comment about having to be the one who picks up the pieces when my love life goes pear-shaped. 'Jas – just so we're clear – you really don't have to take on responsibility for me. I'm making my own choices and, whatever happens, I'm perfectly capable of looking after myself,' I say gently.

'I know you are, but it took you a while to come round after the Tom stuff – him blaming you for everything bad in his life, the phone calls and other weird shit. And because of that you weren't present for a while, I just don't want to lose my best friend. Again.'

'Yeah, I know.'

It was tough after Tom, and he didn't make it easy, but I've moved on now, and don't want to think about all that.

'I just want you to know that I'll be there for you whatever. If he hurts you, or if he's married or—'

'Jas, enough,' I say, and raise my eyebrows in a gentle warning gesture.

'Sorry, I just think—' She can see by my facial expression I don't want to hear this again, and she thinks better of it.

'Perhaps you should go on Meet Your Match?' I suggest, knowing that if she had a new relationship, it might be a distraction and she might worry less about mine.

'No way, I need a break from men,' she huffs. 'I'm certainly not chasing them online. I'm perfectly happy on my own.' She smiles, but her eyes say something different.

CHAPTER FIVE

The following day is a nightmare of red tape and drama, interspersed with Jas sniping, Sameera shushing, and a mess of crumbs all over the desks from Gemma's leftover lemon cake, which Harry brought in for us to comfort eat. The way the day's panning out I reckon we could do with even more sweet carbs – we've eaten everything in sight.

'I think Chloe Thomson's having issues with her mum's new boyfriend and Jack Morris has nowhere to sleep tonight – and that's just for starters,' I say to Jas when she asks if I'm busy.

'Okay, sounds like *my* day.' She sighs. 'I'm tired and was hoping I could go early tonight, but I can see that's not going to happen.'

'Yeah, God only knows when I'm going to leave the office,' I grumble. 'I'd better call Alex to say I'm going to be late.'

'Oh yeah, he's cooking for you tonight, isn't he? Lucky you!' she says, wandering back to her office. She said this kindly, with no apparent subtext and I appreciate that she's trying to be positive for me.

I pick up the phone to call Alex. 'I know you're cooking and everything but I'm going to be working late tonight,' I explain when he answers.

'That's okay. You're allowed to be late,' he teases. 'After all, I was late last time.'

I'm grateful for this, he's so laid-back and isn't making a big deal of it. 'Things are crazy here. We can postpone if you like.'

'No, no! I've been slaving over this hot oven for hours,' he jokes.

'Oh, aren't you at work?'

'Yes, well… I was. I left early, abandoned everything so I could make your dinner.'

I laugh. 'In that case, I'll get there as soon as I can. Is that okay?'

'Yes, absolutely. Just promise me that whatever time you finish, you'll still come over.'

It's so lovely to feel wanted, especially after Tom, who never made me feel that way.

'I will… and, Alex…'

'Yes?'

'Thanks for being so understanding.'

'It's okay, it's the same for me when I'm in court or I've got a big case on. I guess we'd both better get used to it,' he says good-naturedly.

I'm delighted at the suggestion that he sees this as more than three dates – 'we'd better get used to it' is music to my ears. I flush slightly and giggle stupidly.

As I put down the phone, Jas catches my eye from the open door of her office. 'You okay?' she mouths.

'Yeah,' I mouth back. I smile, and get back to Chloe's problematic relationship with her mother's boyfriend and other unfolding dramas.

'Hey Hannah.' Margaret appears in the doorway of our office. She's come up from reception and she's holding the most beautiful bunch of cream roses.

'These are for you, lovely,' she's saying as she walks towards me. I'm really hoping Jas is watching, because the most stunning bouquet is coming my way, and I just know they're from Alex. He knows I'm having a hell of a day, I'm going to be working late, won't get to his until even later – and this is Alex's way of saying it's okay. I just want Jas to see how different he is from Tom, and that she doesn't need to worry about me this time.

'For me?' I feign surprise, I don't want to appear too smug, but I can't help but smile as I take the huge bunch of what looks like fifty long-stemmed roses from Margaret's arms. He must have put the phone down from me and ordered these straight away to get here so soon.

'Looks like you've hit the jackpot with this one.' Margaret smiles.

'I think I have Margaret.' I smile, knowing I'm flushed and everyone's looking at me.

'Ooh, they must have cost a *fortune*!' Sameera says as she wanders over to check them out.

I push my face into the blooms, the smell is exquisite, and I lay them down on the desk while Sameera helps me tear off the gift card. I know who they're from, but I want to read what he says. I'm going to keep this gift card forever, so I can look at it when we're an old married couple, and remember how it was in the very beginning.

'Raj never sends me flowers.' Sameera sighs, caressing the blooms now lying on my desk.

'I don't think Bill's ever sent me flowers, and we've been married thirty years,' Margaret says. 'Don't let this one go, love,' she adds before leaving.

Sameera's still gazing at the blooms, and Harry's smiling at us.

'You'd think you two had never seen a bunch of flowers,' he says, shaking his head and going back to his computer screen.

'Oh, these aren't just "a bunch of flowers" though! Hannah, they're breath-taking… I want Raj to send *me* some too!' she jokes.

I smile and open the small envelope, there's a little card with LOVE written on the front. I look up at Sameera, and we both smile, sharing this little moment. We're bonding because we're both in love and we know what this feels like.

'It might be a proposal!' she gasps.

'Don't be daft, we've only just met,' I reply.

In truth, I wish I could take the note, run into the bathroom and read it in private – after all it is private – but Sameera's looking at me, waiting to see what it says, and it would seem mean to leave with it now. So I open the card and glimpse the message. It's printed, because presumably he ordered the flowers. I settle down to read it. It's just a few sentences, but I want to savour each word. I start to read it quietly.

'*I had to send you these delicate, scented blooms because they remind me of you my darling…*'

I hear Sameera giggle and clap her hands together excitedly. 'This one is SO a keeper!'

I roll my eyes and continue, but as I read, the words aren't coming out right. It doesn't sound like Alex – I know this even this early into our relationship – and I can't make sense of it at first. I stop reading out loud, and wordlessly hand it to Sameera.

They remind me of you because you are the thorn among these roses, and I know what you're up to, you treacherous bitch. You can't ever leave me. I am watching, always watching, you lying whore – every breath you take. Until even that stops.

Always with you. X

'Why? Why would he say something like that?' Sameera's saying, almost tearful as I sit behind my pile of cream roses – a perverse bridal joke.

'It isn't Alex.' I sigh. 'This has to be Tom.'

Sameera puts her hand to her mouth, I'll never forget the look of horror and pity on her face. In the silence, Harry gets up from his seat and Jas comes out of her office.

'You okay, love?' she's asking.

'Tom,' I say, my eyes welling up. 'I thought he'd stopped with the weird shit, but clearly he hasn't.'

Jas picks up the card from the ground where I threw it as I realised what it was. She nods slowly. 'Yeah, *probably* Tom... but then again?'

'*Definitely* Tom,' I say angrily, shutting her down and picking up my phone.

'Are you calling the police?' Jas asks.

I shake my head. 'I'm calling bloody Tom, and *threatening* him with the police,' I say, furious that he's still trying to ruin my life.

Why can't he just move on? He's become so bitter and resentful since we parted – and the only reason I'm not directly calling the police is because I can't actually prove it's him. And in truth because I still feel guilty about throwing him out and I don't want to push him further down. Having been a foster child, I know how it is to be ejected from your home without understanding why, and I still find it hard to reconcile myself to the fact I did it to someone else, but enough is enough. I wait and wait for him to pick up so I can yell down the phone as Jas and Sameera stand by my desk looking a little shell-shocked. But he doesn't pick up so I leave a very angry message threatening him with the police.

'Hell, he really does need to move on,' Jas says.

'I know. For God's sake, he wasn't that bothered when we were together, where's all the passion and inventiveness come from now?'

'Perhaps if he'd shown you some of that then you'd still be with him?' Sameera offers.

'Hardly, he's turned out to be a bloody psycho since she dumped him... if it is him,' Jas says.

Harry goes back to his desk, opening a tube of Smarties and swallowing most of them in one go. 'You don't half pick 'em, Hannah,' he says.

'I reckon that's an understatement.' I sigh, trying to work out why Tom would do something like this.

Looking back, he took our break-up far worse than I expected him to, and seemed genuinely upset and reluctant to leave the flat.

Then a couple of days after he left, I started receiving phone calls in the middle of the night from an anonymous caller. Someone was breathing heavily – it was really creepy and made me feel very uncomfortable, but I knew it was him. Who else could it be? I didn't want to pour oil on troubled waters though and, when I told Jas and the others, we all came to the conclusion that the best thing I could do was to ignore the calls.

'If you phone him up to tell him to stop, then you're giving him the attention he craves,' Jas had said, 'so he'll just keep on doing it.'

So after that I'd just turn off my phone when I went to bed. But then, one night, at about 3 a.m., I was woken up by this shuffling, snuffling noise outside. It was really weird; it sounded like someone sniffing at the front door. I sat up in bed, the hair ends of my scalp prickling, until whatever, or whoever, it was left. After about twenty minutes it seemed to stop, but by then I was in tears, petrified. I thought about calling the police, but would they take me seriously if I called them to say I'd heard sniffing around my front door? After all, it might have been just that. One of my neighbours has a dog, it could have been him. But I've never heard it before or since.

The heavy-breathing calls were scary enough, but this was just plain creepy, so I called Tom the next day. Of course he denied it. He also ranted down the phone that he was glad he'd left and I was mad, then he'd told me I was obviously too scared to live on my own and he hoped I was sorry.

As Jas said when I told her, 'That sounds like a confession to me, babe.' Anyway, she suggested I go and stay with her until he'd calmed down. I don't think Tom would have ever done anything crazy, but Jas was right in warning, 'People who get hurt get dangerous.'

'Come and live in my house,' she'd said. 'No one would dare call me up late and ruin my beauty sleep – and as for someone sniffing at my door, well no one's done that since 2008!'

That had made me laugh. That's one of the best things about Jas – she can always make me laugh.

So I moved out of my flat and into Jas's for a few weeks. She risked her own safety to have me at her place, and I'll never forget that. And even though she isn't exactly excited about my new relationship, I mustn't forget how good she's been in the past.

But it didn't solve the problem with Tom. He clearly couldn't find me at the flat and I'd blocked him on my phone, so he started calling the office, trying to get Margaret to put him through. But she'd been forewarned, so politely fobbed him off. Soon, he started calling Harry, and even Sameera, to ask them if I was okay and if they thought I might take him back. The last time that happened was months ago, and I really thought he had moved on, but it looks like he's still bitter.

Jas takes the roses and throws them in the bin, but I keep the note, I might need it if things continue. I'm so upset, this is just so weird, but since Tom and I broke up I've seen a different side to him. Just goes to show, people can surprise you – even people you think you know.

CHAPTER SIX

It's 7.30 by the time I finally call it a day, and what a day, but even so, I feel guilty, because Jas is still here, and Harry's working late too. He's just taken a call from Gemma, who seems to be giving him a hard time.

'I won't be *too* long. I know, I know,' he's saying in a placatory tone.

I give Harry a sympathetic look as I stand up to leave, and he nods back and rolls his eyes.

'Will you be here much longer?' I ask after he puts down the phone.

He just shrugs. 'I don't know. It just seems to have gone mad, doesn't it?'

'Yeah, Jas's here late too.' I nod in the direction of her office.

'She's not working though,' he says.

I'm surprised. 'Oh, so why is she still here?'

'Well, when I went in about ten minutes ago, she was trawling through a load of guys' photos on her phone. I reckon she's looking for a hot date.'

'She told me she'd had it with men.'

He laughs. 'She's always saying that.'

I grab my bag to leave and, walking past her office, I wave.

'Hey, Hannah, let me walk you to your car,' she says.

'I'm not in my car, I'm going to Alex's. He only lives about fifteen minutes from here, I think. And I don't want to drive. I might want a drink,' I add.

'Yeah, after what happened today I reckon you'll need one.' She sighs. 'Do you want a lift to Alex's?'

'No, I'm fine, I need to call in at the shop on the way.'

'I'm just worried in case that tosser Tom's hanging around.'

'No, he's a coward, Jas, he'll be long gone, probably rubbing his hands together after ruining my day. But I won't let him ruin my night. Although when I get hold of the creep…'

'That's my girl,' she says, waving as I head for the door.

I'm done with Tom, and work and worry now. My day was ruined, but I won't let him spoil my evening – the rest of tonight is about me and Alex.

I step out into the chilly autumn evening. It's the start of November already and it feels like we arrive at work in the dark and leave in the dark – and tonight it's bloody dark. And cold. I wrap my parka around me, pulling up my hood as it starts to spit with rain. I was hoping to go home, have a shower and get changed before I went to Alex's, but I don't have time. Nor did I have the foresight to bring any make-up or extra clothes with me to work in case I had to stay late. I can't believe I'm going to meet Alex, for only the third time, wearing my work clothes and with the remains of the day on my face. So I call him to check it's still okay to come over as it'll be close to 8 p.m. by the time I get to his. Also, he needs to be warned that the glamorous woman he went out with the other night won't be turning up this evening.

'Hey, Alex. It's late – I've only just finished, are you still sure about tonight?'

'Of course. Are you heading over now?'

'Yes, if that's okay?' My old insecurities kick in. Is he just being polite, surely not?

'It's wonderful,' he says, in a husky, urgent voice that warms me.

'I just didn't want to put you to any—'

'I made your favourite, pistachio ice cream.'

I'm so touched by this. 'Well, how can I resist? You had me at ice cream,' I say and he laughs. 'But, Alex, I'm warning you, I look like a dog and I need a shower.'

'Now you're just trying to get me all excited,' he jokes.

'Mmm, if you're sure you want to enjoy a third date with an un-showered woman falling asleep at the table in her work clothes...?'

'Sounds perfect, just how I like my third dates.'

'Okay, but don't say I didn't warn you. I'm ten minutes away,' I say, giggling as I end the call and walk into the shop.

After scanning the limited stock, I find a decent Merlot, it's twenty pounds, but if Alex is providing dinner, the least I can do is bring the wine. While queuing to pay, I spot a container of Smarties shaped like Father Christmas and pick it up for Harry to thank him for all the croissants and cakes he brings us.

I pay for my stuff and leave the shop with my purchases in a thin carrier bag. I've put Alex's postcode into the app on my phone as he suggested. 'It's a bit of a maze,' he'd said. Twenty minutes later, I'm still walking round 'the maze', sure I've seen some of these houses more than once. It's not far from the high street, but this part of town isn't somewhere I often venture, it's a forgotten area of empty buildings and overgrown weeds, and the only houses here seem to be boarded up. I can't help but feel vulnerable, especially after receiving the horrible note today, and as I walk, I keep glancing behind me.

There's no one about, and I'm aware it's getting later and later. I'm just walking around in circles, have no idea where I am and it's starting to feel creepy. I'm tempted to call Alex, but feel like such an idiot getting lost following a map in a city I've lived in for most of my life. But after another ten minutes, I'm feeling slightly panicky, and decide to call after all, when he calls me.

'Are you okay, Hannah? Where are you? I thought you said you were close by.'

'I'm… I'm… not sure. You live on Black Horse Road, right? The app's sent me somewhere else… I'm down near the canal, I think. I put the postcode in, but…' I'm freezing, I hope he can't hear my teeth chattering.

'Ahh yeah, the postcode can be a bit iffy, it messes with satnavs too. Look, I'm coming to find you, but as I've no idea where you are, I'll have to find you by your phone.'

'Okay, but I'm not sure how to do that.'

'It's simple. I'm going to send a request to your phone – you accept it, then I can see where you are and come and get you,' he explains.

'Great,' I say, relieved.

And, sure enough, within seconds a message comes through for permission for Alex to see my location. I click it and hear him say, 'Yeah, I can see where you are, stay there – I'm on my way.' And the line goes dead.

It's now 8.15 on a wintery Wednesday night. The rain's coming down, the street's empty, and I'm shivering, so rather than just stand and wait, I walk slowly along the path to see if there's anywhere I can shelter from the rain until Alex turns up. I spot a bus shelter a little further on and walk towards it. The state of me. On our last date, I'd had my hair done, new dress, make-up, perfume, the lot – and even though it was raining that night, I managed to avoid the worst of it. But the rain's so heavy, even when I've reached the shelter, it's bouncing off the plastic and splashing on my head and up my legs.

Within minutes, a car pulls up beside me, the driver's window opens and I lean in, feeling a tiny bit like a sex worker.

'Thank God it's you!' I say, laughing, as Alex leans over and pushes open the passenger-side door. I almost fall in, rain shaking off me onto the pale upholstery of his Audi. 'I'm so sorry to drag you out,' I say, fastening my seat belt.

'It's my pleasure, no problem at all,' he says. His hands are on the wheel and as I settle in and look up, he's smiling at me.

'I know, I know, I look terrible, but I promise I'm the same woman you were out with the other night, just very wet.'

'And even more beautiful,' he half-whispers, as he leans over, gently putting his lips on mine.

What starts as a peck becomes more and it's only when a car beeps loudly behind us that I try to pull away. But he keeps going, his tongue pushing more urgently into my mouth, his arms now wrapped around me. I wish I could relax and enjoy it, but the car behind's beeping again, harder and longer this time, and Alex suddenly stops kissing me.

'What the f…?' He looks in the rear mirror and his hand goes to open the driver's door. He's about to get out.

'Alex, what are you doing?' I say, looking behind – no wonder the beeping is so loud, it's a bus. 'We're at a bus stop, we have to *move*,' I call anxiously to him. He's now opened the door, and is half in and out of the car. The interior light is on and I can see what looks like pure rage on his face. I put my hand on his arm to stop him getting out, and in a moment, he seems to think better of it.

He moves back onto the seat, and wordlessly turns the key in the ignition, puts his foot down and we roar off down the road. Too fast. In the rain. I'm confused, caught between the afterglow of the moment and his surprising reaction to what just happened. I'm trying to understand it, but feel dizzied by it all.

'What… what were you doing? Were you going to say something to the driver?' I ask, incredulously.

'No, no, I was just looking to see if I knew him.'

'We were at a bus stop. It was a *bus*.'

'Yeah, yeah. I didn't realise until I got out… I thought it was someone I knew.'

I'm confused. When the bus sounded its horn the second time, Alex's immediate reaction seemed to be one of anger, which doesn't suggest that he thought he knew the other driver. And it's dark and rainy – he clearly wasn't getting out of the car to say hi to someone.

'You seemed angry,' I offer quietly.

'God no, not at all – I just thought it was a guy I used to… know.' His voice fades. 'So how was your day?' he asks, changing the subject. I wonder if I imagined his anger – or perhaps it was a moment of road rage and he's a little embarrassed.

'I had a terrible day,' I answer blankly, my mind still on what just happened, feeling that he overreacted; but we've all been there, an angry beep, a two-fingered salute in response.

'Well, hopefully your day is about to get better. You okay?' he asks, probably seeing the questions in my eyes.

'I'm fine,' I say, as he slows down to turn off the road and rests his hand gently on my knee.

Perhaps he did think he knew the driver behind, or perhaps the beeping shook him a little. He's bound to be a bit nervous because we're new to each other and I get the feeling he's the protective type, and perhaps thought that I was upset by the bus driver's reaction. I mustn't overthink everything, he's a nice guy, it's a third date, all I have to do is enjoy it – and settling down into the warm, expensive, new-smelling car, I'm sure I will.

'I don't know how I ended up there.' I smile. 'I couldn't find your road, the map app on my phone is useless.'

'It's the postcode. Like I said, it causes no end of problems.'

We're only a few hundred yards from where he picked me up and he turns into Black Horse Road. 'Oh, I'm such a fool, I was only a few minutes away – I dragged you out into the cold, wet night, I'm so sorry.'

'Not at all, don't apologise,' he says, pulling up outside a gorgeous terraced house. In this rather derelict area, this place is an anomaly, with a potted bay tree either side of the front door and the porch light revealing a tiled step, and a small, neat front garden.

'Is this you?' I say hopefully. This is so nice, the sort of place other people live. But with Alex it could happen to me. This *could* be somewhere I live. In that instant I check myself, I mustn't get carried away.

'Yep, this is home,' he says, pulling on the handbrake.

'It looks lovely, though I haven't a clue where I am,' I add uncertainly.

'Don't worry, I'll drive you home,' he offers, to my relief.

'Thanks,' I murmur and pick up my carrier bag of wine, climb out of the car and follow him through the front gate.

He unlocks the door and ushers me in. 'Welcome to Casa Alex,' he says, his arm on my shoulder as he turns on the hall light.

I'm engulfed in a delicious warmth, the smell of cooking and home as he helps me off with my rather unglamorous, wet parka and hangs it carefully on the hat-stand, like it's the most precious thing he's ever had to care for. He reaches down for my work satchel.

'It's fine,' I say, instinctively pulling it to me. He looks a little taken aback at this and I apologise, explaining that my laptop is in my bag.

'Ooh, are all your secrets in there?'

'No, sorry. I'm acting like I have the world's biggest diamond tucked away in here. It's just instinct to keep it with me. Everything's on my laptop, all my work stuff.'

'Ahh, whatever makes you comfortable.' He smiles. 'There's a shelf here you can leave it on if you like?'

'Thanks, I'll leave it here,' I say. I'm such an idiot, making a fuss about a bloody work laptop.

He gestures for me to go through the hall into the kitchen ahead of him, so I step in front of him, but when I reach the kitchen, I'm suddenly aware he isn't following me.

'Hey, are you coming too?' I say.

'Just a second,' he replies. 'You go ahead.'

I carry on, as he suggests, but turn discreetly to see him fumbling around in his pockets, then he pulls out a key. Unaware I'm watching, he is now putting his face right up against the narrow glass panel in the door. He does this for a few seconds, just staring through. He's absolutely still, and so am I, just a few feet away from him down the hall. What the hell is he doing? I feel slightly creeped out, and wonder if I've been stupid to come here. It's been a weird enough day after the flower delivery, and now this. What on earth is he doing?

After a few seconds, he pulls away and I think he's about to turn round, so I nip into the kitchen and out of view. Then I hear him lock the door once, and then a click as he locks it again.

CHAPTER SEVEN

Shit, he's *double*-locking the door! Is he keeping someone out – or me in? Either way it's unsettling.

I'm standing in the kitchen, but leaning out slightly so I can see him down the hall. And Alex is looking through the glass again! Is he waiting for someone? Checking the coast is clear, what? He eventually moves away from the door and heads down the hall to join me, by which time I make like I'm admiring the grey gloss units.

'Gorgeous kitchen,' I murmur, as I lean against the island, beneath a neat row of pots and pans hanging from the ceiling. It's lovely and looks recently refurbished, but I'm finding it hard to move away from the vision of him in the hall. What the hell was he doing?

I gaze around the kitchen as he checks the oven, it's all very tasteful and minimalist, no clutter, no fridge magnets, no mess – it would be quite calming if I wasn't so disturbed by his strange behaviour in the hall. My kitchen is a bit of a bomb site, and my fridge has so many magnets, every time I open the door several clatter to the ground. I'm probably being sexist, but I'm surprised at how neat and clean it is – and how much kitchen stuff he has for a single man.

I mustn't overthink him locking the door and looking through the glass – I'm sure he was just being cautious. To distract myself from my thoughts, I alight on a set of beautiful crockery, hand-cast; highly trendy, beautiful kitchen units; not to mention those matching bay trees either side of the beautiful grey-painted front door. I've never met a straight man with such wonderful taste. Perhaps it's more a reflection of the men I've previously dated, rather than anything to do with Alex's sexuality, but I have to ask, just in case I've got all this horribly wrong.

'Are you gay?'

He laughs. 'Not that I'm aware of.'

'I didn't think so.' I smile. 'But it's so... stylish, so well put together, so *clean*.' My back is to him as I gaze around, and I turn for his response, but he's just staring at me, expressionless.

He takes a step towards me. He's now so close I can feel his breath on my face, as he gently catches my wrist with his hand. We're face to face now, his eyes are smiling into mine, and I'm melting. He has the most gorgeous face, and standing before me in a blue denim shirt I can see he works out. If it's possible I'm even more attracted to him than I thought – my heart's thumping. I'm here with a beautiful man, in his beautiful home, and I'm trying not to collapse in a heap on what I can only guess are very expensive Fired Earth floor tiles. I desperately try to think of something to say. But my mind's a blank, and he's still looking into my eyes, his mouth perilously close to mine. I want him to kiss me, but I might fall over.

'Is this a safe area?' I hear myself ask. I know it sounds like a weird thing to say at this point, but I can't get that vision of him locking the front door from my head. Before we kiss, I need to know what he was doing, and if I should be worried.

He pulls his head back confused at my complete conversational turnaround.

'I... just ask because it's... There are quite a few empty houses nearby. Do you have much, erm, crime?'

'No, not really.' He seems slightly bemused at my question, and he's looking at me, as if he's waiting for an explanation.

'Oh it's… I just wondered why you double-locked your door. Don't you feel safe around here?'

He hesitates, for a second. 'Yeah – I did, I did double-lock the door, didn't I? Force of habit, I suppose.'

I just nod vaguely, not sure he's really answered my question.

'I mean. You never know, and no harm in being extra careful,' he adds, looking slightly embarrassed.

'Yeah, you're right.'

That makes sense – kind of. But I am an idiot – I've put myself in the kind of situation I would advise any client against. I'm in a man's house, we're alone, and I don't know him. Then again, am I being paranoid? He's made pistachio ice cream for me. Serial killers don't make pistachio ice cream for their victims. Do they? And yes, it's only a third date, but I feel as if I've known Alex for so much longer. I'm an intuitive person. Surely I would have picked up any potential weirdness by now. He's perfectly normal. He's perfectly gorgeous. And he's pouring wine for us in his lovely glossy kitchen. I need to get a grip.

'I just hope you weren't trying to lock me in,' I hear myself say in a jokey voice in an attempt to garner a satisfying explanation.

'God no, I'm not trying to lock you *in*. The keys are *here*,' he says, patting his pocket. But he doesn't take them out and leave them on the side, which would make me feel happier. 'I hope I haven't freaked you out, I just – like to be safe.'

'Not at all,' I lie. 'I was joking. Lawyers aren't *usually* serial killers, are they?'

'Not until now.' He smiles slowly, and for a split second my heart misses a beat, until he starts laughing.

'Okay, *now* you're freaking me out,' I gasp, tapping him on the arm in a light-hearted reprimand.

'I'm sorry for teasing – you're right to be concerned, Hannah. You don't know me and we're in this house alone and, hey, I could be… *anyone*,' he says this in an over-the-top creepy way that makes me smile and roll my eyes.

'Yeah? Well, it won't be good for your business if you do anything weird,' I laugh. 'And all my friends know where I am,' I add, just in case.

'And my friends know where *I* am *and* who with.' He laughs. 'And some of them are policemen, so if you've got any murderous plans, Hannah Weston, think again.'

He pushes a glass of wine towards me, and I laugh, a little too hysterically, as I realise that my friends at work know I'm with him, but they don't know his address, or even his surname. If I didn't turn up at the office tomorrow, no one would check on me immediately, they might think I'm doing a home visit. They might not even realise I'm missing until mid-morning. Jas is always so busy, Harry wouldn't even notice and Sameera's too obsessed with her wedding to wonder if her colleague's about to star in a real-life crime story. So, if Alex does turn out to be the next Ted Bundy, I'm probably done for. I take a large gulp of wine, slightly calmed by the warming red as it hits my throat.

He's checking the oven, so I take another gulp and quickly text Jas his surname and address, explaining it's purely precautionary, so she doesn't think it's a cry for help, then turn my phone on silent. I don't want to appear rude, as if I'm having a text conversation with someone else while he cooks a romantic meal. There's nothing to worry about; I just got myself in a state. I'm a bit on edge because of the roses and the note and the fact that Tom's still at large. But maybe it's more than that too. Maybe it's the job. After being exposed to the very worst of human behaviour day after day, it's bound to leave a mark. As Jas is always warning me, what we do can creep into your personal life and threaten to turn every situation into a crisis, when it really isn't.

Alex opens the fridge to take out some salad vegetables, and I note there's very little in there – which fits in more with my male stereotyping than his bay trees and blue crockery. He's concentrating on what he's doing, chopping a pepper, but he isn't smiling any more. I hope I haven't ruined the mood and made things awkward between us.

'Sorry,' I say.

'Why?' He looks up from the pepper.

'For questioning your domestic security arrangements.' I try to say this in a funny voice, but he doesn't smile.

'I told you, it's *okay*. Now, more wine, or would you prefer a cup of tea?' He's standing by the kitchen island, a bottle of red in one hand, the other gesturing towards a rather stylish tea caddy.

'Wine, if you don't mind,' I say, gesturing towards my half-empty glass as he lifts the bottle to top it up. I watch the blood-red liquid leave the bottle, and decide to take it easy on the alcohol. I'm sure everything's fine, but I don't want to make myself more vulnerable than I already am. Then again, he offered me tea as an alternative, which is vaguely comforting.

'I can just as easily grind some Rohypnol into tea, so your choice?' he says, as if he read my mind.

'What?'

He looks at me with those smiling eyes and I know he's teasing again.

'Sorry, I'm not used to this... Someone cooking for me, being kind, and attentive – I'm looking for the downside. Do you have one?'

'A downside? No. I'm actually quite perfect,' he says, pouring himself a glass now.

'Cheers... and thank you,' I say.

'What for?'

'For being nice, for inviting me over – for not being pissed off because I got lost on the way here, then started quizzing you about locking your own front door.'

'It's a difficult place to find – and a perfectly reasonable question.'

I suddenly spot the carrier bag on the floor by my feet. 'Ooh I have something,' I say, and take out the bottle of wine. I stretch to place it on the kitchen island, but I clumsily catch my glass with the bottle and knock it over. Glass and red wine go everywhere. I am mortified.

I hear him say, 'Shit!' under his breath, and want to die.

'I'm *so* sorry.' I grab at a rather lovely blue tea towel, which looks too nice to mop up spillage, but I give it a go, manically wiping and attempting to pick up shards of glass from the worktop.

'Stop, stop – it's *fine*,' he says gently, walking towards the carnage with a dustpan and brush. 'Just move over there and let me take care of it.' He touches my arm and gently manoeuvres me to the side.

I really don't know what to say. I wish he'd make a joke, but he doesn't, and the picking and wiping goes on for some time in silence, as I stand by. He carefully brushes the floor, then picks up each remaining tiny shard between his finger and thumb, before wiping the counter and giving the floor a final wipe. Eventually, when he's eradicated every sparkle of glass and every speck of red wine, he looks up and smiles. 'There you go.' He moves to the sink to wash his hands. I stand there helpless, like a child.

'Sorry, I'm not usually like this. I bet the glass was expensive, I'll buy you another one, just let me know where...'

His back is to me at the sink, and he puts his hand up in an 'it doesn't matter' gesture.

'I'm so sorry,' I repeat.

He turns around. 'Hannah, please don't keep saying you're sorry, it's a glass – that's all.'

I pull a pained face. 'But it was a *beautiful* glass; it must have been expensive.'

Alex shrugs and taking another lovely tea towel from the side, wipes his hands, and reaches for the bottle of wine I brought, that I've just caused all the damage with.

'Nice,' he murmurs.

'Yeah. I know you like Merlot – well, we both do.'

He holds it for a while and reads the label while I stand nearby wondering what to do with myself. I find myself wondering if it's really worth it. Is any relationship worth all the uncertainty, the foolishness at the beginning, the does-he, doesn't-he, shall I, shan't I? The am I good enough?

'I can't lie – I'm a bit nervous,' I hear myself say into the silence.

'I know, me too. The first few dates are always a bit nerve-wracking. But – I – this—' He pauses and gestures from himself to me and back. 'This feels right.'

I feel a sweep of relief: he likes me, and I like him, and we just have to get over these initially awkward first dates and I'm sure something good will start to happen.

He suddenly reaches down past my legs and picks up the carrier bag that held the wine, then realises there's something inside. 'Sorry, I thought it was empty, I was about to throw that away.'

He hands it to me. I take it off him and put the bag down on a nearby chair. 'It's just some sweets for someone I work with.'

'Oh – is it her birthday?' He wanders over to the oven and checks through the glass.

'No, no it's a thank you – for my friend Harry.'

'Oh yeah you mentioned him before.' He doesn't turn around.

'Yeah, his girlfriend, she works at the café near my office. Have you heard of Brilliant Bakes?'

'Yeah, I think I know it.' Alex walks back to where I'm standing against the kitchen island and leans next to me, both holding our glasses now, like we're drinking at a bar.

'Well, Harry brings me the leftover almond croissants from the café – they're my favourite – bit of a standing joke really. I picked him up a carton of Smarties because he won't take any money off me,' I add.

'That's kind of you,' he says, and I feel his hand on mine, slowly caressing each finger one by one. I like it.

'Harry loves Smarties…' My voice fades, I'm longing for him to kiss me.

Alex's face is now close to mine, his breath hot on my lips. We're about to kiss when he moves back slightly. 'Be careful, Hannah. If a beautiful woman bought me sweets, I might think I stood a chance.' He leaves me to go back to the oven, and I'm surprised how much I want him back here next to me.

'Firstly, I'm not beautiful…'

'You are.' He keeps his back to me as he opens the oven door.

'And Harry's not like that. He's very young and slightly annoying, to be honest. We're friends, we have a laugh, but he's ten years younger than me. *And* he's madly in love with Gemma.'

'I can't imagine for a minute she's as gorgeous as you though.' Alex sighs. 'And what's ten years?'

I laugh, flattered. 'She's very pretty… and ten years is a whole decade.'

I take another sip of wine, feeling like a sixteen-year-old on a first date. 'It's nice, being here. So much better than in a bar or a restaurant with people around,' I say, feeling more at ease now.

'I know, isn't it? I think you can tell a lot about a person by the space they live in. I asked you here because I want you to get to know the real me. I want to get to know you too.'

'I'm not sure you're ready for my flat yet – it's a bit rank compared to this place,' I admit. 'I hope it doesn't say *too* much about me. I'd be horrified if it did.'

He laughs. 'I think I know you without seeing where you live. But I would *love* to see your place. I want to see where you eat, where you relax, where you sleep. I want to know *everything* about you. But I understand, it can make you feel vulnerable letting someone in.'

'Exactly,' I say. Our eyes meet, and I know we feel the same, that we're both looking for something, someone we've never been able to find. Both hoping this is it.

'My biggest fear is that you might be intimidated by my priceless art collection,' he says, gesturing to the framed pictures positioned stylishly on the wall.

'Priceless?' I gasp.

'Originals.'

'Oh wow.'

'When I say *original*, they're original Ikea,' he adds, a twinkle in his eye.

I laugh, feeling a bit silly. I need to be more attuned to when he's joking and when he's serious. But his humour puts me at ease, his home is warm and welcoming, and I'm finally starting to relax.

'Dinner will be ten minutes,' he says and suggests we go into the living room. It's packed with bookcases, and there are lots of photos in different frames hanging on a wall, all clustered together; a look I attempted a while ago, but which just ended up looking a mess. Alex certainly has an eye for detail.

'Are they family photos?' I ask, wondering if any of his previous girlfriends made it to the wall of fame.

'Yeah,' he says.

'I can't see any photos of *you*,' I say, peering at the wall.

'I hate having my photo taken,' he says dismissively, gesturing me away from the photos and towards a dark sea-green velvet sofa.

I sit down, and think of the shabby seating in my unkempt, unfashionable flat, and dread having to invite him over. As he said, you can tell a lot about a person by the space they live in.

I sip on the wine, and feel myself relaxing more as he joins me on the sofa. His thigh is against mine, our shoulders are touching. He tilts his head as he talks about something that happened in court today, and I feel his closeness. I laugh at something he says,

I'm not even sure it's meant to be funny, but he smiles and I feel wonderful. Then, gently, he takes my wine glass from my hand and places it on the coffee table in front of us, and leans towards me.

I think my heart's going to stop as he begins to kiss me softly on the mouth. Every nerve ending tingles, every part of me is touched by this kiss, and every little strand of anxiety, every nuance of doubt disappears, becoming vapour and dancing in the warm, garlic-filled air. I've forgotten about Tom and the roses, about the way Alex peered through the hall window, and Jas's warnings about falling too fast. And even if I did remember, it's too late now – I'm hooked and at the point of no return.

CHAPTER EIGHT

Here, with Alex, I'm in a different world, and everything feels so good – it's that sweet, warm feeling when alcohol hits, or dope kicks in. It's wild and heady. I want to kiss him all night, and never leave this gorgeous, squidgy sofa.

Eventually, we stop kissing, and in the slightly awkward post-kiss silence, I ask him about his day and he tells me about a case he's working on.

'This young guy's homeless and been accused of stabbing his friend. But I believe with all my heart that he's being accused of a crime he didn't commit. I was the duty solicitor on the night he was brought in, and I knew instantly he wasn't capable of such a violent act.' He goes on to explain in more detail, and I'm blown away by his caring, his passion for what he does. 'That's why I went into the legal profession,' he says. 'I want to help people who can't help themselves.'

I totally get where he's coming from. 'I feel just the same in my job,' I say, but looking around this lovely house, I reckon he gets paid a lot more for doing it.

'Sometimes I'm shocked at what some people have to go through, and how any one of us could have found ourselves in a hopeless situation like these poor souls. The wrong parent, neglect, poverty – we're all just a parent away from neglect or abuse,' he says.

I agree, and wonder if perhaps he's speaking from personal experience but know it's too early to ask. I have to wait until he volunteers that information.

'Working with people like this, realising how hard some lives are, it gets to me,' I say. 'I don't trust easily, I'm suspicious of people, and see everything much darker, more threatening than perhaps it is. I was in Tesco the other day, and this woman was shouting at her kid, and I had to resist going up to her and telling her to stop. I even followed her out of the store, at a distance, and watched her go down the road, I was so worried about the child. But when they got to a bus stop the woman took a banana from her bag and gave it to the child. I joined them and pretended I was waiting for a bus and was so relieved when I heard the woman speaking gently to her kid. I guess what I'm saying is, because of what I do every day, and the things I have to deal with, my mind goes there whether I want it to or not.'

Alex doesn't say anything, and I stop talking, assuming he's bored, or worse still thinks I'm crazy for following strangers I see in the supermarket. But then I can see by the look on his face he's silent because he's considering what I'm saying and is listening intently, not talking over me with his story, his theories.

'I probably sound slightly unhinged following a random woman around town,' I say.

'No, you sound kind and caring – and lovely.' He puts his arm around me. 'I wish there'd been someone like you around when I was a kid.'

'Oh?' I say, hoping he'll open up, wondering if there's something difficult in his past. But it might be too soon for him to share it.

'I… I just could never do anything right as far as my parents were concerned. My dad always told me I was a loser.' He sighs and I see the hurt in his eyes.

'Oh God, Alex, that's terrible.' I'm shocked to hear this even though I come up against this most days with my clients. My heart's going out to him even more, realising that, like everyone else, he's vulnerable, fragile.

'I'm over it now. I'm not in touch with my parents. Whenever I went to visit, I hated seeing the disappointment in their eyes.'

'How on earth could they be disappointed with you? You've done so well, a great career, a lovely home…'

'Like I said, I could never do anything right,' he says dismissively. It's clear he doesn't want to continue this conversation and he changes the subject. 'So, what about you? Are your parents proud? Do they have photos of you in your cap and gown all over the living room?'

'Not exactly. They're both dead,' I say. 'Let's not talk about the past, let's leave it for another day.'

'So sorry.' He smiles sadly. 'Yes, absolutely, let's leave the past where it belongs for now. So – how was your day?'

Mentioning today triggers me. I almost flinch thinking about the white roses, the vicious note. As a foster child, you learn not to trust people. Adult guardians can hide a lot behind a smile. Most of them were fine, but some of them were quite cruel, and more than once I was shocked by a sudden temper, a stinging slap, an unkind remark. Even if they never slapped or flared up at you again, the threat would hang in the air like a dark cloud, and you carry it with you into adulthood. To receive those beautiful roses, and discover a horrible message tucked inside, was like the stinging slap of childhood, the nasty remark when you least expect it. Just when everything seems to be going so well, there it is, the ever-present threat of losing everything.

I decide not to tell Alex about the roses. It's too early and the evening's been too good to spoil everything with the idea I have a vengeful ex lurking around the corner. So I stay on safe ground and talk about my job.

'My day was busy, and frustrating. The teenagers I deal with can be difficult to communicate with, especially the abused, neglected kids – and it isn't always easy to help them.'

He nods, listening intently to what I'm saying.

'I often wonder how long I can keep going, and just when I'm about to give up there's a breakthrough and something good happens,' I say. 'I finally rescue a child from an abusive family, a teenager moves out of care into their own flat and with a job, and then – and only then – do I feel like it's been worth all the sleepless nights. Harry always says you watch them like a parent watching their one-year-old take their first steps.'

'Harry certainly has a way with words,' he says. There's an edge in his voice, is he a little jealous of Harry? If so, that's hilarious because as soon as he meets Harry, Alex will realise he's the least threatening, least troubling person for him to worry about.

'The hardest lesson I've had to learn is that some people just don't want to be saved,' I say, returning to the subject matter.

'Yeah. And that hurts.' He sighs. 'People take things the wrong way, they think you're too much, when all you want to do is make things right. I mean, all you're doing is asking them to behave a certain way – you're only doing it for *them*, but they can't see that.'

'You mean with clients?' I ask, unsure of what he's actually saying.

'Yeah… Perhaps sometimes I give too much and, yes, I probably ask too much too. But it's for them – always for them.'

I feel his passion, his caring, and relate to it. But I'm not completely sure he's talking about his work.

'I give a lot – but I expect a lot,' he adds.

'Nothing wrong with that.'

'Mmm, but it often leads to disappointment on my part.'

Again I wonder if he's talking about the people he defends, or something closer to home. Has Alex also been disappointed by love? Has he had his heart broken?

'How long have you been single?' I ask.

'About twelve months now.'

'A year is a long time for someone like you to be single,' I say flirtatiously as I take a sip of wine. He's such a catch, I can't believe he hasn't been snapped up. I glance through the door at the high-gloss kitchen. 'Some women would date you for that kitchen alone,' I murmur, only half-joking.

He smiles. 'Oh no, you only want me for my white goods and worktops?'

I nod. 'Damn, am I that obvious? You give good kitchen, Alex.' I pretend to sigh longingly, and he laughs.

'That's a compliment – I think. Perhaps that's where I've been going wrong with my past relationships. I should have seduced them with my kitchen first.' He's shaking his head theatrically.

'Yeah, might be. Or, like me, you just picked the wrong ones,' I say, opening up the conversation slightly.

He shrugs and I wonder what the story is with his last ex. But I don't get the chance to find out because he quickly moves away from what seems to be a danger area.

'Dinner won't be too long. I'm making this Middle Eastern recipe a colleague recommended,' he says brightly. 'It's delicious, I've made it before – but it takes a little longer than I'd like.'

'It smells wonderful,' I say, and because I'm used to having difficult conversations with clients, I push for more information about his ex. 'So, you've been single for a whole year?' I take a discreet glance at the wall full of photos, hoping to alight on a photo of the one that got away.

Alex puts his head down. He nods, slowly. 'Yeah.'

'Is she... over there on the wall?' I ask, rather clumsily.

He looks at the wall, then looks away. 'No, no I took her photos down. I couldn't bear to keep seeing her.'

My heart dips a little, and I wonder if he's over her.

'She must have meant a lot to you,' I press.

'Yes, she did. I haven't been with anyone else since. I wasn't ready... until now.' He lifts his head and looks directly at me. I feel goosebumps – in a good way.

'Why did you break up?' I ask.

He's now gazing into the distance, and it's a little while before he speaks. 'Why does anyone break up? We'd outgrown each other – she didn't want the same things any more.' He turns to me, and his face is full of pain. 'She ended it.'

'I'm sorry. Don't feel like you have to talk about it if it's too…' I trail off, feeling guilty now for raising this. It's clearly still quite raw, even after all this time.

'No, no it's fine.' But he's shaking his head – it isn't. 'She just said she didn't love me any more. I'd been happily going along, thinking it was great, and then – boom, it was over. *Everything* gone, in a few seconds.'

I think how Tom must have felt just like this when I finished with him, and feel a stab of sadness and guilt, and I'm compelled to touch Alex's arm to comfort him.

'That sounds rough.' I sigh, hoping that Tom finds someone to heal his wounds, like I hope Alex has.

'Oh, people go through far worse. I… I've been told I take things too seriously. I'm always the one who gets hurt,' he adds sadly.

I touch his arm again in a comforting gesture and he acknowledges it with a slow smile.

'Anyway, I'm moving on. I've been there before, I'm used to saying goodbye. I lost my mother when I was nine years old – after that, nothing can really touch you again.'

'I'm so sorry.' I didn't expect him to open up quite as much as this. I also lost my mum when I was young, but don't mention it now, it's Alex's turn to tell his story. 'I didn't realise your mum died – I'm sorry. When you said you weren't in touch with your parents, I assumed…'

'Yeah. My dad's still around, he remarried. I'm not in touch with *them*.'

'Ah, that's not easy, especially for a young child,' I say. I'm used to dealing with the impact of step-parents in the lives of some of my clients and I know how difficult, how damaging, those relationships can be.

'I just expect everyone to leave me eventually. And when my last relationship… ended, I found it hard to come to terms with. It's taken me until now… I hate goodbyes.'

'I can understand that,' I say softly.

'She just went, left her stuff… some of her clothes are still in the wardrobes, she wanted to go that much she didn't even pack properly.'

I sigh, his hurt is tangible.

'When she walked out, I didn't just lose *her*, she took everything else – all the plans we made, marriage, kids, even holiday plans. The minute she left, she took all my tomorrows. You know?'

I nod, realising this was obviously a long-term relationship, a big deal, but not relating to what he's saying. I don't *really* know how that feels, because Tom and I never made any plans, we never had any shared tomorrows, so mine have stayed intact. But seeing the way Alex's eyes fill up as he recalls his hurt, I can't help it, I feel a sharp prickle of jealousy for a woman I've never even met.

He gives a mirthless laugh. 'I flip from hurt to anger when I think about her, and… and what she did to me.' He shifts in his seat. 'I thought I glimpsed her the other day. I was walking through Worcester and thought I saw the back of her walking into a dress shop. And all those feelings, the hurt… came flooding back. I mean, I'm over her,' he adds, looking at me, to reassure me, 'but it's not easy.'

'Oh so she still lives here, in Worcester?'

'She went away for a while – but I heard she's back.'

My stomach dips slightly at the prospect of them bumping into each other and him falling for her all over again. Or her falling for him?

We sit for a while, both in our own silence. I wonder what he's thinking, and given how raw his last break-up seems for him, I also wonder if he's ready to move on.

'Okay, it's after 9 p.m.,' he says, looking at his watch. 'Sorry, that got way too deep. The dinner is late, and probably cremated.' He stands up, holding out his hand to me.

'I'm sure it will be fine. I'm famished,' I say and, taking his proffered hand, stand up too. As we walk towards the kitchen, I tell him I need to pop to the bathroom.

'Up the stairs and second door on the right,' he says, as he heads back into the kitchen.

I run up the stairs, part of me flushed with wine and pleasure while the other part wrangles slightly with what all this means, and the scariest question, is he still in love with his ex?

Pushing the door into the bathroom, I'm soothed by the dim lighting, and impressed again by Alex's eye for design. The walls are grey-and-blue watermarked stone, and ultra-modern vanity units in deep mahogany wood sit side by side. There are *two* sinks, and I note with a sense of anticipation that the shower is also big enough for two. Several large bottles of expensive shower gel stand waiting on a shelf – and even the towels are co-ordinated. Rolled up like the insides of rosebuds, they sit in squares on the wall. Just like the rooms downstairs, this has been considered and meticulously executed.

Having found him to be perfect so far, I really thought his home would be a tumbledown, messy, bachelor pad – not like this. Nothing is out of place, no dirty socks on the floor, no overflowing bathroom bin, the shower is gleaming, as are all the beautiful surfaces.

I wander over to the two vanity units. On top are a selection of dark-brown bottles. I reach for the large eau de parfum – Cuiron, by Helmut Lang. It looks expensive, sophisticated. I spritz the air and as it settles around me, the smell becomes vaguely familiar – it's Alex. I remember melting into that first kiss on my doorstep, a heady infusion of pine, and aged leather. There was something else though, and now I can identify it, a rich smoky aroma secretly winding through the pine-fresh forest. Light and shade, revelations and secrets.

I glance up at the enormous shower head, imagining the two of us together under hot spikes of water, the smell of pine and sweat… then, with a sting, I see *her* with him under the shower. A faceless, nameless woman, her perfect body entwined with his. I brush my fingertips against the softest, fluffiest towels and imagine them wrapped together in a cloud the colour of the Pacific. I am dizzy with jealousy – and desire. Desire for him, for us, for this life together, here.

I don't even own my place, my car is a hundred years old and, if I'm honest, I've never even considered the colour of a wall before. But now there's this man, who has the kind of smile that makes me forget about work and court orders and safeguarding and homeless teens. Here's someone I can escape with, who can take me away from it all with beautiful towels, big hot showers and a fragrance wafted in from paradise.

I move to the basin and wash my hands in heaven-scented liquid soap. But I can't avoid seeing myself in the mirror. God, I'd forgotten that I'd rushed here, hadn't changed or redone my make-up. How has he been looking at this face for over an hour? Among all this minimalism and polished stone, I look like I don't belong. And yet, just beneath the doubt, there's a shimmer of hope, that with someone like Alex in my life, I *could* belong, and achieve everything I want to. After a lifetime of being second best, not quite the real thing, is this someone who might finally make me feel like their number one?

Hoping to find something to comb my hair with, I open the bathroom cabinet under the sink. Inside, there's the usual bathroom paraphernalia – plasters, paracetamol, a tub of moisture cream – but nothing simple like a comb, or even a bit of lip balm to soften the edges of this evening's car-crash look.

I close the cabinet door and spot a black toiletries bag on the side, just sitting there, not out of place, in its spot. Zipped up.

I think about opening the bag. I tell myself I mustn't. I'm in desperate need of a comb, but I shouldn't look in here, it feels too intimate – like opening someone's diary. I struggle for all of three seconds, then open it. Rummaging around, I can't see a comb, but I see more of Alex. His toothbrush is an unusual tortoiseshell, the toothpaste expensive, not like my supermarket-brand cheapie. I reach further in – tweezers, nail clippers, so many grooming tools. But no comb.

I'm beginning to feel slightly ashamed for riffling through this man's personal stuff, but I need to make absolutely sure there's no comb. Anyway, what harm will it do to know what kind of toothpaste he uses? I'm just getting to know him... more.

Suddenly, my fingers alight on something flat, pushed down the back of the bag, and I bring it out between two fingers. I can barely make it out at first, but slowly it dawns on me what it is. A worn photograph – of a woman, but her face has a furious pen mark through it. Like someone wanted to scribble her out.

CHAPTER NINE

I don't understand the photo I'm holding in my hand. The pen mark is running diagonally, and angrily, across a woman's face. She looks around my age, late thirties. Her long blonde hair sits on bare, brown shoulders, she's wearing a strappy top and straw hat. It looks like a holiday snap. The woman is laughing, and holding her hand up to the camera as if to say 'stop'.

I'm shocked. Tonight I learned that if you look hard enough in someone's bathroom, there's a good chance you'll find something unsettling. And this is pretty unsettling. It's probably Alex's ex, which makes sense. I'm sure if you rummaged around at my place you'd find a photo of Tom, though most of them are on my phone – I never got round to deleting them. But this picture is worn, has obviously been looked at too many times, and it's tucked away in his toiletries bag. He's keeping it somewhere safe, so he can easily find it perhaps. But why has the pen been slashed right through her face, like a knife?

I catch myself again in the mirror, holding the photo, and wonder once more if I'm ready for all this. Whether I am or not, I've been up here long enough, I can't delay any more.

I walk back downstairs feeling uncertain, but vaguely comforted by the delicious smell coming from the kitchen. I'm starving, I've hardly eaten all day. So what if he drew a line through the photo of his ex? He admitted he was upset, and he probably did it when she first walked out, when he was angry. Tom's done far worse, and I wouldn't be surprised if he has a similar 'inked' picture of me, several in fact. Let's face it, the mildest of people have the capacity to be enraged when someone they love walks out. It was probably a momentary flash of anger, and he hid the photo in the toilet bag because he was ashamed of what he did to it but couldn't bear to throw it away.

I put on a smile and walk into the kitchen, where Alex pulls out a seat at the table for me to sit down. The table's been laid beautifully, including a vase of autumn leaves and bright-orange Chinese lantern flowers, a stunning contrast against the greys and blues of the kitchen. Hard to believe the same person who created this 'tablescape' also ran a pen through a photo of his ex-girlfriend's face.

I try to put the image from my mind and, touching the papery, bright-orange orbs, ask, 'Did you just arrange these while I was in the bathroom?'

He laughs. 'No, I bought them from the florist yesterday when I thought you were coming over. But when you couldn't make it, I kept them in the utility room, hoping they'd last until today.'

My heart breaks a little at his thoughtfulness, and I push away the image of the woman's laughing face, the ink ripping through the photo. Now I'm getting to know him, I can see he puts his all into what he does, and even for a romantic weeknight supper, he takes care of the table foliage. Okay, so he hates his ex – I can live with that. I can help him move on, to let go of his anger and resentment. In this moment, I just want to live here with him in this beautiful bubble of warm garlic and earthenware crockery. I could be happy here – happy and safe. It would be a proper home.

He opens up the oven. Blasted by the heat, he jumps back, and I wonder how often he really cooks. But soon, he brings the steaming dishes to the table and, placing them down carefully, he catches my eye, and we both smile affectionately. I want to ask him if the woman in the photograph is his ex. I want to know when he tried to scribble her out, and if he's over it like he says he is. I also want to ask if he could ever see himself loving another person. Like me. But instead of these big, important questions, I talk about nothing that really matters.

'It looks delicious,' I say, and ask if I can help, but he won't hear of it.

When he eventually sits down, all he seems to care about is that I'm enjoying the food, that I have wine and water, and that I'm happy. I notice his forehead's shiny with sweat, and I can see by his face when he asks, 'Is it okay?' that this means a lot to him. He needs for me to like what he's put before me. I'm grateful that he cares, and willing to oblige.

'This is absolutely wonderful,' I say. The tasty lamb with chickpeas and fragrant spices warms me to my bones, as does his smile across the table.

'I'm so glad. Like I said, I got the recipe from a friend at work. She makes this a lot and I always love it, so I decided to make it for you.'

I smile through an irrational wave of jealousy at the very thought of him dining with another woman.

'She's obviously very talented,' I say, trying hard not to imagine this 'friend'.

We chat some more, and Alex refills our wine. It's warm and comfortable, he's amusing and makes me feel very relaxed, so relaxed that I eat and drink until I can't eat or drink any more.

'Don't forget I made your favourite ice cream,' he reminds me.

'Lovely! I feel so spoiled.' Despite being full I don't want to disappoint him after he's gone to so much effort, and I can always make room for pistachio ice cream.

'You haven't tasted it yet.'

I laugh. 'Is this another of your friend's recipes?' I ask, subtly digging.

Alex doesn't answer me, but gets up and goes to the freezer, lifts out a Tupperware container, holding it aloft with both hands like a priceless ancient artefact.

'This has been a labour of love.' He sighs as he begins scooping out the pale-green, creamy confection.

'Ahh, that's so sweet of you to go to all that trouble for me,' I say, touched at the way he's placing the ice cream in two glass bowls, painstakingly adding extra pistachios to the top. Just for me.

'Home-made pistachio ice cream,' he says, walking to the table and putting a bowl down in front of me. 'I just hope it tastes okay.'

I can't resist the soft, creamy ice cream topped with crunchy, salty pistachios. 'This is *wonderful*,' I say. 'I can't believe you made it yourself, I wouldn't know where to begin.'

'Well, it's true, I did.' He leans towards me. 'Do you like it, honestly?'

'Yes, yes I love it.'

'It took me ages, I wanted it to be perfect – I want *everything* to be perfect for you, Hannah.' He's looking at me intently as if all that matters is my happiness, and it's both amazing and a little unnerving because I've never had this kind of attention in my life.

My earlier doubts after finding the photo disappear. I figure he may have even forgotten it's in there, because certainly right now he doesn't seem to be thinking about anything else other than me and making me happy. And it's working because I haven't felt this happy for a long time.

As I finish off the ice cream, savouring every spoonful, Alex opens the wine I brought, and I realise if he drinks more, he won't be able to drive me home like he offered. But right now I feel utterly comfortable with Alex, so why not see where the night takes us? I can always call a taxi. And anyway, it's been a long time since I did anything spontaneous.

He fills my glass and, moving the carrier bag containing Harry's sweets, he looks inside. 'I *love* Smarties,' he says, like an excited little boy. 'My mum always bought them for me when I was little, and this,' he says, holding the round Father Christmas container up to the light, 'this is quite an exceptional piece.' He jokes in the voice of a posh antiques dealer, which makes me laugh. 'Yes, a fine specimen from the seventeenth century… the Ming Dynasty perhaps?'

'Mmm, I was thinking it's more the mini Sainsbury's dynasty – the Beech Road area, circa earlier tonight?' I join in.

Without taking his eyes off mine, he slowly begins to twist the Father Christmas head.

'What are you doing?' I ask, surprised.

'I'm opening them.'

'They're for Harry,' I say, aware I sound rather childish.

'I know,' he answers, continuing to twist, still not taking his eyes from mine.

'Don't open them, Alex, I'm warning you…' I say, joking, but wishing he'd take the hint and put them back in the carrier bag. 'I'm going to give them to him tomorrow.' Alex twists once more. 'He likes… Smarties,' I say desperately, as he twists harder and pulls the lid off the tub.

'So do I.' He throws his head back and pours the brightly coloured chocolate sweets into his mouth.

'Alex!' I gasp, surprised and a little pissed off. I wasn't comfortable with him taking them from my carrier bag, but to open and eat them feels like something more. 'I can't believe you'd do that.' I try not to sound angry, but I am.

'And I can't believe *you'd* buy gifts for other men,' he says, smiling through a mouth bulging with Smarties. Then he seems to realise, probably from the look on my face, that I'm not happy. 'Sorry. I was only teasing,' he says, putting the lid back on.

'Yeah I know but I'll have to buy another box now.'

He moves towards me, his arms open, and a rather awkward hug suddenly turns into an embrace and, before I know it, we're kissing and I've almost forgiven him.

'Sorry,' he murmurs in my ear, his warm breath making me shiver. 'I thought it would make you laugh, it was silly.'

'No, it's fine, I overreacted, it's a box of sweets, it really doesn't matter, just don't do it again,' I say with a mock frown, and look at him like a teacher letting a cheeky kid know they've been spotted.

We kiss again, and I tell myself it doesn't matter, it was nothing, he did it in fun, and I can easily buy some more.

Later, we sip coffee together on the sofa, and he asks me about my past relationships. 'So, I told you all about me, and my tragic history with women, what about *you*?' he asks.

'I'm not sure you *did* tell me all about you,' I say. It still feels very sketchy. 'I know you broke up with your girlfriend last year, but you never even told me her name.'

'Does it matter?' he says softly, gazing into my eyes and twisting a lock of my hair around his finger.

'No, I don't suppose so – but it's pretty basic.'

'Helen – her name was Helen. I met her through work. She's a lawyer, a good one, far brighter than me.'

'Do you keep in touch?' I ask.

He shakes his head vigorously, and takes a sip of coffee before answering. 'No, not at all.' He takes a breath. 'So, enough of the Spanish Inquisition – let me interrogate *you* now. How long have *you* been single?'

'About the same as you, twelve months,' I say vaguely.

'Why did you split?'

'I just realised he wasn't what I was looking for. My fault, we were together for two years – I should have realised sooner. Jas says I kept it going for too long, but it's hard to break up with someone when technically they haven't done anything wrong.' I don't point out that Tom hardly did anything right either, it feels disloyal.

'What you're saying about him is what Helen said about me – at the end.' He looks at me with such sadness in his eyes, I feel that pang of guilt again. I'm even taking it on for bloody Helen now – is there no end to my capacity for self-flagellation?

'Tom and I weren't right from the beginning, we had nothing in common. I felt more alone with him than without him, it's just how it was. But the longer I let it run, the harder it was to end it. He wanted me to tell him why, but it was hard to vocalise. He said it hurt to think I just didn't love him, that there was no *actual* reason. His reaction surprised me – I didn't think he'd be that bothered, but he was so upset he cried. I still feel terribly guilty about it.' I deliberately leave out any mention of the way he's been with me since we broke up. I'm tempted, but again, it's too soon to hand Alex my baggage.

'I think I'd have found it easier if Helen hadn't been seeing someone else. Instead she lied and told me she wasn't, but all the time she was – and I just knew it.'

I can see in his eyes that he's capable of feeling such pain, but also love, and real passion, which I crave. I just hope that won't be dimmed by what Helen did to him.

'Helen didn't really understand.' He sighs. 'You see, I don't want half measures, once I fall, I fall. And I'm totally committed – I'm afraid I'm all or nothing, Hannah.' He touches my face with the back of his hand.

'Me too,' I say. 'Being with Tom taught me that it's better to be alone than with someone who can't love me enough.'

'Seems like you and I have both been casualties. I hope I can love you enough.' Before I can answer or even consider what he's just said, he kisses me, then pulls away slightly. 'I can't believe I'm saying this to someone I really only just met, but I do think I'm falling in love with you already, Hannah,' he's saying softly, and I dissolve into him, only vaguely aware that he's slowly unbuttoning my blouse.

His words have undone me and now his touch is adding to the effect. I am lost, all at sea on the velvet sofa, as he carefully takes my clothes off and kisses me all the way down my body. After teasing me forever with his lips, he finally pushes inside me, all the time kissing my mouth, then my neck. He's saying my name, staccato murmurs in my ear, promises, desires. I hear his words, feel his body, as he moves into me, undulating, writhing – all I can think is how this is the most amazing sex I've ever had. Finally – *finally* – I've found what I've been waiting for. Alex is everything.

Afterwards, in a tangle of limbs and spent lust, he holds me, still as loving as he was before, his eyes drinking me in, his hand on my face.

'When I fall, it's forever,' he says. 'I promise I'll *always* be there for you, Hannah.'

I reciprocate by touching his face. I can hear Jas's voice in my head telling me it's too soon, that I'm rushing in head-first. Well, maybe I am, but what he's saying is just what I want to hear. Because I'm falling too – and I've always wanted forever.

There's no mention of me going home tonight, we both just move from the sofa to his bedroom upstairs. I barely take it in, but as we land on the bed, I'm aware of greys and blues, classy, tasteful, sumptuous in the lamplight. During the night, I wrap a blanket around me, and pad downstairs into the kitchen for a glass of water, feeling at home already. There's a full moon, so bright I don't need to turn on the kitchen light. I open several cupboards looking for a glass, and my eyes alight on the bin, where Alex put all the broken glass from my accident with the wine bottle. I peek inside to see the damage, wondering if there's an engraved name on the base so I can buy him a replacement. But underneath the broken glass and dinner detritus, I see something that makes me a little uneasy.

Very carefully, I put my hand into the bin and, clearing away the bits of dinner, my suspicions are confirmed. A screwed up

Häagen-Dazs container. When I loosen it slightly, it's clear to see the label – Pistachio Ice Cream. I really believed he'd made it specially for me. I guess he just wanted to impress, it isn't necessarily a bad thing. After all, who hasn't told a little white lie at the start of a relationship? And there are worse things to lie about than ice cream... aren't there?

CHAPTER TEN

Today, Jas is, as always, keen to know *everything* about last night. And I'm happy to tell her all about my evening – mostly. I decide to leave out the bit about the photograph with the pen across it, and keep up the story that Alex actually *made* the ice cream for me, because I want her to know how much he likes me. I'm sure he *would* have made it himself, he probably just didn't have the time, so it's not an untruth exactly.

'Did he say his ex is still around then?' she says, when I tell her I think his heart's still a bit broken.

'Mmm, she really did a number on him, messed with his head.'

'Is this your new guy?' Sameera pipes up. There's no privacy in this office, it's just as well that we're all friends.

'Yeah, we had the most wonderful night,' I say, remembering how I woke up in his arms; it felt so natural, comfortable. It was a shame I had to get up extra early and rush back to my flat to get a change of clothes, but worth it. 'I just hope his ex doesn't come back,' I say to Sameera.

'I don't think you need to worry about that,' she says kindly. 'Sounds like you're a perfect match, don't you think Harry?' she says dragging him into the conversation.

'Yeah, absolutely,' he replies – he clearly hasn't a clue what we're talking about.

Alex's ex has been playing on my mind ever since he told me he thought he'd seen her in Worcester. I feel slightly paranoid that he might bump into the bright, attractive lawyer – who may still hold a little piece of his heart.

My doubts soon fade when I receive a text from Alex telling me what a wonderful time he had last night. It's the first text of many, along with funny GIFs and heart emojis. I know it's early days, but he makes me feel like a priority already, like I'll always come first in his life. It was never like that with Tom. I can't wait to see him this evening. I'm going to drive over to his, straight from work. I've already packed an overnight bag so I don't have to get up at dawn again to schlep across the city to my flat for clothes. We talked about going to the cinema tonight, but I'd be quite happy to just stay in his lovely house together all evening. It makes me realise, all the times I nagged Tom about wanting to go out to places, it wasn't our social life that was missing – it was us.

It's been a crazy day with lots of comings and goings. Sameera and Harry have been out all afternoon seeing clients, and it's after six but Jas has only just returned from being at the police station with a client.

I pop my head into Jas's office on my way out. 'I haven't seen you all afternoon. I have to get off now, but are you okay?' I ask. She's sitting with her head in her hands and looks up, like she's almost surprised to see me.

'What? Yeah, it's been quite a day.' She sighs. 'I was sitting in that place for six hours, six! What a waste of time.'

'Ahh, sounds like a nightmare,' I say, hoping she doesn't elaborate, as I'm keen to get off.

'Doing anything nice tonight?' she asks, absently.

'Yeah, I'm seeing Alex,' I say, and wait for her response.

To my surprise she smiles. 'Lovely,' she says. 'I'm now dealing with the sodding paperwork, so you get off, don't keep him waiting. Have a good one, love,' she says, and it seems like she genuinely means it.

I call goodbye to the others, and Sameera, who's obviously heard me tell Jas I'm meeting Alex, tells me to 'go for it' and Harry sniggers.

I laugh, we all love taking the mickey out of each other, it's like being back at school – in a good way.

Hitting the freezing night air, I walk quickly to my car. It's so frozen that I can't even unlock it at first. After much jiggling of the key in the lock and breathing on it to attempt to thaw it, I finally get the key to turn and the door opened. I'm so relieved to get into the car, I don't notice it at first, but after closing the door and putting my seat belt on I'm suddenly overwhelmed by the smell of perfume. A strong, expensive smell – so strong it could be aftershave. Am I imagining this?

I sniff the air, not that I need to – it's filling my lungs. Shit. Someone's been in my car. Goosebumps rise on my scalp as, terrified, without moving my head, I let my eyes drift to the rear mirror. It's too dark to see, but… Oh God, is someone crouching on the back seat?

I grab the door handle and, in my haste, almost fall out of the car onto the icy ground. I step away from the car, and watch from a short distance, ready to run straight back to the office if anyone emerges. I stand there for a few minutes but can't see anything, so, holding my breath, I move closer and closer to the car. When I'm near enough, I slowly put my face to the back window and cautiously peer through, standing so still, my heart feels as if it's almost stopped. I give it a few seconds, then leap forward and quickly rip open the back door, hoping to God whoever is in there doesn't jump out at me. But there's no one, nothing. Just nothing. I check over my shoulder, then take a closer look around the back seat and realise I am, after all, alone. I'm breathless, clinging onto the door to hold myself up. Knowing there's someone out there who wants to hurt me is a horrible feeling, and it's definitely playing with my head.

Composing myself, I check the boot, but nothing. I'm overtired and anxious and it's possible I imagined the strong scent. I get back in the car and take a deep breath, and allow my heart rate to slow down for a few seconds before I start the car. I need to get a grip, there's no one here. But even if I imagined there was someone in the back seat, there's no denying the stench of perfume that now pervades the inside of the car. How did it get here? Whose is it? It's definitely not mine.

I don't want to hang around any longer, so start the engine and set off for Alex's. My whole body is shaking with cold and fear, the acrid taste of perfume in my mouth – another person's perfume.

I pull away, and glance again in the rear mirror. As I peer into the darkness behind me I notice the thick blanket that I always keep on the back seat has been moved. I stop the car, put on the interior light and turn around to take it in. It's spread across the whole of the back seat, covering it. And I know I didn't do that. Someone else did.

Arriving at Alex's I get out of the car and walk quickly to his front door. I keep turning to check behind me, just in case.

When Alex opens the door, I almost fall into his arms. He ushers me into the kitchen, soothing me with words and a hot drink, while I tell him about the strong smell in the car, the way the blanket was laid across the seat.

'Do you think that was symbolic?' I say.

He is clearly concerned about this, but as confused as I am. 'Are you sure it wasn't *your* perfume? And are you absolutely sure you didn't lay the blanket across the seat?' he asks.

'Of course I am. I'd remember doing that,' I say. 'And it wasn't my perfume. I like light, floral scents, this was heavy – lilies and musk and dark notes – more like aftershave, really.' I can feel it on me, a cloying stench that I long to wash away, if I was home I'd jump straight in the shower.

'Have you any idea who it might be?' he asks.

For a moment I hesitate. I want to tell him about Tom, but is it fair to blame him for this too? Then again, I hurt him, he's resentful. But why would Tom do that? And anyway, how did he get into the car without breaking a window or lock?

'I don't know, I had a weird delivery at work the other day,' I say, and go on to tell him about the roses and the vile note.

He looks shocked. 'Do you really have no idea who might be sending you something like that?'

'No. I wondered about Tom… But—'

'Tom, your ex?'

'Yeah, I mean he was upset when we broke up. He took it worse than I'd thought he would and there were some late-night calls. I think he might have come to the flat… hung around outside, but I don't *know*,' I add firmly when I see the look of horror on Alex's face.

'You're not in touch with him, are you?'

'No. But I left messages on his phone. He hasn't responded.'

'Well he wouldn't, would he?'

'He was hurt and angry with me, but that was ages ago, he moved on – at least I thought he had.'

'Doesn't sound like it to me.'

'Mmm, but a nasty note, white roses. It's all a bit melodramatic. It just doesn't seem like something Tom would do.'

'Shall we get the police involved?' he asks.

'Not yet, I'll leave it for now. But if anything else happens I'll call the police.'

'Oh babe.' Alex hugs me protectively. 'I'm sorry you've been upset and scared, but you're here with me now.'

'Yeah, thank goodness,' I add with a sigh, as we walk into the living room together. 'Anyway, let's try and forget about it for tonight. I might call the police tomorrow, just for advice if nothing else,' I clarify, hoping I don't sound too paranoid.

'Yeah, tricky though. Not sure how you'd report a crime involving the unwanted scent of perfume and an unfolded blanket.' He smiles, clearly trying to lift the mood.

'Yeah, not sure how that would go down at the station.' I try to play along but I can still feel the sickly scent clinging to me, and ask Alex if it's okay to take a shower.

He smiles, takes my hand and gently leads me into the shower, where he undresses me, then himself, and I stand under the spray of heat, thawing as he covers me in fragrant body wash. I can't get enough of him, and soon the rhythm of his thighs against mine is working with the throbbing heat of the shower.

Afterwards, as we lie naked on the bed, our arms and legs entwined, he says, 'I've never been happier, Hannah. Being with you these last few days has been wonderful, and I never want it to end.'

I smile, it's too soon for promises, but I know I never want this to end either.

I turn over and try to fall asleep, but then I remember the smell in my car. It fills my head and claws at my lungs. I know someone was in there, but who?

I'm woken early the following morning by the shriek of my phone. I turn over, but remember Alex has gone into work early as he's involved in a big court case today. It might be him on the phone, so I pick up, shocked to hear Tom's voice on the other end. He's finally responding to several angry messages I've left on his phone after the flower delivery the other day.

'What the hell is going on, Hannah?' he yells.

I don't want some horrible fight over the phone, while I'm half awake. So I ask to meet him before work, and ten minutes later, I'm sitting in the window of Costa Coffee in the centre of Worcester. The building is steeped in history, from the dark beams and the wonky wooden floor, to the unsettling death mask of a traitor from the Civil War looking down on me from the wall.

Tom works opposite at the guildhall, a beautiful eighteenth-century building right on the high street, where this year's Christmas tree will soon sit in its splendour. As I wait, I imagine the tree, the strings of lights along the high street, and I feel a rush of excitement knowing how different this Christmas will be with Alex.

I sit there a while. Tom's late, he always used to be late for everything. Eventually he saunters in, wanders to the counter and orders himself a latte. He barely looks round to see me, or ask if perhaps I might like a drink. He hasn't changed.

I sip my gingerbread latte and wait.

Tom finally sees me and, in no rush, he comes over to my table by the window and sits down. He doesn't say hello, just stares at me. If I wasn't so angry, I'd be amused – typical, laid-back Tom is clearly fuming that I threatened him with the police, but as usual he took his time to respond.

'What the hell is this about? You don't get in touch for months, and you don't want to know when *I'm* in trouble – but suddenly when it affects *you* you're straight on the phone threatening me with the bloody police!'

'What do you expect me to do when I get shit like this through the post?' I hiss, taking the card from my handbag and shoving it across the table at him. 'And don't pretend you don't know anything about it.'

He slowly picks up the card, reads it, and looks up. 'That's bloody creepy – you should call the police,' he says, pushing it back across the table like it's dirty.

It's not what I expected to hear. Maybe he's calling my bluff. But in truth, he seems as amazed and horrified as I am.

'Oh I *will* call the police, but I wanted to find out what you had to say first before I drop you in it.'

'You really think it was me?' He looks genuinely shocked.

I roll my eyes. 'Tom, who else could it be?'

'Try your new boyfriend.'

'How do you know I have a new boyfriend?'

'I've seen you around. You were all over each other in The Orange Tree the other night.'

'You're not following me, are you?' I ask, genuinely creeped out.

'Hannah, I didn't follow you when we were together, why would I start now?'

I almost smile, and remember that sometimes he could be quite funny, I'd forgotten that.

'Get a grip,' he goes on. 'We live near each other, we work a few streets apart, we socialise in the same, small city with one high street running through it. Of course I'm going to see you around.'

'I haven't seen *you*.'

'Well, I don't spend my evenings licking someone's face in public.'

'It's called being in love, Tom, something you know nothing about.'

He takes a sip of latte, cool as a cucumber, nothing ever seems to move him, even my anger – especially my anger.

'I think you've got me wrong,' he says, putting down his mug. 'Yeah, okay I was pissed off when you dumped me, and kicked me out of my home. Then I was suspended from my job over some emails I didn't write, and I still don't know who did.' He pauses and looks at me accusingly.

'It wasn't *me*, I told you, I swear it wasn't.' A few weeks after we'd split he turned up at the office screaming about how I'd sent emails to everyone at the council (where he worked) accusing him of sexual harassment, or impropriety or something. Apparently there was an internal investigation and he'd been suspended, but I had nothing to do with it.

'Whatever,' he says dismissively, still clearly believing I tried to destroy his life. 'You were the one that dumped me, then you started punishing me… yeah, I came to the office, I was pissed off with you – but, trust me, I am *no* stalker. That' – he points at the card on the table in front of me – 'is different level.'

I'm not totally convinced. Admittedly, he never actually did anything too weird back then, just some heavy-breathing phone calls, but other stuff happened that I still can't explain. Then more recently, there's been the note, and the strong smell of aftershave in my car last night, the blanket on the back seat. It might be nothing. Or it might be Tom.

'Anyway, when have I ever bought you flowers?' he says as an afterthought, and laughs.

I can't help but smile. 'Mmm, you have a point, they were roses too – a bit classy for your tastes. But that note was nasty – and to my knowledge, there's no one else who hates me like you do.'

'I'm over it. And I know this might be hard for you to get your head round, but I'm seeing someone else now. I'm really not interested, Hannah,' he says. 'And, if you ask me, this card isn't from someone who hates you, it's from someone who's obsessed with you.'

CHAPTER ELEVEN

It's been almost three weeks since my meeting with Tom and, tellingly, nothing else unsettling has happened.

I'm not convinced Tom got into my car that night. Perhaps my perfume had reacted in the freezing air and that made it smell stronger, like aftershave even? And the wind may have whipped the blanket up when I opened the door. I'm not sure I believe it, but it's made me feel a bit less anxious, and I can go about my daily life without being too paranoid.

As for the roses and the note, Tom did a good acting job of being surprised when he read it. But for him to say someone is obsessed with me makes me think he *might* just be trying to scare me – and therefore perhaps he did send them. I didn't tell Alex about meeting up with Tom, he'd only worry, he warned me not to make contact, said he was dangerous. Perhaps he is. Fortunately, there's been lots going on recently that has kept Tom's antics on the fringes of my mind, not least my relationship with Alex, which is going from strength to strength.

I can't believe how much my life has changed in a matter of a few weeks. Alex and I spend most of our time at his, weeknights and weekends – it's almost as if we're living together. We cook, binge-watch old movies, listen to music – we both love the same nineties bands, especially Oasis – and we regularly step into that big, beautiful shower together.

We still haven't spent the evening at mine. In fact Alex hasn't even set foot in my flat, and I know I need to invite him over soon. I just worry he'll see my shabby old flat and be totally put off. And, besides, I love being at his, it's a whole house rather than a flat, it's more comfortable. And he spoils me in a way no one has ever spoiled me in my life. This morning, despite having had a large bowl of his wonderful home-made porridge, at 11.30 Alex dropped off a bag of warm croissants at reception. I was out on a visit and actually rather glad I wasn't there when he dropped by. I'd have felt obliged to invite him into the office, which would have been awkward as everyone's always busy, and you never know what they're dealing with. Anyway, the croissants were waiting at reception when I got back, which filled me with a lovely inner glow that rivalled the warm porridge.

'He seemed so disappointed that you weren't here,' Margaret said. 'I think he was hoping to catch a glimpse of you.' She winked.

I walked into the office, holding the bakery bag aloft and announcing that Alex was a sweetie, just as I spotted two large pains au chocolat from the café on my desk.

'I didn't realise you had a new supplier,' Harry joked.

'Yeah, but you'll always be my main man,' I replied.

This morning before work, I'd popped into the Sainsbury's Local and finally remembered to buy a second box of Father Christmas-shaped Smarties for Harry as a thank-you for the pastries. I'd put them on his desk and said, 'A fair exchange for all the croissants?'

'Ahh cheers, Hannah, you didn't have to do that,' he'd replied.

I think he was genuinely pleased, and I was glad I'd kept this new tub away from Alex.

'I'm not sure I can eat dinner tonight after those lovely croissants you sent today,' I tell Alex this evening, when I arrive at his place. He's made a casserole, and insists I have some, but I ask for the tiniest portion.

'So, you enjoyed the croissants?' he asks a little later as we finish eating.

'Yes, they were delicious. So delicious I had to go to the gym at lunchtime,' I say.

'You went to the *gym?*' he sounds horrified.

'Yeah, it's near work. It's nice to get out of the office sometimes and jump on the treadmill. It was busy, though – I reckon everyone's firming up for their Christmas party dresses.'

'You don't need a *gym*. You can work out with me in the garage,' he says. 'I've got everything in there – state-of-the-art treadmill and—'

'Your garage? Isn't it bloody freezing in there this time of year?'

'It's fine, a bit of cold air won't kill you. We can work out together, it'll be fun. Much nicer than a gym full of sweaty people. Besides, it's romantic to work out together.'

I try to resist, but Alex won't take no for an answer and insists we do a mini workout now, so I can 'test-drive' his gym. I have my gear with me, so get changed and reluctantly follow him through the kitchen to the inside door to the garage. He's taking ages to unlock it, and I've never noticed until now, but there's a padlock above the keyhole too.

'Why do you have so many locks? The garage door will keep anyone out, it's electric,' I say, puzzled.

'Oh, you know me, I like to be safe, and now you're here a lot – I want *you* to be safe.'

'I can look after myself. I'm a big strong girl, Alex,' I joke, lifting my arm and flexing my biceps.

'Yes, but after your weirdo ex sent those flowers with the vicious note, I reckon we need double locks on everything.'

I don't like to think about it, it's too disturbing, and as nothing more has happened since I warned Tom off, I reckon it's over now.

'Don't worry about him. He's moved on,' I say, not wanting to get into a conversation about it.

'How do you know?'

'I spoke to him,' I say, knowing this isn't going to go down well.

'You called him?' He sounds agitated.

I don't want to lie, but I also don't want to tell him we met, it will only upset him. He'll think I put myself in danger, when I didn't see it that way. I never thought I'd be one of those women, hiding things from my partner so as not to upset him. I'm not *intimidated* by Alex, nor do I need his approval – it's just easier and will avoid any additional drama this evening. It's true that love makes liars of us all.

'He insisted it had nothing to do with him, he was pissed off that I'd even asked him.'

'It is him though, I'm sure of it. I wish you hadn't made contact, he might think he's in with a chance. He could be watching you, and I hate to think of you being alone and vulnerable. I can drive you to and from work,' he suggests.

'Thanks, Alex, but I'll be fine… I'm tired, let's not talk any more.'

'Hannah, I don't want you to be scared, but I do think you need to take it seriously. Go on, let me drive you to work and collect you. We do similar hours, I can work around you.'

He's mentioned this before, soon after I told him about the note and roses. I like that he cares, but sometimes I think he worries too much. What happened was horrible and upset me, but I don't want to dwell on it, nor do I want to live in a padlocked place and have him ferrying me around everywhere. It's like he's petrified something might happen to me if he's not there. I suspect it might be a legacy of his childhood. He told me that when his mum died, no one told him. She died in her sleep, and he woke to be told by his dad, 'the angels have taken her.'

'I thought she'd been stolen, kidnapped by these wicked angels,' he'd said. As difficult as the concept of death was to his young mind, the idea of a group of angels 'taking' his mother must have been so much harder to comprehend. 'I was scared of angels throughout my childhood, because they came in the night and stole people you love,' he'd admitted. It made me cry.

'The gym's a lot warmer,' I say now, trying to do sit-ups on a mat next to him in the icy garage. As romantic as it might be for some people to work out together, it's not my idea of a couples' night in. Apart from the fact he's so much fitter than me, and I can't keep up, it's absolutely freezing, as I'd feared. 'I think I might give your gym a miss, babe,' I say after an hour of freezing-cold torture. 'I'm tense with cold, my muscles will ache tomorrow.'

'Darling, I'm sorry,' he says. 'What about if I get some heating in here, would you give the garage workout another go?'

'I might,' I say doubtfully, 'but don't go to any trouble, I'm fine with the gym.'

'It's no trouble.'

'You do so much for me, Alex, and you really don't have to, you know. I'm not a princess, I don't need pleasing all the time,' I say with a smile.

We both laugh at this. 'Sorry, I just want to make everything – right. I told you I'm a bit too much sometimes,' he says – a point which was proven earlier this week when he couldn't get tickets for a play I said I'd like to see. I saw the flickers of anger, the fear of failure when he thought he'd let me down. And now, as we walk back into the house, after he's double-locked and padlocked the garage, I know he feels as if he's failed me again because I found the garage too cold tonight.

It makes me feel bad, as if I'm solely responsible for his happiness. I appreciate his attentiveness, but it's quite a responsibility, especially when it seems to be his mission to make me happy. He's even started to fill his fridge with my favourite things. He says I'm a slut when it comes to food, and he's right, but then he moves aside his jars of artisan chutney and pickled artichokes to squeeze in my mini supermarket trifles and ready-sliced cheese. And I know there's nothing that will stop him loving me. And I keep telling myself that's good, isn't it?

*

I tell Jas about the freezing garage-gym workout when I get to the office this morning, thinking it'll amuse her – but she doesn't laugh.

'Anyway, Alex is having heaters installed, so I can't use the cold as an excuse not to work out in the bloody garage,' I add with a giggle.

'Wouldn't you rather go to the gym?' she asks, unsmiling.

'Not really, it's full of sweaty people. Besides, it's romantic to work out together.' I hear myself echoing Alex, but I now think he's right.

'Do you think he's just done that so *you* don't go to the gym?' she says, loud enough for the others to hear.

Sameera asks what we're talking about and Jas tells her that Alex wants to make me a home gym.

'He doesn't want her doing press-ups in tight lycra in front of other men,' she says with a wink.

'Ooh he might be a bit... too keen,' Sameera says.

'No he isn't,' I say wearily, pissed off at Jas's interpretation of Alex's kindness, and the fact she's opened this up to the whole office for debate. I think she's feeling a little rejected because we haven't had a girls' night recently, and now she's trying to rally the troops to judge Alex through her cynical eyes.

'It *might* be that he doesn't want you going to the gym because you might bump into hunky men,' Sameera offers, almost apologetically.

'Is this guy possessive much?' Harry sniggers.

That's the trouble when you spend all your time with people, you tell them too much and they start to create their own narratives. Jas has started this one. I realise it's been difficult for her to see me so caught up in Alex when her relationship has so recently backfired, but I wish she'd be a little more supportive.

'He isn't possessive at all,' I say. 'There's a difference between being *controlling* – which I think is what you're saying – and caring. And, trust me, I *do* know the difference,' I say, perhaps a little sharply.

Harry isn't even listening to my response, he's engrossed in something on his phone.

Jas shrugs. 'Well, it's your life, but I wouldn't like that – I need my own space, I like getting away and being on my own in the gym – or with the girls.'

'Yep, it's my life,' I say pointedly, and it's my turn to shrug.

I'm the one who's with Alex, and I know the truth – not them. They can think what they like. All I know is that since we met, I feel as if I've been living on a cloud of pink candy floss. Alex is kind, considerate, sensitive, he doesn't even leave his socks on the floor or let plates pile up in the sink. Being me, I'm always looking for the problem, nothing is so good that it's flawless. But the only little spot on my horizon is the spectre of Helen, his ex. He hasn't really mentioned her since that first night at his house, and I'd love to know more about her. But all I really care about is that she's in the past. Right now, nothing matters but me and Alex. I've become one of those people who, mid-conversation, smiles mysteriously when they receive a text, and has hushed phone calls in the office. I'm aware Jas doesn't approve, but Sameera and Harry have calls with Raj and Gemma, and Jas never says anything. Perhaps I'm just imagining her disapproval. The old guilt gene again making me feel bad for something when I don't need to.

I am worried about Jas though. She seems in a bad place right now, and it's coming through in her negativity. Being made a widow in her thirties means she carries a lot of baggage, and I don't know how to help her. Only yesterday I suggested we go out for lunch and talk – I understand she may not want to pour her heart out in front of the office. But she said there's nothing to talk about, she's just feeling low, wondering where her life's going and if she'll ever meet anyone again. I understand, because until recently I was the girl who spent her weekends alone, who gazed resentfully, yet longingly, at the 'couple' photos on other friends' Instagram accounts. I used to roll my eyes at the sickly silhouette heart shapes they made with their hands against a sunset, the cute little selfies of two loved-up faces squashed against a camera lens. I hated anniversaries and Valentine's days and dinners for two. No one understands how Jas feels more than me, and I get it: as satisfied as she is with her career, her home, her life – she's ready to share it with someone again.

'I had a bitch of a night last night,' she said to me when I popped into her office earlier. 'So, as you know, I bought a new outfit, got my nails and hair done, trowelled on an inch of foundation and lipstick.'

'Yes how did it go?' I ask, guessing what her answer will be.

'Well, I ended up sitting in Pizza Express on my own. I was that loser, checking her phone and nursing a glass of white wine. The bloody waitress kept asking me if I was waiting for someone, and was I going to order, like you aren't allowed a pre-dinner drink when you're on your own, you have to be in a sodding pair.'

'The guy didn't turn up?' I asked, feeling terrible for her, she'd been quite excited about the date. She hasn't said as much, but I'm sure she thinks if she does what I did and goes on a dating app the same thing that happened to me will happen for her.

'No he *didn't* bloody turn up. The hundredth guy I've been talking to recently who seems to think it's okay to chat online, make all kinds of suggestions and promises, arrange a time, a date and just not turn up. Jesus, it's got to the stage where I wouldn't mind if they just wanted a one-night stand – as long as they actually showed up.'

'Oh, love, it will happen for you. Thing is, you just have to relax and—'

'Don't.' She'd put her palm up in a stop sign. 'If you've got some bloody cliché about ten buses coming at once up your sleeve, keep it to yourself. I don't want to hear it.'

'I know it's annoying, but I meant it. I believe it will happen for you… but you have to open up and stop being so cynical about men.'

'Not easy when time and time again they prove themselves to be the tossers I think they are.'

I shrugged in agreement.

She looked at me, weighing me up for a few seconds and I waited for the comment. 'I bet you spent the night all snuggly in bed with Mr Perfect watching Netflix and ordering a takeaway.'

'No, we just had some bread and cheese,' I said, suddenly feeling defensive. 'We watched some Netflix – but Alex is busy working on a case, so it wasn't quite the love-fest you paint.'

I lied. It was.

I'm now in the office kitchen and Jas is continuing her 'date night from hell' story, by telling me about some messaging thing she started with a guy online when she got back from being stood up at Pizza Express.

'I thought we were getting somewhere, until he sent me his photo,' she says.

'Oh, not a pretty face?' I ask.

'I don't know, didn't see his face.'

'Oh gross.'

We both laugh at the ridiculousness of this as she describes the photo of the man's penis.

'Then that guy in the bank, I've been talking to him on and off for weeks now, I probably mentioned him?'

'Only about a hundred and forty-seven times,' I joke. 'Scott?'

'That's the one. Well, looks like he wanted to talk me into a loan, not into his bed. The loan paperwork landed on my mat this morning – twenty tonnes of the shit.' She'd usually laugh loudly at this, but it's a sign of how low she is that she just rolls her eyes.

'Shame,' I say, sympathetically.

'Yep! He was motivated more by his commission position than by the prospect of any missionary position with me.' She smiles.

I laugh. 'Oh, love, it wasn't meant to be. Someone better's out there, and they are just dying to get you on your back, or your front... or whatever is your preferred—'

'Thanks, Hannah, but please stop now.'

I laugh, and go back to making my hot chocolate. It's so cold in the office it helps to keep me warm. Jas opens the fridge door and tries to find a shelf she can put her sandwiches on.

'Damn Harry and his bloody ten-course lunches.' She sighs, delving into the bottom shelf to make room for her lunch.

'Oh sorry, that's me,' I say, feeling guilty, though in my defence the fridge is tiny. 'Marks and Spencer are doing that dinner at home thing where you buy a meal, a dessert and wine for a tenner.' I try to say this like it isn't a big deal. It is though, because tonight I've asked Alex to come to mine for the first time.

Jas raises an eyebrow. 'Ooh cheesecakes?' She lifts the pack from the fridge, studies it, then puts it back. 'So, are you taking this to his, or is it finally dinner at Casa Hannah tonight?'

'Something like that.' I really don't want to rub her nose in it, and wonder if she thinks I should invite her over to meet Alex. I could stretch the meal for two. It's about time Alex and I started meeting each other's friends, and she's bound to like him because he's lovely.

'Is he ready for the bomb site that is your home?' She giggles, finally jamming her sandwiches into the fridge, and shutting the door.

Is she mocking me? I'm not sure, but either way I immediately change my mind about inviting her over. It's going to be an ordeal anyway having Alex to my place knowing how perfect his is – and I'd be even more nervous with Jas's running commentary on my epic fails as a domestic goddess.

'It's not a bomb site, I tidied my room, Mum,' I say, without a smile.

She picks up on my slight irritation and winks. 'Take no notice of me, I'm a grumpy old cow today. I'm sure you've deep-cleaned it and tidied everywhere...'

Now it's my turn to laugh. 'Yeah, of course I did.' I pour water on the powder, chocolatey sweetness fills my nostrils, reviving me like a warm hug.

'I thought not.' She smiles. 'You've told me how fastidious he is, so leave early, make sure it's spotless, candles lit, something spicy waiting for him in the kitchen – and that's just you!' She laughs at this, her mood has lifted, probably at the hilarious sitcom prospect of clean freak Alex encountering my flat.

I mix the remnants of chocolate powder into the hot liquid with a spoon, then lick it.

'Animal,' she murmurs affectionately. Then she folds her arms. Her jumper's tight across her full breasts, tendrils of black hair escaping onto her neck. 'So, girl... will he be staying for your cheesecake?' She wiggles her eyebrows suggestively.

'Hell yes. My cheesecake is catnip to men,' I tease.

Jas giggles, then leans on the kitchen counter, and as the room's so small, she's blocking my way out, so I stand there holding my hot chocolate.

'Are you sure about this Hannah?'

'What?' I say, wearily.

She holds up both her hands. 'I'm only going off what you tell me, but he seems a bit needy to me. And remember the last time you let a guy into your flat – he moved in and you couldn't get rid.'

'My eyes are wide open, Jas.'

'Really?'

'Yes,' I say, unsmiling.

'I hope so, babe, because the minute Tom got his feet under the table that was it, he was living in your flat, eating your food, it was take, take, take.'

'Alex isn't a taker – and he wants what I want.'

'Until you want what he *doesn't* and he's off with his mates and doesn't come home,' she says with a sigh.

This stings, because Jas knows it's exactly what Tom used to do. I wish she'd stop comparing Alex to Tom.

'Actually, I had to *beg* Alex to go out with his friends last Thursday,' I say. 'He didn't want to spend the evening apart, said he'd miss me too much.'

'And did he go out?' she asks.

'Yes, but only because I insisted.'

I was staying at his and smile at the memory of him leaving reluctantly. Then, when he'd gone and closed the door behind him, he suddenly came back through the door, calling down the hall to me, 'Missing you already.'

'So, Alex goes out with *his* friends, but you don't go out with yours?' She raises her eyebrows and, just at this point, Harry walks in, so she leaves the kitchen.

Shit. Why did I tell her Alex had gone out? I'd promised her the next time I had a free evening we'd have a girls' night and now she's hurt. I feel bad, but I won't be manipulated. I'll arrange an evening out with her soon, but not because she's sulking, because we're friends and we want to spend some time together. It'll be on my terms.

I go back to my desk and try and concentrate on work, but everything's crowding in on me. Jas and I are really close and I always share everything with her, I want to go back to how we used to be, proper besties – but it's like she's putting Alex between us.

A little later, she wanders over to my desk and plonks herself on it. 'Hey, I hope you don't think I was playing the jealous friend before,' she says. It's almost an apology, or an olive branch at least.

'No, not at all,' I lie. 'And I hope *you* don't feel like I'm neglecting you.'

She runs her fingers along the edge of my desk, it seems she wants to stick around, to talk.

'Jas, I know we said we'd have a night out, just the two of us, and we will – we need a proper catch-up. But the night Alex went out, I had to do some work at home. As my boss, I think you'll approve.' I smile. I know I shouldn't have to explain myself to my best friend, but it's a combination of her feeling low and me feeling guilty because I haven't been there for her.

She continues to perch on the edge of my desk. 'Thing is, Hannah, I'm just a bit worried about you, babe. You're completely wrapped up in this guy – which is lovely, but these weird things keep happening, like the roses and the perfume in your car. I hate to say it – but what do you really know about Alex?'

'Look, it was ages ago, the roses were from Tom, and you agreed yourself that the scent was probably my imagination.'

'Yeah, but only so you didn't freak out. I know Tom did some weird shit when you first broke up, but this is recent, and it's happened after you met Alex.'

'I'm busy, Jas, I don't have time for this.' It's true, I have loads of work to do and don't want to get into this with her now. I have to leave the office to meet with Chloe Thomson and her mother at two o'clock this afternoon.

'Since you started seeing Alex you don't have time for anything, or anyone. I'm not just talking about me; I mean you don't even have time for yourself. And now you tell me he goes out for the night and you stay home and work.'

'You're wrong, it wasn't like that – I just stayed at his because he wanted me to.'

'He wanted you to stay because he didn't want you out of his sight?'

'It's called being in a relationship, Jas,' I snap.

'Are you sure it's not called being controlled?' she says in her head-social-worker voice.

'No, it *isn't*. And I resent you saying that,' I snap. 'Really, what gives you the right to comment on my relationship?'

Harry and Sameera glance over; they can hear everything. But I don't care, I'm fed up with Jas sniping one minute, then the next saying she's my friend and wants me to be happy.

'Whoa, I didn't mean… I just—' She moves off my desk. 'I'm sorry, Hannah, but I see red flags with this one, and I don't like it.'

'Well, I don't see red flags, and I *do* like it. So, if you don't mind, I'd like to get on with my work.'

Jas huffs and stomps back to her office and I see a look pass between Sameera and Harry. Is that what they think too, that Alex is controlling? None of them have even met him. We want to spend most of our time together. I stay over at his, and he calls me at work for no particular reason – if those are red flags then bring it on. To my mind, they're signs of a reciprocal, healthy relationship, not that I should have to justify that to anyone. I wish Jas would mind her own business. Because when Alex and I are still together ten years from now, I will say 'I told you so.' And Jas will realise she was wrong to judge Alex by the men she goes out with.

Jas tried to imply that the night Alex went out he made me stay at his house on my own waiting for him, but it wasn't like that. 'I'll only go out with my friends on one condition,' he'd said. 'That you stay here at mine, so I can come home to you.' So I did, willingly; happy to be in the comfort of his home, looking forward to his return, rather than stuck in my flat alone for the night. And when he came home at midnight, instead of being pissed and falling asleep in the chair – like Tom used to – he was sober and loving. And, what's more, he was just so happy to see me waiting for him in what he referred to as 'our' bed. Jas's idea of someone being 'controlling' is shaped by her experiences, and if she sees red flags just because someone cares enough to want to be with me, then I think *she's* the one with the problem.

She's now at her desk, and I know by her flushed cheeks she's angry and upset, and so am I, but things needed to be said. I've had enough of her comments and, thanks to her, it seems the whole bloody office has an opinion on my love life.

I gather my stuff together for my visit to Chloe Thomson. She lives in a village about fifteen minutes' drive from here and, quite honestly, I'm glad of the excuse to get out of this place. I feel as if they're all watching me, listening to my phone calls, judging me, and probably discussing me and Alex. It's really starting to make me feel uncomfortable – I know Sameera and Harry are more curious than concerned, but everyone's comments, especially Jas's, are making me question my relationship. I know in my heart it's right. He isn't possessive, he doesn't stop me from doing things without him, I *want* to be with him.

I'm early for my visit to see Chloe, but I just have to get out of the office. Once I'm in my car I call Alex. As much as I'd like to vent, I have no intention of telling him Jas has pissed me off and called him controlling. One day I hope they can be friends, and I'm not going to drop that bomb and ruin any chance of future harmony, Jas will come round. But, still, I'm feeling vulnerable, and need to be with someone who I know loves me and I can trust.

Eventually, he picks up.

'Hey, I'm missing you,' I say, 'and I wondered if you were free for a quick lunch, I'm early for my meeting and I have half an hour and—'

'Darling… oh darling, that would have been wonderful, but I'm in court all day.'

'Alex, where are you? I can hear water running.'

'I'm… yeah… I'm actually in the bathroom – at court.'

'Oh, have you stopped for lunch?' I ask, glancing at the time – it's 1 p.m.

'No… like I say, I don't really have time, just a quick sandwich.'

'Oh.' I'm disappointed.

'Are you okay, Hannah?'

'Yeah. I just wanted to see you. I'm feeling a bit fragile today.'

'Oh I feel terrible, but I'll see you tonight and make it up to you, just hang on in there, babe.'

I can't help but feel a bit tearful as I drive over to Chloe Thomson's house. It's stupid, I know, and during the drive I give myself a pep talk, I need to be on it for my client, and not distracted by some tension in the office.

Chloe's a child who's been in Children's Services on and off, and considered vulnerable. At sixteen she's entitled to a Social Services Personal Advisor, which is me. So, when five weeks ago, she called in a state, saying her mum's boyfriend had touched her, I called the police, and drove over to their place late at night to support her. But, soon after, she retracted her statement, saying she'd made it all up because she'd had a row with her mum. I can't help but feel this was all too easily erased, and there's stuff Chloe isn't telling us. According to previous records, she became sexually active around the age of twelve – around the time her parents split, and her mother started taking in drug-addict boyfriends. I suspect there are some unresolved, ongoing issues, possibly around sexual abuse, that I now need to investigate.

I know something's going on with Chloe, and I know I can help her if she'll talk to me – she just has to trust me. I also know how hard it is not to be believed. I think about the foster brother who used to threaten me with all kinds of violence as I ate my fish fingers at the tea table. His mum, my foster mum, would smile lovingly at him, but the smile never met her eyes. When, after a particularly painful punch in the stomach, I dared to tell my social worker, the foster family closed ranks, said I lied and I was back in the home. I learnt then about the need to hide things. After that, I made this little box in the back of my brain to hide things so they don't hurt me – the nasty card is now in there, the lid firmly closed.

With all that safely tucked away, my thoughts are now free to wander to dinner tonight at mine. What will Alex think about my basic furniture, my cheap bed linen, my mismatched crockery? It's never mattered to me before. Until Alex, I was too consumed with work to consider what mug I drank from, let alone think up a whole colour scheme for the flat. But spending time at his place has made me realise that these things can enhance your life, and soften the hard edges at the end of the working day. They also project an image about the person whose home it is, and I worry now what impression my cluttered, messy, disorganised space will give Alex of me.

Entering the village of Pershore, I spot a pottery shop with beautiful handmade plates in the window and, feeling spontaneous, I wonder if I could afford two of them for tonight's dinner? I'm still early for my meeting with Chloe and her mother, so I park the car in the little town-centre car park to go and investigate.

Once inside the shop, I'm soon accosted by a well-lipsticked shop assistant, who informs me that not only are the plates handmade, but they're from Italy.

'Made in Tuscany, hewn from local clay, don't you just *adore* that flickering amber shade?' she asks, opening her eyes wide, fake soot-black eyelashes fluttering.

I nod enthusiastically, knowing Alex will love them as much as she does.

'Would you like to look more closely?' She carefully hands me one of the large dinner plates as if it's Ming porcelain. I accept it with equal reverence, holding it with both hands, imagining Alex and me by candlelight, sitting at my rickety little table, crockery thrown by Italian hands, dinner made by M&S, and microwaved by me. I know these plates won't make my flat into a palace, but they'll add a touch of class and effort and show Alex there's more to me than just a tired sofa and chipped crockery.

Even when she tells me the price – a whopping thirty pounds each – I don't drop the plate in shock or say I need to think about it. I picture Alex and say, 'I'll take two please.' I feel like a millionaire.

I'm leaving the shop with a carrier bag full of profanely priced plates, excited about tonight, when I suddenly see Alex. He's coming out of a pub across the street, which doesn't make sense because earlier when I called him, he said he'd be in court all day. Perhaps it's been adjourned? He must have rushed over here quickly – the court's in Worcester and it's at least fifteen minutes away.

All these thoughts are thrumming through my mind as I wave at him, trying to catch his eye between the passing cars. My heart is doing a little dance. After this morning's argument with Jas, I want to run over and fall into his arms. I just hope I don't burst into tears, because despite my surface calm, I'm all wound up inside.

I'm trying to dash across the road to him, but the cars keep coming and a couple of times I step out and have to jump back. Suddenly, there's a gap, and I'm about to cross over when I see that he seems to be talking to someone. A woman. I stop myself from calling to him as he walks on with her, deep in conversation. I've missed my opportunity to cross now the traffic is moving back and forth, so I just have to watch on. I can only see them from behind as they continue down the road. Then, to my dismay, she puts her arm through his.

They walk on, and I'm puzzled, shaken really. Why is he here? Who is she? Why did he say he was in court all day, when clearly he isn't? Further down the road, she rests her head on his shoulder. I don't know what's happening. Is this real?

I stand on the pavement feeling faint, and a woman asks me if I'm okay, and I nod, automatically, without even looking at her. But she's pointing at something on the ground and when I look at my feet, I see the carrier bag with my lovely plates. My brand-new crockery – hewn from Tuscan rock, painstakingly crafted by Italian hands – has smashed into a million pieces.

CHAPTER TWELVE

Picking up the bag of porcelain shards, I don't take my eyes off Alex and the woman as they continue to walk down the street. The noise of the traffic probably drowned out the sound of crashing crockery, so he didn't hear it and hasn't seen me. I guess he thinks I'm back in Worcester, safely at my desk, where I can't see him arm in arm with a strange woman. Had he been with her when I called? Was the sound of running water not from the bathroom at the courts, but from a bathroom in a house? Her bathroom? Who is she? More importantly, *what* is she to Alex?

I desperately try to think of an alternative to the obvious. She may just be a friend. She might be a colleague or client he's helped and she's showing her gratefulness by linking arms with him. I can't say I've ever had a client link arms with me, and whilst I'd link arms with Jas or Sameera, it would be weird to do so with Harry, and he'd definitely think the same. I want this woman to be Alex's sister, but he's an only child. I can't bear this, I need to know what's going on, so I manage to cross over to their side and follow at a discreet distance. It feels weird and wrong. Shouldn't I just trust him, and ask him about it later? Or call out to him and go up to them, rather than sneak behind them? But that would be mad. Along with all the happiness, the anticipation, the warm feeling permanently flooding your veins – this is what love does to a person. It makes you crazy, your judgement becomes clouded and irrational.

They slow down slightly and the woman steps out into the road. For a moment I think she's going to walk in front of a car, but she runs across quickly while looking both ways. My heart lifts slightly, perhaps they've said goodbye? But before I can recover, Alex follows her across the road.

Only half aware of my actions, I take out my phone and call him. It's instinctive, I don't think about it, don't even know what I'll say when he answers. Even though he's run to the other side of the road, I'm close enough to be able to see him react to the ringtone, and take the phone from his coat pocket. He looks at the screen, and I hold my breath, waiting for him to pick up. But he hesitates, then must end the call because the ringing stops and he puts the phone back in his pocket.

I'm devastated. I thought he always answered the phone to me, whatever he's doing. So why is he not answering now?

I stand on the pavement opposite, watching the woman flash her keys at a red shiny soft-top. It's then I get my first glimpse of her face. I know immediately who she is. It's the woman in the photo whose face was defiled by his furious pen. And not only has he just had lunch with her, he's told me he's somewhere else.

I'm not even being discreet now, I've stopped in the middle of the pavement, on a freezing winter's afternoon, openly watching them, as people pass me, giving me angry stares because I'm not moving out of their way. Part of me wants Alex to see me, to rush over, take me in his arms and explain what the hell is going on. But because he's chatting to her, he doesn't see me. Then the woman climbs into the car, Alex gets into the passenger seat, and they drive off. Just like a couple out for a romantic afternoon.

A man walking past almost knocks me into the road, but before he can apologise, I move and stand in the doorway of a charity shop, clutching my bag of broken crockery, feeling like I've been hit by a truck.

After a few minutes, I turn off my phone and head back to the car park. I have to compose myself. Regardless of my problems, I need to go to this meeting with Chloe. I have to be there for this girl who's been let down already by those she trusts. But right now I wonder if it would be in her interests for me to pass her case to someone else, someone who can be more committed, more focussed than I can at the moment.

I think about calling Jas to say I'm ill and need to go home, but I can't do that to Chloe. She has already been passed around the department. Harry was her social worker before me but when she turned sixteen, Chloe had to be moved because Harry only works with kids aged between thirteen and fifteen. She's only just getting over the trauma of not having Harry, how would it feel to dump her because I'm too involved in my personal problems? I couldn't live with myself. No, Chloe's safety is paramount. I have to focus.

I drive to Chloe's house and take lots of notes, make some suggestions, and put a pathway plan together in my head. But it's futile, really, because I know there's something she isn't telling me, so I can't get to the bottom of her problem however much I want to help her. She's recently become surly and uncommunicative, and it hurts my heart and my brain to contemplate what's going on with this troubled sixteen-year-old, who has struggled through school and will probably continue to find life extremely tough. Along with the frustration and limits of a learning disability, Chloe has an addict for a mother, not to mention her mother's new boyfriend. In addition, she's dealing with all the other things a teen has to cope with, from friendship issues, to raging hormones, to boy trouble and there's the ongoing question of sexual abuse, which I can't ignore.

As much as I tried to probe, to my frustration Chloe's mother was present and answered most of my questions on her daughter's behalf. I asked if Chloe wanted to be seen alone, but she just shrugged, so I couldn't insist – but back at the office I'll make an appointment to meet Chloe alone next week.

When I leave the Thomsons' just over an hour later, I get back in the car and immediately check my phone. Alex has called me *seven* times, and sent five texts. The first reads: *Hey, are you there? Think you called me. You okay? Love you.*

There are four more texts of variations on this. I have never ignored his texts, or not returned his calls. But for once I put the phone back in my handbag without responding, start the car, and head back to the office.

As I'm driving, I find myself trying to work out why my boyfriend was having a secret liaison with another woman. Alex adores me, or so he says, but the truth is, it looks like he's been lying to me – and Jas was right all along.

CHAPTER THIRTEEN

'Are you okay?' Sameera asks as she wanders over to my desk.

I'm back at the office, throwing myself into work and ignoring Alex's texts and calls. I daren't pick up or I'll lose it. I'll be upset and angry and I need to concentrate on Chloe.

I nod. 'Yeah, just busy… I'm having a rubbish day, to be honest.' I'm tempted to tell her about seeing Alex in Pershore, but then see Jas pop her head up over her screen and decide against it. I won't be a weeping mess in the middle of the office for Jas to feast her eyes on and say, 'I told you so.' Not yet anyway.

'Did you ever find out who sent those roses?' Sameera asks, leaning tentatively on my desk.

I stop typing and look up. 'No – Tom said it wasn't him.' I shrug. 'Well, he would say that wouldn't he?'

'Yeah, it's not something anyone would be proud to claim as their own.'

'I liked Tom, he was – funny, nothing seemed to rattle him. I can't imagine him sending a note like that. Could it be someone more random, someone you've pissed off and don't even know you have? Like a client, a parent of a client…' The note with the flowers had shocked Sameera. It's obviously been playing on her mind.

'Yeah could be – they can hold a grudge, but then so does Tom.' I sigh.

'Who holds a grudge?' Harry gets up from his desk and joins us, he's eating a sandwich and dropping crumbs everywhere. Sameera reprimands him, and he shrugs. 'You look upset, Hannah.' He's looking down at me, concerned, then he's back to his sandwich.

'I'm okay, just busy,' I say. For now, I'll keep my worries about Alex to myself until I know from him what the truth is. I change the subject. 'I just had a meeting with Chloe and her mum. I reckon something's going on,' I say to Harry as Sameera goes off to make us all some coffee.

'With Carol's boyfriend?' he asks, finishing his sandwich and leaning on the desk.

'Yes, and Carol was in the meeting, so I couldn't speak to Chloe alone. I'll have to though. I really need to get to the bottom of all this.'

As her previous social worker, Harry's all too familiar with the case, and he rolls his eyes. He sighs, and gestures to the files. 'Have you waded through all those yet?'

'No,' I say, feeling guilty. 'I started, but am still wading. I should have gone through them weeks ago, when I first took the case off you. Sorry.'

'Don't apologise, I'm not sure I read every little detail either. I mean, let's face it, they go back years.'

'Mmm, Chloe's had such a tough start. And Carol bringing a guy like that into her home, with a troubled teenage girl – I don't trust the situation at all.'

'God knows what's going on. That poor kid's going to be so messed up.'

'Yeah, I know. As if things weren't challenging enough, her mum is incapable of ever putting her child first.'

'Absolutely, but it's a minefield, be careful,' Harry warns.

'What do you mean?' I ask.

'That kid's been in the system so long, she knows what to say, knows what we're looking for, and if her mother's speaking for her, that might just be because *Chloe* wants her to.'

'Wow, I hadn't even considered that.' Harry's good at his job, and he understands how young people tick. Plus, he was Chloe's social worker for two years, so he knows her well.

'Just let me know if you're worried about anything – or you need me to translate Chloe-speak for you.' He laughs, wandering away.

'Thanks, Harry.' I smile. 'What would I do without you?'

He sits back at his desk, giving me the thumbs up.

My phone is flashing, I pick up and Margaret says, 'Alex on line one, my lovely.'

He can't get me on my mobile, so he's trying the landline. Shit. I don't want to speak to him yet, I need to think and I want to let him sweat. 'Oh, I'm so busy this afternoon, Margaret. Would you mind telling him I'm out of the office?' I ask.

'Actually, love, this is the third time he's called. I thought you liked this one?'

God, even Margaret has a take on my bloody love life. I know she means no harm, but I just wish everyone would butt out.

'I do, but I'm busy and it doesn't do to be too available, does it?' I try to sound light-hearted, don't want her to think it's anything more.

Seeing Alex today with that woman has knocked me for six. I know I should face it, take his calls and ask him, but I'm scared to hear what he has to say. And, besides, I can't have that kind of conversation in the office in front of everyone. I'll call him when I'm ready.

By 6 p.m. the weather's freezing and the forecast is threatening snow.

'Don't stay too late, hon,' Jas calls, 'your drive home won't be much fun if this sets in.' She walks towards me, coat on, holding her scarf, about to leave. She's obviously forgiven or forgotten about our little row this morning, so I will too.

'I won't stay too late, love – just working out the Chloe conundrum,' I say and give her a smile.

'Ah that! Do we need a meeting?'

'Not tonight, let's talk tomorrow, once I've waded through all this. There's loads of handwritten notes from her recent interview with the mental health worker that need to be input.'

'Margaret will do that for you.'

'No, it's fine, I think it will help me get to grips with everything if I do it.'

'Okay, babe, but don't work too hard.' She wraps her woolly scarf round her neck several times and blows me a kiss. But before she leaves, she says, 'Sorry about earlier, I need to keep out don't I?'

'Yes, you do!' I say, longing to tell her about Alex at lunchtime and how I feel, but knowing it would simply be providing her with ammunition and I don't need that right now.

'I'm really sorry.'

'It's fine, we're good. You and I go back too far for a little fight over a man to make a difference,' I say.

'Thanks for saying that, means a lot,' she says. 'Love you, babe.' She blows me a kiss.

'You too,' I say and blow a kiss back as she skips off, whipping open the door, allowing a blast of the frosty evening in.

And then I'm alone in the silence, there's nothing save the clicking of my keyboard. You could hear a pin drop.

My brain is whirring. I should be focused on Chloe Thomson, but I'm too worried about what Alex was doing today to allow anything else in. I may have blown it out of all proportion in my head, but I need to speak to him.

I pick my phone up and put it down several times, before finally summoning up the courage to call him and find out once and for all what's going on. Is he the perfect man I thought he was, or has this whole thing been a lie?

CHAPTER FOURTEEN

Alex sounds pleased, and so relieved, to hear me when he answers the phone.

'Hannah, I've been so worried about you, I've been calling all day. Didn't you get my messages? I sent texts too – where *are* you?'

'I'm still at work,' I reply in a monotone.

'But it's after six. I thought we were having dinner at yours tonight. I went to your flat, but you weren't there.'

Christ, with everything that's happened today, I'd forgotten the glorified ready meal for two still sitting in the office fridge. 'Sorry I… I've been really busy… I just have loads to do.'

'Can't you bring the work home?' he asks.

'No.' I'm stalling. I want to ask him what the hell he was doing linking arms with a beautiful woman today. But I don't want to have the difficult conversation and I don't want to hear him lie to me.

'What's wrong? You sound different. You're scaring me.'

I feel nauseous, I don't know where to begin.

'Why didn't you return my calls, Hannah? I've been in court all day and had to keep coming out to use my phone.'

'You – you've been in court *all* day?'

'Yes, that's what I said.' So he isn't going to tell me. 'I could barely concentrate on the case. An important one too…' he adds as an afterthought.

There's an edge to his voice which makes my hackles rise. How dare he! He's barefaced lying and has the cheek to be irritated by me.

'Well, I've spent the afternoon looking at safeguarding options for some poor teenager who's probably being sexually abused.'

His voice softens at this. 'I'm sorry. Is that why you haven't been responding to my—'

'It's *one* of the reasons. I've had to discuss the case in detail with Harry.' Once I'd gone through the files I sat down with Harry to see what else I could gauge; he was really helpful, and Sameera added some insight too. I was glad of their input, my head was all over the place. 'So, as I said, I've had a few things on my plate today too,' I say.

'Good that you had Harry to chat to about things though.'

'What do you mean by that?' I snap, knowing full well what he means. He seems to have a problem with Harry, or is it any man I happen to be friends with?

'Nothing, just – you don't talk to *me* all day, you ignore my calls and texts, but apparently you have time to discuss things with Harry.'

'You're being an idiot,' I hear myself say. I can't believe he's jealous of bloody Harry. He's totally barking up the wrong tree and, besides, who the hell is he to be pissed off with me for talking about a case to a colleague when he hasn't even told me who he had lunch with? 'Look, I don't want to have this conversation over the phone – I feel spacey, think I need to eat,' I say, segueing nicely into, 'Did you have lunch today?'

'Not a proper lunch, I've been in court – as I said.'

'You didn't even pop out?'

'No. Didn't have time, just grabbed a sandwich in the canteen, never left the bloody building.'

So now I know, Alex Higham, my Mr Right, the gorgeous, perfect man who's clearly husband material tells me lies. And it hurts like hell.

'But I still managed to make time to call you,' he says in a hurt voice, which winds me up even more. 'We're *both* busy people, Hannah – but I found the time.'

I don't respond to this, I'm too angry.

'Hannah?'

'What?'

'Surely you could have found two minutes in your day to return my calls. I don't understand.'

'*You* don't understand? Then that makes two of us,' I snarl.

'What do you mean? What's the matter?' He waits a few seconds, then says in a more panicked voice, 'Hannah, what is it, what's *wrong*?'

'You said you never left the court today,' I hear my voice reading from the script I've been mentally preparing all day.

'Yes.'

'And you didn't even pop out?' I feel like I'm the lawyer, sashaying around the court, questioning the defendant.

'No. Darling, what is this?'

'*This? This* is I know you *did* leave court, in fact you left Worcester. I saw you. In Pershore. With a woman.'

Silence.

His silence is proof he's lied. But why is he lying to me?

I'm vaguely aware the threatened snow has begun to fall outside. Thick, swirling, twirling flakes. I think about the drive home. I think about Chloe Thomson and hope she's okay tonight.

'Oh God, Hannah, I should have told you,' Alex says now.

'Yes you should.' My voice is croaky.

'I'm not hiding anything from you,' he murmurs.

'It doesn't look that way, Alex.' I can barely hear my voice.

Silence, inside and out. No vehicle sounds from the street outside. The snow is covering the windows, as if someone's thrown a big grey blanket over the world, smothering it into an eerie calm.

I'm waiting. I'm scared of what he's going to say. I have to know, but I'm not sure I'm strong enough to hear it.

'I didn't want to tell you because, well, I didn't want to scare you off. Can we talk? Properly? I want to see you.'

My throat constricts. *No, no, not Alex.*

'Just *tell* me, who is she?' I want to be sick.

'It was Helen.'

'I don't know what to say.' I'm confused and hurt and upset, I don't know how to feel.

'But – but you need to know *everything*,' he says. 'And when I tell you, I need to hold you, to explain everything carefully, so you don't get the wrong idea.'

I desperately want to believe this is going to be okay, that Alex will come up with a perfectly innocent reason why he had lunch with his ex today and didn't tell me. The ex he seemed to have a huge problem getting over, until quite recently. I don't say a word, I just want to listen.

'Hannah, please, you mean so much to me…' His voice fades.

'If I mean so much to you, why did you lie to me?'

Again the silence. I was hoping he'd laugh, simply dismiss my fears, tell me I'm being silly, that she was just a client, a colleague – whatever. I want him to convince me there's nothing to worry about. But I *am* worried.

'Meet me, Hannah, let's talk.'

'I don't know.' I sigh.

'Please, I'm begging you, don't throw away what we've got. There's nothing to be jealous of, I promise.'

'Jealous? This isn't about me being jealous, I'm not a teenager. I can understand someone meeting up with an ex – but my problem with it is that you didn't tell me.'

'I… Let me meet you at yours,' he says firmly.

'No, I don't want to meet at mine. But I do want to know what's going on, so let's go somewhere neutral, and then, if I don't like what you have to say, I can just go.'

'Okay, okay, whatever you want. But promise you'll hear me out?'

'I'll try, but I'm promising nothing. Where shall we meet?'

I glance out of the window, it's filling up with snow, covering everything in a sheet of white.

'The wine bar on Foregate Street? Where we went on our first date?' he says. 'I can be there in five minutes.'

'Okay, but you're at my home, right? It's at least ten minutes away by car, and it's snowing, it'll take you longer.'

'Oh. Yeah… I'll… Look, just wait at work for me.'

'No, I'll see you in the wine bar.'

'Why can't I just come to the office…?'

'I have some work still to do, so text me when you get to the wine bar and I'll leave then.' It doesn't really matter if he comes here or not, but I hate it that he sometimes tries to tell me what to do. He has this way of convincing me, browbeating me, in a nice way.

'Why do you never want me at your office?'

'It isn't that I don't *want* you at the office… I just want to be on neutral ground.'

'You never want me there, what are *you* trying to hide?'

What's he on about? I suddenly feel angry and defensive. 'Alex! Really? It's *you* who's been hiding something, so please don't try to deflect this onto me. I'll see you in the wine bar in half an hour,' I say firmly, putting down the phone, angry that he's suggesting I have a reason for not letting him near my office. He's always offering to pick me up from here, but there's no need, and for now I want to keep home and work separate. Plus, from a professional perspective, it isn't appropriate. There's confidential information stored in this office and Jas would have a fit if she thought anyone other than the team were in here after hours. And it would just be my luck for her to have forgotten something, or to come back to check I'm okay, and find him here with me in the semi darkness.

In the shadows of this office are shelf upon shelf of bulging files and locked cabinets. Among the many notes and records of meetings and decisions are the secrets people hide, the things we have to keep safe. Sometimes in this job, we have to let life spill out in all its filth and horror. But in the end it's about making lives better.

I hear something, a movement at the far end of the office. Jas said she thought we had mice. I hope not. There it is again. It's definitely coming from the back of the office. I look round, trying to focus exactly on where the noise came from, but it's so dim I can't see that far.

I try to finish what I'm doing so I can leave to meet Alex, but I can't concentrate. I have this horrible, irrational feeling that someone's in the shadows watching me. I know there's no one there, but I turn again behind me into the blackness, and it's then I see a movement. It definitely *wasn't* a mouse.

I stay very still and stare for a while and realise it's probably just my mind and the darkness playing tricks. I need to stop being stupid and finish filling in the report from today's meet with Chloe and her mother.

I go back to the task in hand, and continue typing, my keyboard clicking in the deep quiet. I hear something and suddenly stop. And wait. Silence. I gaze around. Nothing. I start typing again, remembering the way Chloe couldn't meet my eyes, the way her mother spoke her words for her. As Harry said, maybe there's more to Chloe than meets the eye. Is she the victim this time or the culprit?

I definitely hear something and I stop typing again. I stand up, and my heart starts to thud in my ears so loudly I'm deafened to any other sound. 'Is anybody there?' Just hearing my voice asking this freaks me out.

I wait and I'm met with more layers of thick, snowy silence. I stand for another few seconds, aware I have to finish this report, and yet distracted by something – and nothing. I could kick myself for allowing what happened today to fill my mind – if I hadn't, I'd be finished and gone now. Instead, I'm scaring myself half to death when I should have been home hours ago.

I'm cold and it's creepy and I need to see Alex, so without finishing the report, I click off the laptop, throw Chloe Thomson's files into a carrier bag, grab my coat and shoulder bag, and make my way to the door. I know there's no one here, no one lurking in the shadows, but as I walk towards the door I'm driving myself mad with crazy, intrusive thoughts.

When I reach the outer door, I realise it's locked. Jas must have done that as she left, so no one could get in anyway, thank God. I smile to myself and roll my eyes at my nervousness. But just then I hear something again, and rummage frantically for the keys in my bag. I'm not usually anxious like this, but I've got myself into such a state today. And now I can't find my bloody keys. The more I feel around inside my bag, the more panicky I become. 'Shit, shit,' I'm saying under my breath, I can feel a scream forming in my throat, but swallow it down. Miraculously, my fingers finally grip the keys and I lift my head to put them into the lock when I see the outline of someone's face pressed up against the glass.

Now the scream that's been sitting in my throat is released, loud and shrill. I didn't know I could make such a noise, it's like it's coming from someone else. My heart is now wedged firmly in my throat. Do I open the door and let whoever it is in? Or stay locked inside here, alone in the dark?

The shadow moves away slightly from the glass.

'What do you want?' I shout. 'I'm calling the police.'

The shadow moves again.

I grab my phone from inside my coat pocket.

'Hannah… Hannah? It's me, darling.'

'Alex?' I call back doubtfully.

'Yes.'

I push in the key and open the door, and to my relief, Alex is standing there. He's smiling, his arms outstretched, delighted to see me.

'Why did you come here?' I say, without returning his smile, or falling into his arms, which he now drops awkwardly.

'I… I was worried. I… was already on my way when I spoke to you on the phone.'

'We arranged to meet at the bar, didn't we?'

'What is this, twenty questions?'

'You scared me to death, why have you turned up here?'

'Hannah…' He looks behind me into the office. 'Is somebody else here with you?'

'No,' I say, irritated.

'So you're on your own?' he asks again.

'Yes, *of course* – why are you asking?'

'I was worried… I thought I saw someone.'

'When? Now?' I'm *really* creeped out. Can he see someone behind me? I daren't turn round to look.

'Not at the moment, but I swear I saw someone leave. They were coming from the back of the building.' I feel a shiver run down my spine. 'That's why I came to the door,' he explains.

I was the only one in the building, but I can't help but feel anxious. I thought there had been someone in there too. What if I wasn't alone?

'Let's get out of here,' I say, ushering him out and locking the door behind us. My anger towards him can wait, for now I just want to leave.

We start walking to the wine bar. It's a few minutes away, so Alex leaves his car.

'When you saw someone… leaving just now, were you heading to the bar?' I ask as we trudge through the snow.

'No… I was…' He pauses. 'I was sat in my car. He ran out from the back of the building and through the car park.'

'Are you sure you saw someone? It's very dark.'

'Well, I *think* he ran from your building. I turned on my full beams, I definitely saw someone running away.'

'How long have you been sitting in the car park?' I ask.

'Not long.' He reaches for my hand, but I pull away. 'I was so worried, and when you weren't at your flat, I drove here, to your office. I know for some reason you don't like me turning up at the office... but...'

I stop walking to look at him. 'Alex, why do you keep *saying* that? I don't have *a problem* with you coming to my office, so stop trying to make out I do.'

He shrugs. 'I just feel like whenever I suggest calling by or—'

'I'd rather you didn't. But not for any other reason than it's my place of work and Jas would be really pissed off.'

'Seems to me like Jas gets pissed off very easily.'

I ignore his remark. We plough on through the thickening snow, and if things had been different, this would feel so romantic – Christmas lights twinkling along the high street, white confetti in the air. As we pass the guildhall, I can't help but take in the huge Christmas tree, resplendent in her twinkling ball gown of lights.

'So, Alex,' I start, 'about today?' I refuse to wait any longer.

We're almost at the wine bar, and he gestures for us to keep walking, says he'll tell me once we're inside. It's freezing, my teeth are chattering it's so cold, so I shrug, I might as well be warm while he says what he has to say.

Once inside, I realise it may not have been the best place to come to have an intimate chat. It's early December, but the office parties are already in full throttle. It hurts to remember our first date here and how happy I was compared to how I feel just a couple of months later. It was cosy and romantic then, now it's loud and busy, and instead of the excitement and hope I had weeks ago, now I feel upset.

'Are you sure you don't want to go to mine, where we can talk?' Alex yells as we fight our way to the bar.

I shake my head. 'Here is fine,' I say and, unsmiling, I look away from him so he won't try to convince me otherwise.

We eventually get served, he orders us a glass each of Merlot and, against the odds, we find a table in a fairly quiet corner.

'Talk to me Alex,' I say, sitting down opposite him, placing my handbag and the carrier bag with Chloe's files on the floor, then taking off my coat, and laying it down on the bench next to me.

Alex is pleading with me to hear him out. 'Hannah, I haven't *lied to you...* that's not how I see it.'

'Okay, so how *do* you see it?' I'm impatient, I've put myself through hell today, and only he can stop this horrible, sick feeling in the pit of my stomach.

'I didn't lie. I didn't tell you because I don't want to...' He pauses. 'Lose you.'

I sip my wine, keeping eye contact, but making no attempt to speak. I just need him to talk.

'So. The woman you saw today... with me, yes, it was Helen. How did you guess?'

'I saw a photo – in your bathroom. Someone had... scribbled on her face.' I look right at him. 'That was Helen?'

I see the realisation dawn on his face, and he drops his head. 'Yes, I'm not proud of that. I was very angry back then.'

'So it would seem. You ripped across her face with a pen. And yet there you were today lunching with her – how things have changed,' I say, unable to keep the bitterness out of my voice.

'Things *did* change – when I met you. I was able to forgive her because I'd found someone I really loved.'

I ignore this, I won't be seduced by his words. 'So... why didn't you tell me about today?'

'Because...' Another pause. He takes a drink, I know he's buying time. 'Because – it's complicated.'

'Oh please.' I roll my eyes while discreetly holding on to the table to steady myself. '"It's complicated"? Teenagers put that as their Facebook status, it's meaningless.'

'You're angry.'

'Damn right I am. This morning, before we both left for work, you told me you were in court. And later you lied again, told me you couldn't meet me for lunch because you were in court. But presumably you were in her bathroom!'

'No, no I was in the pub.'

'Even worse. You were speaking to me from a bathroom in the pub because you didn't want to pick up in front of her.'

I take a longer sip of wine this time, and as I put my glass down, he's staring at me. He's really struggling to find the words, and the more he struggles, the more I glare at him, waiting.

'Look, Hannah, I haven't been strictly honest with you.'

'Here we go.' I sigh heavily. 'You spent the afternoon in a hotel room, you've realised she's your soulmate and you're getting back together?'

'No, none of that. But... she isn't my ex-girlfriend.'

'What? Who is she then?'

'She's my wife.'

CHAPTER FIFTEEN

If he'd stood up and punched me in the face, it couldn't have shocked me more.

'Your *wife*?' Is all I can say. 'Your *wife*?' I repeat. My chin's trembling, I'm going to burst into tears any moment.

'I was going to tell you, Hannah.'

I can't bear this any longer, I'm not going to sit here while he attempts to explain. 'I'm sorry, Alex, but this is too much.' I stand up, gathering my bag and coat in my arms, and make to leave.

'Please, Hannah, hear me out, it isn't what you think.'

'What I *think*? What I *think* is that we've been together since October and it's now December. Almost three months – *three* months – and not once have you ever mentioned that you're married.'

'It's—'

'*Please* don't tell me "it's complicated", again,' I hiss, as I desperately try to push back the bench I've been sitting on, which is now jammed against the wall. 'I don't want to hear anything else,' I mumble, on the verge of tears. My mind has been a whirl of doubt and mistrust all day, but even in my darkest thoughts, I never imagined she was his *wife*! I've been totally blindsided, and I'm governed only by primal instinct. I have to escape, like an animal fleeing from pain.

I finally extricate myself from the bloody bench and the table, knocking my drink over in the process.

Alex is on his feet now. 'I knew you'd freak out – but honestly, we're not together now, please listen to me – there's something else. Hannah!'

I can't listen to another word and make my escape, as he continues to call my name. His voice fades as I fight my way through the laughing Christmas throng, twenty-deep at the bar. I'm almost lashing out to get through. I can't bear to be here, where everyone's so full of alcohol and joy, the air thick with pissed happiness. I have so many questions burning inside my brain, but I can't face Alex now. This has come from nowhere and made me question everything about him.

Eventually I reach the door, and pushing through more people to get outside, I gulp the freezing night air and start running down the high street. I don't know where I'm running to, or what I'm running from.

Clutching my coat and shoulder bag to my chest, I run down the street, tears freezing on my cheeks. A gang of girls with Christmas baubles dangling from their ears shout, 'Are you okay, love?' I'm in such disarray, people are staring at me as I pass.

I keep my head down and continue quickly along the frozen high street. I almost bump into a cosy couple, out for a romantic dinner, who step aside and look pityingly at me. They probably think I'm just sad and single and drunk. I want to yell at them for their smugness, and for assuming they're safe in their coupledom. I want to tell them that I felt just as they do twenty-four hours ago, thinking I was untouchable. But Alex is *married*.

I had this naïve hope nestled somewhere inside that when we got to the bar, he'd laugh, tell me the woman I'd seen him with was his long-lost sister. And, in a fleeting Bridget Jones moment, I confess I even allowed myself to hope that he'd taken a female friend to help choose an engagement ring for me. That he'd turn up tonight and go down on one knee, wrapping my worry up in a bright-red bow and handing it back to me for Christmas. But he hasn't. I'm not living in a rom com after all. This is real life. And real life hurts.

I'm shaking with cold, and desperately try to put on my coat without dropping my bag, when I hear someone running beside me in the now sloshing snow. Alex has caught up and he's gently taking my bag and coat from me. I stand there, helpless, as he puts my arms into the coat he's holding, like a parent dressing his child. Once my coat is safely on, he fastens my bag tightly, then puts it on his shoulder before taking off his scarf and wrapping it carefully around my neck.

He stands back to admire his handiwork. He's tidied me up, but the tears are now streaming down my cheeks.

'How could you lie to me about something so... *big*?' I sob.

'Please, Hannah. You ran out without listening to me. That's why I wanted to tell you in person rather than on the phone. I knew you'd be upset.' He holds me by the shoulders and, looking directly at me, speaks clearly. 'Helen and I are *not* together, Hannah.'

'It looked like it to me – you couldn't have been closer, Alex!'

'No. Not like that.'

'But why didn't you *tell* me you were married?'

'I... I don't know. You asked me about my ex, assuming she was my ex-girlfriend, not my ex-wife. I should have corrected you, I *should* have made it clear – but one date turned into another and then another and...' He looks up into the night air, his breath white, like steam. 'I didn't want to lose you.'

'But to find out now is so much *worse*,' I cry. 'I feel like everything I thought we were – we're *not*,' I say clumsily, unable to articulate how I feel.

Alex moves his hands from my shoulders to my waist and tries to draw me to him, but I pull away. 'This doesn't change anything, I'm still me and you're still you,' he murmurs.

'If it doesn't change anything, why didn't you tell me on our first date?'

'Because… it didn't come up. And we had such a great night… I didn't want to risk anything.'

'But by not telling me, you've risked everything. You *lied* – all this time. How can I ever trust you?'

His eyes fill with tears. 'You *can* trust me, Hannah. Please, please don't punish me for being an idiot. It was the past.'

'But it's *your* past,' I murmur into the cold. 'It makes you who you are.'

We're standing in the middle of the high street, snow swirling around us, I feel as if my life's just paused.

'Darling, you're freezing,' he says, attempting to take control. 'Let's go back to mine, where it's warm and we can talk. Our cars are parked at your office, we can collect them in the morning, we've had a drink, and I think we're both too upset to drive, so let's get a taxi and go back to mine.'

He's gently ushering me down the road, and I suddenly feel claustrophobic, I need space to think, and as tempting as it is to climb into a warm taxi, and then a warm bed with Alex, I have to make a stand. I'm not ready to go back as we were yet.

'No, I'll get a taxi home. I'm not completely comfortable with you at the moment,' I say, wiping my eyes with gloved hands.

He looks genuinely shocked. 'I won't let you just go off into the night like this.'

'I'm sorry, Alex. There are big things I don't know about you, and this has made me question everything. I need someone I can trust – I thought that was you, but I don't know any more.'

'Oh, Hannah.' I see tears in his eyes. 'Don't, please don't. You can trust me, I'll do anything to prove it.'

'There's nothing you can do.'

We both stand for a little while in the snow, staring past each other, neither of us knowing what to say or do. He keeps looking at me, but I don't make eye contact.

'Let's get a taxi together at least, and I'll drop you off at yours, you can have some time to think?' he suggests.

I nod, it makes sense and I'm too cold and tired to hang around talking.

He hails a black cab, which, to my relief, stops immediately and we climb in, sitting strangely apart. Alex doesn't speak, and neither do I. It's a lot and I need time to process all this. Within a few minutes, we're pulling up outside my flat.

I climb out of the taxi, try to give Alex a five-pound note, but he's paid the driver and is now getting out behind me.

'Stay in the taxi, go home,' I say, but he refuses. I'm angry, I feel like I've been hoodwinked, the plan was that he'd see me in safely then continue on to his.

'I just want to make sure you're safely home, I can't help but worry. Your ex could be lurking anywhere with another bunch of flowers.' I feel a shiver down my spine thinking about this now, especially after the shadow in the office earlier. In spite of everything, I'm glad Alex is here with me. The snow's falling thicker now, and a gang of noisy lads are singing their way towards us.

'Come on,' Alex says, reaching out for my hand.

I reluctantly let him put his fingers through mine and guide me through the snow to the front door, where I scramble around in my handbag for the keys. I'm desperate just to get inside so I can send him on his way and have some space to think about things.

'Shit.' I suddenly realise I don't have the carrier bag with the folders inside. 'Oh no, I've left the bloody carrier bag in the taxi,' I say, watching it disappear into white oblivion.

'No, you only had your handbag in the taxi,' Alex replies.

'But I remember putting the bag down on the bench in the wine bar... No, oh shit.'

'You think you left it in the bar?'

'I *must* have.' I desperately think back. 'Yes, I'm sure I did. I have to go and get it.'

'You can't – it's late and you're freezing, call them tomorrow.'

'I can't, there are work folders in there. They're highly confidential, from Chloe's mental health worker, I haven't even read them yet.' But now, anyone could pick it up. I have to get it. God, I hope it's still there.

I get my phone out.

'What are you doing?'

'I'm calling the wine bar.'

I google the bar, get the number and for the next few minutes wait for someone to answer. Nothing.

'I'll call a taxi and go back,' I say, in a complete panic.

'No, no.'

'This is too important to leave until tomorrow, Alex.' I sigh.

He gently takes the phone from my hand. 'I'll go back there,' he says quietly but firmly. 'You're freezing cold and upset and it's all my fault that you forgot the bag. I know exactly where we were sitting. I remember now, you put it on the floor.'

'I'm such an idiot.'

'No you're not. I'm the idiot for not being honest with you sooner and causing all this upset. I'll walk back there and I can pick my car up. I only had a glass of wine so I can still drive. If the bag's there, I'll drop it back to you. Don't worry about a thing,' he says, pointing at me and running backwards.

I don't argue with him. I know what's happening here, this is his opportunity to redeem himself, and he's using it. I let him go, it's what he wants to do.

I go inside and, closing the door behind me, the shared hall light flickers on a couple of times, then off again, plunging me into darkness.

'Damn,' I say to myself, as I crawl slowly up the stairs in pitch-black. I make a mental note to call the landlord, the light's been faulty since I moved in a year ago, and it's dangerous.

I open the door to my flat, and then it suddenly hits me what I've done. I'm trusting Alex with Chloe Thomson's secrets, and my career. I wouldn't have given this a second thought yesterday – Alex is my boyfriend, he's a lawyer, I sleep in his bed, I use his shower, and I think I love him and he's someone I can trust. But he never told me he was married and I wonder now how well I really know him, and whether I really can trust him.

I sit in the lamplit darkness of my living room trying to rack my brain for hints he may have dropped or clues he may have accidentally left for me to find. But the more I think about him, the more I realise I don't know Alex. I know what he *allows* me to see, his kindness, his humour, his glossy kitchen and Italian power shower in matt black. I know he loves French food, foreign films and minimalist interiors, but I haven't met his friends, his family – even his colleagues. Come to think of it, despite the wall of photos at his house, there are none of him, and when I asked him who was who he was vague, said they were old friends. But the only photo I recognise is the one of Helen, that he hides in his toiletry bag. So what else is he hiding?

CHAPTER SIXTEEN

The doubts have now firmly pushed their way into what I believed was my perfect relationship. As hard as I try to close the door, they're battering it down and I can't hold them back. I'm feeling extremely anxious about the files too, so I text Harry to see if he knows of any copies anywhere. I've been a fool, only thinking about myself and how I'm feeling – in doing that I've inadvertently been putting my clients second. I've never done that before, and it has to stop now.

My phone suddenly screeches into the silence, making me jump. It's Alex's number and I pick up straight away.

'Where would you like this package delivered to, madam?' he says playfully.

'You've got it?' Thank God. Despite my doubts he's been true to his word this time.

'Of course I got it.'

'Thank you *so* much, you've no idea…'

'I had a pretty good idea.'

'I'd have felt so terrible telling Jas.'

'Well now you don't have to. Are you happy for me to drive over with it?'

'That's really kind, thank you.'

My plan is to thank him profusely and say goodnight; I still need time to think about how I feel. But I'm so bloody grateful when he turns up on my doorstep holding the bag, I invite him in. I almost forgot this is his first time at my flat, and I'm so relieved about the files I'm not even embarrassed about the awful walls, painted circa 1970 when psychedelic orange was 'in' for the first time. And when he says, 'You look totally exhausted, let me make you some tea,' I don't even consider the ingrained stains on the white sink, or the half-eaten croissant abandoned in the fridge a week ago. The flat's shabby, the furniture's old and, unlike a lawyer, my social worker's salary does not extend to beautiful interiors.

I had intended to get back early tonight and fill the place with candlelight to hide some of the torn wallpaper, cracks in the plaster and unmoveable stains. This was to be accompanied by a spritz of air freshener and M&S's finest romantic meal, which is still sitting in the fridge at work. However, that was before I saw Alex and my heart got smashed, along with the most expensive plates I ever owned, even if I only had them for a matter of minutes. It's all gone to shit now and we're both here without the dinner and candlelight but still with the cracks and stains and shabby sofa.

I die inside as he pops his head around the door, holding the stiff croissant between finger and thumb.

'That's one of Harry's.' I roll my eyes. 'Throw it in the bin.'

'With pleasure,' he calls from the kitchen, 'along with the milk. I take it we're drinking our tea black?'

It hasn't taken him long to find the sour milk, which I'd also completely forgotten about. 'Sorry, I'm rubbish, aren't I?'

'Not at all,' he says, walking in from the kitchen holding two mugs. 'You've been staying at mine all the time. I don't know why you even bought milk… you're never here. And when did Harry do a home delivery of croissants?' He puts his mug on the coffee table, slowly shaking his head.

'He didn't, I brought it home from work, ages ago.' I sigh. 'It's been such a horrible, horrible day.' I hear my voice fading as I try not to cry.

As always, Alex instinctively knows how I'm feeling, what I need, and gently puts his arm around me. I know I should pull away, but I'm so emotionally drained after today I don't have the energy.

'I'm so sorry, darling. Can you ever forgive me?' he murmurs.

'I don't know. At the moment I'm just upset, disappointed. I thought you were different.'

'I am, I promise you.'

'I need to work it all out in my head, but I'm so tired.' I lean my head on his shoulder, and in spite of these fresh insecurities, the stabbing doubts, it feels good, and I close my eyes.

'Everything I do is to make you happy.' He sighs. He keeps talking, soft, honeyed tones in my ear, telling me he'll look after me. 'I'll keep you safe,' he whispers, and kisses my head, then moves to my lips, and in the end I find it impossible to resist. Soon he's undressing me gently, saying over and over how sorry he is about everything, and I melt into him. My shabby old sofa suddenly feels like luxury velvet, and for just a little while the world goes away.

'From that first night we met, when we talked about the kind of dog we'd have, the kids, the kind of life we wanted, I knew you were the one for me,' Alex is saying.

'You must have felt the same about Helen.'

It's about 4 a.m. We're in bed – my bed – talking everything through.

Alex is leaning on his elbow, head on one hand, his other arm across me. 'No. It was a long time ago, I was besotted, but it proved to be superficial. What I feel for you goes so much deeper.' He sighs, and I see a vision of my face in a photograph, and for a moment wonder what he'd do to it if I walked out. 'Are you okay?' he asks.

'No. Not really,' I say, shifting the vision from my head. 'I need to process everything, I always do. I'm ready to ask some questions though,' I say, because I need to know exactly what the score is so I can decide on what happens next.

'Okay.'

'How long were you married?'

'We were married for two years. We'd only known each other a short time, and it felt like the next step.'

'And when did she leave?'

'Almost twelve months ago. It was ten days before Christmas. Everything I already told you about me and Helen is true, I didn't lie – I just didn't tell you about—'

'The marriage – which was pertinent, to say the least.'

'Yes. I should have—'

'And the divorce, when is that happening?' I cut in. I don't want any more apologies, I want to know where I stand.

'Soon. We've almost completed proceedings and it should all be absolute in a few weeks, a month at the most.'

'There must be wedding photos, bank accounts, all the things that tie husbands and wives together. You must have actively hidden them from me,' I say quietly. In the last twenty-four hours, I've become the child I used to be, unsure of the person or people I wanted to trust. I'm back to feeling vulnerable, fragile, exposed.

'I threw anything and everything away that reminded me of Helen and our marriage, it was too painful. All I had, and still have, is one photograph of her taken on our honeymoon.'

'The one with the pen across her face?'

'Well, yes… not my proudest moment, but, as I told you, I was hurt and angry. I can't ever imagine feeling like that about you,' he says. I feel his lips on mine, and I melt into his kiss, slightly reassured.

I pull away from the kiss, I won't be distracted for long. 'So tell me about Helen,' I say. 'Not Helen your ex-girlfriend, Helen your wife – and why you were with her yesterday.' I'm aware I'm inviting him to lash me with the details, but I'm ready to take the pain. I need to know the truth, whatever it may be.

'Okay.' He takes a breath. 'As I told you, she walked out on me twelve months ago and last week she called and asked if we could meet up. I thought it was about money, the settlement, the house—'

'*Your* house?'

'Yeah. I... I bought her half off her when she left – she got money and I took over the mortgage.'

'So your house is the marital home? You bought it with Helen?' He nods.

'I assumed Helen had stayed there, like I do. But of course, being your wife...' I stop to think about the implications. I suppose he had to keep the house status unclear because he hadn't told me about being married to begin with. But we've had sex on every stair, in his double bed, a double bed he presumably shared with Helen.

One of the things that made me fall in love with Alex was that he'd prepared his home so lovingly for a future wife and children. I thought the stuff he'd filled it with was him feathering his nest and that he was waiting for the right woman to fill it. But finding out that not only has he already done that, but the nest was created by both of them, from the gorgeous colour scheme, to the shower we make love in, is disappointing. *They* had already made love under that spiky hot water, planned a life and a kitchen together. His home wasn't bought or made with a future *me* in mind after all. And now I feel like the other woman.

I try to gather my thoughts, I have so many questions, but I prioritise.

'So why *did* she want to meet up?'

He takes another deep breath, it seems the truth is a difficult place for Alex. 'She wanted to tell me she made a mistake. She asked me if we could get back together...'

'Oh God.' My throat constricts as I wait in the silence for more. She clearly hurt him so much when she walked out, but I think of the inked photograph he keeps in his toiletry bag. Does he still have feelings for her? 'And what do *you* want, Alex?' I press.

'I want *you*.'

I remember the way Helen had taken his arm in the street, the way he'd got into her car so willingly.

'Are you absolutely sure? Knowing she wants you back makes me feel insecure, there's a shadow hanging over us now.'

'I understand how you feel, and I wish I could say she'll go away, but I'm not sure what she'll do.'

I wish he was more reassuring. I'm filled with self-doubt, which has produced this need in me to reclaim him, to make sure he's still mine. I turn on the bedside lamp. I want to see his face, to look into his eyes.

'Helen's always been hard to fathom,' he says, 'and for now I think it safest if we both stay out of her orbit.'

'What do you mean?' I ask. He seems really intense, even a bit nervous.

He looks at me without smiling, his face unreadable. 'Helen and I are over. And I made it quite clear to her today that I'm not interested, but…' He pauses. 'She didn't take it too well.'

'But she looked happy enough when I saw you.' And so did he.

'It was later, in the car, when she said she still had feelings. But I told her about you… I love *you*, Hannah.'

'And I love you.' I sigh. 'I just feel like there's someone else here now.' I'm unable to call her by name, that way I'll bring her to life and into our relationship. Then again, has she been here all along, just waiting for the gap to form between us so she could step in again?

'No, it's just me and you. We're *forever* Hannah,' Alex says, touching my hand with his for emphasis.

As a child who lived on the fringes of other people's families, I never had forever, and I'm sure Alex knows the power of that word to someone like me. Not having a permanent home growing up messes with your identity, and it's hard to know where I fit in, even now.

Today has reminded me of a time when I was beginning to finally settle into a foster family. Mr and Mrs Rawson were kind and attentive and I dared to dream this might be my forever home. But when their only daughter came home from uni, I realised it was an impossible dream. She was their *real* child, it was *her* home, *her* family, not mine. I'd fooled myself I belonged there, compared to her I was no more than a piece of furniture in the house. They were all very nice, but they'd sometimes stop talking when I walked in a room, Mrs Rawson would take Shelly shopping for clothes, they'd go to the cinema together, and her Dad would take her to football matches. At first they invited me, sometimes, but I think it was easier for all of us when I stayed behind. They had a shared history, cousins, genes and blood – something I could never be part of. No one wanted to put in the effort of cajoling a child who didn't belong to them. I slowly withdrew, eating alone in my room, not joining them on family days out, because I felt like an intruder – a cuckoo in the nest. I feel like that now. I learned at an early age that people break their promises, and however good I am, I'm never good enough to keep.

Whatever Alex might say, whatever his promises, the doubts have been planted. After all, he's already lied to me, and with Helen back on the scene, I feel like there's a timer ticking on our relationship.

CHAPTER SEVENTEEN

Alex pulls away from me and sits up in bed, drawing in his knees and wrapping his arms around them protectively, his head down.

'You okay?' I ask gently.

'Yeah,' he says bitterly, clearly still thinking about Helen. 'I gave her everything, you know, and she just walked out.'

'Some people just don't want to settle down,' I offer, trying not to be catty, after all I've never met the woman, I can't judge. 'Tom was the same.'

'And look where it got them. He's sending poison pens and she's begging to get back with me.'

'Yeah, when you put it like that...'

He seems almost oblivious to my presence, as he stares ahead before speaking. 'We hadn't been married long, when she started taking her phone calls in another room, smiling at texts, talking about some guy at work all the time... Then she started going out. It was just once or twice a week at first, but then it was almost every night. Honestly, Hannah, I sat in our house alone nights on end, just waiting for her to come home, worried about her.'

The reference to 'our house' stings slightly as I'm reminded that he shared his home with someone else before me – his wife. But I'm aware he needs to get this off his chest, it's important for us to be able to move forward.

'I'd be calling and calling, wondering where she was, but she wouldn't answer her phone, said she needed her space. She never let me know where she was. It was like she'd gone missing.'

'Oh Alex, that sounds awful.' I can't believe how selfish and hurtful Helen had been.

'Yeah. We'd bought that lovely house, had a brand-new kitchen fitted because *she* wanted it, filled the house with all her favourite stuff – that blue crockery cost a fortune.' He sighs.

'It's beautiful,' I say, thinking of the rustic, grey-blue chunky bowls I fell in love with on my first visit to his home. But he isn't listening, it's like he's still back there with her.

'I bought the velvet sofa she pined for, the power shower she couldn't live without. I made sure she had *everything* she wanted, because all that mattered to me was her happiness.'

Despite his claims that he didn't feel about her as he does about me, I don't believe him, because that's exactly what he's like with me, constantly trying to make me happy, always giving me things. Little gifts on my pillow, a carton of my favourite pink champagne truffles in the larder. I left my favourite perfume at my place, so he bought another bottle to keep in his bathroom. He fills the house with pale pink roses, because they're my favourite, and he even asked me the other day if I'm okay with the sofas.

'If you'd like something else, we'll get rid of them. You like that blush shade, don't you?' he'd said. I told him I loved the green velvet, which I do, but I didn't know they'd been chosen by Helen. I feel a bit weird about the house and everything in it now.

'If it was all for her, even if she wanted to leave, it must have been hard for her to leave that house and everything in it.'

'I don't know.' He shrugs. 'Makes me think perhaps she was planning to come back.'

This feels uncomfortable. 'She obviously never really left, in her heart at least – and it seems to me like you still have feelings for her,' I hear myself say.

'I'll always care about her. You think you're over someone, and suddenly it hits you. It's like grief, it isn't a linear journey, it comes and goes. But I don't still *love* her, if that's what you mean?'

'I understand,' I say, relieved to hear him say this again. 'I don't love Tom, not sure I ever did – but sometimes, when I think about him, it makes me sad.'

'Why?'

'Because he was part of my life, he did nothing wrong, we just weren't meant to be. And I was the one who ended it. I think that made him realise what he'd had, but it was too late.'

Alex doesn't say anything, he's just looking at me, presumably waiting for me to say more, so I continue.

'I mean, he wasn't caring like you, he didn't show his love – but that didn't mean he didn't love me in his own way.'

A flicker of resentment flashes in Alex's eyes. 'You told me you were unhappy, that you don't know why you stayed so long, that he was indifferent,' he says accusingly. 'And now suddenly he loved you – you were great together.'

'Hang on, Alex, that's not what I said. We were together, and now we're not – end of story.'

'It isn't though, is it? He's clearly still messed up enough to send you vile notes and roses.'

'I think he just gets really angry about everything now and then and can't help himself. But he's met someone else now, so I hope that means he'll move on properly.'

'Do you still love him?' Alex suddenly says.

'No. No, of course not. Like you said about Helen, I care about him, what happens to him, but it's in the past. And as for the note, there's no proof it was him who sent it. Sameera thinks it might be someone I've pissed off through work.'

Alex is about to say something, but seems to think better of it.

'Anyway, this isn't about Tom,' I say. 'We were talking about you and Helen… and I still think you have feelings.'

'How many times do I have to tell you? NO! I don't!'

That sudden flash of anger makes me uncomfortable and I get out of bed and pull my dressing gown around me in the early-morning chill.

'But you still have feelings for him,' I hear Alex mutter from the bed.

I walk over to the window. 'You're wrong, I don't,' I say absently and look down at the white pavements, the black, sludgy road. The darkness outside is punctuated now by mere wisps of white snow, the show's over.

I stand there a while and I'm suddenly aware of Alex's arms around me, he's holding me firm against the window, and whispering in my ear.

'Did you and Tom do it like this?' He pushes against me, nuzzling my neck, but hard enough that my palms are now flat against the cold glass.

'Alex,' I gasp, as I feel him hard in the small of my back.

He lifts my dressing gown, grabs my hips and pushes into me from behind. 'Did he give it to you like this, Hannah?' He thrusts gently at first, then harder as he gets more and more excited. 'Are you looking for him out there on the street, do you think he can see us?'

I'm now squashed against the window and surprised to find I'm strangely aroused. I've never seen this side to Alex, didn't know he had it in him, but rather than feeling weak, used by him, I feel empowered that he wants me so badly when I'd thought he was still pining for Helen.

'Is he out there on the street watching us? Seeing me take you?' Alex is really getting off on this fantasy. 'I hope he knows that you belong to *me* now.' He pushes into me so hard, I almost scream.

In the aftermath, we lie in bed and he tells me how much he loves me, and I say the same. I turn off the lamp and I'm in his arms, wondering what just happened. I'm slightly unsettled by the way we made love, but at the same time it was so exciting, I hadn't wanted him to stop.

'I can't get my head around the fact that the idea of Tom watching us excited you,' I say.

He doesn't answer me at first, and just as I think he must have gone to sleep, his voice creeps over me in the darkness. 'Did it turn *you* on?'

I hesitate. 'It was... good.'

'Did it feel like me?'

'No... it felt different.'

'Like you were doing it with someone else?'

'I... Yes, I guess.'

'Like you were doing it with *Tom*?' he asks.

I don't answer, I want to say no, but I'd be lying if I said I didn't think about Tom, Alex was mentioning his name throughout.

For a few moments we lie in silence, until he says, 'You haven't answered me.'

I don't want to spoil everything, in admitting the truth, that would hurt and make him jealous, so I say, 'No, it was definitely you.'

I smile in the darkness, waiting for the feel of his kiss on my head, the reassuring brush of his hand on my face, but he's still and silent, and then I hear him murmur, 'Lying bitch.'

It's dark and I can't see Alex's face. Is he joking? I'm not sure, so I lie there waiting for him to add something, but after a few minutes I hear his slow breathing as he falls asleep.

Surely I'm mistaken. Lovely gentle Alex wouldn't say anything like that. To me. But like the chorus of an awful song that won't go away, it plays on a loop until eventually I fall into a difficult sleep. *Lying. Bitch.*

CHAPTER EIGHTEEN

This morning, Alex is as loving as ever, but I keep returning to those words he whispered in the dark. It's the kind of phrase that sounds horrific if it's meant, but I mustn't overthink it. He was probably half asleep, in that state between waking and dreaming. At the moment, Alex and I are happy, we seem to be working through everything, and I will, at some point, come to terms with his marriage – so now isn't the time to make something of nothing. I hope that spending time together will help to bond us again and erase the niggling doubts I now have. But remembering last night, being pushed against the window, and Alex's arousal at the idea of Tom watching us, seems rather surreal. It was so out of character. I can't help but think about it – was it just a harmless sexual fantasy or was it something more?

'As it's the weekend, I'm going to make you breakfast,' Alex is calling from the kitchen.

This is the Alex I know and love, the kind, caring guy who only wants to make me happy. So who was that last night who took me without warmth, who murmured that I was a lying bitch? I wish I could wipe away those niggles, I wish I could go back to yesterday morning when I thought I knew the man who shares my bed, my life, my future. But I can't, so I need to try and move on.

'You don't seem to have anything in for breakfast,' he's saying now.

'Oh Alex, I'm sorry. I even left the meal I'd bought for us in the fridge at work.'

'Yes, we were supposed to be dining here last night, weren't we?' He pops his head around the door. 'Come to think of it, no wonder I'm hungry – I haven't eaten since… lunch.' His voice fades on the final word and we look at each other.

'I was too upset,' I say, a gentle reminder that all is not forgotten, and offering to make me a Saturday morning breakfast isn't going to eradicate the fact he lied to me.

'I'll go out and get us something,' he says.

'There's always Harry's dead croissant in the fridge,' I joke.

'No there isn't. I threw it in the bin as instructed.' He pulls on his jeans. 'What's with him and the bloody pastries anyway? He's like your feeder – it's weird.'

'It's not weird. I told you, his girlfriend has the café down the road; he just brings us the leftovers.'

'Well, *I* think it's weird,' he says, walking over to where I'm sitting. 'Does he have the hots for you or something?'

I look up at him and smile. 'Ooh, Alex, I think you might be a little bit jealous,' I say, reaching for him, but he moves away.

'I'm not jealous of some creep at the office trying to lay it on you,' he replies, putting on his jacket.

'You've never met him.'

'I know, but… I just *know*.' His jacket's on now, and he goes towards the door. 'If he ever turns up on your doorstep with a bag of cakes, don't let him in, he'll have you tied to the bed before you can say pain au chocolat.'

'Harry's been here loads of times,' I say, affronted. I'm not playing those games; he may have hidden stuff from me, but I'm not hiding anything from him. 'He used to feed my cat when I went on holiday, before she died. I'd trust him with my life. And he isn't creepy. What's wrong with you, Alex?'

'What's wrong with *me*? I'm not the one who's having little gifts left on my desk by some perv.'

'He's not a *perv*.' I have to laugh at the ridiculousness of the conversation, and Alex catches this and it makes him smile.

He walks back over to where I'm sitting, kneels down and takes my face gently in both his hands. 'I love you, Hannah.' He's looking into my eyes, but it feels like he's going even deeper.

'I love you too,' I say, surprised at this sudden moment he's created, but pleased that he seems to have shaken off whatever concern was making him overreact. I know now that Helen's betrayal affected him a lot, so I can understand his trust issues.

Alex continues to look at me for a while, like he's searching for the answer to a puzzle. Then, just as quickly, the tenderness seems to leave him, and his hands feel firmer on my face. 'Was it Harry I saw running from your office last night?'

'What the hell?' I push his hands away. 'I don't know what's got into you, Alex but I don't like it.' I stand up, almost knocking him over, and head for the kitchen.

He follows me. 'Hannah, I was *joking*, can't you take a joke any more?'

'Yeah. I can take a joke, but you weren't being funny,' I snap.

'I thought I was.'

'Did you? Well, how about this for funny. I was late because Harry and I were doing it on the photocopier when everyone else had gone home, and when we'd finished, he ran off before anyone saw him.' This is not delivered as set comedy, I'm angry and Alex knows it.

'Funny, very funny, Hannah,' he monotones. 'Thing is – I wouldn't put it past him. Total perv,' he says again, but this time in a more relaxed, jokey voice.

'Harry's my friend, please don't call him that,' I say seriously. 'And while we're talking about cheating, please don't you dare question me about what I was doing yesterday,' I hiss.

He looks at me and half smiles, I'm waiting for a playful reply, a little sprinkle of Alex charm. But I don't recognise the man standing in front of me with cold eyes.

'Yesterday you didn't know the situation, so I can forgive you, but now you *do* know – I've told you everything, and it's the truth. So please don't accuse me of cheating,' he says in a steely voice.

This feels like some kind of power game, but he's picked the wrong woman if he wants to play that. I learned young that you have to stand your ground, because if you don't, you risk being taken over and losing control of your own life.

'I thought I knew who you were, Alex,' I say.

'You *do*.' He throws his hands up in the air. 'What do you want from me, Hannah? Shall I just keep saying I'm sorry?'

I don't answer him, and he leaves to go into the living room.

After a few minutes to calm down and compose myself, I follow him, but just as I walk into the room, my phone pings. It's a text from Harry:

> *Hey, are u ok? Sorry I didn't text back, was out. No, I don't have any copies of Chloe's files, you have them all now. Did you get them back?'*

Alex turns, looks at me questioningly.

'It's just Harry,' I murmur, as I text a response.

'Why's he texting you on a *Saturday*?'

'It's about the files. I told him I'd left them at the bar,' I say, matching his irritated tone.

'So, the minute I set off in the snow to get them for you, you were straight on the blower to Harry?'

My heart sinks. 'I texted him last night because I was worried. I hoped you'd get them back for me, but I wondered if he knew if there were copies, just in case,' I say.

'What's it got to do with *him*?'

'He used to be Chloe's social worker,' I start to explain, as I realise I'm trying to justify a text to a work colleague and I shouldn't have to. 'What is this, Alex? What the hell's wrong with you?'

He suddenly looks like he's about to cry. 'I'm sorry, I'm sorry.' He walks over to me, arms open. 'I feel like yesterday was a watershed for us. I told you about Helen and I'm worried it's changed how you feel about me. I know it's made you feel insecure, but the whole thing's made me feel the same – I wouldn't blame you for leaving me, for running off with someone simple and uncomplicated like Harry.'

'Oh Alex,' I say, warmth flooding through me. I reach out to his open arms and we embrace. 'You know it's ridiculous to imagine me leaving you for Harry – right?'

He rests his chin on my head as he hugs me close. 'I've wrecked everything, haven't I? Because I've been cheated on before, I imagine all kinds of stuff, say stupid things. If you want me to leave now, then I'll just go.'

I take his hand and lead him to the sofa, where he lies down and rests his head in my lap. I stroke his hair, like a mother would a heart-broken child, and keep telling him it's fine, *we're* fine, and he mustn't be upset. He closes his eyes, and I put my head back on the sofa and think about the last twenty-four hours and wonder if this *has* changed my feelings towards him, or if I can just carry on as before.

'I want us to get back to where we were,' Alex says. 'Can we forget about yesterday and move on, Hannah?'

I nod slowly and pat him on the shoulder. 'Obviously it will be easier when you're officially divorced, but it might make me feel weird about spending time at your place, *her* place.'

He suddenly seems to come alive, and what we've just talked about seems to be instantly wiped away. 'Then I'll make it *your* place! I can have it redecorated, buy new furniture, change everything. What colour would you like the walls?'

'You don't have to do that.' I smile. 'I just need time to recalibrate.'

'Okay.'

'And if… if she asks to meet you again, will you tell me?'

'I won't see her again. We'll just talk through our solicitors from now on.'

'You don't have to do that, but perhaps if you do ever need to meet for some reason – maybe just take me along?'

He suddenly loses the colour in his face. 'No, we couldn't do that,' he says, looking down at the sofa. He starts to pick at the fabric.

'I don't mean we all do lunch or anything, that would be awkward. But if she suggests meeting, then we could go together. If she meets me, she might get the message that you're happy, you've moved on and there's no going back.'

'She won't, she… she would *hate* that,' he says, shutting it down, horrified.

'I'm not exactly loving the idea myself. But it might help her to accept things.'

He just shakes his head; he doesn't want to even talk about it.

I understand he doesn't want his ex-wife and new girlfriend to meet, it might be difficult, but this is about clarity. I just hope he really was honest and clear with her yesterday, and I hope he's been honest about me.

I don't want to push him, so leave it for now and change the subject. 'You mentioned breakfast?' I say.

'Yeah, I'll pop out for something.'

'I'm not exactly a domestic goddess, am I?' I joke.

'No.' He smiles. 'I did wonder when was the last time you ran a vacuum over this carpet.'

'Wow,' I murmur. I'm a little taken aback, and torn between thinking 'how dare he?' and feeling slightly ashamed. I'm already embarrassed about him seeing the empty fridge and threadbare sofa. But I didn't even *think* about the state of the carpet. Although I only vacuumed it the other day and I've been staying at his since then, so it can't be that messy.

As he kisses me on the forehead and gets up and leaves, I sit for a while in silence, thinking. I don't want to, but I can't help it – I get down on all fours to investigate the carpet. I'm imagining a pile of crumbs I've missed somewhere, but the carpet looks fine, even when I really scrutinise it – perhaps his tidiness threshold is lower than mine. I'm left puzzled over his comment, but since yesterday, I'm puzzled about quite a lot of things regarding Alex.

CHAPTER NINETEEN

Alex is taking ages to shop for breakfast, which is now looking more like brunch. But knowing him, he's discovered the nearby deli and he's buying special cheeses and charcuterie. He'll be poring over every detail, asking about the provenance of the meat and tasting all the samples, taking ages over each little morsel. He adores food, and is a brilliant cook, I happened to mention I was hungry one night, it was after eleven but within minutes he'd whipped up a bowl of the most delicious, garlicky, bright-green home-made pesto and hurled it into a bowl of warm pasta.

As I said to Jas, 'I've never eaten a big bowl of pasta in bed, in front of a man I love before. Who does that?'

Jas said she'd love to taste his pasta, and I mentioned it to him but he wasn't keen.

'I want to just come home and flop, I don't want to be making small talk with people I don't know,' he'd said.

'But I'd love to do something as a couple – what about your colleagues or friends? I'd love to meet them.'

But he didn't like that idea either. 'I spend long enough with them,' he said, 'there's no way I'm spending my home-time with them too. Besides, our time together is too precious – I don't want to share you with anyone else.'

I think about that now, as I sit in my flat. It's like he has no one except me. And I only came into his life recently. But then I know he doesn't get on with his dad and stepmum, and he's got no siblings, it's understandable that he's so invested in me. And is that really a problem or am I just looking for flaws now after the roller coaster of the last twenty-four hours?

I decide to stop overthinking, and to do something. So I decide to get some plates together and make a cafetière of coffee for when he gets back with the breakfast, there's nothing nicer than the smell of freshly brewed coffee through the flat. I open the cupboard door and reach for the cafetière, when my hand alights on a tin of beans instead. I'm a little surprised, because that's where the cafetière lives. I stand on my tiptoes to reach further, but nothing. In disbelief, I search for the cafetière with my hands and my eyes, but the cupboard is stacked with about eight tins of beans and tomatoes. I bought them ages ago, before Alex even, and they've been hanging around since earlier in the year – but in a different cupboard.

'That's odd,' I hear myself mutter. I could perhaps have put the cafetière in a different cupboard by mistake, but the tins standing to attention in a very neat line would suggest this has nothing to do with me. I don't know when he's had the time to move things around, but it's got Alex's name all over it. His cupboards are so organised, I asked him recently if they are ordered alphabetically.

'No,' he'd said quite seriously. 'I just like everything in its place, helps me think better.'

And now it looks like he's imposed that order on my kitchen too. 'What the hell?' I say to myself as I whip open the other cupboard doors in my desperate search for the cafetière. But each cupboard seems to have been 'organised' in the same way. Cleaning equipment is in the one beneath the sink, each bottle lined up with the label facing me so I can see what I'm grabbing, and it's the same with the cupboard above the sink, tea towels stacked so neatly, they look like a pile of envelopes. I can see it's much neater, more organised, but the idea of Alex taking it upon himself to re-order my kitchen is a little unsettling and, actually, quite invasive. Finally, in the cupboard above the kettle is the cafetière. I'm just getting it out when I hear the front door.

'I'm in the kitchen – though not as I know it!' I say as Alex wanders in.

'Ahh you saw what I did? I meant to mention that.' He's smiling, very pleased with himself.

'Yeah. When did you do all this?' I'm feeling slightly exasperated.

'About 6 a.m. I couldn't sleep, and you were dead to the world. I came in here to make myself a cup of tea and decided to try and make sense of it all. Everything was everywhere, and the cupboards hadn't been dusted for a while.'

'It's very kind of you, and it might make sense to *you* – but I can't find anything,' I say. I was going to be cool about this, but I'm now a bit pissed off at his comment about the cupboards being dusty. 'I knew where everything was before.' I can hear the snap in my voice as I now scramble around the cupboard looking for the filter coffee – which has definitely disappeared.

'If you're looking for the filter coffee, I put it in an airtight container,' Alex says, reading my mind. 'Coffee loses its aroma and taste very quickly once you open it, it's due to the roasting process. For every twenty-four hours you leave coffee exposed to air at room temperature, it loses ten percent of its shelf life.'

'Thanks for the Ted Talk,' I murmur, taking down the container that Tom used to keep his maggots in for fishing. 'God, I should have thrown this out.'

'Yeah, it's not exactly Conran, but if you keep it in the cupboard, no one will see it,' Alex says.

'I don't care if anyone *sees* it.' I dig into the brown arabica sand aggressively. 'I just would rather not have my coffee in this container, because it was Tom's and he used it for live bait.'

'Ugh, gross.' Alex pulls a face and then rummages in his carrier bag and places a large paper bag on the kitchen counter.

I pour boiling water into the cafetière and push the plunger down with some force.

'I thought you'd be pleased,' he says, sounding wounded. 'You were saying last night how chaotic you are, and when I looked everything was in the wrong cupboards. I didn't throw anything away... well, only stuff that was obviously rubbish.'

This makes me cross. I feel like I've been invaded. 'You might have thrown something that was *obviously* rubbish to you – but to me it might be precious.'

'Sorry, I didn't think. I was just organising the kitchen for you.'

'Yeah, I know – you were just being kind, but' – I turn to him – 'this is *my* space, you know?'

He nods slowly, as he begins to take items out of the paper bag: fresh baguettes, French cheese, a jar of fancy jam. 'I bought butter... you haven't got any,' he says, holding a packet of Normandy butter in his palm, like a peace offering. And it's probably me being oversensitive, but it feels like a reprimand, a judgement.

'Thanks,' I say, 'but I stay at yours most of the time, so there's no point in buying perishable stuff that'll go off – *that's* why there's no butter in the fridge.' I realise that sounded a bit snippy, and in light of the fact he's emptying a bag of delicatessen loveliness onto my kitchen counter, I'm being quite mean. 'I'll get the plates and cutlery,' I add, opening the cupboard door that *used* to be home to the plates and cups. 'Aah,' I say, slamming the door.

'Sorry, I moved the plates, thought they'd be more convenient near the cooker.'

'*Convenient* for whom?' I can't help asking.

He looks up from slicing a French loaf. 'I only did it to make life easier for you. Can't I do *anything* right, Hannah?'

I sigh, and plonk the plates down on the table.

'Perhaps you'd rather Tom... or Harry was here instead of me?' he says peevishly.

'You're being stupid now,' I say, not wanting to even engage in this conversation.

'Stupid? You come over to mine all the time and yet I stay one night here and you start talking about it being your space, and feeling invaded. Harry's texting every five minutes and I've dared to use Tom's precious container for bloody coffee and—'

'Harry texted once about a work matter and the container isn't a sodding keepsake, I just don't want my coffee stored where live maggots once lived.' I open my arms in despair. 'It's got *nothing* to do with Tom… or Harry, or anyone else for that matter.' I look up into the air. 'I can't even believe I'm having this conversation.'

'What am I expected to think? You don't seem to want me here, but apparently it was okay for Tom to move in, for Harry to have a key and feed the cat.'

'Alex stop,' I say calmly. 'You're behaving like a child.'

'And you're behaving like a *bitch*.'

It hits me in the solar plexus. That word again.

I stare at him. He's not looking at me, just moving the cheese around and opening the jars of chutney, as if he hasn't just called me a bitch. I want to throw the stuff across the room, if only to make him stop, get his attention, make him realise what he just said. And now I think he *did* mean it when he said it last night. I won't have this.

'I'd like you to leave please,' I hear myself say.

He looks up at me, shocked.

'That's total disrespect, Alex, and I won't put up with it.'

He's never given any indication he could *be* like this. Is he just tired or pissed off I found out about Helen? It doesn't matter – whatever it is, I won't allow anyone to speak to me like that.

'Please *leave*,' I repeat.

I see a flash of something indecipherable in his eyes as he slams the jar down on the countertop, grabs his jacket and storms out of the flat.

I stand in the kitchen, angry, hurt and disappointed, so bloody disappointed. I want to cry, but my anger blocks the tears. I know when they come there will be a flood.

In the silence Alex left behind, I boil the kettle, and when, hours later, I haven't heard from him, and I'm sitting in the kitchen nursing a freezing-cold cup of tea, I call Jas.

I don't tell her straight away about Alex and his lunch date and our row over the phone, but later, while drinking glühwein at the Christmas market, it all spills out. I'm upset and she comforts me with her usual refrain about all men being bastards and how she's yet to meet one who isn't. I'm grateful Jas isn't saying I told you so but, of course, she wouldn't. Despite never meeting him, she clearly doesn't like the idea of Alex, but she wouldn't rub salt in the wound.

'I really thought I'd met the one who wasn't a bastard.' I sigh, discreetly wiping my eyes and hoping against hope I don't start blubbing. I feel sick and empty at the same time, and the alcohol and frosty air is hitting my brain quickly. 'He didn't tell me he was married. He called me a bitch. He even said I'd rather sleep with Tom than him *and* implied that I have some weird thing going with Harry, for God's sake.'

'Ooh, that's a stretch.' Jas shakes her head. 'And, no offence, but I can't imagine anyone wanting to sleep with Tom – he was – well, just Tom, wasn't he?'

'You never like any of my boyfriends,' I say. 'I know Tom was a bit meh, but he had his moments.'

'Seeing the card that came with those roses, I can only imagine how revolting they were.' She pulls another face, and suggests we have more drinks. It's dark and freezing, the tarpaulin covering the market stalls is flapping wildly in the breeze and I feel lost. I don't want to go back to my empty flat yet, only to be reminded of everything that's happened with Alex, so I agree, and we order a jug of mulled wine. Warm alcohol is the only answer.

'Thanks,' I say as we sip the next one, 'you're always there for me.' Jas can sometimes be blunt and critical, but her heart's in the right place and she's the person I know I can always turn to in times of need – like now.

'You've been there for me too.'

I feel my eyes well with tears, everything's gone from wonderful to shit in the space of a day.

'Stop crying, you silly cow, he's not worth it,' Jas says, pushing my hair behind my ear with her gloved hand.

'But if you knew him, you'd understand, he's everything—'

'Turns out he isn't *everything* though, is he?' She sighs.

And I have to admit it – it looks like Jas was right all along.

Several mulled wines later, Jas drops me off at my flat in a taxi. I'm a bit the worse for wear and as soon as I get home, I gaze at the abandoned brunch still sitting on the table, out-of-season strawberries, my favourite date chutney – Alex had chosen each item with me in mind, he had chosen with love, and it makes my heart hurt a little.

Then I start to think how everything got out of hand and wonder if I overreacted. What I saw as him trying to take over, invading my territory, was just Alex being thoughtful, looking after me in his own way. In every other aspect of our lives, he makes me happy and comfortable, so he just wanted to do it in my home, that was all.

But then I remember how he lied to me and called me a bitch and then the tears come anew.

I wander the flat feeling slightly wobbly after the many glasses of warm wine. By 11 p.m., I'm a mess. Which is when he finally calls.

'I'm sorry, Hannah,' he says. 'I'm sorry for... for everything.' He sounds as if he's on the brink of tears, his voice croaky.

'You called me a bitch,' I say, still in disbelief. 'I was so hurt, I didn't think it was in your nature. Never in my wildest dreams could I ever imagine you being so vile.'

'I don't know where it came from. And I didn't mean to piss you off. With the cupboards.'

'I know.'

'I thought that's what we did. You move *my* stuff. I mean, only last week you said the toiletries in the bathroom were better on the lower shelf where you could reach them, and you moved them. I didn't even think about it. I wasn't trying to take over or invade,' he says defensively.

'I know, I know.' I'm nodding as I speak. He's right. I move stuff around in his kitchen, sometimes putting things back in the 'wrong' cupboard. He often moves it back, because he's more OCD than me, but he never says anything, in fact he laughs about it. 'I was being unreasonable,' I say. 'And I'm sorry, I'm just used to being on my own here and knowing where everything is – that's all.'

I'm standing in my living room, holding the phone, looking out of the window onto the dark street below. No one's about, the leftover snow is piled in greying heaps, the street light casts an odd yellow tone.

'Hannah, can we draw a line under the last twenty-four hours? Please, let's just move on – and be us again.'

'I want that too,' I say quietly.

There's a pause, then Alex says, 'Hannah. There's something else I need to tell you. About Helen.'

CHAPTER TWENTY

Alex turned up five minutes ago. I've made us some tea and he's sitting with his head in his hands in my living room. I take the two mugs in to where he is and put them down on the coffee table.

'So, what did you have to tell me that wouldn't wait until tomorrow?' I ask.

'When Helen called last week, she suggested we meet for lunch, say a proper goodbye.'

'You already told me this,' I say, getting impatient. Whatever it is Alex was so desperate to tell me, I need to know.

'But the thing is she's now bombarding me with texts and messages, Hannah. She even sent... naked pictures... It's like she's obsessed – I think she's losing it.'

I take a breath. 'Oh God.'

He looks at me helplessly. 'I've spent the last twenty-four hours worrying about it, and whether or not I should tell you. I didn't want to worry you.'

'I'm glad you told me.' I sigh, almost wishing he hadn't, I'm not sure I can deal with any more revelations.

He shakes his head. 'She keeps saying she'll do something stupid, and I'll be sorry.'

'It sounds like she needs help.' I pull the throw around me, horrified at the way this is playing out. 'If she contacts you again threatening to do something stupid, perhaps you could gently suggest she calls a therapist, talks to her GP.'

'Hannah, you don't understand, when she said she might do something stupid – she wasn't talking about hurting *herself*, she was talking about hurting you.'

'You're kidding me, right?' Jas's mouth is open. After what I'd told her on Saturday at the Christmas market, she's doubting my sanity at going back to Alex anyway. But now I've just said his ex is threatening to do something to me, she's horrified, standing in our work kitchen in shock.

'Wow. Just wow, Hannah!' She hits her forehead with the heel of her hand. 'What's wrong with you, honey? He never told you he was married, he called you a bitch, he got jealous of an ex he's never met… He even *accused* you of having something with Harry!' She says this so loudly that Harry – who happens to be walking past – pops his head round the kitchen door.

'Who's having something with me?' he says hopefully.

Jas laughs. 'Hannah's ridiculous boyfriend thinks she's having a secret thing with you – which is ludicrous. No offence, Harry, but I mean, the very idea!'

'Offence taken.' He laughs and, grabbing a cup, makes himself a tea.

'You seem to think this is a bloody joke. It's like you're really getting off on it, Jas,' I say accusingly.

'Not at all. I just knew there was something about him from what you told me. And there it is – he's married!' she announces loudly, and Harry, who isn't actually that interested, joins in with a whistle followed by a sympathetic, '*Shit!*' while the kettle boils.

'And that isn't all,' she adds, oblivious to my discomfort. 'His psycho wife is now hunting our Hannah down and wants to hurt her.'

I pull an awkward face at Harry, wishing Jas wouldn't tell everyone everything, and he looks at me with genuine concern.

'Are you okay, Hannah? I mean, I know I joked about him being a serial killer – but it sounds like his wife *might* be.'

'Yeah. I just hope it's all talk, the heat of the moment – you know?' I mumble, not happy to be starring in the office drama.

'Sounds unhinged to me.' Jas is shaking her head.

'Have you called the police?' Harry asks.

'I was going to. I had the phone in my hand to call them straight away. But Alex said to leave it for now. The thing is, she's a solicitor, any police involvement and she could lose her job, and then she might be even more of a problem.'

'Shit,' Harry murmurs, putting three sugars into a mug.

'Alex knows where she is at all times,' I explain. 'He has an app attached to her phone or something from when they were together. He knows where I am too, so if ever she's nearby he can at least warn me.'

'Hang on! WTAF?' Jas is open-mouthed for the second time in this conversation. 'He's tracking you and his ex-wife, and you're scared of *her*?'

'It's not as sinister as it sounds, loads of people do it – friends follow friends – it's about keeping safe,' I offer.

'That's how the tech companies sell these apps, but how they're used is a different thing.' Harry raises his eyebrows.

'Well, I know Alex is using it to make sure I'm okay,' I say defensively.

'I'm with Jas, I'd be more scared of *him*,' he says. 'And if you ever want me to take that app off your phone, just let me know. Gemma would go ballistic if I put one on hers.'

'She'd be right to go ballistic. It's a digital dog lead,' Jas says, shaking her head, while waiting for Harry to pour the now boiled water on her green-tea bag.

They've made me feel really uneasy about this – surely Alex is just watching out for me. 'You guys are so dramatic – I'm *glad* Alex knows where I am,' I add in a small voice.

Jas looks at me like I'm crazy. 'You really have lost it, Hannah. Have you moved all your cups back into the right kitchen cupboard?' she says, before turning to Harry and filling him in on Alex's nocturnal tidying. 'He basically moved all her stuff around, reorganised her kitchen. *She* can't find a bloody thing. Only *he* knows where everything is – and that's how he likes it.' She clicks her fingers and wobbles her head.

Harry shrugs. 'Actually, in his defence, Gemma's the same. She's always tidying stuff up at mine. Sometimes, I'm actually glad when she goes home for the night.'

'You see,' I say to Jas, 'he's just tidy, that's all.'

'Yeah, but this wasn't just tidying stuff up, was it, Hannah? This was creepy – all the labels were facing the same way!'

'It's *not* creepy, it's *tidy*,' I repeat defensively.

'That's not what you said on Saturday, you said it freaked you out.'

'Yeah well, I was pissed off with Alex then, but now I've forgiven him,' I say, kicking myself for having shared that with her.

'You need to padlock those cupboards next time bae is in your crib!' she says, which makes me and Harry laugh. She loves to use the teen language we all hear from our clients. She's now rummaging at the back of the cupboard looking for biscuits. 'Oh shit, he's been here too,' she says. 'Your Alex has let himself in and tidied away the bloody biscuits.'

Harry's still giggling as he takes his mug of tea and wanders back into the office, where Sameera will no doubt be briefed on the latest headline regarding Hannah's 'weird' boyfriend.

'Joking aside, I'll make sure the others keep an eye out – we all will, mate,' Jas says as we leave the kitchen together. 'We work with hormonal teens, so the psycho ex-wife is a day in the park, isn't she guys?' she calls to Harry and Sameera, who, as I suspected, has already been briefed.

'I'll hold her down and you can kick her,' Sameera offers. 'Seriously though, Hannah, it sounds dreadful – you should call the police.'

'We just need to see what happens,' I say. 'She hasn't actually done anything yet, probably just trying to get Alex's attention.'

'Do you know she hasn't done anything?' Jas asks.

'Yeah... I'd know if she'd tried to grab me in the street...' I start.

'When she says she'll hurt you though – she might not mean physically.'

'Oh God!' The flowers and the vile card.

'Are you thinking what I'm thinking?' Jas says.

I nod.

'What's everyone thinking? Can I join in?' Harry jokes.

'Oh, Harry, do keep up – it's probably the psycho ex-wife who sent the flowers and the note calling Hannah a whore,' Sameera explains.

I don't respond. I hadn't thought of that, but it isn't impossible. If Helen had been aware Alex was seeing someone before she met him for lunch, she may well have sent the roses – perhaps the note was a warning.

Jas looks concerned. 'Mmm, well, I don't want to scare you, but you need to be on your guard.' She sighs, then lowers her voice so the others can't hear.

'Look, you're an experienced social worker, and good at your job. If this was happening to one of your clients you'd spot these red flags a mile off. So why aren't you seeing that this guy is trouble? Are you too close to the situation to see what's happening?'

I shrug. I know what she's saying, and I do see those red flags, but I'm desperately trying not to.

'Hannah, in this job we look after everyone else, we're always on the alert for danger for others – but when it comes to ourselves, we're not always so alert. I should know...'

'I get that, but I'm not stupid, Jas. I can see things aren't right.'

'So why are you staying with him?'

'Because no one has ever cared about me like he does, not even my parents. I want marriage and children, and so does he. Jas, I'm thirty-six – this might be my last chance…'

She looks like she's about to say something, but I stop her. 'And I see it, I see it all.' I feel my eyes welling up. 'I'm an intelligent woman, but this isn't about my head, it's about my heart. Don't you understand? I have no choice. I have to give this a chance, to work through the problems and see what's there. The alternative is that I say goodbye to something that could be amazing. And then it might never happen again for me.'

Her face is expressionless as she clicks her tongue. 'I guess love really is blind,' she says, and stares at me for a beat too long. Then she suddenly smiles. 'Okay, you're a big girl – I guess you know what you're doing.' She sighs. 'So come on.' She puts her arm through mine and we head into her office to discuss Helen and whether she really is a risk.

I don't know why I'm buying into Jas's drama. I think I just have this need to explore the possibilities so I can be prepared. Over the next twenty minutes we assess Helen's current state of mind, theorise about her childhood and come to the conclusion she's straight out of the narcissist's playbook – none of which is based on fact or any knowledge of the woman.

'What does she look like, is she good-looking?' Jas asks.

'Not that you're superficial or anything. It's useful to know just how attractive your best friend's stalker is.' I roll my eyes. 'But yeah, she's attractive.' I sigh and try to describe her. But then I realise she's a lawyer who works – or *worked* in the area – and given that they aren't yet divorced, I google 'Helen Higham'.

I soon find her on Whitney and Partners Solicitors – a small company out on the road to Malvern.

'She's still using Alex's surname then?' Jas says as I hold up her picture on my phone.

'Yes, they're only separated at the moment, but even when they're divorced she could keep his name – Higham – as her surname,' I point out.

Jas screws up her eyes and brings her face closer, then she moves back with eyebrows raised and a strange expression on her face. 'She's very familiar,' she says, this weird half smile on her face.

'What? Oh shit – do you know her?' I ask, dismayed.

She looks right at me, still smiling. 'You can't see it, can you?'

'No, what?'

'She's the spitting image of you.'

I take my phone off her and look at the photo again. It's difficult to see yourself in someone else, but I know what she means, there's definitely a likeness.

'Well, Alex certainly has a type,' she says. 'And don't take this the wrong way – but it isn't necessarily a good thing that you look like her.'

'Why?'

'Oh, love, I hate to say it – but that might be why he chose you.'

'You think I'm a substitute for her?'

'Who knows? Presumably he saw your photo on the app, saw you looked like his ex-wife and—'

'Or he just has a type.' I repeat her original theory, trying to dampen her drama.

Jas raises her eyebrows. 'He might. But at the moment, that's not even the real issue. Does Psycho Queen know where you live?'

'No. Alex said he'd told her about me, but that's all.'

'Because he knew she'd react like a mad bitch?'

'I don't know, I hope not. He says she's just upset, and she'll be fine once she gets used to the idea.' I say this with all the conviction I can muster, but in the back of my mind I wonder if he's just playing it down so I'll stay calm.

'Either way, best be safe than sorry. If I were you I wouldn't stay at Alex's right now – stay at yours a couple of nights, until you know the score.'

'Yeah, that's probably a good idea.'

'I mean, you could be in his place, snogging on the sofa, you look up and she's standing over you both with a kitchen knife.'

'Thanks for that, Jas,' I say sarcastically. She's just joking, but I feel sick. 'It's an empty threat. She's a solicitor. She isn't going to ruin her career to break into another solicitor's house,' I say, 'even if it is her ex's. I'm sure it'll all be fine,' I add, though I'm not sure at all.

'Do you want me to come and stay at yours with you?' Jas asks. 'I'm working late, but I could come over about nine – we could order takeaway. I'll bring the gin. It'll be like old times.' She smiles.

'Thanks, love,' I reply, 'but I'll get Alex to stay at mine, he would have a better chance at fighting her off,' I joke.

She looks disappointed, so to soften the rejection, I smile and say, 'Once everything's calm, you and I must go out.'

'Whatever, but just be careful. Yeah?'

With that, I leave her office, imagining that vision of Helen and the glint of a blade.

CHAPTER TWENTY-ONE

I spend the next two hours setting up a safeguarding plan for Chloe Thomson, and after lunch, Alex calls me.

'Hey,' I say, glad to hear his voice.

'I'm missing you more than usual today.' He sighs. 'Did you pop out somewhere for lunch?'

'Yeah, I just bought a sandwich, ate it at my desk.'

'Ahh, I wondered what you were doing on Foregate Street, I saw you on my phone.'

Thank God for technology. I don't care what cynical slant Jas wants to put on it, he can see where his ex-wife is, and where I am at the same time. And that's fine by me if it means he can prevent something horrible happening.

'Is everything okay, do you know where *she* is?' I ask, feeling on edge just thinking about her at large in the same city as me.

'She's in the town centre.'

'At work? Whitney's Solicitors?'

'How do you know where she's working?' He seems a bit put out.

'I googled her.'

'Hannah, just leave this to me and I'll make sure you're safe, don't go seeking her out, you *must* be careful,' he says.

'That's the second time today someone's told me to be careful. What do you think I'm going to do, run round to her office and ask her if she wants a fight?'

'Who else said be careful?' he asks.

'Jas. She thinks I'm not taking the threat seriously enough.'

'What? I can't believe you've discussed this with Jas. Bloody hell, Hannah, do you have to tell her *everything*?'

'No – but if your ex-wife is on the rampage and says she wants to hurt me, I need my friends to know, so they can be on the lookout. She might find out where I work and turn up here brandishing a bloody knife.'

'She won't, but promise me, if – *if* she *ever* makes contact, don't talk to her. Don't engage with her, don't... don't *tell* her anything. She doesn't know your name, and I certainly don't want her knowing where you live, or anything about you. Be careful what you put on social media too.'

'Okay, okay.' The panic in his voice is making me even more jittery.

'And don't bother with the police. Call me if you're worried; the police won't do a damn thing. Remember I know, I work with them.'

'So do I, sometimes, and I'm sure they'd do *something* if I called and said a woman who'd said she intended to do me harm was following me.'

'Hannah, will you please trust me on this? And don't get the police involved,' he snaps. 'Look, I've got to go, I'm due in court.'

I put down the phone, feeling very uneasy. Why doesn't he want me to call the police? Surely my safety would come before her career – or his for that matter. I know it wouldn't be good for a solicitor to be embroiled in such a drama, but I'm not messing about. If I feel threatened in any way I'm straight onto the police. And I also feel perfectly justified in telling Jas and the others about the situation. What if Psycho Helen befriended one of them, or turned up at the office?

'He's scared to death of you making any kind of contact with her,' Jas says a little later when I tell her about my conversation with Alex.

'Yeah, because he doesn't want me to get hurt, she's very unpredictable.'

'Mmm, so he *says*. I wonder if he just wants to keep you two apart for his own reasons,' she replies.

'Like what?' I ask.

'I don't know.' She sighs, putting her feet up on the desk. We're in her office, it's almost the end of the working day and she's filing her long red nails. She looks nothing like a senior social worker. Jas used to be the singer in a band when she was at uni – I didn't know her then, but I've seen photos. She's very attractive now, but back then she looked fierce. She still has that 'Who Runs the World?' energy about her. 'I mean, what he's saying makes sense. When you're lying in bed at 4 a.m. and hear someone breathing heavily at the bottom of the bed, do take his advice and not *engage* with her. No small talk, no chatting about the weather or who your money's on for *Strictly* this year.'

Even in my darkest moments, she can make me laugh, which I do now. I'm not saying the prospect of Helen standing at the bottom of my bed in the middle of the night doesn't freak me the hell out, but Jas has this way of easing the tension.

Later, I call Alex and suggest we stay at mine tonight, but he says he's working late and wants to go home to make sure the house is okay 'after everything'.

'You're right to stay at yours though. I don't want you alone at mine, she knows where that is,' he says.

My stomach does a little somersault.

'I could come over when I finish, but it might be late – after ten,' he adds.

I can't believe Alex's timing. He does sometimes work late, but having plunged me into this nightmare, I wish he was around to support me. I'm reluctant to be alone tonight, but I can't ask Jas over, then pack her off as soon as he arrives. I have lots to catch up on here, and Harry and Jas are both working late tonight, so

I decide to stick around. I'd rather be here with them than home alone with Helen at large. So I sit working at my desk for a couple of hours. When it gets to nine o'clock, the other two are still hard at it, but I'm so tired, I decide to leave. I check my 'meal for two', still in the fridge from last week. I had vague hopes of resurrecting it for tonight, but when I take it out the lid's opened and what looks like sour milk has dripped into it. And someone's laid a huge carton of orange juice across the cheesecake slices and smashed them. I give up on the idea of a romantic dinner. It'll be too late anyway by the time Alex finishes work tonight.

'Would you like me to follow you home and come in with you?' Harry offers gallantly, but I know he'd rather poke out his eyes. He's clearly exhausted – and I'd bet the last thing he wants to do is drive miles out of his way to watch me open my flat door.

'Ahh, you're sweet, Harry,' I say. 'Thanks, but I'll be fine. Alex should be at mine around ten, so I won't be on my own long.'

'As long as you're okay.' He smiles. 'We don't want any encounters.' He makes a crazy stabbing gesture, and I pretend to laugh, but I don't think it's funny. I'm scared to death.

'Text me when you get home,' Jas calls from her office. 'I'll only worry and turn up on your doorstep if you don't, so it's in *your* interests.' She doesn't look up from her computer, but her hand waves as I leave.

Once home, I open the flat door, and for once the light goes on in the hall. Finally, the caretaker must have sorted it, and now I can see into every corner, around every doorway. I run up the stairs two at a time, and when I finally get inside my flat and lock the door behind me, I feel like weeping with relief. I know I'm being completely irrational, but I check the front door again before heading into the living room. I need a shower to wash everything away, but then I think of the shower scene in *Psycho* and decide to wait until Alex is here.

I'm about to turn on the TV, when I hear a noise, a sort of flicking sound coming from... the bedroom? Yes, it's coming from the bedroom. I remember the shuffling sound at the flat door not long ago. I pick up a bottle of wine off the side and, holding it close, reluctantly walk towards the sound. I stand in the hall, swaying, waiting, unable to control the shaking that starts in my feet and rumbles up to my chest and my head.

Someone's moving about in the bedroom. She's opening and closing drawers, rooting through my stuff, probably trying to find things out about me. My fear is choked by rage, how dare she make me scared in my own home? But then I remember that she wants to hurt me, and probably has a better weapon than my bottle of wine. So I move away, and walking slowly backwards, I head for the front door. Every pore is on fire, my hair ends are tingling. Then, just at that moment, my phone rings. A brash, tinny sound pierces the silence, making me jump. I see Jas's name flashing on the phone just as someone leaps out of the bedroom.

CHAPTER TWENTY-TWO

I don't turn round to see who has emerged from my bedroom, I just scream as loud as I can, and make for the door.

'Hannah, Hannah, it's me!'

I turn around to see him standing there, apparently as surprised as me.

'Alex!'

I almost collapse. I'm leaning against the wall in shock and relief, my phone still ringing, Jas's name still flashing.

'Jesus! You scared me,' I say, almost falling into him. 'How did you get in?'

His arms are open and he hugs me. 'I thought you'd be here when I arrived, I've been here since eight, where've you been?'

'I worked late. How did you get in?' I repeat. If Alex can get into my flat without keys that means someone else can.

'Oh, I grabbed the caretaker guy. He was refitting the bulbs in the hall lights, so let me in through the front door. Then, when I couldn't get in here, he unlocked it for me.'

'I'll have a word with him, he can't be doing that.'

'I told him I was your boyfriend. What is it with you about me being here?'

'It's not about you, it's… For God's sake, Alex, you just told me your ex-wife wants to hurt me. *You* should be pissed off it was so easy to get into my flat too.'

'Yeah, yeah, you're right.' He nods. 'I finished earlier than planned.'

'So I see. I thought you were Helen, come to take her revenge,' I say, sounding like Jas, and wondering why Alex is behaving like there's nothing to worry about. When he doesn't reply, I ask, 'Have you eaten?'

'No, but all the stuff I bought from the deli is still in your fridge, I notice.'

'Yeah, I didn't want to waste it,' I say, feeling a bit put out that he's let himself in, checked my fridge and then my bedroom. But he's my boyfriend, it's okay, I suppose.

'And I can see you're already way ahead of me.' He laughs, pointing to the bottle of red I'm still clutching.

'Ah that wasn't to drink, it was my weapon of choice.'

'Your weapon?'

'Against Helen,' I say, suddenly feeling ridiculous. 'I thought that was her in the bedroom.'

'I haven't heard from her all day, so maybe she's got the message and is starting to move on.'

'Surely not that quickly?'

'That's what Helen's like.' He laughs. 'I told you, unpredict-able – up one minute, down the next. But enough about her. You open your bottle, and I shall prepare a cheese board to out-cheese anything you've ever had before.'

I grab some glasses from the side, while he throws together the deli items on a large wooden platter and walks in with it held aloft.

'Ooh that looks delicious,' I say, as he lays it down on the coffee table.

I pour the wine. We sit close on the sofa, and he hands me a plate and a cheese knife and we tear at the French bread, spread the salty Normandy butter, and cut wedges of soft brie and tangy blue. I sit back to enjoy this unexpected cheese-and-wine evening, when my phone goes again, a shrill, annoying baby demanding attention.

'Leave it,' he says.

But I pick it up to see who it is. 'I have to answer, it's Jas. I promised I'd text when I got in to let her know I arrived home safely. She rang before, she only wants to check I'm safe.'

'I'm here. You're safe, we don't need her interfering,' Alex says, irritated.

'She's my friend and we look out for each other.' I'm unsettled by his apparent frustration, but instead of being pissed off with him because of his reaction, I find myself feeling irrationally pissed off with Jas for calling me and creating tension between me and Alex. 'Jas, I'm fine, I'm *fine*,' I say before she can speak.

'Oh thank God! Harry and I were about to come over. I was so scared, babe, you said you'd text me as soon as you got home.'

'Sorry, yes, I meant to...'

'I said to Harry, why hasn't she texted me? Where the hell is she? We were imagining all kinds of things.'

Alex has now stopped eating. He's not looking at me, but I know the phone call has spoiled things for him.

'Yeah all good – thanks Jas.' I don't expand on anything. Alex says I tell her everything, so to prove to him that I don't, I want to keep it very short.

'Is something wrong? You don't seem – yourself,' she's saying.

I need her to get off the bloody phone. It's been such a stressful few days, and I just want to heal over a bottle of wine and a bit of cheese with Alex. He's now sitting waiting for me to finish my call and I don't need her to keep questioning me.

'No, I'm great thanks, love. Alex is here now, so all good,' I say finally, and roll my eyes at him, which instantly feels like a betrayal to Jas.

'Oh so Mr Alex is there, is he? I see, so that's why you didn't text, you can't when your hands are full.' She laughs loudly for too long.

I'd usually laugh with her but Alex might think we're laughing at him and if I don't put the phone down soon, he's going to be pissed off. I can see his point, Jas sometimes doesn't know when to stop talking.

'Look, Jas, I have to go,' I say. 'Alex and I are having something to eat. Thanks for calling, love.'

'Okay, see ya,' she says in a clipped voice and the line goes dead before I can say goodbye.

'She knew I was trying to get her off the phone,' I say. 'I'll feel bad about that all night now.'

'Hannah, you spend every single day with her, and from what you say, she'd like to spend every night with you too.'

'I think she just misses our friendship. I saw more of her before I met you, and she misses me.'

'Oh I'm sorry, if you'd rather be with Jas...' he says, playing the wounded boyfriend.

'Don't be silly, you know what I mean. I just sometimes feel torn between people. I hate hurting a friend.'

'I know, and I don't doubt that Jas has been a great friend, but don't you think she manipulates you, just a little?' he asks.

'Perhaps – but I think you do too, with those puppy dog eyes.' I smile, softening. 'So stop being a baby, Alex, or I'm going to have to treat you like one,' I say, and play at feeding him lumps of cheese that I force into his closed lips until we're both laughing. 'I know it pissed you off, but I had to take Jas's call,' I say. 'My friends are important to me – and I want them to continue to be part of my life, even though I've fallen in love. I'm afraid you're going to have to accept that if we're going to be together.'

He smiles. 'Of course, I understand, I'm just looking out for you. I'm sure they're all good friends, but I haven't met them. Anything I say is based on what you've told me about them. I'm just sticking up for you. Sorry if that comes over in a different way though.'

'I know you want me to be happy and my friends make me happy.'

'But, from what I see, friends like Jas just use people like you. You're kind and you want to look after everyone, but Jas will suck you dry. Trust me, I've known people like her – and she isn't your friend.'

'Oh, Alex, you're a man, you wouldn't understand the nuances of female friendship. Sometimes she gets on my nerves, yes she can be a bit flippant, a bit bossy, and sometimes I think she's a bit envious – but no one's perfect and a friendship is like any relationship: you have to appreciate the good bits and it's only when the bad bits outweigh them that you have to get out. Jas doesn't suck me dry, she makes me laugh, and we have a lot of fun together. We have a lot of history too. She isn't everyone's cup of tea, but I love her – sometimes I think she knows me better than I know myself.'

'Mmm, well, I hope you'll be very happy together,' he says, taking my phone off the arm of the sofa and placing it out of reach on the coffee table. 'And now, no more work, no more Jas – just me and you.' He runs his hands up and down my back. We start kissing, and lie down on my shabby sofa, and just as I'm about to pull off his jumper, my phone buzzes. I hesitate, for just a moment, but the look on his face tells me this will ruin a beautiful moment, so I ignore the call.

'Bye Jas,' he says in the direction of the phone, as I continue to take off his clothes, and we go into the bedroom, leaving everything else behind. And for a little while I forget Jas, forget that I couldn't get hold of Chloe Thomson today, and even forget that Alex's estranged wife has a desire to hurt me.

But later, when we're in bed, Alex is fast asleep and I nip into the living room. I get my work phone from my bag to check it. Shit, Chloe Thomson's called me three times. I thought she was avoiding me, but she must really need to speak to me if she's called so many times – and this late. Thankfully, she's left a message, so I listen.

'Hannah, I need to tell you something… I don't know what to do, don't know who to trust. I can trust you, can't I?'

I call her straight back, but it goes to answerphone, so I leave her a message saying I'm here, please call me as soon as she can, it doesn't matter what time it is. Then I grab my personal phone from the coffee table. An unknown number's called twice, and left a long, wordless message.

At first I think it's a misdial, or a wrong number, and someone's left it by mistake. But when I listen again, I can hear heavy breathing – and then I swear I hear whispered, distorted words.

'Did the earth move, bitch?'

CHAPTER TWENTY-THREE

I immediately run back into the bedroom and wake Alex to get him to listen. He rolls over, half asleep, and not really in the mood, but I play the voicemail and thrust the phone at him.

'Do you think it might be her?' I ask, as he lies on his back, the phone at his ear.

He shrugs. 'To be honest, I can barely hear it – and I'm not even sure what the voice is saying, Hannah.'

'You *must* be able to hear that,' I say, desperate for him to agree I heard correctly. 'Did the earth move, bitch?'

I play it again. He looks at me doubtfully, and I play it again and again, but now I'm doubting myself and each time it sounds less like words.

Alex props himself up on the pillows, and listens again, but pulling the phone away from his ear, he shakes his head. 'I honestly can't hear it properly.'

'Oh Alex,' I say, snatching the phone off him. 'I'm sure it's her,' I hiss, feeling a little foolish. Okay, the voice is distorted, and in theory it could be anyone, but who else would it be but Helen? Then again, how did she get my number?

'Alex, when you met her, did you ever leave your phone on the table and go to the bar?'

'I don't remember.' He sighs. 'I wish I'd never told you. You've been on edge ever since.'

'Of course I'm on edge – what do you expect? You've frightened me to death saying, "don't engage with her" and "be careful".'

'I still don't think it would be wise for you to engage with her. But what she said – I mean, it was said in anger.'

'She made it clear to you that she wanted to hurt me – and now all this weirdness has started. That can't be a coincidence, Alex,' I say, aware I'm sounding paranoid, but feeling quite justified. 'A woman scorned...' I murmur.

'I just think we need to be vigilant, and not take any risks. If you're going somewhere, I'll drive you and pick you up, and you just need to let me know where you are at all times. And remember, I still have her location on my phone, so even if she did try something, I could be there in minutes.'

I'm about to protest that it would only take minutes for her to do something terrible, but he rolls over, with his back now to me. I feel abandoned, it's Alex who brought this fear into my life, and now he's acting like there's nothing to worry about.

I hear his breathing slow as he falls back to sleep and I'm left sitting on the end of the bed, alone, confused and angry.

I didn't go back to bed last night. After the phone message and the missed calls from Chloe, I couldn't sleep. I called her back several times, but she didn't answer. I listened to the message again, but freaked myself out, so made some coffee and stayed up until it was time to go to work. I left earlier than necessary because I didn't want to see Alex, I needed some space. I left a note asking him to close the door behind him, as he doesn't have a key.

Once at work, I finally managed to get in touch with Chloe's mother, who told me, 'She's left home.' Just like that. I'm not sure I believed her but, either way, I'm concerned for Chloe's safety, and called a contact at the police. Since then, I've spent most of the morning at the police station filling in forms and explaining my concerns for Chloe. I'm not convinced they are as worried as me about a troubled teen leaving home, especially as it isn't the first time, but I can't help feeling there's more going on.

'She called me last night, said she had something to tell me,' I say to the duty officer, 'that she didn't know who to trust.'

Chloe's only sixteen but has a reputation already with the local police, and they don't see her running away as anything new, or dangerous. But I do. She talked about trust, and I understand that, she's run away from home because there's conflict with her mother, presumably over what's been happening with her mother's boyfriend. She obviously wants to talk to someone about it. I've let her down, I should have been there for her. No wonder she doesn't know who to trust any more.

Back at the office, I wait for news of Chloe and blame myself for not being at the other end of the phone when she called.

'Don't beat yourself up, babe,' Jas says. Harry offers equally reassuring words.

'But she wanted to tell me something, and Chloe rarely talks, she seems scared to do so.'

Jas smiles. 'I'm sure she'll talk when she's ready. Don't worry too much. Chloe Thomson can probably look after herself for a night or two; she has before.'

To take my mind off one of my problems, I move to the other and ask my colleagues to listen to the rasping message on my phone.

'Is that a woman's voice?' I ask, and play it on speaker.

Sameera looks freaked out, and Jas gasps in horror, loving the drama.

'It sounds like a joke to me, someone's pranking you,' Harry says, going back to his screen.

'I think it's probably a woman,' Jas says, 'and it doesn't sound like a joke to *me*,' she adds, giving Harry a filthy look for not taking it seriously. I understand what he's saying, the rasping voice sounds really dramatic, but I'm with Jas that this is no joke.

I try to concentrate on work, but it isn't easy, and later, when my phone rings, I jump. Seeing an unknown number, I'm tempted to leave it, but then I remember Chloe and pick up quickly. It is her, thank goodness.

Her plaintive voice on the other end of the phone cuts right through me. 'Hannah? Hannah is that you? I've been ringing...'

'I know, Chloe – and I'm so sorry. Where are you? I've been so worried, love,' I say, wanting her to know that *someone* cares.

She sounds tearful, and can barely get words out. I ask her if this is about her mum's boyfriend.

'Pete's not... Mum says I can't... It's shit, everything's shit and I want to die.'

I look at Jas and Harry, who look back at me with concern.

'It's okay, love,' I say. 'Where are you?'

'I'm near the river...'

'No. Don't do anything stupid, Chloe. I'm here for you, please meet me.' I remember a little coffee shop in Cathedral square, I met her there once before, it's not far from the river. I need to get her away from water in her current state, so I tell her to go there, wait for me, and to order whatever she wants.

'I'm leaving the office now, I'll be there in a few minutes. Don't go anywhere else. Please stay there and wait for me,' I repeat, worried she'll go AWOL.

It's quicker to get into Worcester city centre by foot rather than drive and have to find somewhere to park, so I basically run to the cafe. But as I get near the square my phone rings. It's Alex.

'Hannah, are you in the square, near the cathedral?'

'Yes... I'm just going to—'

'She's nearby. I've just checked and Helen's around that area. Obviously I can't see exactly, but it shows the two of you aren't far from each other.'

I gasp. 'Oh God, no.' I'm desperate to get to Chloe, if I'm late she might not hang around. I was so concerned about her, I'd almost forgotten about Helen, but I doubt she's forgotten about me. My eyes scan the area, I suddenly feel very exposed.

'She can't *do* anything though, can she? It's broad daylight and busy—'

'Who knows? If she's nearby you've got to protect yourself!'

'You're scaring me, Alex.'

'I'm sorry,' he says. 'I'm sure she won't do anything so drastic, but she is potentially dangerous and you mustn't, whatever you do, engage with her.'

'I have no intention of doing that,' I say. I'm really on edge now, my head whipping around to see if she's behind me. To the side, a boy on a bike rides past too close and I let out a little yelp.

'Is it her?' Alex demands.

'No, no, I'm fine – sorry.'

'God, Hannah, you scared me,' he says, then pauses and asks, 'Where are you going?'

'To the coffee bar in the square, I'm meeting Chloe.'

'Well, you know where Helen works, so just make sure you're not anywhere near there.'

'Okay... I'll have to go.'

'I'm watching, Hannah. I'll keep an eye on where you both are.'

'Okay... but, Alex, she won't know what I look like anyway.'

There's a moment where he hesitates to say anything, then obviously decides to be honest. 'I showed her photos of you, when we met for lunch. I'm so sorry.'

'Oh, Alex.' I sigh wearily.

'I know. Stupid of me, but when I showed her your photo I thought she'd be pleased, I never expected... this.'

'Look, I have to go Alex,' I say, not sure what to worry about most, Chloe or Helen.

'Okay, but be aware she's still around there somewhere. I'll keep checking.'

'Okay, thanks, bye.'

I continue to walk cautiously, but quickly, along the high street. I'm scared of Helen, but equally scared of Chloe doing a runner, so I just keep moving, checking every face that passes me, until the inevitable happens. Alex told me Helen was nearby, and just as I'm passing Yo! Sushi, she's walking in the opposite direction – towards me.

I see her face close up, I know it's her, I've seen the scribbled-out photo at Alex's and the clear, professional one on the solicitor's website. Yes, it's definitely her, and for a nanosecond our eyes meet. I contain a horrified gasp and keep walking, as does she. But my instinct is to turn around and check she's not behind me, and as I do, I see her standing in the middle of the high street facing me, staring at me. I turn back and start to walk quickly, my heart now in my mouth, I'm screaming inside, and as I check over my shoulder, she's now walking towards me, very fast.

I hear her calling my name, she's shouting, 'Hannah, are you Hannah?' her voice louder as she gets closer. There's nothing for it, I have to run, so I make a dash for it and hide in a doorway waiting, trembling. I realise within seconds how stupid this is, if she finds me here there's no escape. I have literally placed myself against a wall, out of view from everyone.

I stand there for at least five minutes, which is a very long time when you have no idea if any moment the person who wants to hurt you might appear. I can't breathe, but even now, I'm aware that Chloe will be waiting and I can't let her down again. So I gather myself together and, still breathless, make the short walk to the coffee shop, constantly checking over my shoulder. When I get inside, she's sitting there, forlorn, in a hoodie and jeans, but no coat – she must be freezing. I'm relieved to be tucked inside the coffee shop, where people are drinking and eating and doing normal things. Even if Helen saw me through the window and came inside, surely she wouldn't do anything, there are too many people in here. I'll keep my eye on the door, but will now put what just happened to the back of my mind. This is Chloe's time, and too many people have already let her down, I need to be present for her. So I lock everything else up in that box in my head, brace myself and walk to her table.

Chloe looks up as I sit down. She doesn't smile and I'm immediately struck by how much thinner she looks since I saw her a few days ago. Her skin is paper-white, there are shadows around her eyes, and her lips are cracked and dry.

'Have you ordered food, love? You look like you could do with some.'

She nods listlessly. Hard, dark eyeliner circles her eyes, a grotesque parody of a teenager who, just a few months ago, was beginning to blossom. All she needed was a little support and encouragement, to know someone cared what happened to her. No one understood that more than me, and I loved watching her develop, despite her family and my unease about her mother's boyfriend. I even convinced her to work towards school exams, think about an apprenticeship, but who knows where she's headed now. I just know if I don't do something, she'll be lost, like her mum before her.

'What's going on, Chloe?' I say, looking into her face, trying to comprehend why at just sixteen she's given up on life. 'You said you wanted to tell me something, said you were scared. I want you to know you can trust me.'

She nods.

'So tell me, I want to help.'

'Mum threw me out cos of Pete... he's...' She trails off, her head bowed, not looking at me.

'What's happened?'

'He left, and Mum says it's my fault – I'm causing trouble. She said to bugger off and don't come back.'

She's little more than a child, how any mother could abandon their daughter like that I can't begin to understand.

'Oh, Chloe, I'm so sorry. Anything that happens between your mum and her boyfriend is *not* your fault, whatever she says. You know that don't you?'

A waitress arrives with a Coke for Chloe and I order a coffee.

'You need a brownie to go with that,' I say, knowing they're her favourite.

She shrugs, but I order her one and, in moments, the waitress returns with it on a plate.

Chloe starts to eat, breaking up the brownie into little morsels, tiny mouthfuls, that she forces down while we talk.

'So did something happen, with you and Pete?' I have a feeling she's not telling me everything. Last night when she left the message she said she was scared.

She looks at me, all wide-eyed. 'The bastard hit my mum, so I went for him and then it all went to shit. He buggered off, told Mum he wasn't coming back. I was glad, but then Mum turned on me, said I started it. But, Hannah, I didn't, he was *hurting* her.' She drops the half-eaten brownie onto the plate like it's inedible.

'So that's when she threw you out?'

'Yeah.' She's looking down, I can't see her face.

'Where did you sleep last night?' My coffee arrives, and I thank the waitress.

'I slept down by the river.'

'Oh, Chloe, I'm so sorry. You called me late, and I didn't get your message until—'

'It's not your fault, Hannah. It's mine.'

'No, it isn't, please don't ever think that. We can't have you sleeping rough, love. I'll sort it – make sure you're safe.'

She looks at me warily.

'You told me you were scared, in the message you left on my phone. Were you scared of your situation – or was it someone…? Were you scared of someone?'

For a moment I think she's going to tell me something. But she just stares ahead.

I try again. 'I know you don't think you can trust anyone at the moment – but you can trust me, I promise.'

'I can't.' She sighs, defeated, as if she's given up on everyone, including herself.

My heart breaks, I feel I've let her down. I think about Jas's advice about trying to be more detached – but I don't know if I can be.

'You *can* trust me,' I encourage, 'but I have to know what's happening so I can help. Is there something you want to tell me about, Chloe?'

'No.'

I'm not giving up that easily. 'Is it your mum's boyfriend – Pete? Are you scared of him?'

She curls her lip.

'Is it someone else? Are you still seeing Josh?' She sometimes goes out with an older boy who lives on her estate. He's not exactly a dream date; the rumour is he's a drug dealer.

She doesn't answer me.

I take a breath. 'Okay. Something's upset you, or *someone* has. You were doing so well, what happened?'

Slowly, Chloe begins to speak. 'I can't tell, he says he'll... he'll... lose his job.'

'I don't understand, he'll lose his job because...?' I reach my hand out to her at the table, but she draws hers away.

This bothers me. Everything about Chloe's life bothers me at the moment. Here is a young girl with her whole life ahead of her, a sixteen-year-old who feels lost and confused, like I once had. 'This person... Why would he lose his job? Are you having a relationship with him, Chloe?' She's only recently turned sixteen, if she's been having a sexual relationship with someone lately, she was probably underage. Whoever it is, he could not just lose his job, but go to prison.

She takes another sip of Coke. This is an older, harder Chloe than the one I've been dealing with these past few months. One of the most frustrating things about my job is that child protection plans rarely cover the full range of needs a vulnerable child may have. Work pressures, high caseloads and limited resources mean that kids like Chloe can slip through the net too easily. I watch her now, sipping her Coke, avoiding my eyes, and I know she's hiding something. But if she's in an inappropriate relationship with someone, even her mother's boyfriend, all I can do is strongly advise her against it and offer guidance. I can also offer practical help and find her somewhere else to live where she's less vulnerable to his advances.

'Talk to me, Chloe,' I say gently.

She doesn't speak, just puts her head down.

'It's okay. You can talk to me, you won't be in trouble.'

'No but *he* will be. He made me swear never to tell.'

'That's because he's in the wrong.' I lean across the table so I can ask quietly, 'Is he much older than you?'

She nods, very slowly.

I try to sound casual. 'Okay, so, have you been with him long?' I need to coax it out of her rather than make her feel under pressure.

'Couple of years,' she murmurs, and I try not to register my horror. This means she was thirteen or fourteen when the relationship started.

'Is it a… friend of your mum's?'

She shakes her head.

'If you don't want to tell me Chloe, that's up to you. I can't make you talk about it. I just want you to trust me and know that if he's threatened you, or if you're scared of him for any reason, I can help you.'

She stops sipping on her Coke and looks up at me for a split second then bursts into tears. I watch, surprised, as she falls apart, all the brittleness cracking and melting in the onslaught of emotion. The hurt and confused child emerges from under the hard black-lined eye make-up. I hand her a paper napkin, and tell her I'm here and I can help her, but I'm not sure she hears me.

We stay in the coffee shop for another hour, and I try every which way to get more information from her. But she's been told not to tell, and even my gentle questioning, my offers of help and my reassurances that she will be kept safe don't make any difference, and by the time the paper napkin has been shredded between her thin, little-girl fingers covered in rings and home-made tattoos, my hope fades. It might be out of fear, or loyalty, but Chloe isn't going to tell me anything about the man who's been sleeping with her since she was thirteen years old. I promise her that as soon as she wants to tell me or she needs my help, I'm here.

As the waitress sweeps the floor, and the light fades outside, my thoughts return to Chloe's immediate situation. Right now, I may not be able to find out who her abuser is, and I may not be able to keep her from seeing him, but I can find her somewhere safe to stay tonight.

'So, Chloe, I'm going to call round a few places until I can find you somewhere to sleep, and I want you to promise me you'll stay there.'

'Yeah, yeah.' She shrugs, but I can see her shoulders have relaxed slightly knowing she won't be sleeping by the river tonight.

I get on my phone to call the local hostels, and as I tell her story to each stranger who picks up the phone, she gazes ahead listlessly. Reaching for her glass of Coke, I notice her sleeve rides up, and I see a ladder of fine scars running up her arm. Our eyes meet. She knows I know, and pulls her sleeve down awkwardly, realising that I've clocked the tiny tell-tale stamp running along her flesh. I look at her face, and see my mother's eyes staring back. She's using.

I try to smile reassuringly, but I'm reminded of being a little girl again, in a dark and spiky world. My heart sinks, and another battle begins.

*

It's a fraught walk back through Worcester to the office, my mind so consumed with Chloe I haven't given Helen a thought until I get to the square where I'd encountered her earlier. I suddenly feel vulnerable in the dark, and even though it's bustling with people Christmas shopping, I check behind me every now and then.

As soon as I get back to work I call Alex to tell him about Helen chasing me and calling my name. The others are aghast, and keep saying I should call the police, but Alex has a couple of mates in the police and he says he'll talk to them about it before we take anything further.

'The problem is, she hasn't actually done anything yet,' he says.

'Yes, but she told you she wants to hurt me,' I protest. 'I'm scared, Alex, thank God you told me she was in the area, at least she couldn't take me by surprise.'

'Exactly. The app gives me a rough location, and I know when you're in the same vicinity, sadly I can't pinpoint exactly where you are.'

'So you wouldn't know if she was literally inches away?' I ask, horrified.

'No… not really,' he says awkwardly.

'Shit, Alex, I thought you were going to come steaming in the minute she got too close, I thought you'd know.'

'Not exactly, the technology isn't that good.'

'So I *should* call the police next time she's nearby.'

'No – look, you have to trust me, we don't want to aggravate an already sticky situation. I know the law around this – it's complex, but I promise I've got this.'

'Okay,' I say reluctantly, 'but if anything like this happens again, or I'm even slightly unsure or scared, I'm straight on to the police.' With that, I put the phone down. I hate that Alex has put me in this situation, and I can't believe he made it worse by showing her a photo. She was his wife, he must know her, and he must have guessed how she'd react to the fact he now has a new girlfriend. Then again, I've been surprised at Tom's behaviour since we parted – and I thought I knew him inside out.

CHAPTER TWENTY-FOUR

Sameera's wedding is in early January, so with a week to go before Christmas, we're combining her hen night with our office Christmas night out. It's not strictly a hen night, because Harry's coming along, but he's being an honorary girl for the night and will be wearing the pre-requisite bunny ears, which – worryingly – he can't wait to do.

'I'm not sure you'd get me wearing bunny ears on a girls' night out,' Alex says when I tell him our plans.

'I think you'd look cute.' I laugh.

I'm back at his house after work, he's cooking dinner while I go through my report on Chloe. I managed to get her a safe place to stay through Children's Services, but the problems clearly go deeper. All I can garner from talking to her is that she's in a relationship with an older man who seems to have a hold on her. She's refusing to say anything about him, and I am forming a theory I've just run by Alex.

'What if, rather than Pete hitting her mum, Carol discovered that something's going on between Pete and Chloe, and *that's* why she threw her out of the house?

'Possibly,' he murmurs. He seems distracted.

'Chloe apparently doesn't always tell the truth, but then who can blame her?' I continue, knowing that in Chloe's world, the truth is a horrible place.

'Bit odd though, Harry coming along on a hen night isn't it?' he says, suddenly going back to our previous conversation.

'What…?' Two worlds are colliding, and I suddenly remember what we were talking about. 'No, Harry's one of the girls, and he might bring Gemma anyway. We're going straight from work, so it would be a bit mean if we didn't invite him – not to mention sexist.'

'Fair enough. So, I could come too then?' Alex asks.

I wouldn't mind Alex coming along, but I'm not sure how the others would feel. It isn't a couples' night and as he doesn't yet know any of them, he might feel like a spare part.

'You *could*, but it's a hen do, Alex.'

'Yeah, but if Harry's going?'

'It's… I told you he's an honorary girl. It's also our work Christmas outing. He fits one criteria, you don't fit any,' I half-joke.

'Okay.' He smiles. 'What time do you want me to pick you up from the bar?'

It's been almost three weeks since Helen chased me through Worcester, and I haven't had any more weird messages or perfume-filled cars, but Alex has been driving me to and from work, just in case. But I'm keen to live my life, drive my car, and not rely on Alex quite so much. I'm hoping Helen's started to move on, accepted that Alex and I are together now.

'You don't need to pick me up tonight,' I say.

'No, I'll come for you,' he replies, assertively.

'Honestly, it's fine – we'll all share a taxi back.'

'But, Hannah, this is about your safety.'

'I know, but nothing's happened for a while. Whatever it was she seems to have got over it.'

He faces me, then leans on the kitchen counter, looking at me expectantly.

'What?' I say.

'Why don't you want me to collect you? Are you scared one of your friends might see me?'

'No, don't be silly, why wouldn't I want anyone to see you?'

'You tell *me*? Perhaps you like to pretend you're still single on nights out?'

'Don't be daft! I'd love you to meet them all – soon. But getting a taxi makes more sense. Jas and Sameera live on my way home, and Harry'll probably stay at Gemma's as it's only a couple of streets away from me.'

He lifts his head in an 'is that so?' kind of way, and I'm instantly irritated.

'Look, I refuse to have a night out with my workmates then just wave them off from my boyfriend's fancy car, leaving them on the pavement to hail a taxi in the freezing cold.'

'Okay, then I'll collect *all* of you.'

'I said no, Alex,' I snap, then realise I'm being rude so add, 'Sorry.'

He wants to look after me, and I get that, but I need to make it clear I'm able to look after myself, and what I find most irritating is that Alex won't take no for an answer. This morning, Harry made a joke about 'Hannah's chauffeur' and Jas asked me pointedly if I feel Alex is 'clingy or needy or just weird', and it does make me question the way Alex is. But, after all the Helen stuff, I guess I can't blame the way he is sometimes. Things are finally settling down, my feelings for him are strong and I'm still keen to make this work. I love Alex, I just don't love his ex-wife, and however I try to forget her and enjoy being with him, she's still a shadow lurking in the corner of our relationship. It makes me wonder about the night a few weeks ago when I worked late and felt I wasn't alone. What if it was *Helen* who Alex saw leave through the back door? He said it was dark and assumed it was a man, but there's a chance it was a woman he saw running away from behind the office. And yesterday Harry discovered that the double lock on the back door is broken.

'Do you think she might have got in?' I said to Harry.

'I don't know,' he replied, but I could see by the look on his face he thought *someone* had and was clearly just trying to placate me. I heard the doubt in his voice, the way he glanced at Jas and she looked away.

In spite of everything, Alex and I have made a concerted effort to focus on us. We finally put the Christmas tree up together, and he produced a lovely handmade bauble with our names entwined. He'd had it made specially.

'When I say forever, I mean it,' he'd said, as he placed it on the tree. I watched him, and imagined putting that bauble on many trees in years to come with our children.

On Friday morning, I get up early for work. Sameera's hen night/ Christmas work drinks is tonight and, if we're leaving the office early to go out, I need to fit as much as I can into the day. I have a mountain of paperwork and I need to deal with it. So today I don't have time for random gossip with Jas in the kitchen – and no lunch break.

Alex gets up early with me and makes porridge while I run around the house getting ready. I don't dress up for work but put my make-up and a clean top into a carrier bag to wear tonight.

'Are you wearing that?' he asks as I scrunch the leopard-print top into the M&S carrier.

'Yeah, you said it looked gorgeous when I wore it to the Indian the other evening.'

The expression on his face is saying quite the opposite, his lip is curled and his brow furrowed. 'Oh, yeah it's *okay*, but you might be better with something darker, more slimming.'

'What are you saying?' I'm horrified. 'I'm no skinny model, but did you just say I look fat in animal print?' I'm only half joking.

'No... no, but it's not exactly flattering, is it?'

'I thought it was,' I say, still surprised at his tactlessness.

'What about that loose black top you wore at the weekend?'

I rack my brain to remember which one I wore. 'You mean the big one that's like a bin liner? I can't wear *that* to go out.' I laugh, amazed at his suggestion.

'Well, apparently it's good enough to wear at home for me?'

'I don't wear it for *you*. I wear it for *me* – it's a comfy top I put on for pottering about the house.' I shake my head in wonderment. I can't believe he'd suggest I wear that.

'But you're only going out with friends from work, so why don't you want to wear something comfortable? Why do you need to dress up in cheap leopard print?'

'Cheap? I'm not sure where this conversation is going.' I stop smiling, and look at him, puzzled.

'I'm just saying—'

'Alex, you can *say* what you like, I *won't* wear a big shapeless black top to go out on a Friday night with my friends.'

'Like I said then, good enough for me but not for them,' he mutters under his breath as he places a bowl of steaming porridge in front of me. I'm suddenly not hungry.

'Alex, I *always* try to look nice for you, as you do for me, and I like that we both care how we look. But you're not being fair.' I look up into his face, reach for his hand. I don't really have time for this and I'm aware that I'm attempting to placate him so I can get on with what's going to be a busy day.

'I'm sorry. I guess I'm just a bit down today… It's not you… or what you're wearing.' He sighs and turns away.

'What is it then? Why are you feeling down?' I ask, aware I'm using the voice I usually save for my troubled teens.

'It doesn't matter. It's just…' He turns back to face me and I see there are tears in his eyes.

'Alex. What is it?'

'Nothing. Honestly, it's nothing.'

I get up from my seat and walk to where he's standing, put my arms around his waist and looking up at him. 'Tell me?'

He insists he's fine, but I can see he isn't. I don't have time this morning to deal with his sudden hurt, but I can't just run out of the door when he's clearly distressed, so I keep asking him. Finally, after much cajoling, he says, 'Today was the day Helen walked out. I know it was a year ago, but it still hurts.'

This stings me slightly and brings me back down to earth. 'Okay... I understand, but perhaps it's time to move on,' I say, unable to stop a note of anxiety creeping into my voice.

'It's not about her, Hannah. To be honest, now I'm with you I am glad she ended it. It's just you being out tonight, it'll just remind me of the nights I spent in... waiting for Helen.' He sighs. 'It's not your fault you're going out tonight.'

Why does 'it's not your fault' feel like an accusation? It feels as if Alex thinks I should stay home and hold his hand on the twelve-month anniversary of the end of his previous relationship. I'm not sure it's healthy to have such a date in one's diary, and even if he does know exactly when she left, surely it isn't good to dwell on this.

I move closer to him, put my head to one side, touch his face with my fingertips. Even in sadness, he has a lovely face, long lashes, soft lips, and there's nothing I'd love more today than to just call in sick, stay with him, and kiss that face. His hurt has made me anxious, like Helen's still a threat, still someone he cares about, and now my heart wants to talk this through. But my head knows I can't, because it's after 9 a.m., and I was hoping to be at work by now. I'm running late, with a million things to do, not to mention a 9.30 meeting with Jas to update her on Chloe Thomson.

Chloe's now staying in temporary accommodation I arranged for her. It's not great, but at least she isn't at home with her mother and Pete, who's apparently returned. I hope I can help her long term, but in my job there are few happy endings – there are always kids in danger, who need me to be on top of everything. And there's my partner, here in tears, who needs me just as much. I feel my heart beating faster. It's like when I was a kid and Mum had OD'd, which she did many times. I'd feel like the weight of the world was on top of me, that it was up to me to solve everyone's problems, to take responsibility. I feel that pressure now, and I don't like how it makes me feel. Makes me wonder just how thin I can spread myself before I burn out.

'The memory of Helen leaving must be awful,' I say to Alex now, 'but that was the past, and *I'm* here now. Even though I'll be busy at work today, I'll be thinking about you, and you can call me any time. We can have a lovely weekend together.' I pause. 'I just worry that sometimes…'

'What?'

'I worry that you're not over her,' I admit.

'I love *you*, Hannah. I just miss you when we can't be together,' he says, not really answering my question.

'I love you too,' I answer. 'I don't really want to go tonight and leave you alone and upset like this…' I start.

'Then don't,' he says.

I feel torn, I know Alex needs me, but this is Sameera's big night. 'I can't let them down, Alex.'

'But you can let me down,' he says bitterly.

'No. I'm not letting you down,' I say firmly, aware he's trying to manipulate me into crumbling and staying home tonight.

I'm used to recognising this kind of behaviour. I get it with my clients too. We all do it to some degree, it's part of being human and navigating our relationships. But if it goes too far and one person manipulates the other too much it isn't healthy, because it results in people doing things they might not want to do. Therefore, I *will* go out tonight with my friends from work, and make it clear to Alex that whatever he says, that isn't going to change, but at the same time that I'm not abandoning him.

'I love you very much, but me going out isn't about you and me, it's about me and my friends,' I explain.

He doesn't say anything, but his palm touches my cheek, moving slowly down my neck, softly slipping into my blouse. I feel a rush of lust, but I won't be seduced into doing what he wants, and I gently take his hand from my breast and pull away, grabbing my folders and bag.

'Babe, I will love you *all* weekend,' I say as I pick up my stuff, 'but I don't have time for *anything* this morning.' I turn to him and kiss him on the mouth, which he responds to with vigour, pulling me into him. Again, I carefully pull away.

'But I won't see you tonight.' He sighs, leaning back against the kitchen cabinet, arms folded. He can be quite childlike, which is, at times, endearing – but not now.

I stand on one foot, wanting to leave. 'Look, Alex, I've got to go, but I will see you tomorrow, okay?'

'You enjoy yourself,' he says.

But I know he doesn't mean it, he's pissed off with me – but I continue to the door, blow him a kiss, and leave.

CHAPTER TWENTY-FIVE

After leaving Alex in the kitchen, I'm in a bad mood all morning, totally consumed by our conversation. I'm confused as to why one minute Alex can't live without me and the next he's upset because it's the anniversary of the day Helen walked out. I promised myself no random gossip today, I don't have time, but can't resist mentioning this to Jas at our catch-up meeting about Chloe. It's all going round in my head and I want her detached take on it.

'Do you *know* it's their break-up anniversary?' she says.

'Well, I didn't until he told me.'

'I mean, is he telling you the truth? Is he just trying to make you feel bad about going out tonight?'

'That hadn't occurred to me. But surely he wouldn't lie about something like that?'

She looks at me like I'm stupid.

'Yeah, you're right, of course he would lie about something like that – he didn't even tell me he was married.'

She purses her lips. 'I told you from the beginning, babe, don't be so wrapped up you get blind to him. Before you know it, you're stuck in a shit relationship – and I've got no one to go out with on a girls' night!' She laughs at this, but it's true – on both counts.

A few minutes later, after the meeting's wrapped up and I've got off the phone dealing with a client who's been excluded from school, Alex calls. My heart sinks slightly. I know I told him to call any time, but I'd also dropped a million hints about being busy.

'Hey, it's me!' His voice is sexy and sweet and I find it immediately soothing. My heart is pumping again, as if just hearing him brings me back to life. I am so conflicted about him at the moment. It must be love.

'Hey,' I say softly down the phone, warmth creeping up my body, aware I'm caressing my neck.

Sameera catches my eye and smiles, Harry glances over. I hope they can't see from my face what I'm thinking.

'I was just wondering,' Alex says, 'as we won't be seeing each other tonight...'

A loaded comment. I hope we're not going back there again. I don't answer, my silence, I hope, speaks to him.

'So... as we won't see each other until tomorrow,' he continues, 'what about lunch today?'

I'm now going to have to reject him a second time in one day. 'Oh, Alex, you know I'd love to, but I am so busy today, and I was late in this morning, so I'm playing catch-up. I'm going to be stuck at my desk all day, I won't even *get* a lunch hour.'

'You can't go without a lunch break, you've got to eat something.'

'I'll grab something when I get five minutes,' I lie.

'Okay, see you tomorrow then,' he huffs.

'Yes, shall I come to yours first thing?' I say brightly, trying to lift his mood, erase the sulky air.

'If you *want* to.'

'Of course I do,' I gush, too loudly. Harry turns around and gives me a smile. I roll my eyes. 'Sorry I had to leave this morning,' I say quietly.

'I'm sorry too – but it got to me, you know?'

'I understand. But at the risk of sounding... selfish, it makes me feel a little insecure that you're still grieving for your wife. The one who walked out on you,' I add pointedly.

'Hannah, you've nothing to worry about – but when I fall for someone, I don't just forget them. I still have feelings...'

'I know, I'm the same.'

'You mean with Tom?'

'Yeah. It wasn't perfect, but like I've told you before, I still care about him – so I do understand how you feel about Helen.' But I suspect my feelings for Tom never were remotely close to his feelings for Helen.

'You wouldn't contact him though, would you?' Alex sounds alarmed.

'God no,' I say, reassuringly. 'You wouldn't contact Helen, would you?'

'Not now.'

'I'm glad.'

'Yeah, and after everything, we don't want her chasing you up the high street again,' he says. I feel a slight shiver at the thought of her running after me, the sound of her voice calling my name. I can't bear to think of what might have happened… what still might.

'Babe, I have to go, but thanks for calling. I'll see you tomorrow. Let's make up over the weekend,' I add in a small voice.

'We're good?' he asks.

'Yeah, I think so, do you?' I hear the plea in my voice, recognising the necessary weakness that sometimes comes with love, to break down the other's walls.

'I *know* we are.'

'Good.' I sigh, able to breathe again now we've made up. 'And, Alex…'

'Yeah?'

'Thanks.'

'What for?'

'For asking me to lunch. For caring if I eat.'

'That's because I *do* care. No one cares about you like I do. No one ever will.'

On the surface his words are sweet, but there's something about the tone that makes me feel slightly claustrophobic. Perhaps

I'm just overtired, with a lot on my mind, and overthinking everything.

I put the phone down, and try to focus on what I'm supposed to be doing, but thanks to Alex, I can't concentrate on my work, and I've lost all enthusiasm for tonight's festivities. I feel like shit. I'm only going out for an evening with my friends, when did this all get so messed up?

About twenty minutes later, a call comes through from reception. Margaret's taken the day off to do her Christmas shopping, so a young temp's standing in.

'Someone's here, he says he's your boyfriend,' she says uncertainly.

'Oh?' Alex didn't say he'd be calling in. Besides, he knows how busy I am, so surely he wouldn't, but who else could it be?

'Is he fair-haired, well-dressed? Did he give his name?'

'No, he didn't give his name, sorry. He isn't what you'd call well-dressed though, more casual really. Anyway, he said it's fine, he's been before and he's on his way up.'

'It's not my boyfriend,' I say, and put down the receiver. Alex will definitely be in a suit for work. It couldn't be him anyway. I just spoke to him on the phone.

My stomach drops. It might be Tom. I thought he'd moved on, he seemed pretty laid-back when we met in Costa, but that's what he does, plays it cool then pounces. By accusing him of sending the flowers and the nasty card I might have triggered something again. After all, he's turned up here before, yelling at me about his job, and how I ruined his life. Jas told him to leave, but when he refused she had to take him to the coffee shop down the road and reinforce the fact that I am not the cause of all his problems. She has qualifications in all kinds of psychological matters and can get people to do pretty much anything – and at the time, it seemed she'd got through to him. But he still thinks I'm behind the email that was sent to the council, and it doesn't matter what I say, he will never forgive me for that.

I glance over at her now, she can probably tell by the expression on my face that I'm worried.

'What's the matter?' she says anxiously, moving out from behind her desk and standing in her office doorway, her right arm high on the door frame as she leans out. 'Is it Chloe Thomson?'

I shake my head. 'I think it's Tom… he's here.'

'Shall I call the police?' Sameera asks.

'No, let me speak to him first,' Jas says, moving out into the main office. 'We can't have all that again.' Her long legs stride past my desk.

'The temp says he's on his way up, I'll go,' I say, half-heartedly, but Jas won't hear of it, and before I can argue, she's disappeared through the office doors to head him off.

I feel nauseous, I didn't think this day could get any worse, but it looks like it just has.

CHAPTER TWENTY-SIX

Within a couple of minutes, Jas is back, and my heart's in my mouth.

'Different boyfriend,' she says, and with that steps aside like a magician's assistant and gestures towards someone standing behind her – Alex.

Me, Harry and Sameera are all looking at him with a combination of relief and surprise.

'Nice to meet you, Alex. But call next time? You gave us all a bloody scare,' Jas says, smiling, but I can see she's irritated as she wanders into her office and shuts the door. She would normally want to chat, find out about him, and I'm sure she does, but I presume she's annoyed at the fact he's turned up at the office – and possibly just a little bit jealous. Jas is a great boss, very laid-back and friendly, but she has rules, and one of those rules is that we don't allow friends to come into the office. The nature of our work means that everything is confidential. On the rare occasions we may have clients here, they may be distressed; social workers from other teams could be having private, sensitive conversations, and it just isn't professional. It's a testament to our friendship that Jas didn't just refuse Alex access as she used to with Tom, but it doesn't make me feel any more comfortable about him being here.

I walk over to him, feeling extremely awkward, aware the others are watching. I can't see from where I'm now standing, but Jas is no doubt also spectating from behind her office glass.

'What are you doing here?' I ask, trying not to sound horrified, but I can see from his face that he realises I'm not pleased.

'I brought the mountain to Mohamed – lunch,' he says, holding up a large paper bag.

'Oh… thanks,' I say, forcing a smile.

'What did she mean by, "different boyfriend?"'

'Nothing, we… I thought it might be Tom.'

'He still comes here?' Alex says in a raised voice, causing Sameera to turn around.

'No, no, leave it Alex,' I mutter, embarrassed. I take the bag off him, hoping he'll go, but he makes no attempt to leave.

'Is that your desk?' he says, moving past me and over to where I was sitting when he walked in.

'Yes… yes, that's my desk.' I give an apologetic shrug to Sameera and Harry, who smile and get on with their work. 'So, now you've seen where it all happens,' I add, desperately hoping he'll get the hidden farewell wrapped up in awkward smiles. 'Thanks for lunch.'

But instead of leaving, he moves the papers on my desk, piles them up neatly, and sits on the desktop. 'I see you're as untidy here as you are at home,' he says, playing to his audience of two.

I laugh, mirthlessly, and address the others. 'He's being very unfair, I'm very organised, aren't I, guys?'

Harry rolls his eyes. 'There's stuff under that paperwork that's been there for several years,' he says. 'In fact she lost a Twix a couple of weeks ago, and I'm convinced it's under that pile of envelopes.'

Alex smiles politely, and I feel obliged to introduce him. 'Oh, er, Harry, this is Alex…' I say awkwardly.

Good old Harry steps into the breach, getting up from his desk, wandering over, shaking Alex's hand. Why can't everyone be as uncomplicated as Harry? I'm so grateful to him for easing the tension.

'Nice to meet you, mate,' Harry says, and pats him on the back, while Alex just stands there stiffly shaking his hand.

Meanwhile, Sameera's in mid-stress about a client who's run away from home this morning, not to mention a problem with her bridesmaids' dresses. They're 'too purple' and not the faded vintage lavender she'd imagined when she ordered them online. But she manages a smile and a little wave from her desk when I introduce her, then goes straight back to full on teenage runaway/ too-purple stress.

Harry lightens the mood, and gesturing towards the paper bag Alex is holding says, 'You're letting the side down mate. If my girlfriend finds out you're bringing lunch for Hannah, she'll expect me to do the same for her.'

'Perhaps you should?' Alex says, unsmiling. A moment passes and no one speaks. It feels like forever until he adds, 'You're always bringing stuff in for Hannah. Maybe you should do the same for *your* girlfriend.' He delivers this last comment with a warm smile, and I don't think he means it in the way it comes out, but if you didn't know him it would seem like he's warning Harry off. I can feel my face going red, and Harry looks a little taken aback.

I roll my eyes and try to make it into a joke. 'Alex, Gemma's the one who makes the lovely food, it wouldn't make sense for Harry to take her anything. Coals to Newcastle,' I add rather desperately.

'Well, you're a better man than me, Alex,' Harry adds, walking back to his desk. 'Not sure I'd spend my lunch hour playing waitress.'

Both men are smiling, so I'm going to hope Harry didn't take Alex's comment the wrong way and retaliate.

'Oh – it isn't my lunch hour,' Alex says, replying to Harry, 'I've taken the day off.'

'Ah, I wondered why you weren't dressed in your suit,' I say. 'I didn't know you had today off.' I'm surprised, he never mentioned it this morning.

'Yes you did, I *told* you.'

'I don't remember.' I smile, enquiringly.

'Oh *really?*' It hangs in the air as I remember it's the anniversary of the day his marriage ended. But he never said he was taking the day off to commemorate it.

I'm not sure what to say, and there's a *really* awkward silence. Harry and Sameera suddenly find something important to do and become engrossed in their computer screens. Our desks are all quite close, so they can still hear us, and I know if it were one of them, I wouldn't be able to resist listening, however awkward it was. So now I feel really exposed and just want to get on with my work, but to suggest directly that Alex leaves now would embarrass him. He doesn't seem to realise how difficult this is for me.

'So this is where you come to every day when you leave me?' he says, looking around at the shabby desks, the yellowing walls, the chipped mugs.

'Mmm, it's not exactly Google HQ.' I sigh, opening up the paper carrier bag that Alex brought. 'Thanks for lunch,' I say, again. I'm genuinely touched by his gesture, but the circumstances are clouding it.

Sameera's now on the phone, Harry's typing, and Jas is in her office seemingly knee-deep in paperwork, but I can't help but notice she keeps looking up. No doubt checking to see if Alex is still here.

'Do you have plans for the rest of today?' I ask him, rather pointedly, the implication being that I do – as he well knows.

'No, I'm just going to do some thinking.' He smiles, seemingly oblivious to my discomfort. 'So, shall we eat?' he asks, opening up the bag.

We?

I'm about to protest, to say again how busy I am and he really will have to leave me to work, but before I can even get the words out, he says, 'I thought we might have a picnic at your desk?'

It's a tiny office, we don't entertain our friends here, we don't even let them in, let alone have a picnic at our desks while everyone else works, but before I can say anything, he continues. 'Sorry about earlier. I'm just glad we're okay again,' he says, and leans in to kiss me on the lips.

I am so self-conscious, everyone can see us, and I feel like a teenager – not in a good way. If only I'd just accepted his invitation to lunch earlier on the phone, it would have been easier to slip out and spend twenty minutes in a café on the high street than this. And as I stand like an uncomfortable armed guard by my desk, he's now reaching into the carrier bag and taking everything out. One. Item. At. A. Time. First a punnet of plums, then bagels, cream cheese and a pack of thinly sliced smoked salmon. He's even brought a plastic chequered tablecloth that he's now laying on my desk. Over Chloe Thomson's file.

I feel hot, my face must be scarlet. I can see Jas watching this display from behind the glass of her office with barely concealed horror. What if the regional boss walked in now? She's been known to make surprise visits, especially on a Friday afternoon when she has more chance of catching us on the hop. Today she'd get quite a shock to see one of her senior social workers enjoying a 'romantic' lunch atop a chequered tablecloth with her lover. And the thing is, I'm not enjoying any of this.

'Look, Alex, this is… really lovely,' I say quietly, not wanting to embarrass him in front of the others. 'But it isn't allowed.'

He stops what he's doing with the tablecloth and looks up. 'What isn't?'

'This…' I gesture towards the desk, helplessly.

'What, lunch? You're telling me lunch isn't *allowed*?' he says with incredulity, as if he can't even begin to comprehend what I just said. Then he reaches back into the bag and pulls out a bottle of something fizzy. He twists the cork and loudly pops open the bottle. I am dying.

I see a glance pass between Sameera and Harry. I look at Alex over my pile of paperwork, my flashing phone and a thick layer of stress and embarrassment.

'We can't have alcohol!' I hiss, horrified at the spectacle of him now pouring what looks like bloody champagne into plastic flutes.

'I'm not an idiot,' he says, pleased with himself, 'it's non-alcoholic.'

I nod without smiling.

'I bought the smoked salmon you like.' He's smiling, proud of his selection, spreading the goods out before me, desperate to please. And suddenly I feel such emotion, I want to hug him, he's doing all this for *me*. If he'd taken a picnic to Helen's office, maybe she'd have welcomed him with open arms. I shouldn't take him for granted and behave like a spoiled bitch and keep rejecting him. This guy cares about me enough to bring me lunch, no one's ever done that for me before, no one's ever cared enough about whether I've eaten or not. Even my mother. And yes, it's slightly inappropriate, and to everyone else it might even be a bit weird, but how can I deny this man? I know it's a thoughtful gesture. And I do have to eat.

I reach out and touch his hand, then start to eat the food he brought to share with me. I try to ignore the looks passing between Sameera and Harry. I particularly ignore Jas's obvious glances through the glass. She knows my workload today and like me is probably wondering how the hell I'm going to finish it on time to go out tonight. But I'm entitled to a lunch break, and Alex can be trusted in our office of secrets – he's not a criminal, he's a bloody lawyer, for God's sake.

After we've eaten, he carefully tidies away the wrappings into the carrier bag. I hate to say it, but I'm glad it's over because I've felt under scrutiny by the others the whole time. I don't blame them, it's been quite the spectacle I'm sure. But now I watch him wiping crumbs from my desk and feel mean, for not appreciating him more. He's only done this for me, to make me feel special, loved, and it's all I ever wanted, so why can't I be grateful for that and stop worrying how it looks to everyone else? He catches me watching him and he smiles, a kind and genuine smile, and I remind myself that despite the recent revelations about Helen, he isn't a *bad* person. He doesn't tell lies exactly – he just doesn't always tell me what he thinks might hurt me. I should be flattered that such a lovely guy would be bothered to do all this for me, and I'm sure that behind their smirks, and glances, both Sameera and Jas would love partners who did such thoughtful things.

Alex is standing by my desk now, and I stand up to walk him out, but before I can move, he puts an arm around my waist.

'Alex,' I murmur, 'if Jas sees she'll be really pissed off.'

'Why?' he whispers in my ear. 'You're my girlfriend.' His eyes are twinkling, he's amused by this, and he brings me in for a kiss. A long, lingering kiss on the lips, which I have to reciprocate.

'You're pushing it,' I whisper under my breath, smiling.

'She's not *my* boss,' Alex says as he holds me by the waist with one hand, and waves to her through the glass with the other.

In response, she lifts her hand in a half-hearted wave, and I give her an awkward smile while walking him out.

'I can feel the resentment emanating from her office,' he's saying as we walk to the door. 'She's so jealous – like she can't accept that she's not number one in your life any more.'

'She's not jealous…' I murmur.

'Believe me, she is – that woman is *obsessed* with you,' he hisses.

I turn around and glance back to her office, to see Jas watching me through the glass.

CHAPTER TWENTY-SEVEN

After I've said goodbye to Alex, I go back into the office to find Harry and Sameera deep in discussion. Tellingly, they go quiet as I sit at my desk.

'He seems nice,' Sameera eventually pipes up. Someone has to say something, it's the elephant in the room.

'Yeah, he's lovely,' I say. 'I hope him being here wasn't too distracting,' I add. She shakes her head. But clearly it was.

'Oh my God, what the hell was that?' Jas's voice booms from her glass cage, as she wanders out into the main office. 'Has your butler gone now?'

The others laugh, and I smile but prickle slightly; they're laughing at Alex.

Jas gestures towards the door with her thumb. 'Bloody hell, what's he like? Turning up like the royal butler with his picnic hamper for Princess Hannah.' She laughs again, and the other two giggle.

'Yeah sorry, I didn't know he was bringing lunch,' I say, still not joining in on the hilarity.

'*Lunch?* It was a bloody banquet – and did you see him sniffing the loaf?' She picks up my stapler and puts it to her nose while the others crease up laughing.

I don't laugh. For the first time ever in this little group of people I spend most of my life with, I feel like I don't belong.

*

Later, when I'm alone making a coffee in the kitchen, Jas comes in. 'You okay? You seemed a bit pissed off before.'

I nod. 'Yeah I'm fine. I know you probably think Alex is a bit much… and he is. But it's just that he wants to do stuff for me, and he's only being kind, but the way you were making fun of him – I felt attacked.'

'Well, perhaps next time just meet him somewhere else for lunch and you won't feel that way – okay?'

I know she doesn't like people in the office, for good and professional reasons, but the mean way she delivers this, no smile, just a glint of something in her eyes, makes me wonder – is Alex right, is she jealous?

I don't even get a chance to respond, as Sameera pops her head round the door to ask Jas's advice about a client, and she leaves the kitchen.

I feel stung, and Jas has never made me feel like that before, even when she's had to say something difficult to me regarding work. I can't understand why she'd be so against Alex, and against my relationship, and it makes me sad because I should be able to share with my best friend the fun of being in love.

And it *is* love, not just infatuation or lust, and it's clear Alex feels the same. Even when things haven't been straightforward, I feel like he's magically restored my faith in men and love. I had begun to think there was no one for me, that all men were out for themselves, afraid of the commitment they were unable to give. In fact, I'd been starting to speak from the same script as Jas, which I now realise is negative and pointless. I'm realising a lot of things about Jas – there's no rational reason why she should have taken against Alex like she has. She hadn't even met him and she was telling me to 'be careful' and putting her spin on everything I told her about him. It makes me wonder if Alex wasn't too far from the mark when he said she was obsessed.

*

I'm hard at it all afternoon, but when the others start moving from their desks at 5.30 to go to the wine bar, I still have another hour's work to do, so promise to join them later. To be honest, I'm glad to finally be alone; it's seemed like they've been judging me recently, and today was the worst. I feel myself flush when I think about the way Jas made fun of Alex bringing the picnic – and the other two laughing along.

When I arrive at the wine bar, they greet me like a long-lost friend. I feel welcomed, warm and forget the earlier sense of exclusion. I feel lucky to have them in my life. After a few drinks and the meal, Jas too seems a little softer and we sit together in a little huddle.

'Sorry about before, babe,' she says, touching my arm.

'Oh, it's okay,' I say. 'I just felt a bit hurt and—'

'Yeah, yeah, I was a bit sharp, but you know I love you, don't you?'

'I do.' I smile. 'I can see why you were pissed off, but I didn't ask him to come to the office, he just turned up.'

'I know, I just feel like he's a bit fake… He was looking at me like he'd won some victory over me, do you know what I mean?'

'No, I don't,' I admit. 'So let's not talk about it, I don't want you and me to fall out,' I say firmly.

'Yeah, absolutely. No man will come between me and my sister, am I right?'

We continue to chat, and neither of us refer to Alex or his picnic, we just laugh about funny stuff, times we got so drunk we couldn't stand up, the time we swapped phones and texted men the other one fancied – mature, sophisticated stuff like that. But it's fun, and I'm reminded why we're such good friends: we make each other laugh, and have each other's back.

The evening continues. Jas, as usual, sees a guy who she thinks is cute. He's standing at the bar with his friends and by 10 p.m. she's demanding I go over and talk to them with her.

'I don't want to,' I say. 'Take Sameera.'

'Oh, she won't come and chat up men with me – she's getting married in January, she's no fun.'

'Go to the bar and send him over a drink, that way the barman will do your bidding,' I suggest, poking my finger at her, aware I might be slurring slightly.

'I couldn't do that, it's weird.'

'No it isn't.' I'm waving my arms about. 'Jas... Jas, listen. Go and get what you want,' I slur, now talking absolute rubbish, but as I'm four glasses in, I think I'm a great philosopher and therefore qualified to advise and pontificate at full volume. 'See your prey – and go for it – don't stop until you get it.'

'Hear, hear,' Harry says, raising his glass. He's taking the piss as usual, but he's never mean, it's always with affection.

'You know it, mate,' I say, slapping him on the back a little too hard in my drink-fuelled enthusiasm. 'Look at you and Gemma, you're perfect together, and you had to force yourself to go into the café that day and ask her out.'

He nods, and Sameera points out that she waited four years for her fiancé to even notice her.

'Yes, love, but he *was* married,' Margaret sagely points out, her face taut with disapproval. It's after her bedtime, and she really needs to get back to feed her two cats, but, God bless her, she's sticking it out, 'for the young ones'.

'Yeah, but I knew, I *knew* as soon as I saw him,' Sameera says. 'And, in my defence, she'd already cheated – and they were in an unhappy marriage.' She giggles and Harry giggles and their heads lean together and we're all laughing for no reason when some young girl wanders past and settles on a nearby table with her friend, clearly giving Harry the eye.

'He's taken,' I say loudly, 'so move on, love.' I collapse into giggles.

'Hannah, what's got into you? She can look—' Harry starts.

'But she can't touch!' I slur, and Jas and I laugh long and loud.

'Don't worry about Harry,' Jas says out of his earshot, 'he wouldn't stray, too happy with Gem. I knew she'd be perfect for him when I first saw her in the café – they're so cute. I really have a knack for putting people together.'

'Yeah you're a genius, Jas.' I laugh. 'I just hope they last, they're so young.'

'Yeah, they make me feel old. Gemma's only twenty-two. Shit, I just realised – I'm old enough to be her mother.'

Yeah makes you feel ancient doesn't it?' I nod, feeling quite tipsy, and clearly so is Jas, but we've hit a low point, we're not laughing at everything any more. 'It's like drinking,' I say. 'This prosecco's really getting to me, is that because I'm getting old?'

She laughs. 'No, you're just not used to going out on benders any more. That's what comes with being in a couple, you don't go out drinking like you do when you're single. When Tony was alive, I hardly ever went out drinking – didn't need to.' Jas looks a bit sad.

'I reckon I'll always want to go out drinking,' I say to bring her round a little, don't want her to be upset thinking about her husband. 'I just wish I didn't feel so pissed so early, it's not 10.30 yet.'

'Don't you worry, I've got your back,' she says, putting her arm around me. 'And if you get too pissed, you can always stay at mine.' Then suddenly she stops smiling. 'Well, what a surprise.' She nods her head over at the bar.

My eyes follow where she's looking, and there he is.

Alex is sitting at the bar, having a drink.

CHAPTER TWENTY-EIGHT

'How long's he been there?' I ask Jas.

'No idea, I only just noticed him. Bloody weird him turning up on your office do.' She pretends to laugh, and winks at me like she's making a joke. I know she isn't.

I tell her I'll be back in a minute and leave the table to go and see him. I'm not sure how I feel about him turning up like this.

'Hey, what are you doing here?' I say, approaching him and going in for a hug as he climbs off his bar stool to greet me.

He hesitates. 'I know you said you didn't need a lift, but I was worried about you. I texted and called, but you didn't answer. I thought something might have happened.'

'I'd turned my phone off because I wanted to get work done. I must have forgot to put it back on,' I say, taking my phone out and switching it on to see a *lot* of messages and missed calls. All from Alex. 'Alex, when I'm out, or if I'm busy, you mustn't be worried if I don't answer immediately. There must be twenty texts here,' I say, holding out my phone.

He shrugs. 'But if you don't answer, what am I expected to think?'

'That I'm out enjoying myself and that's why I'm not answering?' I'm trying to be firm, but it isn't easy as I'm aware the room's spinning slightly.

'I'm sorry, I didn't realise it annoyed you.' He sits back on the bar stool.

'It doesn't – but I'm out with my friends. If I answered every text and responded to every call, I wouldn't get a chance to join in would I?'

'Just go back to your friends and "join in" then. I'll go home, you clearly don't want me spoiling your night.' He turns away and faces the bar, as if he can't bear to look at me.

'Oh, Alex, stop playing the victim. All I'm saying is you can *trust* me... That's what this is about, isn't it? Helen hurt you and you're expecting me to do the same.' I lean back on the bar to face him, pushing my face into his rather inelegantly, my spatial awareness impaired by prosecco.

'Actually, it isn't about me not trusting you,' he says, pulling away from me.

'Oh, so what then? Did you think Helen had got me down a dark alley? I can defend myself,' I half joke.

'Thing is... she was here tonight.'

'Here? In the bar... this bar?' I'm finding it hard to speak.

'That's why I've been trying to call and message you all evening. I saw on the app that she was in the area, probably this bar but of course it's not that accurate. I was worried she might do something.' This feels like a sharp slap through the alcohol haze. I'm aware this is bad news but can't articulate how I feel. Then my legs start to buckle.

'Is she... is she here now?' I gaze around, but everything's blurry.

'No, it was earlier,' he says.

I'm now leaning on him as he sits on the bar stool, aware I should really stand up unaided, but not sure I can.

Alex holds me gently by the upper arms. 'Are you okay?'

'I'm not sure.' I'm upset by what he's just told me. I'd hoped it was all over, that she'd moved on. But in my drunken state I'm unable to comprehend what it all means, or even form words.

'You can see why I had to be here can't you? I was so worried,' he's saying. 'I think it best if we get out of here, I'll drive you to mine when you're ready.'

Even feeling like I do, I'm aware he's taking over, making decisions about what I'm going to do. But I can't let him. 'I can't just abandon everyone,' I say.

'You don't have to, I said *when you're ready*. I'll just wait here for you until you've finished with your friends.' He discreetly glances over at our table, adding, 'I *care* about what happens to you, unlike your boss, who's giving us daggers.'

'Is she?' I turn quickly to look, and catch Jas's eye.

She mouths, 'Are you okay?' and I nod. Then she turns back to chat with Sameera.

I turn to Alex, who's smirking. 'See?' he says.

'She's only checking if I'm okay, she's not giving us daggers.'

He shrugs and orders me a drink, a large glass of Merlot, but I'm currently sharing a second bottle of prosecco with Jas and I told her I'd be back in a minute. I realise that we've gone from me being out with my friends and going back to my place to him being here, drinking with me and planning to go back to his. I feel like protesting, but at the same time, I'm feeling very tipsy and if Helen's on the prowl, the last place I want to be tonight is at my place on my own.

I glance back at my friends. Jas is really animated about something, and Sameera's looking doubtful, and it makes me think how strong Jas can be – and how manipulative. She's probably convincing Sameera to change her whole wedding colour scheme, or the honeymoon. Jas really does love to be involved in everyone's business, and where I've always thought it's because she cares, Alex has made me see her from a different perspective. He says she likes to be in control, arranging everything and everyone around herself. I hadn't realised this before, but tonight, for instance, she chose the venue, the timing for the meal, and even ordered a round of Porn Star Martinis – her favourite cocktail – for everyone. And glancing over at her now, with the others, across the bar, everyone wearing bunny ears – it was her idea. She's kind and fun and bought a pair for everyone, but it's funny how Jas's are the biggest and the only ones with flashing lights. I wouldn't have even noticed that before, but now I see there's more to it. She makes herself the centre of attention, being loud and hilarious, making everyone laugh, as they dance to her tune. If you didn't know, you'd think it was *her* hen night.

Alex is now chatting away, his hand on my knee. He passes me the large glass of wine and, as I take it from him, I almost drop my handbag. He picks it up and helps me onto a stool, which I'm finding more precarious than I'd thought, and I'm glad he's here because he's basically holding me up.

I take a sip, a large one, and feel Jas's eyes boring into the back of my head. 'I should go back,' I say, gazing over.

'Darling, of course, but you seem very tired – or drunk. Don't you think it might be time to go home?'

I do feel ready for bed, and even if I stay, the last thing I want to do is stand outside in the freezing cold waiting for a taxi. In fact, I'm not sure I can stand at the moment full stop. A ride home in Alex's warm car is definitely a better option.

'I want to go, but it's a bit awkward. We were having a nice time, Jas and I were bonding – again,' I admit. And it had been nice. She'd seemed less bitter, less confrontational tonight... until Alex had turned up.

'That's good, but you need to make it very clear to Jas that what *you* want has to come first sometimes. I'm happy to give them all a lift home, if that helps?'

I take another sip of Merlot just because it's there, I don't want it, I know I've had enough and the room is already swaying. 'Okay, so I'll go over and say, "Alex has come to collect us, so if Jas wants a ride home, she'd better be nice to him",' I say loudly.

Alex smirks. 'I don't think she's going to take that too well. Perhaps save it for another time,' he says, patting my arm. 'Actually, I'm not sure I can fit everyone in the car, and we don't want to be waiting for them to finish their drinks and say their goodbyes. The state you're in, I don't think we should hang around. They can make their own way home can't they?'

He's looking at me with such sincerity, I can't help but feel grateful he's here. After all, Sameera's fiancé hasn't offered to pick us up, but Alex has come out to make sure I'm okay, and he did offer to try and fit everyone in the car. I realise I am really, *really* drunk, and it's making me feel a bit vulnerable and clingy, and I just want him to take me home and tuck me in.

'I'm sorry I didn't check my phone earlier, babe,' I slur, feeling a bit wobbly. 'I'm glad you're here. I feel safe and… I've never felt so… cared for… so loved,' I add. 'I love being with you,' I gush.

He puts his arm around me, looking down into my eyes, and I feel happy, even though I'm experiencing the sensation that the floor is coming up to meet my face. I automatically take another sip of Merlot and Alex looks a little surprised.

'Steady.'

'I'm fine.' I try to sound sober, but I'm finding it increasingly hard and this latest glass seems to have just about wiped me out. 'I'll just finish this and then we'll be off,' I say, attempting to climb down from the stool I've been barely sitting on.

Alex is smiling indulgently. 'Hannah, I don't think you're going to make it.' He holds out his arms to me as I teeter on the stool.

'Shall we get the others over here to have a last drink with us?' I say, about to beckon them over.

Alex shakes his head and helps me down from the wobbly stool. 'I hate to be the party pooper, but I think the only thing you're fit for is bed,' he says.

'I'm only a little tipsy,' I say, aware that the word tipsy isn't coming from my lips, just a strange jumble of sounds. I finally manage to climb down from the stool with a lot of help from Alex. 'I'm just tipsy, that's all,' I repeat, but again it's just an attempt at sounds, and the sober part of my brain knows that the more I say it, the less convincing I am. 'Jas kept pouring prosecco into my glass,' I say, then I giggle. Too much.

'Oh did she now? I'll have to have a word with her,' Alex says, disapprovingly.

'It's okay, you don't need to have a word with her. I'll just tell her next time not to keep filling my glass… I can look after myself, Alex,' I slur as I almost trip over my handbag.

'Hannah, you can't look after yourself right now. Bloody hell, it's a good job I'm here,' he says, concern written on his face as he picks up my bag from the floor.

'Thank you.' I look up and his eyes are on mine. I know even in this state he wants to kiss me. I can see it. I want to kiss him too, but I'm moving between happy, tipsy and slurry, to nauseous. I can feel it building and I must be pale because Alex has stopped smiling.

'Do we need to get you outside?' he asks gently, and the act of nodding makes my head hurt and something rises quickly up my oesophagus. I start to retch, and I'm aware of Alex moving me firmly away from the bar and guiding me through the crowded restaurant. At speed.

Once outside, the freezing night air hits, nausea overwhelms me and I throw up. In front of him. Spectacularly.

As I lift my head, I almost faint, and despite feeling so terrible, I am stung by deep embarrassment. How could I let myself get like this? I still feel quite sick and I'm worried there may be more. I try to say this, but I can't, I'm unable to form words. Prosecco's never done this to me before.

Through all this, Alex is wonderful; I don't know what I'd have done without him. He takes off his jacket and puts it around my shoulders. I'm irrationally tearful, I've seen men do this for other women, but until now, never me. And with my puke on the floor, and the strong possibility of more to come, I'm filled with such love for Alex I just start crying.

'I'm sorry, I'm sorry,' I keep repeating.

'Darling, really, it's fine. These things happen…'

'I'm embarrassed.'

'Don't be. I'm here for you. I love you whatever you do, you know that. Now let's get you in the car.' He walks me round the back to the car park, where he carefully folds me into the passenger seat. 'Let's get you home, safe and sound.'

'My friends?' I say. 'I should say good… good… bye.' My head feels like lead and it drops forward involuntarily. My eyes close, even though I don't want them to. I've never felt as drunk as this before.

'Give me your phone and I'll text Jas and let her know you're leaving, otherwise she'll be calling you every five minutes.' He opens my bag and takes out my phone. 'What's your pin?'

'Pins?'

'To get into your phone, so I can let them know you're safe and going home.'

'Oh… all the fives. Are we going home then? Tell Jas she can squeeze in here next to me…' I mumble. I can't think straight, nothing makes sense, and suddenly Helen is chasing me down the high street, she's screaming at me, and darkness is washing over me like a big, black wave, obliterating us. And everything goes black.

CHAPTER TWENTY-NINE

I wake up the next morning in Alex's bed with the worst headache I've *ever* had.

'I don't know how much I drank last night, but I've never felt as bad as this in my whole life,' I say, as I slowly sit up.

Alex is standing over me with a breakfast tray that he places carefully on my knees. I look up into his soft, kind eyes and again feel a flash of resentment for Jas calling him my butler. It's December, but he's managed to find the sweetest strawberries, and also on the tray is a plate of pancakes with wedges of lemon, a bottle of maple syrup, a cafetière and two cups. I want to hug him for caring so much.

'That coffee smells good,' I say, as he pours the steaming brown liquid into the mugs and joins me back in bed, where we eat breakfast. Saturday morning, no work today, outside it's frosty and inside under the duvet it's warm. Our bodies touch as we eat, and I can feel Alex's heat, the smell of last night's aftershave, musky, with a syrupy balm, and that echo of secret smoke, that I'm sure only I can detect. 'Pancakes and coffee – best ever hangover food!' I say, pushing the sweet, spongy dough into my mouth.

'A hangover? Is that what you have?'

'Yeah, but this is helping.'

'Hannah…'

'Yeah,' I say, a mouthful of strawberries now accompanying the pancake. He's not eating, he's just watching me and drinking coffee.

'You didn't drink that much last night, did you?'

'No. But it wiped me out totally. I don't remember much. I think I was sick, then nothing.'

'Yes you were very sick.'

'God. I haven't been sick with alcohol since I was at uni – I can usually take my drink.'

'Yeah, I know. We've shared a couple of bottles of red at home, and you've been fine, and everyone else at your table seemed relatively sober from where I was sitting.'

'Oh no, did they?' I feel even more embarrassed now.

'I don't know – it doesn't make sense,' he's saying, 'and it wasn't just the sickness, you couldn't stand up.'

'Did you bring me home?' I ask.

'Of course. Good job I was there, the others were oblivious, just carried on drinking, didn't seem to register how bad you were. You blacked out in the car. I was in two minds whether to take you to the hospital but brought you here and kept an eye on you all night.'

'Aah thanks, what would I do without you?'

'I thought the same.' He pauses. 'It made me wonder if…'

'What?' I stop chewing.

'If someone spiked your drinks?'

This hadn't even occurred to me, but I definitely felt much worse than I normally would after a few drinks. 'You mean someone in the wine bar, the restaurant? But who? I mean, why would anyone *do* that?'

'Who knows? There are some weirdos about. I worked on a case once where a waiter put drugs in women's drinks, and when they were really out of it, he'd drive them home – and rape them.'

'Jesus.' I shake my head in disgust.

Alex shrugs. 'I know. And I honestly don't think it was just drink that made you like that last night Hannah. You should be careful, especially if you go out with a group of people again.'

'What are you saying?'

He leans on one arm and looks at me. 'What do *you* think?'

I immediately assume he's talking about Helen. 'Oh my God. You saw her on the app, she was nearby, she might have come into the bar and... But could she...? Could Helen be capable of...?'

'Perhaps,' he says. 'But then again, I can't say she was actually *in* the bar, and she moved away from the area pretty early on, long before your second bottle.'

'So you were there, in the bar – Alex you must have been there all night.'

'I don't know how long... I just drove over as soon as I saw Helen was in the vicinity.'

I take a breath. 'That's good... I think, but...' I'm about to say that he can't spend his life looking at the app and checking where she is. But I guess while there's still a chance she's upset about us, it's just as well.

'She could easily have seen me go in...' I start, but he interrupts me.

'I don't think that's Helen's style,' he says. 'No. I was thinking – now don't get angry with me – can you think of someone you work with who might want you to be so out of it you go back to theirs?'

And it hits me. 'You mean Jas, don't you?'

'You tell me? I don't know her – but if someone were to tell me that one of them had tried to get you really out of it for a laugh, I might think Jas – or Harry, or the other one, Sameera is it?'

'All my friends basically,' I say, annoyed now. 'What about Margaret? She's sixty-five with a heart condition, but I'm sure she's got the odd date-rape drug knocking about in her handbag. So why don't we throw her into the mix too?'

Alex sighs. 'I knew you'd get angry.'

'Of course I am. Why on earth would any of my friends do that? It's not like it's even funny.'

'*Jas* might think it's funny. Harry might see it as a way of getting you vulnerable and—'

'Stop this now, Alex, it's ridiculous and hurtful. These are my good friends. I've known them longer than I've known you. What would any of them gain by me being out of it?'

'I don't know. You said Jas is always telling you how much she misses you. She might just have thought if you were in a bad way, you'd have to go back with her and stay over, and she'd have you there with her, where she wants you. Doing her bidding.'

A vague flash of memory hits me from last night. Jas putting her arm around me, saying I could stay with her. I feel a shiver now. 'I woke up this morning to loads of messages and missed calls from Jas, asking where I was,' I admit. I'd immediately texted her back. I know how she worries, but this does make me think.

'Yeah. I was going to text her from your phone when I got you back here, tell her where you were, but she beat me to it, and called you. When I picked up, she kept demanding I put you on the phone, kept going on about your safety, like I'm some serial killer.'

My heart sinks. 'You were nice to her though?'

'As nice as one can be when someone's virtually accusing them of kidnapping their own girlfriend. It wasn't like she didn't know where you were. When we left the bar after you were sick, I actually left you in the car – I locked it – and went back in to let them know you were with me and I was taking you home.'

'Oh?'

'I couldn't find them at first, but then I found Jas by the bar. I told her I was taking you home and if she wanted a lift home, she could have one.'

'Was she on her own?'

'No, she was with a group of guys. I'd never seen them before, and I don't think she knew them. She was all over them, though… ugh.'

'She gets like that sometimes when she's had a drink. She's been through some tough times. I think she misses Tony and is looking for a shoulder to cry on, I guess. She's had a difficult life.'

'Yes, so you've told me, but it's no excuse. The way she was going on, she had her arms round one of them, making all kinds of lewd suggestions.'

I have to laugh. 'Alex, you sound so pompous! She was probably only messing around.'

He smiles. 'You're right, I'm sometimes a bit much I know, but I just hate the way some people sleep around.'

'Enough, Judge Judy,' I say, and give him a gentle slap. 'Hopefully Harry and Sameera were looking out for her.'

'Well, your friend is a grown woman. I suppose it's up to her who she molests in a wine bar.' He sighs.

'Whatever gets her through the night,' I reply.

He's looking at me, like he's thinking about something, then he says, 'I'll never understand how you two are friends – you're so different.'

'We're not so different.' I sigh. I hope he wasn't too short with Jas – she seems to antagonise him without even trying, and vice versa. Is it too much to want my partner and my best friend to like each other? I guess it's the kind of people they are, both strong and both quick to judge. Both very much alike, come to think of it.

'You know,' he starts, making himself comfortable, 'Jas didn't know I would come along to the wine bar, so if she did spike your drink, you'd do everything she wanted you to. You'd go back with her, and also hang around with the guys she was with.'

I wish he'd leave this, he's totally barking up the wrong tree. 'Alex, she didn't spike my drink – no one did. I must have eaten something dodgy, or my body reacted to the drink – that's all. And Jas doesn't need *me* to pick up guys.'

'Well, I hope you're right – and I'm wrong. But do me a favour, and just be careful if you go out with them – especially Jas – again.'

'Alex, don't, they're my friends,' I say softly, so he knows I know he's gone too far. 'I think I'm being a bit of a crap friend myself at the moment where Jas is concerned. I rarely do anything with her any more.'

'I know. I just… I've seen stuff like this through work, people do dangerous things when they're scared of losing what they love, Hannah. The courts are full of neglected and abandoned people,' he adds dramatically, 'and if Jas is feeling like she's lost you, because of me, then she might… do something out of character, something weird.'

'Hang on, Alex.' I feel quite angry and defensive of my friend, I also feel he's being a hypocrite. 'The only person doing anything weird around here is your ex-wife.'

'I just want you to be safe, Hannah.' He sighs. 'And as much as I worry about Helen being a danger, I'm not convinced Jas has your best interests at heart.'

'Who does?' I ask, peevishly.

'I do and you know it.' He looks at me earnestly. 'Just remember what I said, be careful.'

'Okay, I *will* be careful next time I go out with her,' I say, sure he's wrong.

CHAPTER THIRTY

'Did you say Alex is working late this week? Perhaps you and I could have one of our legendary girls' nights out?' This is Jas's opening gambit the minute I walk in on Monday morning. She's already called me several times over the weekend, and when I explained in whispers from the bathroom why Alex had turned up at the wine bar, she laughed out loud.

'So that's what he's doing now is it? Pretending Helen's on the loose, so he has an excuse to be wherever you are?'

'No.' I sighed, unable to have a proper conversation because he might hear and then say again that I tell Jas too much. I do tell her most things, but she's my best friend and that's what friends do, it's what we've always done. But her calling pissed off Alex, because the first time we were trying to watch a film together, then she called again when we were having dinner, then she called later when we were making love.

'For God's sake, does she never stop?' he said, each time my phone rang. It made what should have been a lovely, relaxing weekend very tense. It seems that after meeting her in the office, then seeing her with some random men on Friday night, has turned an irrational dislike into something far worse.

'So, what night are we having a girls' night?' Jas asks again now. 'After all, it's Christmas next week and we need to get festive.'

'Let's sort something out,' I say vaguely. I don't want to say no to her, but I have a lot of work to catch up on and as Alex will be working late this week, I was hoping to do it then. I'm planning to spend a couple of nights at my place. I haven't been there for what feels like weeks, except to pick up clothes, and I'm looking forward to spending some time there. I love spending time with Alex, but I find it hard to concentrate with someone else around. It's bad enough at work being distracted by Jas's latest dating disaster, Sameera's constant wedding planning, and Harry teasing us and waving bags of croissants in my face. I don't really want to give up a precious night alone at my flat.

'So give me a day – when are you and I going to hit the town?' Jas has her head to one side, a smile playing on her lips.

How can I say no? And would she ever stop asking even if I did? I agree to go out with her on Wednesday and Jas seems happier.

'I just feel like we need a big catch-up,' she says. 'I miss you, and Alex took you away early on Friday, just as we were having fun.'

'Yeah it was great, but I wasn't well. I felt really rough after just a few glasses,' I say. I don't think for a moment that Jas had anything to do with that, but I can't help but think about what Alex said and discreetly check her face for any tell-tale twitches. Immediately, I'm ashamed of myself for even thinking my friend might have spiked my drink.

'Could have been something you ate?' she offers half-heartedly.

'Yeah, probably. Anyway, I promise I won't get wasted on Wednesday, just pleasantly pissed,' I say.

She giggles. 'Me too!'

I watch her bounce back into her office, curly black hair caught up in a scrunchie, her long legs clad in thick woolly leggings, and the usual 'Conversed' feet. She looks good; she doesn't look forty-two – she dresses like an eighteen-year-old and carries it off. I love the way she doesn't care, she is who she is and she wouldn't change for anyone. At the same time, she wants a relationship, and recently I feel like she's gone from booty calls to wanting so much more. Despite her bravado, I think she'd love what she once had with Tony, and what I have with Alex. She went out on a date almost every night last week, but didn't like any of them. She says she doesn't want another Christmas alone, but I tell her a lot of it is down to luck, the right man, the right time and all that.

As much as I'd like to share my happiness with my best friend, I try not to push it in her face. Sometimes I find it easier to talk about Alex to Sameera, because she's loved up too and we can forgive each other for boring the world about our boyfriends. Last week, I told her how he leaves little notes around the house saying how much he loves me, and she squealed with delight.

Harry overheard and started smirking. 'I could leave you guys notes around the office if you like?' he said. 'They could say things like, "Stop gossiping and get on with your work."'

'Mmm, perhaps not, eh?' I giggled. 'But, Harry, don't you ever leave romantic notes for Gemma?'

'No.' He shook his head as if it was the most ridiculous thing he'd heard, and Sameera and I laughed. If it hadn't been for Jas, he wouldn't even have asked Gemma out. She's quite the matchmaker and perhaps she'd be more accepting of Alex, if she'd literally put us together. I know she saw him on the app, but it isn't quite the same, and she isn't as invested as she might have been.

Her criticism of Alex isn't something I should take personally, though. Jas needs my friendship and support, she probably always will, so if it means swapping a night of peace and quiet at home to spend the evening laughing in a wine bar with her, then it's a no-brainer.

Over dinner at his, I tell Alex I'm going to spend a couple of nights at my flat this week while he's working late. 'I thought Wednesday and Thursday – I know you're busy too, it would be good for both of us to give some time to work,' I say.

'But I love having you here. We can work *together* in the evenings?' he says, and I smile at the glimmer of a sulking bottom lip.

'Alex, I love being here, but I need to make sure my flat's okay, and you're going to be working late and I've really got loads of work too and…' I feel a sense of rising panic just thinking about Chloe. She's still in temporary accommodation, but for how long? I called her mum, Carol, who in truth, seemed concerned about her daughter, and was at least able to talk to me without snarling. But when I asked what she knew about Chloe being in a relationship, she said she had an idea, and even hinted it might be one of Chloe's teachers. She was adamant that nothing was going on with her own boyfriend Pete, and took offence at my extremely subtle suggestion that Pete might be the one getting too close to her daughter. Carol did say she felt bad for kicking her daughter out, but complained that 'she caused trouble' between her and Pete. She said she hated the idea of her sleeping rough and would like her to go home, but when I rang Chloe with the good news she refused. And I'm convinced her not going home has something to do with this older man she's been seeing.

Meanwhile, there's a boy of thirteen called Jack, who is worrying me. We've been contacted by the family GP who suspects he's being physically abused by his father. I've visited the home, the family's now on our radar, but the boy isn't telling us anything. That's the problem working with families, even if you're there to help you're the outsider – they tend to protect each other, even when that 'protection' leads to harm – or worse. Perhaps that's why I chose this career, I've always been outside looking in – my experience as the outsider allows me to observe a family unit objectively. But with individuals it's different, my days are tied up with horrible little knots of life that need undoing, and some days my head is filled with a montage of abuse and hurt and suffering. That's what I need to detach from, that's why Jas, quite rightly, says I need to detach. But on the few occasions I turn off my phone and try to enjoy some downtime with Alex in the evening, I'm always aware that some of my clients are suffering. And however much I tell myself it's okay, because this is home and that's work – it isn't. Not for me. The abuse doesn't stop after 5 p.m. when I leave for the day. I can't shut the door on these kids when I get home and pretend everything's okay. And with Christmas round the corner, it can be an especially difficult time. Where the season is fun and exciting for many teens, it's something far darker for others. This is my job, and it's also my life, and I understand it can't be easy for Alex, who must sometimes feel as if he's taking second place to my work, and the mess of human life involved.

'You understand, don't you?' I say now. 'I just need some time to sort everything out.'

'I have stuff too,' he says. 'I'm working on a big case. It's important, but not more important than you,' he huffs.

'Whoa hang on, Alex, I'm not saying my work's more important. But you have to understand the kind of work I do is sometimes 24/7 – it *has* to be, because troubled kids don't do nine to five.'

'Now you're being sarcastic.' He sighs.

'I'm just saying it isn't office hours, and sometimes I need to have some space, to be able to *think* about what's happening, to make and receive private phone calls.'

'*Private? Space?* But I'm your partner, aren't I?'

'Yeah, but it wouldn't be ethical to make client calls in front of you. Even at the office, we have a small room we can go in to make confidential calls out of respect to our clients.'

'I understand that, but I don't see why you have to go back to your flat to have some space, there's plenty here. And you have to strike a balance – being a social worker doesn't mean you can't have a personal life. There are emergency helplines, you know.'

'Yes there are. But I didn't become a social worker to only be available during office hours – these kids need to know I'm there for them. With someone else, they might feel unsafe… betrayed.'

Alex comes over to me and puts his arm around me. 'I understand, my work's confidential too, but you could just go into another room, or I could?'

'No, I don't want you to feel like you have to leave a room in your own house because I'm working there, it's not fair on you. And I just need the space, the peace… you know?'

First Jas, now Alex. All I want is some 'me' time to focus on my work and my clients. I'm beginning to feel slightly claustrophobic in my own life.

'Of course, I understand. You need to be alone somewhere quiet to work, it's the nature of what you do. I can see that,' he says, finally giving in. He squeezes my upper arm, and kisses my cheek.

'Thanks, sweetie.' I kiss him back, surprised at how easily he accepted this; he usually doesn't take no for an answer.

'So you're going to work from your flat Wednesday and Thursday evening. Is that what you said?' He's picking up our mugs.

'Yeah. Well – I'm actually going to work on Thursday night, but I'm going out tomorrow with Jas.'

He stands up straight, still holding the mugs, still smiling, but it's slightly stiffer now. 'You're going out with *Jas*? But I thought you had work to do. I thought that's the whole reason why you're not staying here.'

'Alex,' I moan, 'stop. I just want to spend a couple of nights in my flat. And I can tie it in with a night out with Jas.'

'I don't understand why you'd want to spend an evening with her and not me. You said last week she was getting on your nerves, that she was bossy.'

I am exasperated. Can men ever understand the subtleties, the complex bonds, the conflicting feelings around female friendships? 'Sometimes, I don't *like* her. But she's my best friend, and I love her. It's difficult to grasp, I know, but we have such a laugh when we're together, and as I said at the weekend, I've been a crap friend and neglected her since I met you.'

'I'm sorry about that,' he says genuinely.

'No, don't apologise, it's my choice, I want to be with you, I'd rather be with you. But I do enjoy her company, and I think she's feeling abandoned, especially now I'm in a healthy relationship and she's still going on dates and sleeping with men she doesn't love. She's not a bad person, she just hasn't found what she's looking for.'

He puts the mugs back down on the coffee table, sits next to me, pushing his arms around my waist. 'I'm sorry, I sometimes forget that other people don't have what we've got.'

I smile, I feel the same, like we've known each other forever.

'And I don't blame Jas for feeling neglected,' he adds. 'We both want you to ourselves.'

I rest my head on his chest. 'Thanks for understanding.'

'But keep your phone on so I know where you are, won't you?'

I nod, grateful he hasn't turned this into a big deal.

'I could come and collect you both?' he offers.

I sigh, it's like a loop going round in my head, and I'm actually thinking a couple of nights recharging on my own is just what I need. 'No. No it's fine – in fact, I thought I might even drive there from work, so Jas won't put me under pressure to drink. As much as I need to spend some time with her, I also need a clear head at the moment with work.'

'Yeah,' he says. 'Makes sense for you to drive.' As he stands up, takes my hand and leads me upstairs to bed, he adds, 'Just be careful. If I'm not there to watch you, anything could happen.'

CHAPTER THIRTY-ONE

I come straight to Alex's after work today like I usually do, but am surprised to see his car in the drive when I arrive – he's supposed to be working late this week. When I walk in, he's on the phone, and while I hang my coat up and take off my boots in the hall, I can hear him talking.

'No, she's not here all day or evening tomorrow, so you could come first thing when she's gone to work,' he's saying. 'She usually leaves about 7.30 in the morning, so if you come at 8, the coast will be clear...'

I'm standing on one foot taking my second boot off when I lose my balance and fall against the coat rack.

He obviously heard as he ends the call and the next minute he's shouting, 'Darling! Are you okay?'

'Yeah fine,' I say, embarrassed and, after gathering myself together, go into the kitchen, where he's put down the phone and has started dinner. *The coast will be clear,* he'd said. Has Helen insisted on meeting him here?

He asks me about my day, he tells me about his, but as I lay the table, I keep going over what I heard, trying to put it into different contexts. I ask him if he's busy tomorrow, giving him the opportunity to tell me who he was talking to on the phone, but he offers nothing. He obviously doesn't realise I'd heard him. And I can't help but come to the conclusion that Helen is coming over, and he isn't telling me. I wonder if she's putting pressure on him to see her – is she threatening to do something to me if he doesn't agree? Does she want to get back into the house they once shared? Or is there another, far less dramatic explanation? Is he meeting a client here? Or a colleague? But if so, then why not mention it to me?

So, a little later, I try again, as we eat chicken risotto at the kitchen table. 'How's tomorrow looking for you?' I ask casually, grinding pepper on the creamy rice.

'Good, good,' he says absently, then looks up from his dinner. 'And you? Are you heading straight to the office in the morning?'

I nod, and continue eating. He definitely wants to make sure I'm out of the way.

As we drink coffee on the sofa in front of some TV drama, I can't concentrate. I'm on the brink of just telling him I heard him on the phone and asking what's going on. But it makes me look sneaky and I've asked him to trust me, so it also makes me a hypocrite – people only listen to their partners through doors when they don't trust them. Which now begs the question, do I trust him? After the whole Helen revelation, how can I?

I tell Alex I don't feel great and I'm going to take a shower and have an early night. His face shows some concern, but I can see he's enjoying the TV and really wants to get back to it, so I go upstairs to be alone and think.

When I said I was going to my flat for a couple of nights this week, he'd tried to change my mind. He was desperate for me to stay here with him – so is he punishing me for leaving him, by inviting Helen round? God that would be sick, surely he wouldn't?

A little later, when he comes to bed, I pretend to be asleep. I'm angry and hurt but now isn't the time to start questioning him. I'll go to work early in the morning, spend the next couple of nights at mine, clear my head and be 'me' for a while. After that, I'll come back here, and if he still doesn't mention it, I'll ask him about it, and I'm hoping he won't lie to me. But for now, I've just got to trust him.

*

I came into work this morning feeling horrible. I couldn't even face Harry's daily gift of a leftover almond croissant. It's still sitting on my desk uneaten, and buttery grease has now seeped into the paper napkin. It's making me feel nauseous. I'm going to have to get rid of it without him seeing, but I'm too busy trying to sort out a care order for Phoebe Cross, a new council flat for Craig Jackson, and, worryingly, I can't seem to get hold of Chloe Thomson. Meanwhile, Jas has scheduled an 11.30 meeting with me that I don't have time for. I just hope it's not one of her 'vital' meetings that turn out to be a detailed discussion on what we're both wearing tonight. I don't care what anyone wears, not with everything else on my mind. Jas clearly feels differently though, and I notice she's brought her huge make-up bag and an overnight holdall into work, containing, no doubt, a selection of outfits.

'Have you never heard of a capsule wardrobe?' I said, as she staggered in with all her bags.

'There's no such thing. A capsule wardrobe is work clothes pimped up. And what I wear to work is what I wear when I don't care. Oh, how quickly you forget, Hannah.' She smiles. 'When you're single, you have to dress like every night might be "the night".'

'Hate to piss on your bonfire, Jas, but I doubt George Clooney'll be in The Orange Tree tonight,' Harry laughed.

'You never know. Amal might be busy working on a big legal case. Alex is, isn't he, Hannah?' she said.

'Ahh, I see, so while poor old Alex works late, you two are going on a girls' night out? Look out, lads, the girls are on the pull!' Harry clearly thought the idea of me and Jas out on the town was hilarious.

'We are not on the pull, as you so delicately put it,' I rolled my eyes.

'Speak for yourself,' Jas said, staggering under the weight of the make-up bag and holdall.

'Yeah, but...' I started, about to remind her I'm taken, then remembering not to rub it in.

'And if I bump into that cute guy who works at the council and he has a friend, I need you to play along. I don't want you talking about your boyfriend and ruining everything,' she warned, like she'd just read my mind.

Two and a half hours later, I'm not surprised to find myself at our 11.30 meeting doing exactly what I didn't want to be doing. We are discussing what Jas should wear, while I get her take on the phone call I overheard Alex making last night. I wasn't going to mention it, I know she'll just use it to create a narrative where he's the baddie, but I wanted to bounce it off someone and she was there. She was opening up her holdall and laying all her outfits on the desk, and I just blurted it all out between the scarlet jumpsuit and the sparkly wool dress.

'Oh, love, I'm sorry,' she says, folding the dress, and resting her chin on both hands on the desk. 'That doesn't sound too good, does it? "Come when the coast is clear."' She bangs her fist on the desk and I see Sameera glance over and say something to Harry, who then looks over more obviously.

'It might be nothing,' I say, immediately regretting opening my mouth, because it's made this more real. 'It could be anything...' I try to play it down.

'Okay.' She's talking to me in her social worker voice. It's slightly patronising and I can feel myself becoming defensive. 'So what do *you* think the reason might be for him saying, "she goes out early, come over about eight, so the coast's clear"?'

'I don't know. I don't know *what* to think, but I don't want to jump to the wrong conclusion. I don't want to ruin something good, Jas.'

She raises her eyebrows and clicks her tongue. 'Sounds to me like he might have done that already,' she says, slowly shaking her head. 'I wonder if the wife is a permanent fixture, and all this talk of divorce is just that… talk?'

'No. No,' I say. I hadn't thought of it like that.

'You sure you're not the other woman, Hannah?'

After that conversation, I go back to my desk and feel even more paranoid. Has Alex been seeing Helen all along? I consider going straight over to his house and having it out with him. But if I'm right, there's a chance I'll walk in on them, and I couldn't bear that. I have to protect myself. I'll stick with plan A, and deal with this on Friday when I go to Alex's after work as we planned.

My phone pings, announcing a text from Alex. It makes me jump, which amuses Harry.

'You're a bit jittery today, Hannah,' he laughs.

'Just got a lot on my plate.' I then add quickly, 'Workwise.' I don't want everyone knowing every single part of my personal business, it's a small office and we already know too much about each other's lives.

I check my phone.

Hey gorgeous, have a great evening tonight. And don't forget, if you change your mind about driving, I'm free to play chauffeur. I'm home all evening. Xxx

This text gives me a glimmer of hope. Why would he offer to collect me if Helen or anyone else is staying over? It doesn't make sense.

'I might go to Alex's place after we've been out tonight,' I say to Jas a little later. I can't bear the not knowing, the constant tumble dryer of possibilities whizzing around my head.

'What? Why? Just go back to your place. Better still, come back to mine. Then you can leave your car here and—'

'No, no. It's stupid to think I can just ignore this. I'll drop you off after we've been out and go straight to his house. I'd rather deal with whatever's going on than torture myself about it. The irony is I wanted to take time at home to do some work, but I can't even think straight.'

'I thought you were taking time away to come out with me?' She looks a little hurt.

'Yeah, of course. That too,' I say.

'You guys okay?' Sameera asks, as I leave Jas's office.

'Yeah, you two seem to have lots of girlie secrets today,' Harry teases.

'Oh it's nothing, I wouldn't begin to bore you with it.' I sigh. Jas means well, but I think Alex might be right, I think she *does* want to spend more time with me, and it's affecting her assessment of the situation. She just wants to push the idea that Alex is up to no good – then again, all the evidence is pointing to that.

This is the problem with meeting someone online, however much you think you know, you don't – you don't know their history, their lives, their friends. When we met, Alex presented me with a picture of his past and present, but he left out what he felt didn't fit, like his marriage. And hearing him on the telephone last night makes me wonder what else he's left out of the perfect picture?

CHAPTER THIRTY-TWO

By 4.30, I've managed to do everything I need to do, except I still can't get hold of Chloe Thomson; her mother's not answering her phone either. I don't want to leave it any longer, I saw her a couple of days ago and she wasn't good. I reckon she's still using, even though she denied it, she's emotionally vulnerable and will need support to get off the drugs. I still don't know who she's seeing, but if it *is* her mother's boyfriend, it all makes sense. Chloe's refusing to talk to me about it and I think that's because he's threatening her. I'm not sure what worries me the most: the drugs, the self-harm or the fact Chloe's embroiled in some kind of relationship with an older, abusive man.

As I can't get hold of her, or anyone connected to her, I start calling everyone else, from the police, to children's agencies, to the homeless hostels. Nothing. By 6.15 p.m. in a last-ditch attempt to find her, I start calling the hospitals.

My first call is to Worcester Royal Infirmary, the biggest hospital in the area, and I'm put through to various wards to confirm if a Chloe Thomson is there. Eventually, I speak to someone who can give me some information. It seems Chloe was brought into the A & E Department at two-thirty this afternoon as a suspected overdose. She was found in a squat just outside the city centre. Her mother has been informed and is now with her. Chloe's alive, but she's in a coma.

I dash over there immediately, but I'm not allowed to see her because she's in ICU. I talk to one of the nurses who tells me that she was found this afternoon by a fellow squatter, who thought she was dead. Judging by her condition, doctors seem to think she OD'd last night. At this stage no one can tell me anything more, or provide any kind of prognosis, and after a while I decide to leave, and come back tomorrow.

I return to the office and google her condition, I can't find anything that helps, except that the longer a patient remains in a coma the poorer his or her chance of recovery and the greater the chance that he or she will enter a vegetative state. This is heart-breaking, and all I can do is hope. And with this in mind, I optimistically try to plan for a good outcome and request a mental-health social worker for if and when she comes round.

'I'm behind you on this,' Jas says, 'and as her care-co-ordinator it's up to you to put everything in place for her. But, babe, you must know it's not looking good.'

'I know, but I have to have hope. I feel like I dropped the ball, Jas,' I say, honestly.

She puts her arms around me and gives me a much-needed hug. 'Babe, we are sometimes on the fringes – they won't or can't let us in – and you did everything, everything you *could* for Chloe. You involved the other agencies, you put safeguarding in place – but sometimes things happen outside our control. You've been doing this job long enough to know that. So please don't beat yourself up.'

'I don't want her waking up to no one. I've told the nurses to call me if there's any sign of her coming round, and I'm going back first thing tomorrow. I just feel like I failed her, Jas.'

'You didn't, you were brilliant with her, and things were going well. She'd come on leaps and bounds with you guiding her, but we can't be there all the time. All you can do is be there for her going forward.'

Ever since I spoke to the hospital and had it confirmed Chloe was there, I've felt responsible. I can't help but feel if I'd been more present, more focused, maybe this wouldn't have happened.

I suggest to Jas that we take a rain check on our night out, I'm really not in the mood, but classic Jas, she says it's even more reason to go out.

'You need some downtime and a few drinks. I know that might sound heartless given Chloe's situation, but this is our job – it isn't our life. And if we stayed home feeling guilty every time something like this happens, we'd never go out.'

She's right, but I feel it's wrong somehow to be out enjoying myself when Chloe's in this state.

Harry made me feel a bit better. 'Chloe's been here before,' he said, 'and bless her she'll probably be there again. And like all the Chloes before and after, we can only do so much for them. She's a tough cookie, if anyone can pull through, she can.'

I hope he's right.

'So, have you thought seriously about your plan to go and gatecrash his romantic evening?' Jas says as we walk to the car park later. I can't help but be stung by the cruelty in Jas's words. She seems to be enjoying the idea of Alex having a night with Helen while I'm away, and I choose to ignore her comment. I think she's being a little caustic because she's not too chuffed that I'm driving and not drinking, but I won't be swayed by her. I want to be in control, I'm shaken by what's happened to Chloe and the last thing I want to do is drink. I also want to drive over to Alex's at the end of the evening and find out what the hell is going on. And I definitely need to be sober for that.

Once we're both in the car, I put the keys in the ignition and hear the sound no driver ever wants to hear, a sinister click.

'Oh shit.' I sigh. I had it serviced last week, so this doesn't make sense – shouldn't the garage have spotted this?

We both look at each other and Jas clicks her tongue, but there's a smile on her face.

'Looks like you're drinking with me after all, babes!'

The sensible thing would be to call the breakdown people, but, as Jas points out, it's freezing and it will mean us standing around for at least a couple of hours and this is our night out.

'Let's go now, get the drinks in. You can stay over at mine tonight and I can drive you in tomorrow. We can call the break-down then and get them to fix it while we sit in a warm office.'

She seems hell-bent on me drinking with her, and staying over at hers, which she wanted me to do last Friday when we went out. I'm also trying really hard to push away Alex's weird suggestion that she might have spiked my drinks then too. But I remind myself that I've known Jas for several years and she's only ever been a good friend to me, so who is Alex to tell me to be careful of her? Christ knows what he's up to. The truth is I'm feeling very unsure and starting to drive myself mad.

'It's safe here in the car park, it's locked at night, and it's probably only the alternator,' Jas is saying.

'Since when did you get to know words like *alternator*?' I smile, warming slightly to the idea of a dimly lit bar and a few cold drinks.

'That guy I went out with – Carl? Craig?' She genuinely can't remember, which makes me smile. 'Anyway, he was a mechanic, he showed me how to do things in cars.'

'I bet he did,' I say as we start walking towards the high street.

We're just walking onto the main road when a car whips past, splashing us both, which makes us squeal, and then laugh. Then the car pulls up, almost causing the car behind to hit it.

'Look,' Jas says loudly, 'that's Harry's car, is he okay?'

We both run over and Harry pulls the window down.

'Do you have whiplash?' I ask.

'No. That dickhead was right up my arse.' He laughs. 'Where are you two off to? I thought you were *driving* to the wine bar, Hannah?'

We explain the situation and within seconds Jas and I are sat in the back of Harry's car as he drives us the short distance to The Orange Tree.

'One of you could have sat in the front with me,' he says. 'I feel like a bloody taxi driver.'

Jas giggles. 'That's because you are.'

He drops us off outside, and we're so grateful, we invite him to join us for a drink, but he says with a twinkle, 'Gemma's waiting at home with something hot.'

Jas sighs. 'Stop bragging.'

He rolls his eyes. 'Will you two crazies be okay getting home later?'

'We'll be quite safe, thank you,' Jas says, 'we'll get a taxi to mine.'

'Well, if you're stuck, no problem picking you up.'

'Ahh, that's sweet of you, Harry,' I say, 'but we'll be fine.'

'Hey, and Hannah?' he says, as I climb out of the car.

'Yes?'

'Don't worry about Chloe Thomson, she'll be fine.'

I'm touched at this. Harry always seems like such a lad on the surface, smirking, making fun of everything, but his concern moves me. Chloe may not be his client any more, but because he's good at his job he still has a connection, and most importantly he still cares.

'I hope she'll be okay,' I say, 'but she's in a bad way.'

'Miracles can happen.' He smiles, and I think how mature and caring he is for a guy in his twenties.

'If I were ten years younger,' I murmur to Jas as we walk into the bar.

'He's such a boy,' she says, 'you need a *man*.'

I smile. 'I thought I had one. And talking of which, you know you said to Harry that we'd get a taxi back to yours later? Well, I still think I need to go to Alex's.'

'Oh don't, Hannah. Honestly, you don't want to go bowling in there and find him with her – *imagine*! Forget about all that, stay at mine. We can go to that new nightclub, have a dance and a laugh – go *on* it'll be fun. You need to let your hair down, you've had so much shit recently. Don't ruin a good night out for a man, he's not worth it, babe,' she says.

I think again of something Alex said about her not having my best interests at heart. I feel like she's trying to push the evening in the way she wants it to go, not considering my feelings. 'Let's just enjoy the night,' I say, 'and whatever happens, happens.'

The Orange Tree is warm and festive, the walls are smothered in fairly lights, and a trendy twig tree sits in a corner, spiky and white, with fake snow and silver baubles. I feel a rush and think about the weekend and mine and Alex's plans to do final Christmas shopping, then watch Christmas films. But I remember with a jolt that I may not be with Alex by the weekend.

Meanwhile, Jas orders four Porn Star Martinis – two each, they're two for one, she's in for a big night – and this terrible wave hits me. I'm lonely. I miss Alex. It's like homesickness – something I lived with as a child. I'm being really bloody stupid not asking him outright about the phone call. I've been trying to spare myself the pain, hoping desperately that if I left it long enough, he'd say something about it, but he hasn't, and I've realised the real pain is in not knowing.

'I'm going to just call Alex,' I say to Jas.

'For God's sake, Hannah, can't we just have an evening together without him being all we talk about?' Then she softens slightly. 'I'm only thinking of you, love.'

'Okay, I'll call him later,' I say, because she has a point, it's not fair to make our girls' night about him.

By 11.30, we've both drunk a lot of Porn Star Martinis and Jas is making eyes at the barman, which is making us both laugh, because after so many cocktails, everything is funny. Then, suddenly, in a blur of fairy lights and Porn Stars (the martinis!), my phone vibrates. It's Alex.

'Hey, are you having a good time?' he asks when I answer.

'Yeah... kind of. I just – I just... Alex,' I start, moving slightly away from Jas, who's now trying to look sober while talking to the barman. I can barely hear him with all the noise, and 'I Wish it Could be Christmas Every Day' has just started playing, very loudly. I cover my free ear, but it doesn't help.

'Sounds like you're having a great time,' he says.

'Yeah, I needed cheering up,' I say and tell him about Chloe.

'Oh, darling, you've worked so hard to keep her safe.'

'A hazard of the job sadly – you win some, you lose some.' I sigh, trying to sound casual, but Chloe's situation has been whirring through me tonight.

'I'm so sorry. Don't beat yourself up, you couldn't have done any more.'

'Thanks for saying that.' There's a silence, and I'm compelled to speak. 'Alex... there's something else worrying me.'

'Okay, what is it?'

'Did you... Did Helen come round to your house today?'

'No.'

'I heard you, on the phone yesterday. You were telling *someone* to come over after I left for work.'

'Oh?'

'You were saying they should come over at eight in the morning.' My head is slightly fuzzy, but I've gone over this so many times in the past twenty-four hours, certain words and phrases are imprinted on my brain.

'I'm not sure what you're talking about?' he says.

I tap Jas on the shoulder to say I'm moving to the doorway, to get away from the music and the chatter. She nods, and goes back to flirting with the barman. I end up having to go outside because of all the noise and I'm now standing in the cold and rain, and I'm freezing, but at least I can hear Alex.

'*Yesterday*, I heard you,' I repeat anxiously. 'You were telling someone what time I'd be leaving for work, and inviting them over… you said' – I feel tearful now – 'you said, the coast would be clear.'

'Oh… oh that.' I hear him laugh slightly. Then silence on the other end of the phone. All I can hear is lashing rain and the faint echoes of 'I Wish it Could be Christmas' thumping from inside. I'm trying to shelter in the doorway, and someone suddenly whips open the door almost knocking me over. I turn to see a young guy in his twenties, staggering out, followed by a more sober friend.

'Hello, gorgeous,' the drunk one says and almost falls into me. The sober one rolls his eyes and pulls him away. 'Sorry, love.'

'It's okay.' I smile.

'Who's that?' Alex's voice is tense on the phone.

'No one, it's no one.'

'You're beautiful!' the drunk guy says, and his friend smiles at me.

'Ignore him, he always gets like this after a Babycham.'

'I drink pints, me,' he's saying in mock bravado, banging his fists on his chest.

I can't help but smile, I deal with teenagers every day, and these guys aren't much older.

'Shall we walk you home? Shall we walk her home?' he says to his friend.

'I'm good thanks.' I smile. 'Night night.'

'Yeah, she's fine, Josh, you need to walk yourself home.' His friend laughs. 'Night, love.'

'Christmas kiss?' the one called Josh is saying as they walk past me to set off home, but his friend is dragging him away, laughing. I turn away from them and shelter more in the doorway, and all of a sudden, there's frantic movement, and it looks like the boys are fighting each other. It all happens so quickly and before I can see what's happening, the drunk guy slumps to the floor, making the noise of a wounded animal.

'What the f—?' the more sober guy says.

I scream, and someone grabs me, holding me too tight. 'Get off!' I'm yelling and kicking, my face is now in his chest, and it's then I recognise the warm, smoky scent on his jumper. It's Alex.

'Darling, it's okay – it's okay. It's me!' He's shouting into my face, his hands holding my upper arms too tightly.

'What... what happened?' I'm confused, in shock.

'Mate, what have you *done*?' The sober guy is on the floor, trying to wake up the other one who's flat out.

'He was about to assault you, there were two of them,' Alex is saying.

And then I realise – Alex was the one who hit him.

I look down. The lights from the pub are shining into the rain and lighting up the scene. The guy's lying on the floor, and mixing with the rain rippling along the ground, and into the gutter, something red is ribboning its way through. Blood.

CHAPTER THIRTY-THREE

'Is he… is he okay?' I'm shaking, probably from shock.

'He's fine, I only pushed him,' Alex says.

'You *punched* him, in the head!' the other guy's screaming.

'Alex, what the hell!' I'm now yelling, hysterical.

'But… he was assaulting you…'

I slam Alex out of the way with both hands and bend down to see if I can do anything. Close up, it doesn't look good, and his friend's in tears, shouting, 'Get an ambulance, somebody get an ambulance.'

'He looks… he looks…' I'm about to say dead, but I can't get the word out.

'Let's get out of here,' Alex is urging, pulling me by the hand.

'No, we can't leave him, we have to get help.'

'No, Hannah! He's okay, he's breathing, he's just knocked out, that's all.'

'NO, Alex.'

The boy – Josh – is stirring and groaning now, to my great relief.

'Look, he's coming round.' Alex is trying to pull me away.

A couple emerge from the wine bar and ask what's going on.

'Shit,' I hear Alex mutter at my side, as the friend tells them his mate's been thumped. The woman gets out her phone to call for help.

'It was him there,' the guy yells, pointing at Alex, who has his head down and is trying to drag me away with some force.

'Alex, NO!' I yell again.

More people arrive and sit Josh up, propping him with their coats. He's still groaning, now holding his head – and all I can think is thank God he isn't dead.

'I can't be here, I CAN'T!' Alex is saying as he pulls me off the pavement and out into the road. I'm now in tears. I have no idea where we're going, or why he's here. Then suddenly, I see his car parked across the road and he's pulling me towards it, cars beeping as he drags us blindly into the oncoming traffic. He opens the passenger door, and almost pushes me in, then runs around to the driver's side. Within seconds, he's started the car and we're driving too fast down the road.

'Alex, we can't just drive off.' I'm still slightly drunk, and can't get my head round what just happened.

'We *have* to.'

'Alex, what the hell is going on? Why did you do that? Why were you even there?'

'Hannah, stop! I need to *think*,' he snaps. I've never seen him like this, he's scared, petrified. Angry.

I glance back up the street and a crowd has now gathered around the poor guy lying on the pavement.

'Alex, what's wrong with you? You might have killed him!' I say through tears.

He doesn't answer me, but I'm looking at him in the flickering light of traffic and street lamps and see his jaw tense. We keep on driving until the pub has disappeared from his rear mirror and there's finally no yelling, no screaming, and no 'MERRY CHRISTMAAAAAS,' thumping in my head.

When we pull up outside Alex's house, I'm shaking. Alex turns off the engine, and we sit in the dark silence of the car for a long time.

Eventually I say something. 'Why, Alex? WHY?'

He just stares ahead for a while and finally turns to me. 'I told you. I thought he was hurting you.'

'He wasn't, they were going home. They were laughing, so was I. You *must* have seen that.'

He puts his head in his hands. 'I don't know what I saw. I sat there, waiting for you in the cold, wondering if you'd ever leave that bar…'

'What the hell were you doing there? We hadn't arranged for you to come for me. I told you I didn't need you to pick me up, I was fine. I thought we'd talked about this?'

'I know, I know. But I checked my phone and Helen was in the area – and I started to worry. Then I worried that Jas might put something in your drink like before for a laugh, and I… I'm so sorry, I just panicked, and jumped in the car.'

'You were following me,' I say, staring straight ahead, unable to even look at him. I remember what Jas said about him using Helen as an excuse to turn up unannounced everywhere – I think she might be right. I can feel an anger bubbling in my head.

'I totally overreacted,' he's saying, 'but I'm worried Helen might do something, and the way Jas can't stop calling you and *obsessing* – and then those guys.'

That reminds me, I left Jas in the bar. I'm such a crap friend! I immediately text her to ask if she's okay and tell her I've gone home, that I had a terrible headache and had jumped in a waiting cab, but would see her tomorrow.

'Who are you texting?'

'Jas,' I say. 'Once more it seems you've whisked me away from an evening out – only this time Alex you went too far,' I hiss.

'I was protecting *you*, Hannah.'

'I don't want *that* kind of protection, Alex. I didn't even know you were there. I mean, what the hell? And leave Jas out of this. You're being ridiculous and paranoid about bloody spiked drinks and weirdo ex-wives – I'm beginning to wonder if it isn't Helen but *you* who's the bloody weirdo, following me everywhere, and checking up on me!'

My phone buzzes, it's Jas saying she's chatting to the barman, he's cute and she's fine and will see me tomorrow. 'Thank goodness Jas isn't pissed off with me, she'd be quite justified if she was,' I snap, texting her back, telling her to let me know when she's home so I don't worry.

'Hannah, I'm so sorry.' He's trying to grab my hand.

'Don't touch me,' I yell.

'I'm an idiot, I've ruined everything.'

'Yes, you have, and you ran away from what you'd done back there like a coward, with no thought for that guy, just yourself.'

'I did. But you and I couldn't be found there if the police came. I'm a solicitor, you're a social worker – imagine.'

'That's hardly the point. Besides – *I* didn't *do* anything.'

'No, but you'd be a witness, or… seen as an accomplice.'

'We both know that isn't the case. But what if… what if he's seriously injured? Does that mean anything to you?' I'm finding it hard to reconcile this cold, selfish guy with the one I thought I loved.

'Of *course* it means something to me – shit, I don't know if I could go on if…'

I have every intention of phoning the police myself tomorrow, but I don't tell him this because he's already upset.

'I'm just so… I'm so wrapped up in you, I can't do anything,' he's saying. 'I can't bear not knowing where you are, if you're okay. I just want to look after you.'

'But it's not healthy, Alex. You don't need to be with me 24/7. Why do you have to be like this? It spoils you, it spoils *everything*.'

'Don't say that, please… I just feel deeply, always have. That's why it was difficult with Helen. Once I fall for someone, it's forever.'

'I get that, you're committed and I love that in a partner. But you're too much.'

'I know, I know, I am. You're not the first person to say that to me, but please don't…'

'I can't do this, Alex.' I hear my voice, and find it hard to believe. 'I really love you, but what happened tonight...'

'No, no please.' He starts to cry and I feel so helpless.

'Alex, I just think we need some time. I need space.'

He reaches out to me with both arms, and I find myself being held as he cries. I'm unable and unwilling to comfort him. I'm just numb.

'I know I expect a lot from a partner. I think I need help, Hannah. I used to watch him hitting her, he used to bang her head against walls. I can still hear that thud; it makes me want to puke.'

'What? Who are you talking about? I don't understand. Alex?'

'I can't forgive myself, all those years she suffered, and I never did a thing.'

'Your mum?'

He nods. 'I've never told anyone... Me and my sister used to hide in the wardrobe when he started. Mum always told us to go there. I was very young; at first, I didn't understand. But even as a little child, I could hear her screams, and later, my sister would bathe her wounds. Dad would act like nothing happened. *He* was a coward, and so am I.'

I didn't know any of this, I didn't even know he had a sister.

'God, I regret what happened tonight, you've no idea. But when I saw him going towards you, I saw my mum, and all the times I didn't save her.'

'I had no idea. You said your mum died when you were nine.'

He nods. 'Mum died of cancer.' He pauses. 'But he's still around. I don't speak to him, I've never forgiven him for what he did. My sister is a better person than me, she was able to move on, but I'm still so angry. She visits him now – and I don't see her either. It was a lifetime ago, but if I saw him, I'd kill him.'

I look at him, and the look on his face causes a shiver to run down my spine.

'Alex, don't say that.'

'I just want you to understand why tonight… happened. I feel terrible, I don't know what to do, Hannah.'

'We should contact the police, tell them what happened. You need help, Alex.'

He nods, and turns to me. 'Will you help me, Hannah?'

He could have said anything else and I would have just walked away, but asking for my help is something that gets to the very core of me. I have always wanted to do the job I do because I want to help people. I can never turn down someone who's suffering – and right now, Alex is suffering. What he did tonight was appalling, he lashed out without thinking, he was out of control, but he was urged on by the anger and pain of his childhood. He must have felt so helpless watching his father attack his mother, and he carries that and the guilt with him now, it explains why he is what he is. And apart from the pieces of him that reacted tonight and caused someone to be seriously hurt, I love who he is. And I don't know if I will ever be able to walk away.

'Will you stay tonight?' he asks, his voice still croaky with tears. 'I can't be alone.'

I nod. 'Yes, but we need to talk. I suddenly feel like I did when I found out about Helen. I'm seeing you from a different perspective. You have to tell me everything before we can even think about moving on, or staying together.'

'But I have, you know everything about me now.'

'I didn't know about your childhood, or why you're so over-protective of the people you love. We all find it hard to let go, but you held onto the idea of Helen coming back for a year, and even now I wonder.'

'I've told you, I'd never want her back now, I have you.'

I sigh. 'Stop the lying. I told you we can't move on if you keep lying to me. The phone call I overheard. You were arranging to meet her, weren't you?'

He starts to laugh. At first it's a small laugh, then it gets bigger, more out of control. He bangs his head on the steering wheel, and I realise Alex isn't laughing any more. He's crying.

I sit and wait for this to end. It's a panic attack, mild hysteria, I've seen it before with some of the kids I've worked with, you just have to hug them or leave them to work through it.

Eventually, he stops crying, and I touch his arm.

'You okay?'

He shakes his head and laughs, tears still streaming down his face. 'I'll probably never be okay, but if you leave me, Hannah, I don't know what I'll do.'

'I'm not leaving. Not tonight. Let's talk some more. Let's discuss what we can do to make you feel better. First is trust – you need to trust me, but I also need to be able trust you – and we have to have complete honesty between us.'

'Did you really think I was meeting Helen?'

'Yes, I still think that. That you invited her over to your house. I don't know why. But I wish you'd told me.'

'I wasn't meeting Helen, I was organising something for you. Come on,' he says, getting out of the car, 'let me show you.'

CHAPTER THIRTY-FOUR

I climb out of the car and follow him up the path. The front door is decorated with a beautiful Christmas wreath. It makes me sad to think how we'd put up the tree, planned Christmas. But now I feel like I'm in a parallel universe. We've just run away from a bar where Alex hit someone and left him for dead.

My phone pings; it's Jas. I have three missed calls from her. I text her back to ask if she's home yet. It occurs to me that she might still be at the bar and I wonder if she's aware of the fight, and does she suspect something? There's so much going on in my head, I really can't be bothered with Alex's 'surprise', whatever that might be, but he's hell bent on showing me, and ushering me through the door quite excitedly. It's like nothing happened, like he didn't just punch a man to the floor, like all that matters is what happens here, in his home between the two of us. That's his only reality.

'Come upstairs.' He's beckoning me from the bottom step. He's just opened up to me in the car, laid himself bare, and I'm not sure he has the strength to handle a rejection from me at this point. So I reluctantly follow him upstairs, and he stands on the landing, waiting. 'Now, I'm going to cover your eyes,' he says, which makes me feel a little vulnerable. I've never felt like this before with Alex, I've always trusted him implicitly, but now? I'm not one hundred percent sure, but what can I do?

'You're not going to throw me in a room and keep me there tied up, are you?' I say, with a mirthless giggle. I'm not even sure I'm joking.

'Shush, walk this way,' he says, guiding me forward. As we move, I instinctively open my eyes, but I'm unable to see anything through his hand.

'No peeping,' he says, as I hear him open the door. I'm so nervous my mouth is dry and I find it hard to swallow. In the silence, I hear him close the door behind us.

I feel him firmly manoeuvring me to stand on a spot he's obviously planned, and I wait nervously, unsure I even want to see what the 'surprise' is.

'You know you said that you can't work here because you need a desk, and privacy and a phone and...' With that, he takes his hands away. I'm standing in what was the spare room and is now a luxurious office space, with two matching desks, looking out onto the back garden. There are two anglepoise lamps, casting a warm, yellowy light onto 'his and hers' Apple Mac computers. There are framed black-and-white photos of the two of us on the walls, and a small sofa against the wall opposite the desks, with a coffee table, a coffee machine and a mini fridge.

'Oh!' I say, because I'm not sure how to feel. I'm glad it's something so normal, because I was imagining all kinds of weird things – a freshly painted dungeon, a padded cell. No, this is very Alex – and I know it comes with kindness, I have nothing to fear – but I'm slightly overwhelmed.

'The phone call you heard, "the coast being clear" was me talking to the decorators,' he says, with a beaming smile. 'I also had to arrange for the computers and desks to arrive,' he adds proudly. 'Now you and I can work from home together – side by side.'

'Oh, it's... great,' I say uncertainly. He is so delighted with what he's done, and he so wants me to be happy I can't crush him, and I don't want to seem ungrateful. But he's missed the point. The main issue I had was that I want to work alone, and I need privacy.

'Oh, and if you're thinking about when you have to make those confidential calls, don't worry, you can send me out.' He smiles. It's as if he can read my mind.

'Okay,' I say slowly.

He wanders over to the coffee table, he seems oblivious to my reaction. Either he isn't picking up on my lack of excitement – or he doesn't want to.

'We could live in this space, and never want for anything,' he's saying, arms open wide, encompassing his little world, the universe he's created here for the two of us. 'Imagine it, Hannah, I could work from home, and you could do a course. I remember you saying on our first date, you'd love to do a Masters in Social Work some day?'

I shift from one leg to the other. 'Yeah, yeah I *would*, I've talked to Jas about it – but I'd do it while I work, the council might even pay for it.'

'Darling, when we're married and I become partner at my firm, you won't *need* to work. And I'll pay for any courses you might want to do, we don't have to rely on the council.'

'But there'd be no point in *doing* a Masters in Social Work if I wasn't a social worker – and I love my job, I don't *want* to leave.' I feel slightly panicky at this.

'Okay, whatever,' he says dismissively. 'So long as you know this is your sanctuary, I made it for you. I want you to be happy and have everything you need.' He's excited, exhilarated even, I've never seen him like this. 'Look, I even had the walls painted in that blush pink you love.' He runs his hands along the wall.

'It's lovely,' I murmur, unable keep up with him. It's all too much.

'So?'

I look at him, slightly puzzled.

'So, Hannah, will you move in with me?'

I don't answer him, just gaze around the room.

'If you want to totally redecorate, new kitchen, new anything – that's fine with me. It will be your house too, Hannah. Hannah?'

I'm listening to him talk. He's like a salesman, and he's selling me the dream I've always yearned for: a home of my own, with someone who loves me. I think about our first date when we talked about children and dogs and white picket fences. And I believed him, in spite of Jas's doubts I knew I could trust him, and he's never wavered. He didn't go cold, he's never lost interest, and his passion and plans for our future are as strong as ever. And from the beginning I've longed to live with him in this beautiful home, my clothes in the wardrobes, my photographs on the walls. I've imagined summers watching roses bloom in the garden, Alex and I together in each other's arms on long dark wintery nights safe and cosy in this lovely house. I'm still that foster child looking for her forever home, and I really thought I'd found it – but now… I'm not so sure.

Alex wanders over to the desks, sitting side by side. Two perfect desks. But all I can think is *two perfect coffins*.

'And that's not all,' he's saying. 'I have a few other surprises for you. I was going to make them Christmas presents but was too excited to wait.' He takes my hand and walks me over to the small sofa by the coffee table. On the table is a brochure for what looks like a very upmarket holiday company.

'So, the yellow Labrador is on order, but before we collect him after Christmas – oh his name's Kevin by the way, I had to give him a name so they can get his shots and everything, apparently vets need a name. I thought Kevin was quite funny.'

I nod slowly. I'd wanted a girl dog, I wanted to call her Rosie.

'I thought you'd have been more excited, darling. Remember we talked about having a Labrador on our first date?'

'Yes, but I would have liked to go and choose one – when the time's right.'

Alex puts his head back a little, in mild surprise. 'Oh... okay, well, I guess we can cancel Kevin and when you think the time's right, we can order another one.'

'No – I didn't mean—'

'So we *keep* Kevin.' He beams, all eager again.

'Alex, I don't know, just stop, this is a lot to take in.'

'But we talked about all this – on our first date, you told me your dreams, and I'm making them come true. Like I said I would.'

'I don't know any more. I feel slightly overwhelmed, to be honest.'

'Oh, I'm sorry, I've done it again, haven't I? I can't ever get things right.' He's crestfallen, and I feel awful. I look at his puppy-dog eyes, while at the same time remembering the punch, the heavy landing, the blood trickling along the pavement, mixing with the rain.

'I just think I need time to think about what I really want,' I say quietly.

'Oh.' The sadness on his face is difficult to bear. He's obviously been so excited about the home office, and the dog, and as much as I want time to think, I don't want to ruin it all for him. Maybe he didn't punch that guy tonight. He said he only pushed him. Perhaps it was just bad luck that he fell and banged his head. And when we left him, he *was* coming round.

'Can I have some time to think about moving in?' I ask. I don't want to hurt him, so I say, 'It's more to do with logistics, and—'

'Yes of course, but I don't see why logistics come into it. This is closer to where you work than your flat – which, let's face it, is run-down.'

I nod, I don't have the energy to talk about this now. 'It's a big decision,' I say. 'It's very late, I have work in the morning, and I'm so exhausted. I just want to sleep.'

'And Kevin?' His face lights up like a child's. 'I never had a dog as a kid, I was so excited about collecting him.'

'Okay, let's go with Kevin,' I say, unable to say no to the thought of a lonely puppy not being collected. I know he's doing this for me, but Alex wants this too, and it's a small comfort knowing that if I decide not to move in, at least with a new puppy around he'll have a companion.

'I know you're tired, darling, but...' He's now wafting the brochure and I can't help but feel slightly panicky at what new 'surprise' he has up his sleeve. 'On our first date, along with the dog and the three kids – we also talked about spending a holiday by the sea in Devon.'

I'm sitting waiting for this, knowing what the surprise is but not as happy as I should be.

'And this weekend, you and I are going here,' he announces.

'I can't just run off to Devon, Alex. I have stuff to do.'

Ignoring me, he opens up the brochure at a picture of the most beautiful little cottage. It's a traditional pastel-coloured fisherman's cottage on the outside, but further pictures show the inside is contemporary, with everything one might need for a romantic winter weekend away. It's perfect, but right now it doesn't feel *right*.

'Don't worry about food and drink, I've made an order from this amazing deli near the cottage. I called them today and they'll deliver as soon as we arrive on Friday.'

I'm almost breathless. 'Alex, I'm sorry, I can't just take Friday off, it's our last day before we break for Christmas. It's a busy time.'

'Don't worry,' he says, 'I think of everything. I called Jas earlier today and told her you need to take Friday off.'

'I don't... Look, Alex, I'm sorry. I just don't like surprises. I need to know what I'm doing. Surprises and sudden change freaks me out – it stems from being a child in care – when someone comes into my life and starts telling me I have to move, or go somewhere, I feel like I'm losing control. I know it's hard for you to understand, it's just the way I am. I'm grateful, and appreciate your thoughtfulness, but I feel very uncomfortable at what's happening now.'

'Oh.' He puts the brochure down on the table, deflated. 'Sorry. I'm so bloody thoughtless, what an idiot.'

'No, you're not. You can't know how I feel about everything.'

'I'm your partner, I *should* know. I should know *everything* about you. I'll cancel our Devon trip first thing tomorrow, I'm so sorry.'

I sigh deeply. 'Don't apologise, you were being kind and thoughtful. It's just the way I am. Have you paid a deposit?' I ask.

'Yes, but it doesn't matter.'

Now I feel even worse. 'Let's sleep on it and talk in the morning, eh?' I need time to get my head around everything that's happened tonight. Right now, I'm feeling bombarded and unable to make a decision about anything.

'Yes okay. I'm a bit rubbish, aren't I?' he says, his brow furrowed, the earlier exhilaration and hope now crushed.

'No, you're not, you're not rubbish at all,' I say, but deep down I'm beginning to think I don't know who Alex even is.

Later, in bed, we hold each other and Alex talks about all the things we can do in Devon.

'Fish and chips, romantic walks along blustery beaches, the cottage, warm and welcoming. Oh, Hannah, all this trouble with Helen, and me doing that stupid thing tonight, I feel like we've become disconnected. A long weekend, just the two of us – it's just what we need right now, please say yes.'

And in my almost sleep, I can see us hand in hand, skimming stones, wrapped up warm, a bottle of Merlot drunk by a roaring fire. And I know I'm beaten.

'Sounds perfect,' I whisper, before falling into an exhausted, troubled sleep.

CHAPTER THIRTY-FIVE

This morning, everything felt back to normal with Alex. He was loving and funny and bright. I didn't want to ruin the mood, but I was keen to know if he still planned to contact the police about what happened last night.

'Of course,' he said, a coffee in one hand, toast in the other. 'I'm going to go in there today, see my friend at the station, tell him everything, and see what we can do.'

'You don't mean try to get out of it?' I'm still uneasy about what happened last night.

'No, but there might be a way I can come clean, come to some private arrangement with the guy – compensation or something?'

'Okay, fair enough.'

'After all, I can't be unemployed now, I have a future wife and kids to think about.' He beams. 'Not to mention keeping Kevin in dog food!'

I don't answer him. He's talking about a wife, but I don't recall a marriage proposal – or me saying yes. Alex gets so carried away with his plans, and he's so meticulous he's basically made it impossible for me *not* to go on the trip to Devon. On the other hand, what harm can a couple of days away do? Perhaps spending time together, with no distractions, will give me a chance to decide what I really want. If I start to feel okay with him again, then perhaps we can work things out? If not, then I have to find my way out of this.

*

I call the hospital to ask about Chloe. They've moved her from ICU so I should be able to see her, so I leave the house and head straight there. So much has happened since yesterday I feel like it's been weeks since I saw her, and a little part of me is desperately hoping to arrive and find her sitting up in bed. I take her a box of brownies and a fashion magazine, but the nurse on the desk tells me there's been no change. As her social worker, I'm granted access, and the nurse shows me into her room.

'Has her mum been in?' I ask the nurse, knowing that for someone in a coma, friends and family are encouraged to sit with them, talk to them.

'Yeah, she's only just gone home to change her clothes, she's been here since yesterday,' the nurse says.

Looks like Carol has finally started to step up, which is something, even if it is too little too late.

I'm shocked when I get into the room to see Chloe covered in tubes and monitors. A machine is breathing for her and her skin is white, like porcelain. Only the monitor above her bed gives any sign of life, and I know the chances are slim for Chloe right now.

Being in here reminds me of the first time I came into a room like this, years before, when I was much younger. My mum lay in a tangle of tubes just like this. I touched her white, papery flesh, the dark skin around the eyes – the track marks – before I said goodbye. I can't bear to say goodbye to Chloe though – I can't let her slip through my fingers too.

'I can only let you have a couple of minutes,' the nurse says, before disappearing.

I sit next to Chloe's bed and touch her hand. 'I think I've let you down, Chloe,' I say, 'but I promise, if you wake up, I'll be here for you.'

I open the brownies and put them near her face, hoping the aroma of chocolate will wake her, but nothing. I talk to her as I flick through the glossy magazine, knowing she likes this kind of thing – fashion, celebrities, a totally different world to the one Chloe lives in.

Ten minutes later, the nurse comes back and tells me I have to go. I leave the magazine, and ask her to give Chloe's mum my regards, and say I'll be back tomorrow. I doubt Carol will want to see me, she doesn't like social workers. Harry said she was a nightmare when he worked with Chloe, so I know it isn't just me.

I leave the hospital feeling like a failure, desperate for Chloe to wake up, to pull through, so I can prove to her and myself that there is redemption, hope – a future.

As soon as I arrive at work, Jas grabs me. 'Hey, did you see anything last night?'

'What?' I ask.

'When you left the bar? Apparently, some guy almost killed another guy on the pavement outside.'

'Oh no… it… must have been after I left,' I lie, hoping she can't hear my heart loudly thumping.

'Yeah, they brought him into the bar. He looked awful, blood everywhere.'

Nausea sweeps through me. 'Oh God. Was he okay?'

'Don't know, they called an ambulance.'

'Did they… get the guy who did it?'

'I don't think so. I mean he was talking, but I don't think he knew who it was…'

'Talking… Was he talking to the police?' I feel the blood rush to my head.

'No, the police weren't there – I meant he was talking, as in, he wasn't dead. He wouldn't even get in the ambulance, he walked off.'

'Oh good, good. So he wasn't too badly injured then?'

She shakes her head. 'No, there was a lot of blood but when he left he looked fine to me.'

I'm so relieved I feel my eyes well up and have to make like I'm looking in my handbag for something so she doesn't see. It could have easily been so different. Alex hadn't even stopped to think, he'd just reacted and lashed out.

'So what happened?' Jas presses.

'I don't know anything. I told you it must have happened after I'd gone.'

'I wasn't talking about the fight, you daft cow, I meant what happened with you and Alex? The phone call telling someone when the coast was clear? Did you confront him about it?'

'Oh that.' Again, relief sweeps through me. 'Yeah, so he was arranging to have decorators in and equipment delivered. He's turned one of the bedrooms into an office.'

'WTF?'

'I know.'

'Is he planning to set you up as some kind of homeworker and lock you in the house?' she jokes.

I just roll my eyes, I'm really not in the mood.

'And so...' She looks at me for a reaction to what she's about to say. 'Why did he call me at five-thirty this morning to ask if you could have tomorrow off?'

My stomach lurches. 'He wants us to go away... to Devon for the weekend. But last night he said you'd approved it already. That he'd spoken to you and you said it was okay for me to have the day off.'

She's slowly shaking her head. 'Nope, he woke me at dawn and asked – and it's fine. I just wondered why you didn't ask me.'

I feel awkward, I should have been the one to ask for time off in my job, not my bloody boyfriend. I know how this looks to Jas, and I need to explain before she accuses him of taking over my life *and* my work and treating me like a 1950s wife. This isn't quite how it looks, and in the great scheme of things it isn't a big deal, but he *told* me he'd already phoned her when he hadn't, and I am left wondering yet again why he seems to hide so much from me.

'Devon was meant as a surprise,' I say. 'But when he "surprised" me last night I told him I couldn't go, because I had to be at work, and couldn't just take it off. But then he said he'd already asked you.' I raise my eyebrows, indicating that it's as difficult for me to understand as it is her.

'Wow, he really is a *lot*,' she says.

'Mmm.' Then I realise something. 'I didn't even know he had your number,' I say. I'd never given it to him. Why would I?

'My number? Oh yeah when he picked you up from Sameera's hen you were out of it and he came back in the bar to tell me he was taking you home. I gave it to him then, asked him to call me to let me know you were okay.' I nod. Then she turns serious. 'I think you should know, when he called this morning, he hinted that you guys are talking marriage.'

My stomach lurches again. 'Did he?'

'Yeah, he didn't actually *say* anything, but there were some heavy hints. You're sure about this, aren't you?'

'I'm not sure of *anything*, Jas,' I admit. 'But I'm going to go away and see how things are between us. Thing is, I feel like I don't know him… He seems to keep so much to himself, then suddenly springs it on me.'

'Like what?' She gets up and closes her office door, her tone instantly changing. 'Christ, he already sprung his previous marriage on you. What now?'

'Oh nothing that affects us really – just that he told me last night his mum was the victim of domestic violence and he used to hide in a wardrobe when his dad was hitting her. He's never mentioned his mum or dad at all before. He even has a sister, and I'm sure he said he was an only child!'

'Ooh.' She screws up her face in a painful way. 'He does sound a bit messed up, love. And it's a bit convenient the way he can produce stuff out of a hat like a magician when he needs it,' she says, inspecting her nails.

'I don't think he makes stuff up – I think he just wants to impress me, he wants to please me, and so he tries to present himself in this perfect way.'

'And he's not perfect – who is? So it backfires?' she says.

'Exactly. And then I'm disillusioned and he feels like crap and we argue. I just wish he'd be more… honest.'

'Yeah, but the real problem is he wants to be everything to you, and he doesn't want anyone else around. Like… whenever you go out without him, he seems to turn up. He's always sitting there at the end of the bar or the end of the night. And last week at Sameera's hen party – and then there was the picnic he produced in the office.'

I cringe slightly at the memory of this.

'And don't you think it's weird that he doesn't want you to go to the gym?' Her face is screwed up, her lip curled, she really doesn't like him.

'Well, he never said he didn't *want* me to go, he just thought it would be romantic to work out together,' I say defensively.

'Romantic? Claustrophobic, more like. I mean look at it, Hannah. He can't let you go out without him, he's put an office in an upstairs room, a gym in the garage, he doesn't *ever* want you to leave the sodding house, love!'

I think about the two desks side by side, the sound of the guy's head hitting the ground, the blood and rainwater. I tell myself to stop this, I'm overthinking again. Alex hit him, yes, but he fell over, that's what the bang on the head was. And as for Alex, he's going to the police today, and he'll bring it all above board and sort it out, no hiding. I just don't want to explain all this to Jas, I feel like I'm always explaining Alex to her, so I continue to keep what happened last night to myself.

'After he'd shown me the home office last night,' I say, 'he told me he'd ordered a yellow Labrador. Jas, he just wants to make me happy.'

She purses her lips disapprovingly, then leans forward. 'Look, Hannah, I don't pretend to know what's going on in your relationship, but buying gym stuff, office stuff, pedigree dogs and a weekend in Devon? When you say all that it sounds okay... good even, but can't you see it for what it is? All he's really doing is building you a gilded cage.' She sits back. 'And good luck getting out of *that* once he locks the door.'

I feel very uneasy. Both Jas and I have a different interpretation of Alex's behaviour, I see love and kindness where she sees possessive and controlling.

'Just be careful, Hannah – I don't trust him,' she says.

Which is exactly what he says about her.

CHAPTER THIRTY-SIX

As we're now going away, I abandon plans to spend Thursday evening at my flat, and after stopping at mine to pack a suitcase, I go back to Alex's after work. When I arrive, he's in a very positive mood, and confirms what Jas told me about the guy he hit being okay and walking away.

'I saw my mate Dave, the police sergeant. I told him a client of mine was worried he might be dragged into this by witnesses, but he didn't do it. So he checked with the desk and no one's reported anything so far.'

'Thank God. So in theory that's it?' I ask, not sure about him lying to the police, but he's a lawyer, Dave is his friend. Perhaps the lines are blurred? Besides, as long as no one was hurt, perhaps he's learned a lesson and we can move on.

'Yeah, I mean, obviously, if in future the guy decides to press charges, then that's a different matter,' Alex says. He's sitting on a stool in the kitchen and shifts in his seat, clearly uncomfortable with the truth, because he only ever wants to give me totally good news. I actually like that he's being honest, he's saying 'it's okay at the moment but let's not be too "blue skies" about it'. Perhaps there's hope for us yet.

'I'm hoping he woke up this morning with a hangover from hell,' he continues, 'and neither he nor his mate remember what happened, or who did it. And before you say anything, it doesn't excuse what I did, and I shouldn't walk away scot-free. But I donated five hundred pounds to a domestic violence charity this afternoon – call it guilt money, if you like, but some good has to come of this awful thing I did.'

This is more like the Alex I know. Essentially he's a good man, what happened was out of character and it's clear he feels bad about it all. I believe this has been a wake-up call for him, and perhaps now he will realise that he can't always be where I am. His less than flawless approach to the truth has always been about me, about presenting a perfect picture for me to love. And there's a lot to love. He's been in many ways the best, most loving, most attentive partner I've ever had, and who doesn't have problems in their relationship? No one's perfect. You have to decide if the good bits outweigh the bad, and in this case I think they might. I have to at least give this one more chance before I throw in the towel. I'm not a quitter and it would be such a shame if I ended everything, and lost him because of a few issues we might be able to work on.

'Alex, I do love you—' I start.

But he interrupts me. 'I don't want to lose you, Hannah.' He sounds upset.

'If – and the emphasis is on "if" – we're going to stay together, we have to address a few things, and there have to be some changes, Alex.'

'Whatever, I'll do whatever it takes… I can change,' he says, gently putting both arms around me.

'You have to be honest with me, and not hide stuff because you think it'll make me see you in a different light. And you have to stop worrying about me, turning up places where I am. And we need to speak to Helen. You and I have to face her, talk to her and ask her to stop.'

He looks doubtful. 'We can try…'

'We *have* to, Alex. It's the only way I can even think about continuing with this, because at the moment I'm really not sure about the future.'

He nods eagerly. 'Whatever you want. If it means you'll stay. Let's talk about it over the weekend while we're away.'

'Okay, let's do that,' I say, going along with it, hoping the weekend will provide the answers, and I'll know where to go from there.

We set off first thing on Friday morning. The journey from the Midlands will be at least three hours, and as snow and sleet is forecast, it could take longer, but Alex is confident we can get there by noon.

'We'll find somewhere lovely for lunch,' he's saying as we hit the motorway.

He loves nice food, nice things – and he only wants nice things for me too. So why is this not making me happy? I'm trying to think of the positives, to get that feeling back, to love him like I did yesterday, but I keep hearing the thud as that guy hit the pavement. Alex's fear, his cowardice. The blood ribboning through rainwater. Can I ever get over that?

I think about what Jas said, the gym garage, the home office, the way he wants to drive me everywhere, how he turns up on my nights out with friends. The subtle, almost intangible ways he makes me feel slightly uncomfortable to be with anyone else but him. Do I want this for the rest of my life? Some women might like the attention. Helen ran away once; perhaps she felt like I do now? But she soon realised she'd made a mistake and came running back. I'm sure she'd love to be in my position now, as the object of his affections gazing out at the garden from behind her state-of-the-art Apple Mac, no pressure to work, just to hang around all day being worshipped. Alex would love his partner to be safely at her desk in the spare room never venturing out without him, or talking to other human beings. But that's not for me, and I won't change for him. He's either got to accept me as I am, be happy with my independence, and learn to trust me, or we won't be able to move forward.

I gaze out the window, the scenery is peppered white with snow, but becoming more rugged. I need to stop looking for negatives, and turning kind gestures into something other. I take a deep breath, and as the white sky meets the white ground, I tell myself to embrace this romantic, Christmassy weekend – and give Alex another chance.

But then my phone pings, and he shoots a look at me. 'Who is it?'

I look down at the screen. 'Jas.'

'Shit! Can she not leave you alone? Honestly, Hannah, it's like she's with us everywhere we go.'

'She's only asking me if we're there yet,' I say.

My phone pings again, and Alex sighs and grips the steering wheel a little tighter, which irritates me. I don't want to start a row while he's driving, but accepting Jas as part of my life is something else I need to address with him.

Babe, text me the address of where you're staying. Harry and Gem are visiting friends in Somerset this weekend, so if things go pear-shaped, you can always get a lift back with them.

I text her the address. I'm not expecting things to be bad enough that I'll need a lift back, but always better to be safe than sorry.

'She's so *bloody* jealous,' Alex is saying. 'She'd love to be you, heading out on a weekend away.' He overtakes a car in front a little too fast.

'Watch it, Alex,' I say, as the car swerves slightly. Everywhere is turning white before our eyes, and the road is becoming slippery. 'And don't flatter yourself, Jas doesn't want to be heading out for a weekend away with *you*,' I say nastily, my anger getting the better of me.

'She *would*,' he insists.

It's the way he says it that gets my attention. 'What are you talking about?'

He sighs. 'I wasn't going to say anything, but Jas – she told me she *likes* me.'

'*Likes* you? In what way?'

'Likes me, as in she *fancies* me.'

Surely he's teasing, it couldn't be further from the truth. 'You're not being serious, are you, Alex?'

'Yes.' His eyes are on the road, so I can't see them, but his voice is serious. 'She told me. When you all went out on your works do, and I left you in the car and went back into the bar to tell her I was taking you home.'

'Yes, but you said she was chatting with a group of guys at the bar.'

'Yeah. And I told you she was all over them?'

'Yes,' I say, feeling increasingly uneasy.

'Well, it was true that they were there, but it was *me* she was all over. I was disgusted. You said when I told you about it the next day that I was pompous or something, but that's why I said she was vile, because that night, she would have done *anything*... but not with them, with me.'

'No, no. She was messing about, she didn't mean it,' I say trying to convince myself as much as him.

'You really don't know her, do you?' he says, staring at the road in front of him. 'She told me she fancied me before you even met me.'

'What?' I'm puzzled.

'Said she was with you when you both saw my photo on the Meet Your Match app. She said she told you to go for it because I was so good-looking.'

'What the hell?' I'm shocked, and horrified, but mainly because what he's saying is true. I've never told Alex that Jas and I went through the app together looking for a suitable match for me, it felt slightly disrespectful, like we were trawling a meat market. And she did go on about how good-looking he was.

'She said she figured if things didn't work out between you and me, she'd be interested, that she didn't mind your sloppy seconds.'

Oh God, she did. She *did* say that. I remember it too clearly – we were in The Orange Tree, she pushed the app at me, found Alex's photo and said if it didn't work out, she'd have my sloppy seconds. It was typical Jas. But she was joking – wasn't she?

I am in shock. 'She wouldn't, you're my boyfriend.'

'Do you think that would stop her? The fact I'm with you makes me more appealing to a woman like her. And, let's face it, she'd love to break us up. I wasn't going to ever tell you – but you have to know. I've said before, she doesn't have your best interests at heart. I *know*, Hannah… she tried to kiss me.'

For a while we sit in silence. He wouldn't know any of this, so he must be telling the truth – and if he *is* telling the truth, then she might have come on to him. I think about Jas's warnings against Alex, her desperation to find a partner, and begin to wonder just why she's constantly tried to ambush my relationship with him all along? It had never occurred to me until now, but does she want Alex for herself?

I feel bruised, like my skin's tender from thinking too much. Not long ago I would have trusted Alex and Jas implicitly, and now I don't know who I can trust. Can I even trust either of them? Here I am on a romantic break with a man who left another man for dead because he says he was protecting me, and my best friend is constantly telling me my boyfriend can't be trusted because *she's* the one protecting me. I genuinely don't know who to believe any more.

We arrive at the cottage, and it's as lovely as the brochure's pictures. It stands alone in acres of green, currently covered in snow, and looks just like a Christmas card. Once inside, I'm enchanted by the wooden beams, an open fire, a huge, soft, feathery bed. And in the lovely little kitchen with the Aga and chintzy tea towels, the hamper of food and wine from the deli is waiting – just as Alex promised.

I watch Alex lighting the fire, and feel happy and cosy; the snow's outside, and he's making this fire for us, for me. And as the flames begin to leap, and we thaw in front of them, I think about how home isn't a place, it's a feeling. Right now, here with Alex I feel like I'm home.

'Let's open some wine and warm up a little?' he suggests. Within seconds we're sitting in front of the fire, a glass each in our hands, it's warm, and I feel safe. Here is the clean canvas I hoped for.

Back in Worcester I was caught up in Jas's criticisms of Alex and despite defending our relationship to her, the comments had got under my skin and I'd been confused. But being here with just him now, I feel I've been right to give Alex a chance, and think we might just be able to overcome everything that's happened, and be happy. I can't excuse his actions the other night and there are things for us to work through, but I turn to look at him, his eyes flickering in the firelight, and I know in that moment no one has or possibly ever will, love me like he does.

We start to kiss, and right on cue my phone starts to buzz, and the 'new' Alex pulls away. 'Do you want to get that?'

'No. I don't,' I say, and reach for him. Soon we're making love urgently, the snow falling thick outside, the fire flickering inside, and the two of us finally coming together, erasing all the doubts and fears and hurt.

'Are you happy?' Alex asks, afterwards.

'Yes, this is exactly what I dreamed of,' I say, as we lie together on the floor in front of the fire.

He pours the rest of the wine, and pads into the kitchen to get us something to eat from the hamper.

'Bring it all,' I call through, 'I'm starving.'

'Let me at least put it on a plate, you heathen.' He laughs, and I hear him unwrapping the contents, no doubt inspecting every jar, scrutinising every ounce of pâté.

That's my Alex, I think – and like how it sounds – *my* Alex.

Knowing he'll be a while, I idly check my phone, to see if there's any news about Chloe, but I'm irritated to see loads of missed calls and messages from bloody Jas. Even *she* wouldn't usually call so much when I'm away, especially on a supposedly romantic weekend. Perhaps, as I haven't got back to her, she's worried Alex might have told me about her trying to kiss him. She's probably panicking that I've finally realised what she's up to. I open the latest message – which has an attachment.

Please tell me you're okay? Text me. I'm worried. I just found this – remember the night we got your profile on to the app? We were in the wine bar, we took selfies? Well, look at this one.

Puzzled, I open up the attachment, and see me and Jas leering into the camera, all lip gloss and cocktails. At first, I think she's simply sending the pic to remind me of some of the good times we've had as friends. I wonder if it's damage limitation in case Alex has told me she tried to get off with him. But looking again, I see she's put a red ring around something in the background – and the closer I look, the more unbelievable it is.

Alex, the man I wouldn't even go on a first date with until several weeks after the photo was taken, is standing behind us – and he's looking straight at me.

CHAPTER THIRTY-SEVEN

I look at the photo again and again, completely freaked out. I instinctively know to keep this to myself for now, but Alex is calling to me about 'the deli feast' being almost ready, so I tell him I'm popping to the bathroom, where I lock the door and text Jas back.

WTF? Why was he there? I don't get it.

I wait for her response.

I Know! Weird. Looks like he was stalking you before your first date? Soooo creepy. Are u ok?

I'm about to text back, but where do I start? I don't know what this means, but I know the bubble has definitely been burst now. Another text comes through from Jas.

Do u want me to call the police? she texts.

NO! All fine I'm sure. It's not a crime to photo bomb. But will ask him about it.

I don't believe it's all fine, I just want to stop her worrying so she'll stop texting and I can think. Could it be a coincidence that he was there that night?

'Hannah? Where are you, darling?' I jump at Alex's voice. He's standing outside the bathroom, I can hear his hand brushing up and down the door.

I flush the toilet, turn my phone on silent and put it in my jeans pocket.

'Be with you in a minute, Alex,' I call, unsure of how I feel, unsure who to trust.

I run the taps to buy more time, and see his toilet bag on the side, the one that used to have Helen's scribbled photo hidden inside. I don't know why, but I feel down the side of the bag to see if it's still there, but my fingers touch something else, something cloth. I slowly pull it from the inside pocket where it's hidden, and hold it in my hand. It's a napkin. But not any napkin, I recognise the lipstick – it's my napkin from our first date, the one I saw him put in his pocket as we left the restaurant. I feel further down into the bag, and there's the coffee spoon, my coffee spoon. Are these mementos – just reminders of a wonderful evening, or something else? I can almost hear Jas's voice, 'He's a serial killer and those are his trophies. GET OUT NOW!'

I am terrified, but know I have to come out of the bathroom, so I compose myself, and try to wander casually into the living room. The fire's still blazing, my glass of wine has been refreshed, there's a platter of delicious food on the little coffee table, and Alex is there by the fire. I take it all in for a moment, this could have been so different, so wonderful, the start of a life I've always dreamed of. I still want that so badly that, against my instincts, I dare to wonder if there's still a chance for me to grasp at this future. Perhaps there's a perfectly innocent explanation for why Alex is in the background of a photograph of me and my friend – before I met him? I can't think of one, but in a last-chance bid for a happy ending, I brace myself, aware that what I'm about to say might change everything.

I sit down next to him, and cross my legs. I want to be in control, I don't want him fobbing me off.

'Alex—' I start.

'Yeah?' He drags his eyes away from the fire and reaches out for my hand, but I pull it away quickly. He looks alarmed. 'What is it?' He sits up, and looks into my face. 'Hannah?'

I take out my phone, open the message and show him the photo.

He takes the phone from my hand. Looks from me to the photo, puzzled.

'It's from Jas,' I explain.

'Oh, I see, *another* text from Jas. What's she trying to do *now*, split us up?' he snarls.

'You tell me. That picture was taken before we met. What the hell, Alex?'

He's studying the picture, really closely, like he's trying to think of a reason.

'Please don't try and tell me it's a coincidence, because I'm not an idiot,' I say.

'Yes, okay it is me, of course it's me – I saw you that night, thought you were the cutest girl I'd ever seen,' he says, staring intensely at the photo.

I'm taken aback by his honesty – but then how can he even try and deny he was there?

'So, you're admitting it? You *stalked* me?'

'You really do spend too much time with Jas – she's so dramatic.' He's shaking his head.

'Just *tell* me what you were doing there, Alex,' I say, ignoring his bitching about Jas.

He sighs, and looks at the platter of food. 'She's spoiled everything. Again.'

I don't respond to this, just continue to glare at him, waiting for the explanation.

He sighs. 'Hannah, you want me to trust you, but when are you going to trust me? I'd gone for a drink. I was actually looking for Helen. I'd heard she'd come back from Scotland, and thought she might be in The Orange Tree. But she wasn't there, and I was about to leave – and you walked in.'

'And...?'

'You sat with Jas – your annoying friend at the bar. She was loud and kept ordering too many drinks, and you seemed lovely, really pretty, but you looked a bit sad. I overheard you both talking about a dating app so... I bought a drink, and sat near enough to hear everything you said. Telling you this now does, I'll admit, sound a bit creepy...'

'You bet it does!'

'But it really wasn't. It was just an overheard conversation in a bar – and by the time you'd set up your profile, I was in love.'

'On the rebound more like,' I say, imagining him going to the bar that night hoping to see Helen, and when she wasn't there, attaching himself to the first blonde woman who looked vaguely like her. Me!

'No, I promise I wasn't on the rebound, we'd parted months before. I just saw you and felt relieved, invigorated. It was like I knew because of you that I could love someone other than Helen – it was liberating.' His eyes seem to sparkle at the memory of this.

'You can't know you're going to love someone you see in a bar,' I murmur, unsure how I feel about this.

'I did. I'm a romantic. I believe in love at first sight, and that's what it was with you. And when I overheard you talking about Meet Your Match, I downloaded my photo and bio and left the rest to fate.'

'But that isn't fate, Alex. You heard me tell Jas what I wanted in life, I remember it clearly. I listed it – a kind boyfriend who'd give me attention, a yellow Labrador... three kids... weekends in Devon.' I look around the room. 'And here we are.'

'Yeah, but, Hannah, you're making it sound sneaky, but we fell in love. The ends justified the means – I simply used the information I had to help things along,' he says with such sincerity, as if he really doesn't understand what the problem is.

'But, Alex, it's *dishonest*! You let me think we wanted the same things – but you'd just copied everything I'd said. Love isn't a shopping list – it's about two people being honest and open with each other, and you're not, you never have been,' I cry, realising from the start this relationship has been a lie.

'How can you *say* that?' His eyes are pleading with me.

'So many reasons, and apart from hanging around the bar before you knew me, ticking off my list, there was also that small matter of you not telling me you were MARRIED!' I yell out of frustration and anger and hurt. 'There are always so many layers – so many lies with you, I can't believe I've let this go on so long, just thinking you'll change, that we have a chance.'

'Hannah, don't say that. I just sometimes find it hard to tell you everything, because I think you'll fall out of love with me. Please don't end this – please! I just want to love you, and for you to love me back,' he's saying, grabbing both my arms with his hands, making me face him, trying to make me look at him. 'And I didn't lie about wanting the same things as you do – for the record, I really *love* yellow Labradors, I want three kids. And Devon seems pretty lovely.' He's breathless, his face is in mine, his hands still gripping both my upper arms.

'You've never been to Devon before?' I say into the thick, tense silence.

'No, not until today, but that doesn't matter. I know I'll love the place as much as you do. I already love it as much as you do.'

'That's not the point though… you lied, you told me you loved it here.' I try, but he's not listening, he's bearing down. His eyes are on mine, but he's not *seeing* me.

'I bet she couldn't wait to send you that photo. She's been trying to split us up all along.'

'Alex, why aren't you getting this? It isn't about Jas, it's about *you*. I've spent the last few months believing I love you, wanting to be in love so much, that I've ignored the red flags.'

'There are no red flags. And I've told you, I'll change, just tell me what to do,' he urges. 'What do you want, Hannah? I'll do *anything* to keep us together – I can't live without you.'

'I thought I loved you, Alex, but now I don't know. Perhaps I just fell for the man I met on our first date. But I'm not sure he exists.'

Tears are forming in his eyes, and I know this is killing him, it's killing me too, because I do still love him, I can't just turn it off.

'I can understand how finding out that I saw you before and never said anything—'

'And lied about dogs and... Devon and so much more,' I interrupt him to say.

'But, Hannah, think about it, if you had a Facebook page, I might have looked on there and seen similar things, your likes and dislikes, your dreams. I didn't do anything harmful, or creepy – honestly.'

'But the fact you didn't tell me makes me feel that I can't trust you, Alex. I feel like I start to trust you and then something else comes along and all that trust goes again.'

'Hannah, please, please don't let this tear us apart, it's just Jas being jealous and twisted and trying to make me look weird. I would have told you about seeing you in the wine bar...'

'Would you? You mean, like everything else you didn't tell me?'

He looks down, starts caressing my hand. I don't respond, I just stare ahead into the fire that's now smoking rather than flickering.

'I'm going to make pasta for dinner,' he says. 'You'll love it. I thought it would be nice to hole up in here, eat ourselves stupid, drink wine and lock the world out. It's going to be perfect, Hannah, just you and me.'

He hasn't heard a word I've said. He thinks if he makes everything cosy and cooks a meal it will erase all the problems. I used to think that too, and as someone who once dreamed of a home and a family, I believed that a future with a loving partner in a beautiful house was worth everything. But it isn't, and all the cosy nights in and home-cooked meals in the world aren't going to smooth away all the bumps in our relationship. I can feel the pressure of his hand on mine, and glance at the wooden cottage door that he made sure to lock when we got back from the beach. And I wonder where the key is – and what he'd do if I tried to leave.

CHAPTER THIRTY-EIGHT

Alex is in the kitchen preparing the pasta bake when I text Jas back.

I'm not sure what's happening here. I'm ok, but A didn't take photo too well. Will stay in touch x

I go into the kitchen, where Alex is now slicing peppers and humming to himself, it's the picture of domestic bliss. But that's all it is – a picture.

'God, I love this place,' he says, as I walk in.

'Me too,' I say, trying to sound like I mean it while watching the knife go into the peppers like butter. 'Just going to the bathroom,' I add, leaving the kitchen and heading upstairs to see where he's put the front door keys. I know from experience, he usually puts his house keys in his jeans pocket, but he's wearing jogging bottoms with no pockets, so the keys must be somewhere. I pick up his jeans, folded neatly on the bedroom chair, I push my hand into his pocket, and there they are! I slip them into my hoodie pocket, while trying not to creak the bedroom floor.

'You know, I was thinking—' he calls from down in the kitchen.

I drop the jeans and head to the bathroom, flushing the toilet so he thinks that's where I've been. I don't want him to know I'm in the bedroom, he might put two and two together. He knows I'm not happy, and he's hoping bloody pasta bake's going to change everything, but it isn't.

'Hang on…' I call, coming down the stairs. 'What were you saying?'

He turns round as I walk into the kitchen and smiles at me. 'There you are. I was just saying, babe – we could move out here, buy a nice little cottage, raise our three kids by the sea.'

I nod. 'That sounds good,' I say, but inside I'm screaming NO!

He laughs, almost to himself. 'I mean, we've already got the dog, we're picking Kevin up next week… I make dreams come true, don't I, babe?'

'You certainly do.' I smile, and head back to the living room slowly, as if I'm just pottering, but once in there, I push the keys under the sofa seat.

I don't know what to do next. He also has the keys to the car, and God knows where they are. I'm wondering how quickly I could get outside and get the car started before he realised and came after me, when I pick up my phone to see several missed calls and a text from Jas in the last few minutes. Christ, why did I leave my phone here? He obviously came in when I was upstairs and he must have seen the first few lines of her text, which says:

Get out of there asap!

I can hear the sound of chopping and Alex singing to himself in the kitchen, so I quickly open her message. She's sent me a news link, and for a moment my heart stops, thinking it might be about Chloe, that the police have arrested whoever gave her the drugs, or, worse still, that she hasn't pulled through. But when I open the link, it's a news report on a man being *killed* outside The Orange Tree wine bar on Wednesday night. *Killed?* He turned away the first ambulance that came, insisting he was fine, and walked home, but was later found and taken to hospital, where he died of his injuries.

I look through into the kitchen at Alex still humming. Does he *know*?

I read on, apparently police are seeking a man who fled the scene. I'd never told Jas about that night, and Alex said he'd seen his policeman friend, who said the guy was fine.

I immediately text Jas back.

How did you know?

The guy said it was a businessman in a suit who attacked him. I guessed. You were quite jumpy the next day. I knew something was up. Now you HAVE to tell the police. x

Just as I put down the phone, Alex walks in. I'm sitting among the cushions by the fire and he comes and stands over me.

'Who's on the phone, Hannah?'

'No one.'

'Must be *someone*?' He's smiling, but it's frozen on his face. He's still holding the knife he was chopping the peppers with.

'Do you *know*?' I ask, looking up at him.

'Know what?'

'That he's dead – the guy you punched.'

He takes a deep breath, then nods, slowly. 'Yeah, I know. It was on the news this morning…'

I gasp. 'I only just saw it. You have to call the police.'

'I can't. Hannah, you have to understand – I'd lose everything – including you.'

'You've already lost me,' I say.

'No, I haven't. I need to work it out, but just give me some time. As soon as I knew I called the cottage company and booked the cottage for another two weeks. In a different name.' Then he looks at me with such a strange expression. 'Please tell me you haven't told that idiot friend of yours where we are.'

'No, I haven't,' I lie. 'But we can't hide here. We need to call the police.'

'We can't – we just need to lie low and it'll all die down… No one knows it was me, we left before anyone else turned up. Hannah, we can have Christmas here,' he says excitedly, as if nothing's happened.

'Alex, are you out of your mind? You're talking about Christmas – a man is dead, you *killed* him. This is something you can't hide from, the police will find you.'

'It's okay, don't worry. If they do ever find me, I'll say I hit him because he was trying to assault you. I saved you, and you can vouch for me, say how scared you were – you could even say he roughed you up a bit. Then we'll say you were so distressed I had to get you away from the scene.' He says this like he's reading a well-prepared script. 'But it's an outside chance that anyone will ever know it was me,' he says, holding out his hands as if he's waiting for me to congratulate him on his story.

'Whoa, hang on,' I say, standing up. 'That's all lies and you know it.'

He lifts both hands as if to calm me down, but given he's got a kitchen knife in one of them it's having the opposite effect. I don't dare take my eyes off it as he talks to me slowly, as if I'm a child who doesn't understand.

'Hannah, listen to me, we have to keep to the story here – and if we say it was done in self-defence, everything will be fine. I'll get away with it.'

'But it's *lying*, Alex, it's *perjury* – we have to tell the truth. You didn't mean to kill him, it was an accident.'

'It's not a solution,' he says, beginning to pace the floor. 'They'll do me for manslaughter. I'll still be locked up for years. I won't see you, I won't be able to look after you,' he says, sounding like a child who's about to lose his favourite toy. 'Someone might take you away from me, or you might leave me.'

I get up from the floor where I've been sitting by the fire, and sit down on the sofa. When I'm sure he's not looking, I reach under the seat cushion, keeping my eyes on the glint of knife still in his hand.

'You're not going to leave me, are you, Hannah?' he says, alarmed, as he suddenly stops pacing and turns to me.

'I… No, no I'm not,' I say, discreetly retrieving the keys while still keeping my eyes on the knife – it's down by his thigh. He's twisting it with his fingers, and I'm only too aware that one swift movement, one wrong word – and the knife could be in my chest.

I have the front door keys in the palm of my hand, but he's watching me intently.

Suddenly a buzzer goes off in the kitchen, making us both jump.

'The pasta,' he murmurs almost to himself and turns away for a split second.

I see my chance, and make a mad dash for the door. I push the key in hard, it's stiff, and takes all my strength to turn it and then heave the wooden door open. I can't believe I did it, and I'm yelping as I get through the door. But Alex is shouting my name and running towards me. Just as he gets to me and tries to grab me, I slam the door in his face – hard. I hear him shout out in surprise and pain, but I'm already running through biting wind in slippers and a thin jumper.

It's dark and freezing, but I don't care. I feel nothing, just an urgent need to escape, to survive. I just need to get far enough away from him and call the police. I'm heading out onto the main road now, a coastal road, where the wind is bitter and relentless, but I keep running. I'm not used to this exertion and, eventually, just a few hundred yards down the road, I have to stop, even though he may be close behind me. I stand behind the trees on the side of the road, my hands on my knees, my breath short and rasping. I'm holding my phone, ready to use it, but suddenly, my stomach tilts and I vomit into the frozen grass. I wait in silence. The road's empty and black in front of me, and behind me there's only the whispering of trees. After a little while, when I'm sure there's no sign of Alex, I click on my phone and try to call the police, but I've got no signal.

The wind's whistling, and the little spots of frozen rain are now snow, landing from a great height, a silent blanket on the world. It's then I hear him calling my name, it's softened by the snow, but I hear the loss, the desperation, the grief in the darkness.

He has the knife and I remember his words, when we were happy and in love and the world was a different place. 'People do dangerous things when they're scared of losing what they love, Hannah.'

Who knows what he'll do now? So I stay by the tree, waiting, his voice faint in the distance. He can't find me, and like a lost child he's becoming more desperate, more distraught. Then, suddenly, I see a car in the distance. Is it more dangerous to stay here by the trees with no hope, and die of cold, or wait for Alex to find me and take me back to the cottage, and hold me there in some horrible parody of love that turns into weeks, years? Or do I run out into the road and wave the car down?

I make a snap decision. It isn't even a rational decision made by my brain, my body just shoots out into the road, my arms waving. I'm crying, and calling for help. As the car approaches, the headlights block my view, and for a moment I think it might be Alex coming from the other direction in the car, to fool me. I hold my breath, knowing my fate is in the car, but then I hear Alex in the distance calling my name again.

I run towards the car. I know he's behind me, I just hope who-ever's driving lets me in and drives off without asking questions. If we don't get away, Alex might attack them too. He's already killed one man and now I know that he'd do it all over again.

The car stops, and the driver's door opens, and it's Harry, waving. 'Hannah, Hannah is that you, mate?'

I almost collapse with surprise and relief. 'Harry, Harry.' I am sobbing now, and he runs round to the passenger door and helps me in. Climbing into that warm car is the best feeling, I feel weak from running and crying and cold.

'I've been up and down this road looking everywhere for you.'

'Thank God. But how did you…?' Then I laugh. 'Jas?'

'She called me, said she was worried about you.'

'And you and Gemma are in Somerset this weekend?'

'Yeah, it took me less than an hour to get here, then another half an hour to find the cottage, but no one was there.'

'Jas knew something wasn't right.' I gasp, still out of breath from the cold and the running and the fear.

'Yeah, she called me to tell me about the… the fight… the guy died.'

'Yeah, I don't—'

'And that photo of Alex watching you guys in The Orange Tree – Jesus!'

'I know, it was so weird that he was there…' I don't finish the sentence. I can't even begin to explain Alex to a nice, sane person like Harry who doesn't stalk someone to become his girlfriend or kill people outside wine bars.

He pats my arm. 'It's okay, Hannah, we don't have to talk about it.'

I'm flooded with relief. 'I can't thank you enough, Harry. If you hadn't come, I might have… I was so scared…' I start crying, and I know he finds emotions a bit much because he's a guy in his twenties, but he turns to me and talks calmly.

'Hannah, please don't cry. I hate it when girls cry. I don't know what the hell to do.'

This makes me smile in spite of everything, and I rest my head on his shoulder, and squeeze his arm, desperate for a comforting hug. He has one hand on the wheel, and is hugging me back as best he can, when a car suddenly pulls up in front of us, and Alex gets out.

'He's got a knife,' I squeal to Harry, who central-locks the car.

'It's okay, we've got this. He's not hurting anyone,' he says calmly, never taking his eyes from Alex, a dark figure silhouetted in the headlights, arms in the air.

He walks closer, comes around to the passenger window, and it's then he sees Harry. The realisation makes his mouth fall open in surprise, and he starts banging hard on my window, as if he's hitting me in the face.

I flinch and yell, 'Drive, drive,' and Harry puts his foot down, swerving on the icy road, the snow adding extra slide as the wheels spin, giving Alex time to get back in his car. I watch him in the side mirror, shouting at Harry to 'go, go,' and eventually we start to move and slide along the ground, with Alex tearing after us.

Harry is as scared as me, and driving so fast I'm worried for our lives. On the coast road, the sheer drop is terrifying, but on black ice, it's treacherous. We can't see a thing in the dark, and Harry's having trouble keeping the car on the road. We turn a bend and almost go over the edge, and Harry's so frightened he pulls up at the next visible gap in the road, with Alex right behind us.

'Harry – we can't stop here.' I glance behind me to see Alex pulling up a few feet away. 'Harry! He's getting out of the car! Please drive,' I'm begging him, terrified.

'No,' he says calmly, turning off the engine, the lights. 'I'm going to talk to him.' And he opens his door, the icy wind whips through the car, cold and dangerous, and he steps out into the darkness.

'NO!' I'm yelling at the top of my voice. But he's gone, and has closed the car door behind him and locked the doors. I watch him in the rear-view mirror walking back a few yards to where I presume Alex is waiting. I can't see him, and now I can't see Harry either.

I sit and wait, wondering if I should have got out of the car and helped Harry. I know he wanted to talk, but Alex may have turned it into a fight, and I've seen how angry he gets. Two of us might have overpowered Alex, but on his own, I can't imagine Harry standing much of a chance if Alex starts on him. Harry's always said he's a lover not a fighter, and whereas he thinks talking will work with Alex, I'm not convinced. I hope to God it isn't Alex who returns and finds me locked in the car, a sitting target. I check my phone to call the police, but there's still no signal out here. I have nothing to protect me, and if Alex hurts Harry, and returns with the knife, I know my life is over.

Eventually, I see someone in the rear mirror. They are walking towards the car, and I swear I see the flash of metal. It's Alex, he must have stabbed Harry and now he's going to get me. I duck down, lying my head on the gearstick, unable to breathe I'm so scared. I hear the thud of the lock being opened by the key fob, and hear myself gasp, then I hear a whimpering noise, and realise it's me. The door opens, and a blast of freezing wind whips into the car and I slowly lift my head to see who it is.

'You okay?' It's Harry, and as he climbs in, I grab him and hug him too tight.

He hugs me back and we sit there for a long time just holding each other, as I sob into his chest.

Eventually, we pull apart. 'Did he hurt you?' I ask, but he doesn't answer, just sits with his head on the steering wheel and for a few moments he seems shaken.

'Harry, what happened, where is he?' I say, looking behind the car – my relief was temporary, I'm now scared again.

Harry turns on the interior light, he's visibly upset. 'Hannah, I can't believe you were with that guy. You should have heard the stuff he said, the creepy way he talks – the things, the terrible things he was planning to do to you in that cottage.'

My stomach plummets. I'm not wholly surprised, but it's still not easy to hear. I look behind again to see where Alex is; he may still be planning those terrible things.

'Let's go,' I say. 'He might try and ram us off the road if he feels he's got nothing to lose now.'

'No, he won't, I promise you. I've had a serious talk to him, I think I made him see sense. From what he said, he's more likely to take his *own* life.' He sighs.

'Oh no.' I start to cry, even after everything I don't want something terrible to happen to Alex. I won't be in his life, but I don't want him to die.

'Hey, hey, I'm sure he'll be fine. It's you I'm worried about,' Harry says.

'I just… I don't know… I can't imagine what might have happened if Jas hadn't called you.'

He nods. 'Yeah, yeah. Hey, don't cry,' he says gently, and wipes away my tears with the cuff of his jumper. 'I called the police, they're on their way. We have to wait for them here, you warm enough?' he asks, and I nod, but still he takes off his coat and puts it round me.

'Thank you, I owe you and Jas such a lot.'

'A lot of *alcohol*.'

I smile and grab his hand, I just need to feel the warmth of another person. 'I didn't know him – I thought I did, we were talking about marriage. But he's a stranger to me.'

'Well, you dodged a bullet there, mate.' He smiles, and starts the car to keep us warm. 'I've explained as much as I can to the police on the phone, but when they get here, they'll want to talk to you.'

'Yes, of course. Do you think Alex will make a run for it?' I ask.

'Nah, he's broken.' Harry sighed. 'He knows what he has to do. I left him sitting by the side of the road, he knows the police are coming, I reckon he'll go quietly.'

A few minutes later, we hear sirens and flashing lights.

'It's all over, Hannah.' Harry smiles. 'The police can deal with him now. And after we've talked to the police, I'll get you home.'

'I feel such a fool, Harry.'

'Don't,' he says. 'You just fell in love with the wrong guy – let's hope next time it'll be the right one.'

CHAPTER THIRTY-NINE

Alex meant what he'd said about not being able to live without me, and today I said goodbye to him for the last time. I'm still finding it hard to come to terms with what happened, but it seems that on realising it was over, on that cold, snowy night, just days before Christmas, he took his own life.

Harry and I waited, parked on the road, until the police arrived, assuming Alex would still be further down the road where Harry left him. But when they got there, the police couldn't find him, and said he must have made a run for it. Until the next day, when a body was recovered by a lifeboat crew at the bottom of Salcombe Cliffs. Harry said he just knew the way he was talking that he'd come to the end, but although I knew he was desperate, the shock of hearing Alex had taken his own life still left me feeling sad and guilty. I never realised just how troubled or tormented he was. I thought I loved him, but I didn't really know him. I just wish I could have helped him.

It's been so difficult and sad trying to sort out Alex's life in death. Each day I learn something else about him, proving how little I really knew him. Sadly, it seems that I'm the closest person to him, as he would have been the closest to me. We were little more than children without roots, both searching for a family and a home, and believing we'd found that in each other.

I found details for his sister, Lara, and invited her and anyone else from his family to come along to the funeral. Lara wrote back to me saying he'd been deeply affected by the death of their mother and had always struggled emotionally. She said her father was too ill to attend the funeral, and she couldn't leave him so neither would be there. This broke my heart, to think the closest person at his funeral would be me, someone he knew for less than a year.

The funeral was horrible, and to make it worse, throughout the service I was aware of Helen standing like the black widow at the back of the church. I barely heard the vicar's words, I just wanted to get it over with. I was terrified she might blame me for his death and have some fresh vendetta against me. The last thing I needed was the vengeful ex-wife hunting me down.

Me, Jas, Harry – and of course Helen – were the only people at the funeral, which was heart-breaking. Even Alex's former colleagues didn't come along. Again, the fact he was wanted for the death of a young man didn't exactly have them flocking to celebrate his life, or commiserate his death. I understand that, but still, it was upsetting to think his life had meant so little to so few.

After the funeral, Jas stood by me like a security guard as Helen approached. I held my breath, dreading a confrontation.

'So you're Hannah,' she said, holding out her hand.

I cautiously offered mine and we smiled awkwardly.

'Thanks for coming.' I shrugged, not really knowing what to say.

'I know Alex could be a little – impulsive, but I was surprised to hear about what happened. I mean, suicide? It's just not him, he always had such optimism… blind optimism really. How does someone like Alex take his own life?' she said, confused.

'Yes, it's shocking what darkness people have inside,' I said, amazed that Helen appeared to be so warm and friendly.

'I hope all that stupidness with you has stopped now?' Jas went straight in, no subtleties.

'What? I don't know what you're talking about,' Helen replied.

I don't know how good an actress she is, so I wasn't sure if her confusion was real.

'The roses with the note, the heavy-breathing phone calls, the threats you made about hurting me,' I said. 'I understand, I know you wanted him back, but you made my life a misery, Helen... and his too.'

She clutched her chest, a look of absolute horror on her face. 'Oh, Hannah, you have this all wrong,' she said, shaking her head vigorously. 'I never made any threats, or calls... roses?'

'But you *told* him... you chased me through Worcester... you called out my name, you—'

'Yes, because I wanted to talk to you.' She still seems completely blindsided, and she's either a brilliant actress – or she's telling the truth.

'You invited him for lunch, told him that you still had feelings... didn't you?' I ask, not sure any more.

'Yes. I'd asked Alex if he and I could meet for lunch a few months ago, but not because I wanted to get back with him. God, no. I was relieved when he said he'd met someone. He showed me photos of you on his phone, he seemed so happy. I didn't want him back. He was a good guy, kind and caring – but too caring, he wanted all of me, and what started as a lovely relationship became claustrophobic.'

I listen, realising she felt the same as me. She too had been seduced by his apparent warmth and kindness into a relationship she didn't want.

'He became too controlling, so possessive,' she said. 'I hate to say it given the circumstances, but I never wanted to see him again after I'd walked out – I had to escape, some of my clothes were still in the wardrobe. I just ran.'

It reminded me of how I felt that day in the cottage. I just ran too.

'So when you saw me in Worcester that day, why did you want to talk to me?' I asked.

'I thought you might be able to help by convincing him to move out of the house.'

I don't understand, and I must look puzzled as she suddenly smiles. 'Ah, I get it... he had to make you think I wanted him back and I was *threatening* you. He had to make you scared of me because he didn't want to risk us ever talking.'

'I don't understand...'

'He was hiding stuff from you. He did the same with me.'

'Yes, he wasn't always completely honest... but why did you want me to get him to sell the house?' I asked, still not sure I believed what she was saying.

She shook her head. 'It wasn't about *selling* the house – my friend wanted her house *back*.'

'But he bought the house from you when you split.'

Again, Helen shook her head, and rolled her eyes. 'No, the house wasn't ours, it belongs to my friend from uni. She had this great job working abroad and let me rent it from her while she was away, but then I left Alex, and she allowed him to continue to rent it on his own. She didn't want the hassle of re-letting, especially to someone she didn't know. Besides, he was the perfect tenant. She knew he wouldn't trash the place; quite the opposite, he was a neat freak. So while she was away he was the perfect tenant – all her stuff was in that house, you see. Her crockery, photos – even her books – we were just staying there, really. We didn't buy a stick of furniture. Probably as well, because when we split up there was nothing to share, no mine and yours and messy money matters, just the divorce.

Anyway, my friend's job ended at the start of November, and she moved back to the UK and wanted to move back in, but he'd refused. So I arranged to meet Alex that day to tell him he *had* to move out – it was all rather embarrassing, her being my friend and all. Thing is, she'd already been round a few times, and he wouldn't even open the door. He'd not only changed the locks, he'd put double locks on everything, even the garage. My friend knows some dodgy people who'd have made mincemeat of Alex, but despite several threats he just refused to move out. But when I saw him, he said you loved the house and he wanted to stay there for you. I had a feeling he might have told you it was his, which is why I hoped that, if I could catch you in Worcester that day, I could ask you to get involved, make him move out. But typical Alex wanted to make everything perfect even if it was all a façade – he was desperate to make a nest, even if it wasn't his nest to make.'

I was shocked at the revelation. I realise now that the phone calls, the notes, were all Alex trying to scare me off contacting Helen. Perhaps even the earlier incidents before I knew of her existence, the smell of perfume in my car and the roses, were him preparing the ground, planning to set her up as the jealous ex.

This also explained why he always double-locked the front door when we were home, why he was looking through the glass that first night I went for dinner. Later I'd assumed it was because he was worried Helen 'our stalker' might turn up on the doorstep. But I believe Helen, and it looks like he was scared the house owner would send someone to evict him, or hurt him even.

'We should have talked sooner, Helen.'

'He wouldn't have allowed that.' She smiled. 'It seems like every moment was meticulously planned in his relationships with both of us.'

'Even after I'd left he still couldn't let you go,' I said, knowing if he'd lived he wouldn't have given up on me easily. I told her about him using a phone app to know where we both were at all times, and how he'd listened to my list of likes and used them on our first date.

'Yeah, that's Alex.' She nodded. 'Creepy that he knew where we were, but he had to keep us apart, he was living so many lies. He was like a blank canvas, and it may sound harsh but when I was with him, he never seemed to have his own thoughts, opinions, just seemed to echo mine. He even started drinking gin because that's what I drank, he said it was "our" drink, but I once overheard him telling a friend that he loathed gin.'

I thought about '*our*' drink, the bottles of Merlot we shared and he professed to love, and wondered again if anything about Alex was real.

'He seemed like the perfect partner at first.' She sighed. 'We had some good times, but looking back, from early on I felt like he was testing my feelings for him.'

I thought for a moment and realised what she meant. 'Yeah, our first date was wonderful, but he made me wait before he asked me on a second date, not long, just enough to introduce some doubt,' I said as a memory came flooding back. 'And he was late for our second date, and I had to wait ages in the freezing rain.'

'Yep, that was Alex.' She smiled. 'I mean what a test – keeping you waiting in bad weather, just to see if you like him enough to stay. He was probably watching you from across the street.'

'God, now you come to mention it – he said "where's your umbrella?" like he knew I'd had one while I was waiting for him. So he must have been hanging around,' I said, surprised at the lengths he went to.

'That is classic Alex,' she said. 'He kept me waiting at the registry office, and let slip later he'd been there an hour before. Just his way of making sure he'd really got you.' She chuckled at the memory.

'I think it was because he felt he wasn't good enough, that he couldn't believe anyone really cared about him,' I said.

'Oh, Alex – he wanted so much to please, didn't he? I think it stemmed from his childhood. His mum died when he was young, his father was very cruel, you know.'

I nodded, acknowledging this flake of truth in the middle of all the lies, and I'll never forget Helen suddenly looking serious, and touching my arm. 'But Hannah, you know what? I loved him, and in spite of everything, there'll always be a little place in my heart where Alex is.'

And we both smiled at each other in recognition of this, because, in the end, Alex just wanted what any of us want, to love and be loved – he just went about it the wrong way. His lies were usually an attempt to make things seem better, but in the end they just caused more hurt.

Sadly, I've discovered even more of Alex's lies since his death. It turns out that he wasn't actually a lawyer, he was a legal assistant and he'd been let go from his job just a few weeks after we met. It seemed he lost focus, made some mistakes and regularly didn't turn up for work without even letting them know. I often wondered how he'd found the time to work on complex legal cases and still cook lavish meals when I came home in the evening, but it seems he'd basically abandoned his job to look after me. With no income in his last few months, he died owing a fortune in credit cards, spending on extravagant dinners out, the renovated gym garage, home office, and romantic weekend away. It makes me sad to think he did all that for me, I always wanted someone who cared, but Alex cared too much.

Saying goodbye to Alex was hard, and I miss him, but I don't miss the constant texts and calls, the way he seemed to dislike all my friends, was jealous of anyone I gave attention to.

'He really didn't like me, did he?' Jas said the other day.

'You never liked him either,' I pointed out. 'I know you were only looking out for me, but I used to be irritated by your comments about red flags and always saying I should be careful. Somehow you saw through him, I guess you were far more intuitive than I was,' I said, but then again, I was in love, and love is blind. I saw nothing until it was too late.

I've never told Jas what Alex said about her trying to kiss him. I feel like there's no point in bringing it up now, it will only hurt her. We're rebuilding our friendship now and besides, I trust Jas again, I doubt very much she came onto my boyfriend, it's not what best friends do. Me and Jas are as strong as ever and we're back on the Porn Star Martinis every Tuesday night down The Orange Tree – though we're not doing any online dating for now.

After Devon, I even spent Christmas with Jas. It was a little difficult, thinking about how things could have been with Alex, but Jas did her best to take my mind off things. And work too has been keeping me busy. I go to the hospital every day to check in on Chloe. After Alex's death, seeing Chloe is still a struggle, but I'm determined to be there for her. Carol, her mum, seems to have gone back to her old ways now Pete's back on the scene and checks in maybe once a week, so I feel even more committed to being there for Chloe. I know it's going to be a long road back for her, and she's going to need someone by her side, someone who isn't going to let her down or walk away. Alex and I both had difficult starts in life and it shaped what happened for us both and I want Chloe to have a chance in life, and the support and guidance I never had. She's been in the coma three weeks now, and it's not looking too good, but, as the doctor said, 'miracles do happen' and I'm hoping for a miracle.

CHAPTER FORTY

I've always loved her. Beautiful, blonde Hannah with the long legs and the infectious giggle. She thought we were just friends, but I knew one day we'd be together, I just had to wait.

They all wanted her, but none of them loved her like I did. Like I do. I was always there for her, waiting in the shadows. I'd stay late at the office, follow her home, make sure she was safe.

When she finished with Tom, I was ready to leap in there, but he kept calling her, and I was worried he might wear her down. 'I feel so guilty,' she kept saying. 'He's done nothing wrong.' But let's face it, he'd done *nothing*, period. My elation at their split turned to fear that she'd bump into him again and they'd end up back together. Hannah can be quite easily manipulated, and I knew he wanted her back. Why wouldn't he? So I decided to put a spanner in the works and sent everyone at the council a global email from a group of women Tom had 'sexually harassed', saying we wanted the council to take action. It was all very strident; I captured the essence of enraged #Metoo women foaming at the mouth and demanding his imminent death. I ended on a flourish, saying he was a danger to women and we were all taking legal action. I figured if he lost his job at the council, he'd leave the area and go back to where he came from.

Apparently within council walls, my email went nuclear; everyone was talking about it. My friend who works there said it was the talk of the place. I didn't have long to wait for the fallout, because Tom turned up at our office, he was a mess, really pissed off and angry accusing Hannah of sending the email. Hannah was upset, but he was almost crying. really showed himself up. It was all very embarrassing. Apparently, the council had to suspend him while they investigated, and for a while it looked like he might be sacked, but sadly, with no proof, no outraged victims prepared to speak, and no real evidence, he was kept on. It wasn't a complete failure though because she and the rest of the office had witnessed his rage, and after that, she assumed the heavy-breathing phone calls and anything else weird was Tom. Which meant she avoided and feared him, so it worked, even if it wasn't quite as I'd planned.

But seeing her, watching the way she licked her lips, the way she threw her head back when she laughed, and the way she looked at me over her coffee cup, was agony. So near and yet so far. But I told myself I had to be patient, didn't want to make any sudden moves and freak her out. But watching her type, brushing past her in the kitchen, breathing in her perfume, shampoo and sunshine – sometimes I'd stand by her desk and chat, just so I could breathe her in. It was like a sickness, and sometimes it felt so bad, the only way I could feel better was to be close to her. Some nights I'd go and stand across the road from her flat, just looking up at her window, usually in the middle of the night.

I sometimes looked after a friend's dog – I'm good with pets, and I'd take the dog for a walk late. It could be raining, snowing, whatever, and I'd drag that little dog round to Hannah's.

Once, someone hadn't closed the outer door properly so I got inside her building and stood outside her door for a long time, just pressing my cheek against the cool wood, imagining it was her face. I started to think about her in there, lying in bed, naked, and I'll admit was quite turned on. But then the bloody dog started running his snout along the bottom of the door, making this sniffing sound I was sure would wake her up, and it was a matter of time before he'd start barking and drop me in it. I should be clear, I meant her no harm and was only doing this to check on her, make sure she was okay – and I locked the outer door on my way out, so she'd be safe from passing weirdos.

After a long time loving her from afar, I knew my feelings were reciprocated when she bought me a big carton of Smarties shaped like Father Christmas. 'I know how you love them Harry,' she'd said, which I knew was her way of telling me she loved me. I was over the bloody moon. It was around the time she started seeing *him,* and I reckon it was her way of saying she was sorry, that I was the one she wanted, but I was with Gemma by then so she assumed I was taken. But that didn't stop her flirting. She even said to me once, 'What would I do without you, Harry?' She was such a tease, with her long blonde hair and that secret smile she sometimes gave me across the office.

I finished with Gemma weeks ago, but no one noticed. I only went out with her in the first place because Hannah was living with Tom and I wanted to make her jealous. I ended up stuck with Gemma for almost a year. The only plus point was that she lived near Hannah, so it wasn't far for me to go and check on her.

I let Gemma hang on during Hannah's Tom period, planning to end it and turn to Hannah for a shoulder to cry on. No way was I going steaming in with Hannah, she was too special, so I was going to make it so that Gemma dumped me and Hannah, who's the kindest person I know, wouldn't be able to resist my sad, puppy-dog eyes. But while I was planning all this and being mean to Gemma so she'd dump me, Hannah went on some app and met the idiot Alex. I was so pissed off.

I'd really worked on her, let her tell me all her problems with Tom, bought her almond croissants every day, even fed her bloody cat until it died. And no, I didn't kill it, I don't do clichés. Besides, it was useful feeding old Tiddles, because it gave me access to her inner sanctum, and the chance to look through her stuff, get *really* close to her. Sometimes, I'd take something of hers, nothing big or important that she'd notice, just little things, like a hair bobble, a lipstick. Anyway, after all that, she starts shagging some dickhead she picked up online. Unbelievable!

Alex. God, I hated him. Rich and posh and stupid – mind you, I heard he wasn't that rich after all – like I said, Hannah can be easily manipulated, she's a bit naïve, but that's part of her charm for me. I want to protect her, keep her safe, but I felt I'd let her down when she met him. I loathed everything about him, even before I met him. It was 'Alex says this and Alex thinks that' and I'll admit I was jealous. I used to lie in bed at night thinking up ways to torture him. But I kept telling myself I had to play the long game, and if I waited long enough, I could fix it. Patience was the key.

When she first started seeing him, she'd come into the office all flushed and girly, just crushing on him until I had to go to the bathroom and literally vomit. I couldn't stand by and watch this car crash, I had to get involved, even if it was petty – it was the only way to stay bloody sane! She'd put a romantic meal for two in the fridge at work, and the idea of the two of them eating this and probably having sex afterwards just ate away at me. So I tore off the lid and poured sour milk in the beef whatever-it-was, and then, when no one was about, I stood on the box of cheesecake slices. I ground my boots into the box until they were paste – then put them back in the fridge under a big carton of orange juice. I can't tell you how much pleasure that gave me.

She always left her car keys on her desk, and one day, I couldn't resist taking them. I wanted to scare her, so spent a fortune on some fancy unisex perfume from Creed to stink out her car. It was the kind I thought Alex would wear and I wanted her to think it was him checking up on her. Hilarious. I'll never forget that night when she went out to her car. It was dark, and I watched her from the back door. I hate to admit it, but I got quite excited seeing her all frightened and helpless. And that perfume was worth all the money, because later, when she found out he was married, the fact the perfume wasn't gender specific made her think it might be Helen, his ex, stalking her. Yes, being permanently scared made Hannah vulnerable, which I found very attractive – it also stopped her getting too cosy with anyone. She just didn't know who to trust.

Another time, I blew a hundred pounds on roses, printed out a card, sealed it and asked the florist to deliver it with the flowers. Jas and Sameera had been going on about how controlling Alex was, so I thought I'd just ramp it up a bit to make it look like he sent them. But that didn't work so well, as Hannah thought it was from bloody Tom, which made her lean more on Alex – major backfire and a hundred pounds down the drain.

Anyway, just after that, she told us his ex was a psycho who wanted to hurt her, which was a gift to me. I made calls from a pay-as-you-go phone, so Hannah would think the ex was stalking her, and be so scared she'd dump him.

Despite always knowing she was the one for me, there were moments when I questioned her feelings, wondered if I was wasting my time. But then she'd smile at me a certain way, or say something nice about me – and I was back there. I'll never forget Jas telling me that Alex thought Hannah had 'a secret thing' for me, I laughed about it but was secretly really chuffed. I mean if her boyfriend thought she had a thing for me, then she must. And when we were all out on our Christmas drinks do, I saw for myself how jealous she got when some girl was giving me the eye. 'He's taken,' she shouted. Yeah, she definitely had the hots for me.

Look, I haven't been perfect, and there are things I'm not proud of, but I only ever did it for her, like that same night of the Christmas do when I thought she was going back to her flat alone. I was planning to take her home myself, so I admit, I spiked her drink, but it backfired because *he* turned up and took her home instead. It might seem wrong to do that, but I wouldn't have *harmed* Hannah, I just wanted to spend the night with her.

Then another time, when she was going out with Jas, I messed with the alternator in her car so she wouldn't be able to drive there. I stuck around outside work and turned up out of nowhere to give them a lift. Jas said I was the taxi driver – cheeky bitch. I was hoping to do the same later, when they were leaving – just turn up outside, say I was passing, and take Hannah home. Thought she might invite me in for coffee and I'd tell her how I felt, and she'd fall into my arms, but her sad boyfriend ruined that *too*. He couldn't stay away, and this time he turned up and got himself into a right state when he saw some bloke outside The Orange Tree talking to her. He just got out of his car and punched him, then ran off dragging Hannah with him – coward. Anyway, the bloke was okay, just a bit pissed so he fell over when wimpy Alex threw his spineless punch. I saw it all from my car, which I'd parked just up the road, hoping to casually be around and offer 'the girls' a lift home. I got out of my car and hung around for a bit while some snowflakes called an ambulance, but when it arrived, the bloke wouldn't get in. He was fine, just drunk, and by now he was sobering up so was a bit embarrassed about all the fuss. After a few minutes he and his mate disappeared off down the road, and something told me to follow them. After about ten minutes, they split up. There was no one about, it was very late, very dark, and I took him by surprise and just punched him. I hit him in the head, like Alex had *tried* to do, so he'd fall the same way he had earlier, and the bruises would match. Only this time I made sure to do some proper damage. Poor bloke hit his head on the pavement – again – and by the time some more snowflakes found him the next morning on their way to work, he was a goner. Even if there were no witnesses to identify Alex from the night before, people saw him leaving the scene, including me. I would say I was passing and have helped the police by providing the registration number of his car. But I didn't need to, because things started to move quickly when the police assumed the injuries that killed the bloke were inflicted by the man who'd hit him outside the bar. Shame really, the dead bloke was quite young – but stupid for getting done twice, if you ask me.

Meanwhile, back at work, things weren't going quite so well. There were problems with a client, which at one point looked like it might derail everything, including me! Thing is, Chloe Thomson *always* had the hots for me when I was her social worker. I didn't encourage her – hell she didn't *need* any encouragement, believe me. At first it was just flirty, and okay, I might have spent a bit too long on visits when her mother was out. Then we kissed, and one thing led to another. I mean, she wanted it, really wanted it, the little slapper. I knew I shouldn't, bloody hell, by then she was still only fifteen, so was underage *and* my client – I'd have had the book thrown at me. But she was gagging for it and I know it's no defence, but she looked eighteen with make-up on.

Then the worst happened, and Chloe was taken off me and given to Hannah – if she opened her stupid little mouth to her I was ruined, in so many ways. So, in order to stop her blabbing, I kept Chloe dangling, and at first, I thought I'd got away with it. But then Hannah told me she'd been sent some information from Chloe's mental-health worker regarding a recent interview and I was really worried. What if Chloe had said something? I asked Hannah if she'd had a chance to read it, which she hadn't, but I prepared the ground by saying, in a nice way, that the stupid little bitch didn't tell the truth. I also dropped heavy hints about the mother's boyfriend to anyone who would listen, so if Chloe had said anything about having sex with an older man they'd look there. I knew I had to get hold of whatever was in the files sent to Hannah, so one night when I thought everyone had gone home, I crept into the office via the back door hoping to take them. But Hannah was there, and I had to stand there in the dark corner of the office just watching her. Normally I'd have enjoyed that, I might have even made a noise to scare her, but this time I was too worried about getting my hands on the files.

I tried not to make a sound, just praying she'd leave, but she must have heard me, because she started saying, 'Hello? Hello?' I thought, shit, if she sees me, I won't ever be able to explain this, so I left. But as I left, I saw him, sitting in his fancy car outside the office, bloody stalker, and I'm sure he saw me running away. I hid across the road, and when they left together, I followed them discreetly to the pub, where to my deep joy they had quite a nasty row. But the icing on the cake was that she walked out on him and left the files on the floor! I couldn't believe my luck, I was straight in there – took the files into the toilets, removed all the notes where Chloe's mental-health worker reported that she'd told her she was 'having a relationship with someone older in a position of authority, but refused to name them'.

I didn't stop seeing Chloe, I couldn't because it kept her happy, and more importantly, kept her quiet. Besides, it wasn't exactly a chore – she had a good body, well, what teenager doesn't? But I'm no paedo – I actually prefer older women, like Hannah. Chloe was just a bit of fun, a diversion while I waited for the real thing.

Finally, after a short honeymoon period, it looked to me like things were in danger of going pear-shaped for Hannah and Alex, and I was ready to dump Gemma, so I'd be free for when Hannah dumped Alex. But there was Chloe, and if I didn't handle her right, she could blow everything wide open, so I sat her down and said I really cared about her but she was too young. I fed her some rubbish like one day we'd be together when she was older, thinking she'd swallow it. But I hadn't reckoned on her being a right little bitch. 'But Harry, I *am* older, I'm sixteen now,' she'd said. I told her she was still too young and it had to end – and that's when she really turned. The stupid little cow threatened to tell her mother about us, and her social worker – Hannah. She said she'd tell them how we had sex when she was fifteen, how I'd made her do it – which I didn't – and she'd tell them I'd given her drugs, which I'll admit on occasion, I had. I had to hold on to my temper, and trust me it wasn't easy with her being so bloody childish and unreasonable. Next thing I know she's gone missing and Hannah's looking everywhere for her, and I know I have to find her first.

So, I asked around the homeless in Worcester, some of them are former clients – and I eventually managed to track her down. She was so pleased to see me, nearly broke my heart the way she clung to me, like a little puppy she was. And she was so grateful when I gave her some stuff, I almost stopped myself, but then I thought of Hannah, and how much I had to lose. She choked a bit as I lay her down on this old coat by the river, I knew it was a matter of time, so told her she was a lovely girl, and I was sorry it had to end this way, but I was in love with Hannah. I explained that I couldn't let her ruin everything by blabbing about us – I mean, what would Hannah think?

I thought my problems were over, and Chloe Thomson would become another statistic in the homeless-deaths-from-drugs chart, God rest her soul. But the next day, Hannah announces through her tears that Chloe is in hospital, in a coma but still alive. *Still alive!* I didn't believe it, when I'd laid her down by the river she was virtually gone. So I phoned the hospital as one of her 'concerned social workers' and almost wept with relief when I was told her outlook wasn't promising. Thank Christ! She's been in a coma for three weeks now, and as long as she's asleep, I'll be fine. Also, the longer she remains in this catatonic state, the less chance there is of her coming round, and the *more* chance there is that at some point they'll seek permission to turn the ventilator off. Then I'll be home and dry, and the pretty nurse I've made friends with broke it to me sadly that it's just a matter of time.

I had visited Chloe a couple of times but was dragged away from her bedside when Hannah went to Devon with that madman. I went down the same day they did, so I could be there if anything went wrong, okay – *when* it went wrong. I knew that by Friday afternoon the dead bloke would have been found, everyone in the pub would be questioned, and an anonymous witness (me) would have sent in the car registration number of the murderer. So I casually mentioned to Jas I was staying with friends in Somerset for the weekend, and if she was worried about Hannah, to let me know as I wasn't far away. Jas assumed Gemma was with me, which of course she wasn't; I'd dumped her ages ago. So, alone I checked into a Travelodge in Somerset, ordered takeout, put on the TV and waited for the cry for help. I must admit, I hadn't expected Alex to turn out to be quite the psycho he was. God, I would have stepped in sooner, and certainly wouldn't have let Hannah go away with him if I'd known.

When I saw Hannah in the headlights, it was a dream come true, and she was so delighted to see me, I couldn't have asked for more. My car was warm and clean – I'd had it valeted that day, just in case, so it was ready for her. She was so frightened, and when Jas called me saying he was 'crazed', I was a bit scared myself, to be honest. I didn't know just how 'crazed' he'd be when I got to him. But I left her in the car, and 'bravely' went off into the night, and there he was shivering on the side of the road. It was dark and windy and he wasn't quite so big and posh any more.

The first thing he says to me is, 'What are *you* doing here?' Like I was dirt on his shoe. I didn't say anything, just stood and stared. We'd locked horns before, I think he'd always known instinctively that I was a threat, that Hannah and I were more than just colleagues. He said he knew he had issues, he could be controlling, possessive, but he loved her blah blah.

I said I didn't want to hear it. I said, 'All I know is that you've got a knife and she's scared.' That, by the way, was another amazing thing he did for me – carrying a knife! Alex really was the gift that kept on giving.

'You don't understand, I was slicing peppers, I had it in my hand in the kitchen. For God's sake I wasn't *chasing* her with it,' he said in his stupid, posh voice. He went on and on about how he'd never use it as a weapon. Ponce. On and on he went. And I just couldn't take any more of that whining voice, so I whacked him across the face. I wish I could say it was planned, because let's be honest – it was the perfect murder, but I did it in the moment. And while he flailed around in shock at the smack I'd just given him, I pushed him. With just the tips of my fingers. I didn't break a sweat. And before I knew it, he'd fallen backwards, and disappeared over the cliff. And that was it. I couldn't believe how easy it was, and how quickly it happened. But as always, I thought on my feet, calling 999 immediately, and telling the police that I had the bloke they were looking for, who killed 'that poor man' outside that pub in Worcester. I said he'd just confessed – told me he couldn't stand the guilt and was threatening to throw himself off a cliff.

'Hurry,' I said down the phone, 'I can't keep him here any longer, he just wants to go.'

It was that easy, and a few minutes later, when I climbed back in that car, the hug I got from Hannah was *everything*.

EPILOGUE

'So you don't want a Labrador then?' I ask, with a smile.

'No, I'd much rather have a red setter,' he says.

Another first date in another restaurant. And it's going well, he's funny and kind and fun. But the real bonus is that this guy obviously hasn't secretly stalked me before the date, because he's not matching me at all – he just told me he wants FOUR kids!

I'm laughing a lot and having a lovely time. I just have this feeling that tonight is the first of many, and no I'm not talking too soon, and yes, I have learned my lesson. This isn't just some random handsome stranger I met online, this is different. How did I miss this? Who knew you could work side by side with someone for years and suddenly realise they're kind, funny and actually *very* attractive?

Thing is, I'd always thought of him like a brother, an annoying, teasing little brother, who's also ten years my junior. But that night, when he turned up in Devon and took charge, I saw Harry in a completely different light. He just stepped in, calmly took control of the situation, and probably saved my life. I think it was during all the drama and fear that feelings were sparked for me. I remember it felt so inappropriate, to suddenly want to be near him, and my instinct that night in his car was to bury my head in his woolly jumper. I obviously resisted on that occasion, but tonight I want to make up for that, I want to hold him, and kiss him and I can't wait to sleep with him. It's like something's awakened inside me that I can't ignore – and I don't want to because this time it feels *so* right.

Harry told me after Christmas that he'd broken up with Gemma, and I could see he was hurting. But through it all, he's been so supportive and kind in the aftermath of Alex and I could feel things change between us since that terrible night in Devon. Harry says he felt it too.

Of course, Jas is doing the usual, even today she said, 'don't go on this date tonight, you can't start a thing with a colleague, it'll be embarrassing when it doesn't work out.' She even had the cheek to say he might not be as innocent as he seems, and that I'll fall too quickly, and regret it – again.

But, as I said to her, 'Just because you were right about Alex doesn't mean every relationship I start will end in murder and mayhem. I mean, this is *Harry* we're talking about.'

I realise now, she says these things because she finds it hard when I'm in a relationship and she isn't, she doesn't want to lose her best friend. And she won't, I'll always be there for her like she's always been there for me.

'I don't want to be presumptuous, but I wondered if – on Friday, you'd like to try that new Indian restaurant on Foregate Street?' Harry's saying now, with a twinkle in his eye. 'If you're free?'

'I am,' I say, feeling a familiar rush, like I'm about to embark on an exciting journey. My head's telling me to hold on tight, but my heart is jumping right in. After everything, you'd think I'd be reluctant to start another relationship, but this just feels right to me. As if to confirm this, Harry reaches over and squeezes my hand.

'Who'd have thought it?' He sighs. 'Both with other people, getting on with our lives, we didn't even notice each other – and yet, here we are.'

'Yeah, and we had to go through quite a lot to get to this place,' I say.

'Do you think we'll tell our four kids about *everything* that happened to lead us to this?' he asks.

'Perhaps not *everything*.' I pull an alarmed face, and he laughs.

Then my phone starts to beep.

'It's the hospital,' I say. 'Must be Chloe.'

He looks at me anxiously as I answer the phone, I can see he's as desperate as I am for news, both praying for her to be awake and well again.

'What?' he's mouthing, as I nod into the receiver.

'I'm on my way,' I say, into the phone, as he stares at me desperate to know.

'You'll never guess…' I start, as he stares at me, unsure if the news is good or bad, not knowing how to react.

'Chloe's woken up, and…' I pause. 'She's *talking*, Harry.'

The blood has drained from his face, and I can see it's been as big an ordeal for Harry as it has for me.

'It's okay, the police are with her,' I add breathlessly. 'Apparently she knows the guy who gave her the drugs, he was the one she'd slept with – and right this minute, she's telling them *everything*.' I look into his eyes and melt to see tears.

'Come on, you old softie, let's go and see her,' I say. I'm unable to wipe the smile from my face as I get up to leave. 'Harry, we've got our miracle!'

A LETTER FROM SUE

I want to say a huge thank you for choosing to read *First Date*. If you did enjoy it, and want to keep up to date with all my latest releases, just sign up at the following link. Your email address will never be shared and you can unsubscribe at any time.

www.bookouture.com/sue-watson

I loved writing *First Date*. As an author who also writes romantic comedies, I wanted to explore how something that seems on the surface like the perfect romance can, when peeled back, be rotten inside. My editor came up with the idea of a woman meeting her perfect man on a dating app and discovering on their first date they share the same likes and dislikes, even the same dreams. It seems almost too good to be true – but in psychological-thriller style, it isn't long before happiness fades and darkness creeps in.

So if you go online dating, I wish you every success, and I hope it leads to wonderful earth-shattering love, and a big happily ever after. But don't be swept away too quickly, think of Hannah, and always remember, if it seems too good to be true, it usually is…

I hope you loved *First Date* and, if you did, I would be very grateful if you could write a review. I'd love to hear what you think, and reviews make such a difference helping new readers to discover one of my books for the first time.

I love hearing from readers, so please say hello! You can get in touch on my Facebook page, through Twitter, Goodreads or my website.

Thanks,
Sue

 suewatsonbooks

 @suewatsonwriter

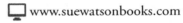 www.suewatsonbooks.com

ACKNOWLEDGEMENTS

As always, my enormous thanks to the wonderful team at Bookouture, who give so much to each and every book.

Thanks to my editor, Isobel Akenhead, for coming up with the original idea for this book, for walking me through the maelstrom of online dating, and once more helping me to turn my reams of words and thoughts into a novel.

Thanks to Kim Nash, Noelle Holten and Sarah Hardy for their hard work in getting my books out there and to Jade Craddock for her wonderful copyediting and Lauren Finger my brilliant proofreader from Down Under. An extra special thanks again to Sarah Hardy for reading this at an early stage, and providing her wise and invaluable insight. Huge thanks also to Ann Bresnan for kindly going through each chapter with her forensic eye, coming up with some fab ideas – and missing nothing!

An enormous thank you to Lisa Horton, for creating another amazing stand out cover that gives me a rush every time I see it.

I wrote this book during lockdown, so big hugs to my husband Nick and daughter Eve who had no choice but to join me on my writing journey. They shared the highs and lows, the inspiration and desperation, and the final Porn Star Martini celebration, when lockdown eased, just around the time I wrote *The End*.

Made in the USA
Las Vegas, NV
11 November 2021